THE TUDOR COURT BOOK IV

THE SON IN SHADOW

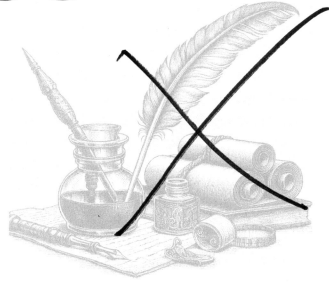

KAREN HEENAN

E-book ISBN:  978-1-957081-24-3

Paperback ISBN:  978-1-957081-25-0

Hardcover ISBN:  978-1-957081-26-7

THE TUDOR COURT BOOK IV

# THE SON IN SHADOW

# KAREN HEENAN

For all the readers who thought
Will deserved his own book.

He thanks you very much.
So do I.

## PROLOGUE

My life has been spent in the shadows of powerful men. Some people flourish in shadows, but I have not; shadows are cold, and those concealed in their depths are not clearly seen by those who live in the light.

I wish to be seen.

# PART I
## 1568

## Chapter 1

THERE WAS ONCE A time when there were two queens in England. Whether I was fortunate in working for them both depended entirely upon your point of view. My opinion varied from day to day, but I had little choice in my continued service of two mistresses, and therefore tried not to think about it too often.

"The queen will be there ahead of us at the rate we're moving," my man shouted as our horses splashed through a wide, shallow river.

"I doubt it." I looked over my shoulder at the group riding behind me. "They have to take care and choose a place where she'll be welcome."

We were lately come from Scotland and our journey was by necessity more leisurely than if a royal warrant had been available to grant us a change of horse at each stopping place. As we made our way south, a pathetic straggle of men ostensibly loyal to a vanquished queen, I took careful note of what was said at the inns and in the halls of the great houses where we lodged.

The other men of the party complained at our slow pace, but I had experienced far worse, and unlike the queen whom I had served until recently, no one on either side of the border was baying for my blood.

It was by this time mid-May, and the worst of the spring rains had passed. The ground was boggy in spots but having made this ride in the torrential rains of autumn years before, my mind registered nothing more than weariness and a mild concern for our horses. I was glad to see a village appear below, with an obvious tavern by the side of the road.

Handing our mounts over to an eager young lad whose hand flashed
out for the coin I threw him, we ventured into the room—dark even on
a bright day, with the remains of a fire low on the hearth. Several tables
were occupied, and we settled at an empty one near a rowdy knot of
young men, hoping for gossip. Sometimes we asked outright about the
Scottish queen and others only waited for news to be dripped into our
waiting ears. And news there was this day, as we quickly learned.

"Defeated at Langside," said a young man in a dirty brown coat, his
elbows resting on the scarred table. "Not even a fight."

He had been there when we arrived, along with several others, already
well into their cups. By their rough garb, they were apprentices or land
workers cleaned up for a ride into the village.

"Were they so outnumbered?" I asked, hoping for more.

"Melted away into the hills is what I heard." He slammed his empty
cup on the table. "Left her standing there with her teeth in her mouth."

We were told that even though her Protestant lords had made it clear
she would never be permitted to regain the throne, Mary had nevertheless mustered a force of some six thousand men and faced down her
son's army. When they were defeated, she fled south with a scant handful
of supporters and was rumored to be making for England—which, of
course, we already knew.

"Good fellows, not wanting to be associated with an adulteress,"
Robert Sturgis put in, his voice insinuating. "Or a murderess."

"Ha!" The man threw his head back, calling to the maid. "More ale
here for my friends."

Not ten years past, I had been part of an English embassy sent to welcome Mary Stuart back to her own shores after the death of her French
husband. But the beautiful young queen, whose reign had showed such
promise, mis-stepped at every turn, impetuously marrying the abusive
and lecherous Lord Darnley, and then standing back when he was mur-
dered, as he had held her back when his men tore apart her Italian
secretary, accusing him of being her lover and the father of the child in
her belly.

Now, having refused advice from all corners, Mary had been forced
to abdicate in favor of her infant son. After nearly a year of imprison-

ment, separation from her third husband, Lord Bothwell, and a rumored miscarriage of their child, she grew desperate to escape from Lochleven Castle.

Despite her imprisonment, she had been allowed visitors. I was not the only man who had left Lochleven with letters and tokens for the English queen. When I received word of a successful escape, I gathered a handful of previously selected men, and we left Scotland to pave her way. Prior to that, my instructions were to test the temper of the people of the north, to ascertain whether their opinions were just that—opinions—or beliefs strong enough to become actions.

There were six in our party, plus assorted servants, all come from the Scottish court, though fully half of us worked for the English queen. Only I knew with any certainty each man's allegiance, although Dennis, my manservant, likely knew as much or more than I did.

Robert and Peter Sturgis kept our spirits high with their continual sniping and sparring. The brothers had been raised Catholic, as I had, but their faith was flexible, and their belief in England's right to rule itself without popish interference was infallible.

Charles Mannion was a staunch papist who did not believe Mary Stuart to be Catholic enough but deplored her half-brother, the Earl of Moray, and hoped the queen could be led in the direction of Rome.

Hugh Talcott was a priest fallen so far from God's grace that he was often seen creeping out of ladies' chambers before dawn. He kept himself to himself and caused me little concern.

The third Catholic, young Jamie Welldon, was my special protégé, a fact that gave me no small worry on his behalf. He was half in love with Mary Stuart and wholly in love with God. It pained me to use him, but his ingenuous views were helpful when cynicism overwhelmed my thoughts.

The instructions I had been given, so far as they knew, were to move slowly and sample the mood of northern households on our way to London. We stopped at houses both Catholic and Protestant, our welcome guaranteed by whichever of our band led the approach. When the men complained of the delay, I reminded them that we were under the queen's orders, and they subsided into grumbling.

It was not a complete falsehood. My underlying orders stemmed from Sir William Cecil, and thus from Queen Elizabeth herself. But when things began to go badly, I had also spoken to Queen Mary. "You have faithful supporters in England," I reminded her. "Allow me to depart for London, to visit them on your behalf, before attempting to plead your case with Queen Elizabeth."

"You will take letters," she said in French. "Not only to the queen, my cousin, but also to the Duke of Norfolk."

That the duke was a strong supporter of both Mary and the Catholic faith was known in England, but I wasn't clear on how much Mary knew; in any case, his intentions would do him little good until she was untangled from Bothwell. I shrugged off my concern and accepted the missive; the duke would be at Howard House in London and her letter, although locked and undoubtedly ciphered, would be opened, read, and reproduced, with edits, by a member of Cecil's team before it was delivered, as Mary's letters to the queen would also be read prior to the monarch's receipt.

"Master," called Dennis, cantering up beside me. "The weather is turning."

"Nonsense." The sky ahead of me was as blue as the Virgin's robe, with streaks of pale cloud hovering above the horizon.

"Look."

He tugged at my cloak, and I turned to see that behind us, the sky had darkened, thick bands of gray stacking up in ominous fashion.

"We can outride it." It was hours until full dark; the horses had at least two hours in them, as did we, and I wasn't yet certain where we would lodge for the night. "What's the worst that can happen?"

"We get soaked for no reason." Charles Mannion spoke up. He was a great hunter whose tanned face showed his familiarity with the outdoors, but he was also a practical man; with no beasts to chase, he would prefer to be dry and in a warm hall with a fire and a jug of ale and a pleasing wench within arm's reach.

"Fine." I slowed Dart at the top of the hill, scanning the area for a likely stopping point. Other than one obvious location, there was little nearby that could offer us shelter. "If we keep on, there is a village about ten miles ahead."

Dennis's mount came up on mine, dropping its head to crop grass. "Is there no nearer place?"

"No." I wheeled around, and his horse skittered backward, nearly tipping him off.

He righted himself, jamming his hat securely on his head. "But there's—"

"I said no." Touching my heels to Dart's flanks, I started down the hill, away from the small, pleasant manor that lay a few miles to the east.

Dennis fell back, and I didn't miss him until the first drops of rain spattered my face and Robert appeared at my shoulder. "Your man says there's a house."

Damn him. "There's not," I said.

"There is," Dennis sang out cheerfully. "Not fifteen minutes away, just over there."

And damn his excellent memory. "I haven't been there in years. The owner may not be in residence."

The rain grew harder. "And he may be," Robert said roughly. "You may take the high road and drown if you like, Hawkins, but I will find this house and beg their hospitality." He touched spurs to his horse and it bolted away, spraying clods of wet earth at those who remained behind.

The others followed, shouting derisive comments. I stayed for a moment, letting the rain soak into the wool cloak over my shoulders and then, shaking myself like a dog, I rode down the hill toward a house I had not visited for over a decade.

The Bower was a small manor of two stories, set in a park with abundant gardens on either side and a wide, circular courtyard in front. Made of local gray stone, its plain face was covered by dark green serrated leaves: the wild rose which had given the property its name. A drift of pink petals, torn off by the suddenness of the storm, covered the ground near the house.

Our arrival had been noted. A boy ran from the stables to take the horses while I led my party toward the door. "I would rather we had sheltered elsewhere," I told them, "but as we are here, I would ask that you remember the house is owned by a lady, and to mind your tongues and your manners."

There was a muttering of assent, and I let fall the knocker. The servant who answered was unfamiliar, but when I said we were on the queen's business and had been waylaid by the rain, he gestured that we should come inside.

"We are for London," I said, following him into the hall, "and ask for food and the comfort of this room for the night. If the lady is agreeable."

"The lady has always been agreeable." A feminine voice cut through the murmur of conversation. My men scrambled to their feet, tearing off hats and bowing in her direction. "Is that not correct, William?"

I removed my hat more slowly, and as it passed my face, I beheld the sight of Lady Rose Caxton, sixty-five if she was a day and yet as blooming and vivid as the tavern girl who might have turned my men's heads if we had but ridden to the next village.

"My lady." I wove through the chamber, stepping around benches and dogs—she always had dogs—to kiss her hand in greeting. "You are well?"

"As always." She continued down the last two steps to stand beside me, the trimmings on her elaborately worked cap barely reaching my shoulder. "And you?" Casting her gaze around the men making free with her hall, she asked, "Who are these gentlemen?"

"*Not* all gentlemen," I said apologetically. "But they will be respectful of your property. We are for London, as I said, coming from Scotland."

Lady Rose caught the servant's eye and an unspoken conversation occurred. She turned back to me, smiling in the way which had always been hard to resist, despite what she'd done to my family. "Tippett will take care of your friends. Come with me. I want you all to myself."

I followed her to a small, private chamber off the hall, where a young maid was hastily laying a fire.

"This is unnecessary, Lady Rose." I looked around at the familiar comforts of her home. "The hall is good enough for the others. I am content there."

She sat in a tall, carved chair by the hearth, her sea-blue skirts spreading across the swept floor. Her movements were purposeful but halting; she had slowed since our last meeting.

"I am not content to sit among such a rough gathering," she said. "Nan, when you are done here, bring us wine." Her keen gray eyes looked me up and down until I felt no more than a raw boy. "And some of whatever Tippett will have prepared for the rest." Nodding sharply, she added, "Take Master Hawkins's cloak and hang it by the fire."

"Yes, my lady." The girl relieved me of the offending garment and scurried off before she could be given another task. Before the door closed behind her, a disreputable-looking hound sidled in and stationed itself by her chair.

"Do you need a change of clothes?" she asked. "You don't appear too wet—"

"I am fine." I had no desire to see whatever masculine garb she had stored away in her cupboards.

"Still too proud for your own good, eh, William?" Her over-familiar words grated on my exhausted sensibilities.

"I do not know what you mean."

The girl returned bearing a silver tray laden with a jug and two cups and a meal of manchet loaf, cheese, and cold meat. I moved a small table in front of the fire, which had begun to flicker and put out warmth, earning a grateful smile from the maid. Seating myself across from Rose, I poured two cups of wine, placed one before her, and drained mine in a single swallow.

"William." Her tone was disapproving. "You did not give me a moment to toast the return of the prodigal."

I refilled my cup, not caring how mannerless I appeared. "I have not *returned*. I am traveling through Yorkshire because I must. If you think I'm setting foot on Hawkmoor, for all that it's over the hill, you aren't as canny as I thought you were."

Her silvery laughter filled the room, making me remember all the times I had run to her for refuge as a boy, before I knew better.

"Enough sparring." She drank, watching me over the rim of her cup. "You are riding for London. You have spent the last several years at the Scottish court. Are the rumors true—did the Scottish queen marry her husband's murderer? Did he really abduct her and"—her voice dropped—"have his way so she would be forced to accept him?"

I shook my head at the breadth of her knowledge. Had I been speaking with my friend Robin Lewis and his wife, I would not have been surprised; as a former member of Queen Elizabeth's court, Robin was kept fully informed whether or not he wished for the knowledge. But Lady Rose lived an isolated existence, with few neighbors and little contact with the world beyond the nearest estate—and the lord there was no longer an active member of court.

"How do you know all this?" The dog nudged my leg, and I pushed it away.

"Never mind how." She snapped her fingers and the beast slumped at her feet. "Is it true?"

"All of it and none of it." I brought out my knife and cut a chunk of bread, keeping it well out of the hound's reach. "She married Bothwell after he was acquitted of Darnley's murder." It was difficult to determine whether he *had* abducted her last year. It could have been an elopement, rape, or something in between; after her experience with Darnley and her public affection for Bothwell, Mary's pride would not allow her to admit another marital mistake. "It does not matter. He has been exiled."

Mary had been shocked by both Protestant and Catholic reaction to her marriage, then, upon the arrival of a letter from Elizabeth, from whom she had expected support, she raged and then fell into despondency. Having become close to one of her ladies-in-waiting, I had read the letter. It was signed by Elizabeth but undoubtedly composed by her all-knowing secretary.

*"For how could a worse choice be made for your honor*
*than in such haste to marry such a subject who, besides*
*other notorious lacks, public fame has charged with the*
*murder of your late husband."*

Even after those blistering words, Mary believed Elizabeth would help her regain the throne. I had been one of the voices to whom she had refused to listen when she formed her plan to flee. Mary was no ardent Catholic, but England at this time was as divided as Scotland, split between a Protestant government and the old, noble Catholic families who might make common cause over a queen who could be molded to their will. I did not see how it could end in her favor.

"Here, LeRoi." Lady Rose speared a bit of cheese on the point of her knife and fed it to the dog, who wolfed it down with slobbering appreciation. "Has she come to England? Is that why you're here?"

It was, but I couldn't admit that to an elderly woman with a circle of informants worthy of Cecil. Perhaps I should recommend her to him. He didn't like using female agents, but if the situation warranted, he might make an exception in her case.

"I am acting as a courier," I lied. "Carrying messages to London. Nothing as interesting as all that."

"Hmm." One eyebrow raised. "It's been a fair spring. A man could get there quicker by ship than horseback. If he didn't mind being seen to leave." She looked at me appraisingly and I remembered she had always been able to see through me. "And a courier doesn't need a half dozen armed men, not unless the messages he's carrying aren't for everyone's eyes." She raised her cup. "Your secret is safe with me, William. Whatever it may be."

We stayed idly chatting until she retired for the evening. I allowed her to catch me up on county gossip and refer discreetly to certain family members, but our conversation never again strayed to the topic of the Scottish queen. Then, having rejected her invitation to take a chamber for myself above stairs, I returned to the hall where my men were sprawled on benches and floor, exhausted by the ride and no doubt an excess of Lady Rose's ale.

When I came close to the fire, Dennis raised himself up on his elbows. "You've rejoined the common folk, have you?"

Kicking him lightly, I retrieved my dry cloak and sat on a bench, folding it on my lap for later use as a pillow. "I should feed you to that abominable hound."

"That would be a waste of my talents." He lowered his voice so the slumbering men would not hear us. "I got them drunk and kept them talking so they wouldn't wonder *why* you wanted to avoid this place, much less realize there's another estate across the moor and who it belongs to."

I covered my face with one hand. "All right, I'll protect you from the dog. It's the least I can do."

He leaned against my bench. "Did the lady ask you to visit Lord Kelton?"

"She did not." She had hinted mightily, but I pretended first to be obtuse and then to be sleepy, and eventually she gave up. "And don't you dare suggest it."

Dennis laughed quietly. "I would never. The last time I saw your lord father, he swore at me and threw a boot at my head."

# Chapter 2

Fifteen years ago, I loved a girl and broke her heart. Or perhaps not. I had no insight into the state of her heart, only the knowledge that mine would not have survived the wreckage of our marriage and so the relationship was better ended.

Cecily, her name was. Cecily Farr. A young woman with sparkling eyes and rosy lips and smooth, dimpled hands. I knew her through my Uncle Henry, with whom I had lived since the age of ten, and as a boy, I thought marriage would be a fine thing if I could have a girl like Cecily.

My parents agreed. Their match had been arranged by the king, but in my mother's eyes it was a love match. Because of that, she insisted that their children, with the exception of the firstborn, who must marry for dynastic reasons, should marry where they loved. Mother was as hurt as Cecily when I refused the match and wept when I could not articulate my reasons.

"I cannot love her," was all I said.

"Oh, Willie!" Her large blue eyes brimmed. "Why must you be so hard? Tell me what's wrong and your father will make it right."

Father was well-born, powerful even before King Henry knighted him and granted him the manor of Kelton in addition to our family lands in Yorkshire. He treated our family as his own small kingdom, with my mother as queen and the rest of us not as children, but serfs, vying for attention and favors.

He was the last person in the world who could make it right, but I could not say that to Mother, who was as beautiful and sparkling as

Cecily Farr and who had been passionately in love with my overbearing father all the days of their marriage. He swore when Mother told him of my decision and called me to account in the hall in front of everyone, roaring at me that I was a disappointment as a son. I stood with my hands behind my back and let his words wash over me, secure in my decision even as my heart ached with loss.

I could not marry and be made a cuckold by my father.

The past years had not been wasted on regret, other than the regret of being born my father's son. I ended up at court on the introduction of my mother's brother. Their family was Catholic, and while my father followed the new religion, upon King Henry's death, Lord Kelton retired to the country, having no interest in the backbiting court of the child-king, and even less in the grim world of Catholic Mary that followed.

In early 1556, not too long after I parted ways with my expected future and this time at my brother's recommendation, I took a job in Queen Mary's government, rounding up traitors and heretics to face royal justice. It was good work for an angry young man, because the accused did not matter—why would I care about them when my whole life had been blighted?

I did my job, riding back and forth across England through fair weather and foul, fetching in men who fought and swore or begged and bribed, remaining untouched by the business. One man took his life while we waited for him to make ready, and I had his body slung over a horse and brought in anyway. He was judged guilty; self-murder allowed no chance of innocence.

My steadfast efforts garnered praise and an offer to stay in London to do more of the same. I resisted being trapped in the city, afraid of running into people I knew. It was not until a cold November two years later that I was shaken from my stupor. I rode into Yorkshire in a driving storm to bring in a minor gentleman, one of the many Protestants who'd exiled themselves during Mary's reign. Robert Lewis's unexpected return set off rumors of a northern uprising in support of Princess Elizabeth, but as he had a history of working with Cromwell, the official charge was heresy, as it took less effort to prove.

He was taken into custody without incident, but over the next week, as we made our slow and muddy way toward the Tower, he methodically dismantled everything I believed and built me anew in a shape I no longer recognized.

Uncle Henry once said that the art of war is knowing when to change sides. Before we reached London, our party was met with the news that Mary was dead. In a moment that defined my life, Robin Lewis shrugged off captivity like an ill-fitting coat and turned toward Hatfield, and I followed. He immediately ceased to regard me as an antagonist, adding me to the party and seeing that I was presented to Elizabeth. After the coronation, I joined him in the offices of the queen's principal secretary, William Cecil.

I worked for him still, although these past years had seen me in the erstwhile employ of the Scottish queen. No longer a fraud, but an agent of the crown, keeping an eye on things north of the border and sending detailed accounts by courier whenever the official accounting and reality showed a marked disparity.

It had been a good life, but my loyalties, such as they were, were to England.

## Chapter 3

THE FIRE HAD BURNED low, and my feet were like two blocks of ice. Around me, men snored, wrapped in their cloaks. I shook the sleep from my head and pushed myself upright, catching up my boots in one hand and making my way to the door. A startled maid, coming in to build the fire, shrank back out of my way. I laid a finger to my lips and slipped outside.

Standing on the cold stone step, I shoved my feet into my boots and strode around the back of the house. If anyone saw me, I could say I was there to piss.

A pale band of light stretched along the horizon. It would soon be dawn. As I picked my way across the yard and past the outbuildings and the empty mews, memory took hold and led me to the spot I sought. Mist swirled around my ankles, and as I stationed myself against the trunk of a tree to wait, I wondered if it would be too foggy to see anything.

When I was a boy, Lady Rose had told me that rowan trees meant protection against enchantment, but witches were never among my boyhood fears.

I loved this tree—in full, saw-toothed summer leaf; in berried autumn, covered in birds; in winter, with its smooth gray wood and remaining scarlet fruit; and in spring, as now, when the fragrance of the densely clustered creamy blossoms nearly overwhelmed the wild garlic underfoot.

The sky brightened, the mist lying in tatters in the low-lying areas. Hawkmoor came into view across the fields. It was a bulky, unattractive place, thrusting aggressively from the surrounding landscape. I had not found it beautiful as a boy, when it was the only home I knew. Later, when I no longer belonged there, I saw its true ugliness.

How much of those feelings stemmed from the man who made the house his principal residence I could not be sure; I had feared my father even in childhood, when I still loved him. It was his father who had acquired the house when he came into prosperity serving the seventh Henry.

It took almost an hour for a short-legged boy to make it from Hawkmoor to The Bower; once I had a pony, I could escape more easily and arrive to take the midday meal with Lady Rose. As a child, I had been baffled that an elegant lady would choose to live alone in a secluded house by the moors, but she said that after her husband's death, she wanted no more of London and chose to come to a place where she could know her neighbors.

"It is a small life, Willie," she had told me, "but it is enough for me. The house is protected by the rowan tree, and I have all I need."

Those needs were met by one of her neighbors. This fact was unknown to me at the time, and I wished to God it had stayed that way.

Behind me, the house was coming to life. Servants' voices rose and fell, and horses nickered in the stables as they were given their morning feed. I would check on them on my way back, to give a reason for my absence, if it had been noted.

As I turned away, several windows in Hawkmoor's second story glowed into life. Someone was awake. Perhaps a governess or another servant seeing to my niece; I did not recall my father's rooms being on that side of the house. I watched for a while longer, then turned my back on the past and returned to the house.


We reached London without incident four days later. It had been three years since I was last in the city, and though I had expected it, it was shocking to pass beyond the walls and be surrounded by a din that was more than street noise and the sound of industry. The air, recently so green and soft, became foul, reeking of sewage and tanneries and smoke.

"Does all of London smell like a midden?" Jamie Welldon inquired in choked tones.

I looked back; he'd tied a kerchief over the lower portion of his face. "On a good day," I said. "On a bad day it smells worse."

Dennis went to scout out beds for us at Whitehall, and the other men dispersed on their own business. I put in an appearance in the offices of the principal secretary. Cecil was with the queen at Hampton Court, I was told, but Sir Edward Pickering was at his desk and greeted me as if I were his long-lost son.

"Hawkins!" Ned pushed himself up and threw an arm around me, pounding my back until my bones rattled. "You took your damned time."

"At your direction," I pointed out. Reaching into the inner pocket of my doublet, I produced the letters given to me by the Scottish queen and dropped them on the cluttered surface of his desk. "I'll need to deliver that one to Howard House as soon as it's been dealt with."

"Good boy, Will." A wide smile spread across his face as he shouted out the door. "Come!"

Within moments, a young man skidded in. "Yes, Sir Edward?"

He waved the letters. "These need to be opened and copied immediately. Do you know when Cecil returns?"

"Not until the next tide, sir." The young man looked with sparkling eyes at the papers in Ned's thick fingers. "I'll fetch Alleyne, sir, and the supplies."

Once he was gone, Ned returned to his seat and nodded at an empty chair. "Sit, Will. Tell me what you've heard."

I gave him a thorough detailing of our travels: the humor of each innkeeper, tapster, or lordly host; their opinions on Mary Stuart's situation; whether my men had sniffed out an illicit chapel in any of the great houses or sighted someone who might be a priest in disguise; a distillation of truth from rumor and speculation.

"There is sympathy for her in the north," I said. "With so many Catholic families, how could there not be? But the two together... I don't believe there is a great risk that they would attempt to overthrow Her Majesty."

"Barring his lordship the Duke of Norfolk." Ned's fist struck the locked letter, cracking the scarlet blob of wax. "Who treads a fine line in both sympathy and religion. Damn his eyes."

That was true enough. Thomas Howard was a complicated man: the queen's cousin, a Roman Catholic with a Protestant education, and the wealthiest landowner in all England. He should have been content, but he complained without ceasing that the queen undervalued him, while giving power to lowborn men like William Cecil.

The first young man returned with another, who bowed to me and introduced himself as William Alleyne. He carried a sheaf of paper of different thicknesses, while the other man held a tray with a jumble of ink and quills, colored waxes, and a small box containing a collection of seals.

"One of these should do the job, sir," Alleyne said, setting up his materials on a small side table. "Pettigrew, you do the fair copy and I'll sort out what's needed for the reproduction."

I sat back, watching as Alleyne picked up the letter to the duke—a tightly folded affair no longer than my finger—and broke the seal. He carefully tore away the strip of locking paper, murmuring, "Spiral lock," to Pettigrew, who nodded agreement.

Once its seal was broken, the letter became a wide bifolium sheet with the queen's slanted writing on both sides. A thick, creased margin ran down the middle, with a narrow rectangle missing at the top where the locking strip had been cut out. The paper was perforated in several places where the strip had been threaded through its folds. In theory, a locked letter was impossible to tamper with—once broken, the strip could not be reattached—but it appeared that Secretary Cecil had skilled workers on hand with the materials to reproduce the letter as we watched.

His eyes closed, Alleyne ran his fingertips over the letter, then sorted briskly through the stack of papers before him, choosing a sheet of the same approximate size and color. He produced a small paper knife from a pocket and trimmed the sheet to match the original, then put it aside to focus his attention on the inks. Three quills were dipped into three separate pots, with samples being drawn on the trimmed portion of the paper.

A murmured conversation took place between the two young men. I looked at Ned, and he grinned like a proud father. "Any given day, there's a half dozen of them about. Useful creatures. Let's leave them to their magic and get a drink, shall we?" He rose, taking his cap from a nearby cabinet and settling it on his sandy hair. "Transcribe the original," he directed, "but save the copy until I return. Let no one in here."

"Yes, sir," came their voices; they never looked up from their work.

I would have rather stayed and watched the process, but Ned brooked no disagreement when he decided it was time for a drink. It always surprised me how far he'd progressed while remaining in Cecil's good graces; the principal secretary was not a man to overlook dissolute habits in those who served, but Ned never allowed his ways to interfere with his work, any more than he allowed his wenching to interfere with his marriage.

He was not someone I would have chosen to follow, but when I changed my allegiance from Mary to Elizabeth, I had fallen in with him and Robin as a way of proving myself. Initially, Ned appeared to be no more than a womanizing blowhard, a surprising choice of friend for a man like Robin, but I soon saw the keen mind and calculating ambition beneath the blustering exterior. It made me like him less; Ned would take care of himself, first and foremost.

Robin retired from the court almost three years ago, pleading ill health. I would have followed him again if I'd been able, and if there had been a place for me. But what place could there be in their tight Yorkshire household of a man, his wife, and two small children, living not a day's ride from my father?

I stayed in Edinburgh and built a life there, watching the queen, writing my ciphered letters, and wishing for something more.

In addition to his comfortable house on Lothbury Street, Ned kept rooms at Whitehall. We installed ourselves there for an hour while his men did their work. Wine was brought at the snap of his fingers, followed by a tray of meat and cheese and all manner of good things. The number of sweets explained Ned's expansive girth; his hand traveled steadily from plate to mouth as he caught me up on court gossip and made discreet mention of our own craft of secrecy.

"We will keep a close eye on Norfolk," he said, licking sugar from his fingers. "Especially once he reads this letter." He washed down the sweetmeat with a swallow of wine. "We've got a man in his household."

Of course they did. Every known Catholic-leaning noble house in England had one of Cecil's men, if not more.

"Are there any others you're watching as closely?" I cut a piece of cheese and took a half-hearted bite. After a journey, I wanted a change of clothes, a wash, and a proper meal, not these tidbits; I could achieve the first two before riding to Howard House, and I hoped the duke would show his gratitude for the letter by feeding me.

"Not in the upper ranks." Ned drained his glass and his lids drooped. "I suppose we must go back. I need to read the letter before it is copied for you to take to Norfolk." He looked me up and down. "Have you got rooms yet? You smell like you've spent a week in the saddle."

"I have done," I reminded him. "And I came straight to you, so I haven't had time to wash."

He nodded slowly, his chins resting on the small, starched ruff at his neck. "Don't bother," he advised. "Let Norfolk think you're his first stop."

"I'll need to tell him I came first to court," I said. "The letter to the queen, remember?" No matter the urgency of Mary's message to the duke, logic said that I would deliver Elizabeth's letter first.

"Right." He trotted down the corridor, eager to see the letters now that his flagging energies had been restored. "Go on, then. Take care of yourself and come back to me in an hour."

By that time, the letter would be copied and locked, and I would have no idea what was in the original or what amendments had been added. I sighed, but it was not my place to ask; I was an agent, a courier, not one of the men who controlled the spiders' webs stretching across Europe.

Howard House, once the great Charterhouse monastery, was bustling with activity when I arrived. The courtyard seethed with men and horses, almost as if the duke were about to depart, but when I caught hold of a fellow in the Howard livery, he said that his master was inside, though he intended to venture to Hampton Court within the hour.

I presented myself to a harried servant indoors and Jamie and I waited in the hall before being fetched into the great man's presence.

"I'll have to leave you out here," I said apologetically when I was called at last. Jamie nodded understanding, turning to study one of the mammoth tapestries ornamenting the wall.

Norfolk was alone in a small, over-furnished chamber. Though the day was warm, he stood before a crackling fire, a furred cloak over his shoulders. Was the man unwell, I wondered, or was he proud of his inherited wealth and liking to show it off? I'd known enough men like that.

"Yes?" He looked up from the small volume he was perusing, irritated.

I bowed low. "William Hawkins, my lord."

"Yes?" he said again. "What do you want?"

He was a few years my junior but with the pettish tones of an older man. His father had been executed by King Henry and his grandfather ought to have been. With a history like that, he should have been more amenable, but he seemed to take the opposite approach.

"I come bearing a letter from a lady."

His expression altered. "Hand it over," he said sharply, his palm extended. "Have you read it?"

I brought forth the folded and sealed missive, suitably creased and scuffed as if by a long journey in my pocket. "No, my lord."

"You may go." He glanced eagerly at the letter. "Can you take a reply to the lady? Where may you be found?"

"At Whitehall." Ned and his men would be eager to read any response I might be given. "But I do not know where to find the lady at present. She is... traveling."

Norfolk gave me a wolfish smile. "Your news is out-of-date, Hawkins. The lady crossed the Solway Firth into Cumberland yesterday."

# Chapter 4

Word of Mary's landing had reached court during my brief absence. The young men in Ned's offices were abuzz with the news, as well as the detail that the Scottish queen had escaped in a fishing boat, having cut off her hair and disguised herself as a man. Although I was impressed by her methods and curious about the identity of the sixteen remaining supporters who fled with her, a small part of me wondered how the queen's vanity had fared, watching her glorious hair being sheared away. No doubt it had been done by the lady-in-waiting in charge of such matters.

Mary Seton had been with her mistress since childhood and could weave magic with the queen's hair. For that reason alone, the queen did not wish to sacrifice her favorite waiting woman to marriage and insisted on keeping her close. As her twenties passed and her bloom faded, the occasionally resentful Mary repeated gossip heard in the queen's chambers in exchange for the scratching of an inconvenient itch. I scratched willingly enough, both as a requirement of my employment and for expediency, but bedding Mary Seton brought little pleasure to either of us, I thought.

I shook off thoughts of a time of which I was not proud and presented myself at the outer door of Ned's office, only to be told that he was unavailable, being locked away with the principal secretary. I made my way to Cecil's offices, a larger, grander suite of rooms than those belonging to Ned Pickering, and waited for a good half hour, listening to the rise and fall of their voices on the other side of the heavy wood panel. When Alleyne passed, I called out to him.

"You delivered the letter?" His eyes were bright with pride at a job well done.

"To Norfolk himself," I said, then added, "He did not read it in my presence."

He shook off his disappointment. "It is the result that matters. Wait here and I will tell Sir Edward of your return."

He knocked and opened the door, and I heard no more than my name before he scuttled back into the outer chamber. "Sir Edward will speak with you when he and Secretary Cecil have finished their discussions."

In any other instance, I would have been hauled immediately into Ned's presence, but the matter of the Queen of Scots took precedence over all, even a locked letter embedded with a specially crafted hook to catch a noble fish. Discussions of that sort could take hours, and my stomach was rumbling. I rose from my seat, and despite Alleyne's protests, I told him that as it was near to suppertime, I could easily be found in the great hall when Sir Edward had a moment for me.

The hall was crowded, servants moving among the tables with laden trays upon their shoulders. I took the nearest seat, looking around for familiar faces. Many of those I had known in the early days of Elizabeth's reign, before I was sent to Scotland, had moved on—to marriage and family life away from court; to elevation or promotion; in some cases, to missions not unlike my own.

The chamber was boisterous, chatter rising in waves above the clink of pitchers on cups and knives on plates. I recalled from my sister Nell, who had been one of Elizabeth's maids of honor before her marriage, that the queen took her meals in the privy apartments, which meant that everyone not in her direct service had this stretch of time unmonitored, with no expectation of being called into the presence chamber.

A tray of steaming hot mutton made its way down the table. I cut off a thick slab and put it on my trencher, realizing as its rich scent reached my nose how many hours had passed since I'd last taken food. The ale I drank upon sitting down was weak, but too much of it before I'd eaten would leave me in no fit state for a conversation of the sort bound to be required of me before too long. I tore off a piece of bread and chewed, my eyes roaming over faces as my ears were pricked for words which might prove useful.

I often wished that I could close my eyes and block my ears and go through life as no more than plain William Hawkins, younger son of a northern lord, but that was what had drawn me into this life to begin with. My average height and looks made me invisible to most people, as had my training with Robin Lewis, who showed me that if you were unobtrusive and did a job no one else wanted, eyes would glide over you as if you were part of the paneling. Being of few words made it easier to be forgotten.

And I had, apparently, been forgotten, for no one greeted me or called my name across the chamber throughout the entire three courses. It made for a quick meal, but I would have enjoyed even a superficial conversation, just for the novelty.

My trencher clean, I wiped my knife and then my mouth with my napkin and stepped away from the table, bidding farewell to those seated nearby. I could return to Cecil's offices, I thought, or perhaps go to my room and sleep for an hour before I was summoned. As I walked through the hall, a waft of sweet air from outside caught me and I found myself wandering out the door and into the late afternoon sunshine.

Whitehall was a river palace, with abundant gardens—private ones for the queen's use and larger ones for courtiers—and a broad walk along the Thames. A barge had arrived, and men in livery were swarming over the walk, tying the vessel securely and bringing stairs alongside so those on board could alight more easily. I leaned on the edge of a marble column and watched the spectacle of a dozen women in flower-bright gowns, clustering together on the paving stones, waiting for the gentlemen of their party.

When the group was complete, they made their way, in pairs and small groups, toward the palace. I stayed at my post, watching to see if I recognized anyone, and my gaze was taken by one of the women.

She was older than me, possibly forty, although discreet cosmetics made it difficult to be certain. Her black hair was threaded with pearls, not silver, and her eyes were dark and lustrous. She was very familiar, but I had no idea why.

"Sir?" A page appeared at my elbow, and the woman was lost in the crowd. "Are you William Hawkins?"

"I am."

"Sir Edward Pickering requests that you come to his office, sir." The boy bowed and turned to scamper away, and I caught his shoulder.

"Do you see that party there?" I asked, gesturing toward the group going into the palace.

"Yes, sir."

"Do you know the woman in the green gown? With the black hair and the pearls?"

"Yes, sir." The boy puffed up with knowledge. "That is Isabel, the wife of Lord Humphrey Ferren."

My eyes closed, and I saw her face, younger, on the inside of my eyelids. Isabel, after all these years.

I need not have worried about the ale I'd drunk; Ned was none the better for drink when I reached him and had another full glass of wine at his elbow. "You took your time," he said, as I bowed and seated myself. "I've been waiting."

"As was I." I softened my words with a smile. "I went to the hall. I wanted to see if anyone was talking about the Scottish queen."

"They'd better not be," Ned said grumpily. "The news has only arrived."

"Norfolk knew when I gave him the letter," I said. "So his sources appear as swift as yours."

Ned's flush deepened. "Damned rascal. He's no better than any other member of that damnable tribe."

"Is Norfolk an active threat?" I asked.

He raised a meaty shoulder in a heavily padded doublet. "Aren't they all?" Ned took up his glass, swirling the red liquid so it lapped up the sides. "I have work to do before I can even attempt my bed tonight," he said. "Take yourself off, but don't go too far."

"I have a room here at Whitehall," I told him. "If I venture out, I'll leave word."

We spoke again a few days later, after encountering each other at the midday meal. Our conversation there was general—who I'd seen since my return, Ned's son's recent engagement, a letter from our mutual friend, Robin. I thought I was safe until he rose from the table, shaking crumbs from his napkin. "Come to me in an hour, Hawkins."

I lingered over the remains of my dinner, wondering what task they had for me now. Their intent, I believed, was to send me north, once Mary's location had been settled, either to serve her or to work for those with whom she lodged, to keep her firm in the belief that William Hawkins could be trusted with her secrets.

"We've taken her into protective custody," I was informed. That was a fancy name for arrest, but they wouldn't call it that any more than they would dare to mistreat her. Despite the threat she posed, Mary Stuart was an anointed queen.

"Where is she being held?"

"Bolton Castle, for the moment," Ned said. "A more permanent situation is being discussed."

As a northerner, I knew Bolton well, and thought that Lord Scrope, whose ancestral home it was, would make a decent keeper. The place, while a prison, would not disappoint a woman raised at the French court. My sole objection to being sent there was that it was two days' ride from Hawkmoor.

"Who is with her?"

"Knollys," he said, referring to Sir Francis Knollys. "We've already heard from him. He says it is far more secure than Carlisle, taking half the number of soldiers to watch over her."

Mary would not like being guarded by soldiers; she had eluded even her own men on occasion, going out into Edinburgh to experience the city and its people. I had accompanied her on one such excursion, attempting in my way to provide security for her and her women, and had found the queen as difficult to control as a toddling child.

"Sentiment in Yorkshire is fair split," I said. "Will that be a problem?"

"We'll see." Ned's eyes narrowed. "But it's further from Scotland. Would you believe"—he pounded his fist for emphasis—"she refused to be moved until someone guaranteed she could continue her correspondence with Scotland?"

"I would, honestly." I fell quiet as one of his young men came in, placing a ribbon-tied folder on the desk and conferring quietly with Ned. When he had gone, I continued. "She is a woman accustomed to having her way."

"Damned papists," Ned said conversationally. "All of them, not just the French tart. More threats than we have watchers." He studied the backs of his hands, then clenched them abruptly. "She's not what keeps me wakeful."

"No?" I couldn't imagine anything keeping him wakeful, not with the amount of wine he consumed.

He opened his hands again, spreading his palms flat on the desk. "It's the little men with their little plots that we don't hear of until they make contact with someone like Norfolk. Mary is like tinder and all those men are flints, waiting to light her on fire."

It was an unpleasant image. There were men like that all over England, discontented by religion or the thought of an unmarried queen or the queen's possible marriage to a Frenchman, or a Spaniard—anyone but a good, plain Englishman; if men like that were keeping Ned up, he'd never again get a full night's rest.

"Can't keep a near eye on every one of them," he said, as if reading my thoughts. "There are too many."

"No," I agreed. "I imagine not."

"But you." He tilted his chair back, looking over my shoulder into the open office area and giving me a broad, unsettling smile. "You have a cousin named Matthew Darcy, do you not?"

"I do." He knew very well that I did, but the mention of Matthew's name set loose a feeling of disquiet in my belly. We had been close as boys, but in recent years, the only news of him was in my sister's letters.

"That last letter you sent down before leaving Scotland, the one with the new cipher..." Ned lifted his cap and scratched his head.

He was going to make me lead him through whatever this was. "Yes?"

"It took us a while, but we broke it," he said with a satisfied smile.

That was no surprise; as I had already witnessed, Cecil had an array of code breakers and cipherers at his disposal. Ned, on the other hand, couldn't find a cipher with both hands and a flaming torch, much less break it.

"What has this to do with my cousin?"

The chair came down abruptly. "A lot, as it turns out. We recently foiled a plot against Her Majesty's life. Your cousin's name has turned up repeatedly, in that letter and several others."

"Are you certain it's the same man?" Matt would never involve himself in such matters. He'd had his obsessions, certainly, but never anything that would put his life or his family at risk.

"Quite certain." His tone made clear that I should not inquire how he came by that knowledge.

I was so tired of secrets.

"What would you have me do?" There was a plan, else I would not have been summoned so quickly.

"Be a good cousin." His joviality masked something darker; it often did. "Pay a visit, see what the young man is up to." Ned looked at me squarely. "If he's helpful, and gives you some names, perhaps we can leave him out of this."

I tried to imagine that conversation and flinched. Matthew was not always serious, but he was stubborn as a mule. "And if he chooses not to share information with me?"

"I think you know the answer to that question." Ned's patience was gone. "Feel free to let him know the price, if it will sway his decision."

## CHAPTER 5

THERE WERE EXPECTATIONS IN my family, the same as in any other. When my brother and I reached a certain age, we were sent to live with relatives to learn how to be gentlemen, to fight and to serve, to act as squires to our lords, to court women, and take down an enemy. Harry went to our father's cousin, Lord Moreton, and I went to my mother's brother, Henry Darcy.

Matthew Darcy and I had grown up together in his father's house, and I was fonder of him than my brother. Part of that feeling, if I was honest, was because he made me feel stronger and more confident; despite a bright intelligence and a loving family, Matt was always a bit lost. He found purpose over and over again, the way my sister Nell found love, but his fancies never lasted.

When I turned sixteen, there was a stretch of formal education. Like my brother, I spent two years at university. I enjoyed the convivial atmosphere and Cambridge's numerous taverns, but I cannot say with any certainty what I learned. After that, like my brother, I was sent to Paris to conclude my education. Paris was far superior in matters diverting to a young man. I met with my tutors and attended lectures during the day, but after dark I roamed the streets with the other students, sampling the varied pleasures of the city.

When we were at Cambridge, Matt wanted to become a lawyer—or a priest. When we were in France, he attached himself to our classmate, Jacques, and thought the best life would be that of a country nobleman, growing grapes and making wine. After we came back to England and

I entered into—and out of—my engagement with Cecily, Matthew returned to his family home and married the young woman of his parents' choosing.

We'd had little contact since then, for no reason other than that our paths had diverged, and while I was eager to see him again, I dreaded the conversation that needed to take place. To keep from worrying over the matter as I traveled up the northern road, I asked Jamie Welldon to accompany me. He had been in Scotland for so long that he proclaimed England to be unfamiliar, and it seemed to me that educating him on his home country would provide a good distraction when thoughts of Matthew's potentially treasonous behavior threatened to overwhelm.

Jamie reminded me of Matthew Darcy in his wide-eyed approach to life and his painful sincerity. There were times when he reminded me of myself, but I tried not to remember that young Will, so easily bruised.

"Pretty as a princess, that one," Dennis muttered, rolling his eyes as we readied ourselves to leave. "Rides like one, too."

"He's not that bad," I said, refraining from commenting on the boy's looks. Jamie *was* uncommonly pretty, with milky skin that blushed easily, vivid blue eyes, and a fringe of lashes that any young miss would be proud to claim. He was an adequate rider, and if we were not pushing ourselves, he would acquit himself perfectly well.

"He'll be trouble," Dennis said bluntly. "And don't you have enough on your mind with your cousin?"

"Sir Edward must be overreacting," I said. "You remember Mattthew as well as I—do you think he'd stay the course long enough to do any damage?"

He shrugged and took my horse's reins so I could mount. "Perhaps he's grown up?"

Matthew wouldn't be so stupid as to involve himself in a plot against the queen. Would he? It had been years since we'd had more than a passing conversation, but from my sister's letters, I knew him to be a contented family man who rarely ventured far from home. Would such a man risk all in the name of religion?

The answer, I found out five days later, was yes.

"She is nothing but a bastard heretic," he declared, his joy at my sudden visit falling away when he learned of its purpose. "She leads England away from the kingdom of heaven, away from God."

We were settled in the small, paneled room from whence Matt ran his estate; I had led him away from his loving wife and three younglings in the hall, turning down a tour of the gardens and the mews because I wanted our conversation to be private.

"Perhaps the pope will excuse such opinions," I said, pushing my glass away in disgust. "Mayhap even God. But Elizabeth, she will not, nor will Cecil and his men. Have a care, Matt, for what you say and to whom."

The bright gleam of fanaticism in the depths of his gaze made him look like a stranger. "Are you threatening me, Will?"

"No!" I reared back. "But they would. I am simply warning you that your existence is known to them." You don't want that to happen, I added silently.

Matt shook his head as if in wonderment at my advice. "I heard that these past years you were in the service of the Scottish queen."

"I was," I said. "I am. But she sent me away when it became clear she would have to flee Scotland. And I have friends in London, one of whom brought your name to my attention and counseled me to speak with you."

He bounded from his seat, resting one hand on the carved mantel. "I care for my immortal soul, cousin. Let Elizabeth's men do what they will, as I will do what I must."

Our conversation was disturbed by shouts from outside and the rumble of wheels on cobbles. Through the closed window, I caught a glimpse of a gleaming black conveyance, and my heart sank in my chest. "I believe that is my father's coach."

Matthew leaned toward the window and nodded confirmation. "He often breaks his journey between Kelton and Hawkmoor by staying with us." His smile then was crooked, an expression from our youth. "You are still not comfortable with him?"

"I am not," I said, "and never shall be while we both draw breath, but I am a guest in your house and will be on my best behavior." I rose, brushing the front of my doublet. Father would be sure to point out any flaws in my appearance. "I cannot promise the same from him."

I stayed behind as Matthew gathered his household to greet my father. Their mingled voices filtered through the door, but I remained where I was, nursing a cup of wine and a thirty years' grudge.

It was too much to hope that my father would remain unaware of my presence in the house. Within fifteen minutes, the door opened again, and Matthew's voice reached me. "...and there is someone here you will be interested to see, uncle."

Even in his traveling clothes, my father was a striking figure—not overly tall, but muscular, even in his seventies. He kept his hair longer than was fashionable and had been, all my life, clean-shaven.

I rose reluctantly and made my bow. "Father."

"William." His voice hadn't changed, either: pure velvet, concealing not a blade but a blunt instrument. "I thought you had changed allegiance and disappeared north of the border?"

"The Scottish queen has come south," I reminded him. "She sent me to London on her behalf."

Matthew's head came up. "And London sent him to me."

"Not now, Matt." I cut a glance his way. "We can speak further tomorrow."

My father sprawled in the nearest chair, booted legs stretched in front of him. "After I have gone?" he asked lazily. "I was going to leave after breakfast, but perhaps I'll extend my visit."

"You would be more than welcome, uncle." When he turned the warmth of his smile on my father, it hurt more than it should have. Matt had never taken the difficulties between us seriously, perhaps because his father was kind and mine was not. My inability to convince him that my father hated me was mirrored by my inability to convince him that actions had consequences. "How many in your party?"

"Just myself," he said. "And Jane's new governess."

"How is Jane?"

The girl—my niece and his granddaughter—was a safe subject. Jane had lost both parents and infant brother to the plague before she was old enough to remember them. Her father's family didn't care to take on a girl child and so she had been brought north, living first with my sister Elizabeth, and then with my father, who claimed only he could care for her properly.

Father was never the same after Nell died. He had doted on his youngest daughter, lavishing on her all the affection he failed to show the rest of his children. My abiding love and protection of her was the one thing about me of which my father approved. After her death, we had nothing in common save his name. I would surrender that if it relieved the pressure of measuring up to his exacting standards.

Jane was the image of her mother and grandmother, and the light of my father's life. Her sweet nature was the sole reason she was not insufferably spoiled.

"Very well," Father said. "Blooming, in fact. Her mind is such that I wanted her to have a proper governess."

I remembered his criticism of Elizabeth, who stole books from the library at Hawkmoor—books which were never opened in his lifetime—and dared to contradict him. She married a man who had no interest whatsoever in her brain and allowed her to read as she chose, so long as his children were mothered, his house well-run, and a blind eye turned to his infidelities.

"And who have you found?" Who could possibly be good enough for her? And when had his opinions changed so drastically on the subject of female education?

My father sat up, brushing an invisible speck of dust from his black breeches. "Do you remember Arthur Rowan?"

I searched my memory for a face to go with the name. "Was he a... physician?"

"That's the one," he said. "Presentable, well-educated—her father's daughter in that regard—but at a loose end because she turned down a proposal and the gentleman didn't take it well. Rowan wanted her out of reach, and knowing of Jane, he wrote to offer the girl's services."

"What did the girl have to say?"

My father's thick black brows raised. "I don't believe she was asked."

"In what way was the gentleman upset?" Matthew asked curiously. "Did her refusal deprive him of a significant dowry?"

"Not at all!" His laugh was harsh, as if this young woman's life was barely worthy of discussion. "Rowan may be a doctor, but he's not a wealthy man. The fellow was apparently willing to take her for very little, but she disagreed. Violently, from what I heard. Her parents wouldn't force her."

His tone said that he would have done otherwise, but none of my siblings had been forced into marriage, something I credited to my mother's influence.

"He's taking it badly," he continued. "Veiled threats and all sorts of muttering. For her safety, as well as theirs, Arthur wanted her well away." He looked at his empty cup and Matthew hurried to refill it. "As if one girl is that different from another. Why not marry a willing one instead of chasing after one who does not wish to be caught?"

"I forgot your high regard for women." In my father's presence, it was difficult to maintain my promise of good behavior.

"William." The velvet bludgeon again. "You are a child."

"I'm thirty-five." The words came out clipped; I didn't want to shout, nor did I want my voice to shake.

"I stand corrected." He nodded, almost gracious. "A thirty-five-year-old child."

Matthew's wife, Anne, appeared in the doorway, saving me from what surely would have been a response so inadequate that I would have regretted it for years to come.

"Uncle," she said, looking at him with the same dazed smile that all women turned upon him. "Your room is ready, should you wish to rest before supper."

"Plenty of time to rest after I'm dead," he said, rising with the ease of a younger man. "But I'll wash off the dust of the road and change into something less offensive to a lady's sensibilities." Kissing her hand, he nodded in our direction and followed her out.

For a moment, my eyes met Matthew's and we could have been boys again, made to feel small by our elders. Then his expression darkened as our interrupted conversation returned to the fore.

"I'll not turn heretic for safety's sake," he said when we were again alone. "Nor risk the souls of my family."

Souls were important but lives even more so. His refusal to see sense made me try again.

"I'm not asking for you to do that," I said gently. "I would not tell you what to believe, Matt. To me, it is all the same—God is God and I hope someday we learn that the manner in which we worship is unimportant—but until then, men are in charge, and men are violent, unpredictable creatures." I heard Robin Lewis in my speech and wondered that I could reproduce his words so easily. "My request, out of love and concern for your family, is that you worship with your head down and stay out of the plots of men who would use you for their own purposes. They will bring you no closer to God by doing so."

Matthew nodded, his face softening. "I understand, cousin. And I will try, for the sake of Anne and the children." His hand went to his neck, touching the crucifix I assumed to be hidden beneath his shirt. "May God keep us safe, even as the heretic queen and her ministers burn in the fires of hell."

# CHAPTER 6

THE DARCY HOUSE HELD to the custom of supper at six of the clock, which gave me adequate time to recover from both my discussion with Matt and the confrontation with my father. I remained in my chamber until the smell of roast meat ventured through the door and drew me forth.

"I'll be eating with the servants, then." Dennis straightened my collar and brushed my shoulders with more force than was necessary.

"As you should." I softened my words; I was the one, more often than not, who treated him as a friend and traveling companion. "How else will I know what goes on here? My cousin will tell me nothing now."

"The usual?" he asked. "Habits of worship, opinions on the Scottish lady? Plant ideas if it is safe to do so?"

"Yes," I said, "and if you can get them talking, any visitors in recent months. Particularly those in the service of the Duke of Norfolk, but anyone they see as out of the ordinary."

He would get them talking; Dennis was a social sort, far better at winkling information from people than I was, and generally more easily liked.

"A better job than you have," he said, opening the door for me. Momentary concern weighted his voice. "Do not let him torment you. It is a meal, not a bear baiting."

His words stayed with me as I descended the stairs into the pit, where my father awaited, along with Matthew, Anne, Jamie Welldon, and several unfamiliar faces, all of whom turned to look at me as I entered. Their scrutiny made me glad of Dennis's vigorous attentions.

"Cousin," Matthew said, coming to my side. "Allow me to present Lord John Christopher, our neighbor, and his wife, Lady Christopher, and"—his voice dropped respectfully—"Father Francois deReve, recently arrived from France."

Jesu! A priest staying in the house was something Matthew should perhaps have mentioned earlier. I wondered if I would be able to omit that from my report. Jamie stared at the man as if he'd stepped down from the cross, replete with the scent of heaven's incense upon him.

I bowed, murmuring what I hoped were appropriate greetings, noting that Matthew avoided my eyes when presenting the priest.

The Christophers, on whom I focused, were a pleasant-faced older couple who lived on the next estate.

"Our son, Thomas, has been assisting your cousin on some building work with the house," Lord Christopher said, gesturing to a thirtyish man speaking to Anne Darcy.

"William wants to hear none of that," Matthew interrupted. "Do tell him about your horses, John. My cousin is a great rider."

The older man brightened. "Are you, sir? I've a scheme to breed a superior mount, one that could travel forty miles a day with ease."

"Have you?" Save me, I thought, from these old men and their breeding programs. Once they were done siring children, their focus always turned to horses. My father was the same. "That would be a great help, indeed."

It would, actually; far too often I had been held up because my horse was exhausted, and there were no changes available. I doubted that this old Lincolnshire gentleman would be able to achieve this feat in my lifetime. The Arabs, it was said, had superior steeds—stories had reached England during the Crusades of war horses performing enviable feats of strength and courage—but whatever breeding had taken place since then had not given the same results.

"On about your horses again, Christopher?" My father shouldered his way into the discussion. "My son here seems to spend his life on horseback. He has no real home to speak of."

Christopher looked at me curiously and I said, "I was until recently living in Scotland. My esteemed father is not up to date on my living arrangements."

"I am up to date on more than you know." His chin jutted a challenge.

Ignoring him, I addressed Lord Christopher. "Maybe I would be able to visit your stables before I return south."

"Certainly." His smile encompassed us both. "Perhaps I can provide a tour to both father and son?"

"No," we said hastily, and in unison.

"I return to Hawkmoor on the morrow," Father explained, nodding in the direction of a new arrival in the hall. "I am bringing a new governess to my granddaughter."

The Rowan girl—had he said her name?—was slim and pale, with honey-colored hair tucked under a plain cap. Her gown was gray and without ornamentation, a far cry from what I was accustomed to seeing at either the Scottish or English courts. She kept behind Anne Darcy, her eyes lowered, the very picture of a penitent daughter sent away for her own good. I wondered how such a demure girl would cope with a man like my father.

My attention was drawn from her to the priest, who spoke to Matthew and Jamie in quiet French. My cousin would not repeat the conversation, but when tedium set in on the next leg of our journey, Jamie could be led in that direction. If not by me then by Dennis.

As the guest with highest rank, my father was seated to Matthew's right, and Lord Christopher to his left. Strict precedence would have put me beside my father, but being an observant woman, Anne had put me between Lord Christopher and the priest. Lady Christopher was on her right and Jamie on her left, which put my father's unfortunate governess between young Christopher and Jamie.

"What is the news from Paris?" I asked Father Francois, as bowls of spiced pottage were put before us.

He turned, spoon hovering in mid-air. "Je ne comprends pas, monsieur."

I had heard him speak English earlier, but I obligingly switched to French, asking the same question, and saw in his sharp brown gaze something I did not entirely understand. Not fear, nor the expected cunning of a man infiltrating a country mostly hostile to his kind. It was,

I realized, the same belief which burned in Matthew, and I trembled for my cousin.

The priest's eventual response was innocuous: he spoke about the weather and his crossing but failed to mention the high feeling in the French capital after the treaty of Longjumeau, which ended the latest round of religious wars. Protestantism had been legally recognized and Huguenot worship would be permitted, in limited fashion, so long as there were no threats to the crown. Reality, however, was different from paper. There were men in the field on both sides, and no one expected the treaty to last.

When I questioned where he intended to stay after leaving my cousin's house, he made a great business of admiring a platter of lamb, then turned to speak to Lady Christopher on his other side.

That left me with Lord Christopher, whose limited conversation I had already exhausted, and who was in any case engaged in energetic debate with my cousin over a disagreement between local landowners.

I looked across the table at the girl, whom I had heard my brother's wife call Katherine. Her head was down, focusing on her plate, but Tom Christopher spoke steadily to her, and Jamie was doing his best to break into the conversation. I pitied her; she had left her home to escape male attention, and my father, who should act as her protector, was paying her no mind at all.

The hall was overheated, and the conversation—and my worry over Matthew—did little to improve matters. Before going upstairs for the night, I took myself outside and walked around the back of the house. Ever since boyhood, a visit to the stables had been a way to settle myself. The idea proved less than calming as I encountered my father emerging from the stables, having had the same idea.

"Sir." An owl, hunting its prey, hooted somewhere in the trees beyond the outbuildings.

"William." He reached up to brush hair from his eyes. "They are all well-settled, if you were concerned."

"I have no concerns for my cousin's stablemen," I said. "I needed air, and to be away from the house."

He fell into step beside me. It was one of few times in my life I could recall my father actively seeking my company. "Why is Matthew so upset?"

I hesitated to speak of it; although my father was Protestant, he'd never forced my mother to change her faith, and my sisters Barbara and Agatha had married Catholics. Because we'd never seen eye-to-eye, he would likely take my warning to Matthew as interference.

"Matt has been putting his family in harm's way," I finally said, couching it in those terms to appeal to his finer feelings. "Those in power do not concern themselves with Catholics unless they've found a way to make themselves stand out."

"And he has." My father's expression was considering. "His family has always been strongly papist."

"I take no issue with his beliefs." I paused at the stone wall that separated the stables from the rest of the grounds. "It is how he professes them, in a time when loud professions of faith are unlikely to be ignored." I met my father's eyes. "It is from concern for Anne and the children that I spoke to him."

"He's always been rash," he said slowly, "ever since you were boys." He nodded. "I'll keep an eye on him myself."

"Thank you." I hadn't expected this visit to end with any sort of fellow-feeling toward my father. "He respects you, and I hope will listen."

Father cocked his head. "More than my son, I warrant."

The moment was gone, as quickly as it had come. I took a deep breath. "I give respect where it is deserved."

"As do I." He began to walk again, circling the house and heading back the long way around. "At your age, I was married with two children," he said. "The king had given me Kelton, along with its title. What have you done to prove yourself worthy of respect?"

"Your father died when you were five and twenty," I pointed out. "You haven't given me that same consideration."

"Insolent puppy," he said, almost without rancor. "Whether I continue to draw breath or not, it will make no difference. Your brother inherits all."

"I don't care," I told him. "I don't want what is yours."

Windows began to darken inside the house. If we stayed out any longer, a servant would have to stay up to wait for us. Not that my father would care; in his world, servants should not complain about being kept up but bless him instead for giving them work.

"Speaking of what is mine," he said. "I heard you paid a call on Rose."

"I did not realize she would tell you," I said stiffly.

He would rub that in my face; I had discovered The Bower and Lady Rose years before I'd understood her relationship with my father. It was not until I'd come home on a visit in my twelfth year and witnessed him coming over the hill one late afternoon, following the same path I took, that I made the connection and ceased to wonder why a beautiful widow would choose to live an isolated life in the country, with no near neighbors but my family.

"Rose and I have no secrets." His tone made it sound as if he still made that journey over the hill to plow his furrow on the neighboring estate. "Are you working for England or Scotland?"

I remained silent. He would do what I asked for Matthew without knowing all my secrets.

"England, then," he said, sounding satisfied. "At least you're on the right side."

"I didn't realize you took sides," I said, stopping at the front door. "I thought you remained aloof."

He pushed past me into the house and turned toward the hall table, which was littered with plates and cups, the servants not yet having begun to clear. Choosing the nearest cup, he filled it to the brim and tipped it back.

"I left court after Henry died," he said when it was done. "He was my friend, if one may be friends with a king. I had no interest in what came after—it was all religion and persecution, with no joy to be had anywhere."

Father poured more wine and offered me a cup. I nodded, hoping he would continue—he'd never spoken this plainly before about his reasons for staying in the country. But he leaned against the edge of the table, seemingly content to drink in silence.

"So you stayed at Hawkmoor with your mistress conveniently stashed over the hill." I wanted to drain my cup, but all my wits were needed to contest with him.

"With such a happy situation, what sane man would leave?" He could have been a boy boasting over the conquest of a tavern wench.

"You've hurt so many women—" It was pointless to challenge him, but his arrogance pricked at me.

"What women?" He towered over me, his face flushed with drink and arrogance.

"All of them!" Arguing with him had always made me feel small.

"I've never forced a woman." He sank back into a chair, reaching again for the wine. "Never had to. They came to my bed gladly."

I pushed that thought away, remembering a particular gladness I had once witnessed. "What about Mother?"

"She was the most glad of all."

I wanted to strike him for what I saw in his face. "I meant that you hurt her, with all your women."

The chair flew sideways. He stood, slamming his fists on the table so that the cups rattled. "She never knew—and if she did, she got her part of the bargain. A house full of brats, status, and all of me when I was there."

"But—"

"You have the standards of a fainting maid, William," he spat at me. "And I've never found much appeal in a fainting maid."

I lingered in my bed the next morning, sending Dennis down to make certain my father was gone before I set foot in the hall. His presence leached energy from me; every conversation felt like a duel where I was constantly on the back foot. Although things were not easy between Matt and myself, when my care for him came up against the unyielding bulwark of his religion, there were years of history to fall back on.

Before we left the following day, I found a moment to speak to Anne Darcy. She was at the back of the house, supervising the tending of a vegetable garden, watching indulgently as her son, a boy of about six, attempted to help.

"You are off tomorrow?" she asked, shifting her baby to her other hip. Its swaddling bands hung loose around its kicking legs. "Matthew will be sorry to see you go."

"I think he won't." We had spoken again after breakfast, and I made the mistake of warning him of the danger of keeping a priest in the house. It had ended in shouting on both sides.

"What is wrong between you?" she asked. "Matthew has told me of your closeness, ever since childhood."

"Careful," I said to young Henry as he tried to heft a spade taller than himself. "We disagree on matters of religion."

Her lashes fluttered, dark against her sun-flushed cheeks. "As do many in these troubled times."

"Your husband's name is known in London, which worries me," I told her. "I do not judge him for his faith, Anne. I but warned him to keep away from those who would involve him in their intrigues."

"He would not," she said with certainty, but sat down hard on a battered stool near the kitchen door, the babe on her lap. "He would not."

"I hope not." I squatted beside her, reaching out to take hold of the baby's tiny, waving foot. "But he is fierce in his beliefs, and I fear they may overpower his common-sense." I noted the tears gleaming in her eyes. "Try to make him see reason."

Her arms wrapped protectively around the child, making it squeak in surprise. "I will."

"And get the priest out of the house, if you can." If she needed me, I said, she had but to send word to London.

"What if my letter is read?" she asked. "Would that not also be dangerous?"

Her perceptiveness surprised me; I would not put it past Ned—or Cecil, for that matter—to read my letters if they suspected I had not told them the entire truth. "You are right. Direct any letters to a tavern called The Minstrel's Arms," I told her. "They will know how to reach me."

My first introduction to the tavern had been with Robin Lewis and his wife, but I had returned many times to listen to the owners, former royal minstrels, as they played and sang for their devoted customers. I was friends with their son, Harry, who ran the place, and upon my return to London would give him a way to reach me.

"Thank you." Anne rested a hand lightly on my arm. Her nails were bitten to the quick; mine was not the first worry she bore. "You are a good friend to us."

"I will do my best to protect him." I leaned my head against the rough surface of the wall. At that moment, with the morning sun warm on my skin, I almost believed we could keep him safe.

# Chapter 7

Ned's house on Lothbury Street was a family house unoccupied by a family, as Lady Joan rarely ventured into the city from Surrey. Lacking a wife's civilizing influence, the detritus of his existence was strewn on every surface, resisting all attempts by the servants to keep the place presentable.

When I arrived, I was shown into a small, windowless chamber off the hall where Ned was having his portrait painted. He was seated in a heavily carved chair, wearing an unfamiliar dark red doublet with jeweled buttons and an elaborate starched ruff. One thick-fingered hand, with a prominent ruby ring, lay possessively on the cover of a leather-bound book. The other held a quill over a virgin sheet of parchment. He looked like what he was: a wealthy, middle-aged man with aspirations to power.

Whatever else he might be was invisible.

Seeing me in the doorway, the artist paused. "Sir Edward?" he said, gesturing with his brush.

Ned's unfocused gaze snapped into alertness. "You may go."

The man bowed, swiftly gathering his brushes and paints and backing out the door.

I waited until he had gone before advancing fully into the room, pausing to look at the abandoned canvas. "A good likeness."

"That's what I fear." Ned climbed stiffly down from the chair and turned to blow out the extra candles needed for the artist to see properly. He stopped beside me in front of the painting. "You could serve me at a Christmas feast with an apple in my mouth."

I would not have said he was so fat but sweat shone on his brow from the heat of the closed room, and the comparison was apt. I hid my smile before he could see.

"Sit down, Hawkins," he said. "I'm glad you were able to come by."

"I didn't realize I could refuse." A small table had been pushed into a corner to make space for the work of painting. I took a seat there.

"It was not." Ned dropped into the other chair, and it groaned in protest. He raised his chin, gesturing at a flask of wine on a tray. I poured two brimming cups. "You've been a bit of a problem," he said, "ever since your return from Scotland."

"How is that?" I had given a mostly faithful account of my visit with Matthew, doing my best to convince Ned and Cecil that my cousin's activities amounted to no more than some ill-judged conversations. They appeared to believe me, but in the weeks since, as I lingered at Whitehall and was reminded how unsuited I was for life at court, there had been no calls for my services.

"Your history with the Scottish queen makes your use in certain circles... difficult."

"But you—or rather, Secretary Cecil—sent me there." I should have returned to London after the initial embassy, but other uses were found for me, and I had shuttled back and forth between the two courts ever since.

"And it was necessary at the time." He shrugged. "But she is here now, and it has been decided that sending you back to her household straight off would be a mistake."

I took a deep swallow of wine. "What would you have me do?"

"That's being discussed," he told me. "Come to the principal secretary's offices tomorrow at noon. We'll explain then in more detail."

"Why summon me this evening?" What point had there been to leaving me wondering for the whole night?

Ned clucked disapproval at my tone. "Wanted to give you a bit of warning," he said, waving his cup in my direction. "Thought you'd be grateful."

I collected Dennis from the kitchen and told him we were returning to Whitehall.

"Already?" He reached out to straighten my collar.

"Did you have any other suggestions?" I twisted away; the man could never let me be. Ned would benefit from someone as dogged as he was.

He raised one shoulder. "It's been a while since we've visited the tavern. Didn't you say you wanted to speak to Harry?"

My mouth was already sour with Ned's wine. The last thing I needed was more drink. I sighed. "Fine. Cheapside *is* on our way back to the palace."

The bells had begun to ring as I hurried through the crowded public spaces of Whitehall, through doors and passages into the less crowded private spaces. The principal secretary's offices were inconveniently located, especially for a man with a blistering headache and no clear memory of how he'd been returned to his bed the night before.

When Dennis caught up my crumpled shirt, he had given me a knowing smile—but not before I'd caught the scent of stale sweat and a hint of perfume. What had I done? I searched my memory, but after a certain point—and a certain amount of Harry Minstrel's excellent ale—things became fuzzy.

The Minstrel's Arms was not the sort of tavern where one ran across prostitutes; Harry's mother, who was unwell and had not been there last night, kept a watchful eye in that regard. Had we stopped somewhere else before returning to the palace? It was entirely possible. Despite my threats, Dennis did no more than grin; he would wait for a more inopportune time to tell me what had actually occurred.

Arriving at the office doors, I announced myself and took a seat while the young man went to tell them I had arrived. I sniffed discreetly at my underarms; though I had washed, I fancied I could smell ale.

"They are expecting you." A young man—yet another one—stood before me.

I followed him through a series of interconnected chambers until we reached the office of William Cecil, the man who knew more about what was happening in England and on the continent than anyone else in the world.

He was seated at an imposing desk, a man of middling size with a long gray-brown beard and the pouched and worried eyes of a spaniel. Those eyes flicked up at my entrance and then back down at the papers he held in one hand.

"Hawkins." Ned emerged from an interior doorway. "Cutting it rather fine, aren't you?"

I made my bows. "You said noon, Sir Edward." The assorted bells outside chimed their last and I met his eyes with more challenge than I felt. "It is noon."

"We don't have time for this," Cecil said in irritation. "Hawkins, Sir Edward tells me you have been at loose ends since returning from Scotland."

"I have not received a new assignment, that is true." I would not call it loose ends, more the situation of someone waiting to be given a purpose.

He nodded. "We have been discussing you, and because of your history with the Scottish queen, it is not advisable that you return to her household immediately." He folded his hands and looked at me blandly. His knuckles were swollen; these damp river palaces must have caused him great discomfort. "Give people time to forget any supposed allegiance on your part."

"I understand." I hesitated. "Then what am I to do with myself?"

"We've come up with an excellent plan," Ned interrupted. "You shall be a royal messenger."

I tried to take it in. It was a respectable job: messengers stayed in royal service for decades. But it meant near constant travel, by horse and ship and foot, if necessary.

"Yes." Cecil's eyes were as sharp as his appearance was aged. "We'll start you off with a letter to Bolton Castle, which you can deliver directly to Mary Stuart. Convince her of your allegiance and that you have taken this inferior position to stay connected to her, and those faithful to her."

Mary would believe the tale; she preferred to think well of people and gave far more chances than were warranted.

"When would I leave?"

"When we order it," Cecil snapped. "Have you so much life here in London that you require time to settle your affairs? Sir Edward informed me that you were without attachment."

I objected to this description. "I have family, sir."

"In the north, and no fond relations of which I am aware." Cecil blinked slowly, like a turtle. "Am I incorrect?"

The room had grown very close. I both desperately needed a drink and never wished to drink again.

"Not entirely," I hedged. "I am close to my sister, Elizabeth Fremantle, and my niece. They are both located in Yorkshire, not too far from Bolton."

"Pay them a quick visit, if you must, after you have dealt with the Scottish lady," he said. "When you return, you will be assigned a route as a second."

"A second?" Parroting his words made me feel stupid, but the scant foundations of my life had been kicked from under me and it was difficult to gather my thoughts.

"A junior man," Cecil explained. "Messengers tend to travel in pairs, for safety. It will give you an opportunity to learn the routes and from his experience."

The door cracked open, and a man put his head into the room. "Secretary Cecil, sir—a summons from the privy chamber!"

With a sigh, Cecil stood, brushing the front of his immaculate doublet. "Her Majesty calls. Sir Edward, I leave it to you to finish this business."

I was no more than business to these men, a pawn in their never-ending chess game with the world. I addressed Ned. "I don't understand. I could take this message to Queen Mary and give her the same story without new employment. Why have I been chosen for this?"

Ned came around the desk, parking his ample buttocks on the edge and disarranging a stack of papers. "It's what Cecil said, man. It's your lack of attachments."

"Why is that so important?" I felt my lack sorely enough without having it made a qualification for employment.

"It's what I find so useful about you, Hawkins. You're free. You can be gone indefinitely without anyone looking for you." Ned smiled broadly. "Do you know how rare it is to find someone with no ties whatsoever?"

## CHAPTER 8

Before riding north to begin my latest deception, I received a badge and a letter identifying me as a messenger traveling on the queen's behalf. Those two things would alleviate the complication of changing horses and requesting shelter along the route and would guarantee we would make Bolton in under a week.

On the morning of our departure, Jamie Welldon sought me out. My heart sank when I saw the small satchel of possessions under his arm.

"I am to return to Her Majesty's household," he said with a blazing smile. "How wonderful that you are riding to her at the same time."

"It's very well timed." I suspected his presence was no accident, nor had he been added to our party for the sake of convenience. "I'm happy to have company on the journey."

Dennis appeared with the horses in time to hear my words. "Am I not company enough?" he grumbled. "Back and forth across this country I've gone with you—how many times now, do you think?"

"More than I can count," I shot back. "And your conversation was used up long before that."

He made a rude noise but refrained from further comment, strapping my pack on the back of my horse and fiddling with Jamie's things before swinging up onto his mount, which was laden with goods sent by Elizabeth to her Scottish cousin. "I shall be mute, then, all the way to Bolton."

"We should be so fortunate."

Jamie laughed, the high, innocent laugh of a boy, and I thought again how I hated that he was involved in all this. Perhaps along the way I would be able to discreetly share some of what I knew, so that he would keep from digging himself a hole and falling into it headfirst. But it was near-impossible to keep myself from the court's intrigues; Jamie would have to learn to protect himself.

The more I thought of this latest assignment, the more sides I saw to it. There was nothing dishonorable about being a royal messenger—it was a position I would not be ashamed to speak of before my father—but I had not sought it out, nor was I the most qualified man for the job. Still, it gave me reason to be in and out of London and any number of great houses, and back and forth across the Narrow Sea to France and the Low Countries. My tendency to pass unnoticed was a handy qualification for someone in my line of work.

I had encountered royal messengers over my years with the court, many of them involved in intelligence work. Now I would be one of them, involved in—and aware of—situations of which I might very well want to remain ignorant. But there was no way out of it that I could see. As Ned said, I was free. I might as well use my life in traveling and serving my country as I was so little in demand.

Jamie proved a pleasant traveling companion without a group of older, rowdier men to intimidate him into silence. Another younger son searching for his place in the world, he landed in Scotland when his Northumbrian father sent him there on business and simply stayed on.

"No one needed me," he said, and his words made a home under my rib cage. "If I could have been a priest, I'd have been happy, but Father would never agree to that."

"Your family is not Catholic?" I guided my horse closer. Dennis did not need to hear every scrap of conversation between us; his ignorance of details often led him to develop more and separate information.

"No, they are." Jamie lowered his voice. "But he says being Catholic is risk enough in these days without becoming a priest."

"He is right." I let a mile go by before speaking again. "What will you do for Queen Mary?"

Jamie looked abashed. "Secretary Cecil told me she needs another secretary. I know he does not approve of our queen"—a confiding glance included me in that *our*—"but he cannot prevent her from having the number of servants to which she is entitled."

William Cecil could do exactly that, which meant Jamie's appointment to the household served the English queen as well as the Scottish. I assumed there was some underling already installed in the castle who would scan any letters he prepared for her and report back to London.

"Of course not," I said. "And you are just the man, Jamie. She liked you, I saw that well enough in Edinburgh."

My flattery cheered him further, but rather than continuing his confidences, he burst into song, drawing laughter, and eventual harmony, from both Dennis and me.

When we stopped that night at an inn, our party was told that there were no available beds. A flashing of my badge saw two groups of travelers lumped together and the prime room at the back of the building given over to our rest.

"I could get accustomed to this," Dennis said, handing off our bags for the inn-boys to carry upstairs but keeping the queen's gifts to watch over himself.

"Don't," I cautioned. "You may not even be with me on all my travels—that remains to be seen."

His face fell. "And what am I to do if that happens?" he asked. "Hie myself back to Hawkmoor and throw myself at Lord Kelton's feet saying, 'Please, sir, take me in. Your son has no further use for me.'"

"I do not know if that will be the case." I cuffed him lightly. "If it is, you will remain at Whitehall, or wherever else I may be living, until my return." I shot him a glance. "It will give you time for your favorite pursuits, without my intervention."

At Jamie's confused look, Dennis elaborated. "Drinking and womanizing. Master William here has no appreciation for either." Returning my pointed glance, he added, "Except when he does."

There it was. I had known that at some point, Dennis would choose to torment me with my activities on the evening of my meeting with Ned.

"Out with it," I ordered. "What exactly are you trying to say?"

"I'll see to the room," Jamie said, hastening inside after our luggage.

Dennis grinned at me. "Nothing at all."

I caught hold of his sleeve, then his arm beneath it, the strength of my grip telling him that my patience had been lost somewhere on the road. "Try again."

"Very well." He shrugged, and said, "You drank a bucket of ale and griped about Sir Edward. After that, you staggered into the alley, puked it all up, and came back and drank more." Shaking his head, he added, "Harry and I tried to get you into a coach, but you were legless at that point."

"What happened next?" That was embarrassing but didn't explain the scent on my shirt.

"Harry called his sister to help—he thought you'd be less trouble in front of a lady." Dennis began to laugh, holding to the corner of the building. "He was right. You dropped to your knees in front of her and told her she looked like your mother, or an angel, or your mother who was an angel." Squinting at me, he said, "You weren't very coherent."

His words brought back faint, but unmistakable memories. I wouldn't be able to go back to the tavern again—I could never face Harry or his sister after such a miserable performance. "Why didn't you stop me sooner?"

"Because you're as hard-headed as your father when you're like that," he said flatly. "And I didn't fancy getting struck for my pains." He ducked through the door, leaving me alone with a sick feeling in my stomach and the knowledge that I had to be deep in my cups before I could approach my father's level of authority with servants.

For all his failings, my father's drinking did not change who he was. We had argued many times over the years, with varying levels of violence, but he was the same man drunk or sober—high-handed, arrogant, often uncaring, but consistent in his behavior.

I shook my head and went inside, avoiding Dennis and sitting on a bench near the wall. Despite the inn's proximity to the road, the July evening came in sweetly through the open window. I accepted a cup of ale and a bowl of some sort of stew and closed my eyes, listening to the bedtime songs of the thrushes and wrens in the nearby trees, with the occasional distinctive, rising call of a curlew.

The scrape of a bench called me to myself. Jamie seated himself across from me, tipping his cup in my direction. "Eat, before it gets cold."

"Yes, mother." I dipped a piece of bread in the bowl; it was lamb, or mutton, not too skimpy on the meat. I took a bite. "All set upstairs?"

He nodded. "A clean bed, and the door latches."

I had stayed in far worse places over the years, sharing a room with a half dozen others, or sleeping, wrapped in my cloak, before the fire. It was all one, in the end. Just part of the journey.

"We'll be there tomorrow," Jamie said. "Bolton."

"Yes." The ale was as good as the stew. "Mid-afternoon, I'd guess."

Jamie hesitated. "Dennis says afterward, you're going to visit your family."

"I might." Damn Dennis for a gossiping old woman. "Why do you ask?"

His cheeks flushed. "I thought you might perhaps pass along a greeting to Mistress Rowan."

"Who?" My eyes were fixed on Dennis across the room, regaling a cluster of townsmen with tales of London life.

"Katherine Rowan," he repeated. "The young lady your father was bringing to care for his granddaughter."

I'd nearly forgotten the shy young woman who'd had so little conversation at Matthew's house. "You were seated by her at supper, weren't you?"

"Yes." His gaze dropped, studying his knife. "She's lovely."

She had been a pretty enough girl, from what I'd seen, but there'd been no chance to speak with her without encountering my father unnecessarily. No woman was worth that. "And you want me to speak to her for you?"

"If you would," he said. "Do you think she would object?"

"I have no idea," I said, laughing at his eagerness. "I've not said two words to the girl, but she's just escaped an engagement. Her mind may not be on matrimony." And my father's mind would hardly be on losing his new governess to the likes of a young Catholic secretary to Mary Stuart.

"I understand that," he said with a sigh. "But if you could bring my name into conversation—if there is some way to manage it—and write to me of her response, I would be very grateful."

## CHAPTER 9

THE NEXT DAY BROUGHT bright skies and, as anticipated, an arrival at Bolton Castle while the sun rode high above our heads.

Bolton was high-walled and imposing, set among extensive gardens. It had been built to withstand Scottish raiders, if not outright invasion, and had, thirty years before, been set alight on the king's orders, after a previous Baron Scrope gave aid and comfort to a runaway abbot during the Pilgrimage of Grace.

I was a boy when it happened and did not remember the fire, only the ferocity of my father's reaction, informing us that no sanctuary would be given within the walls of Hawkmoor. He would not have his home torched for any man who drew breath, not even if the pope himself appeared on the doorstep with a begging bowl.

My mother, distressed by the news of the burning, as well as the threat to her fellow Catholics, had sobbed, my sisters told me later, but he was adamant. Our home remained untouched despite the waves of violence that passed repeatedly over the north of England.

Once Bolton had sheltered an abbot; now it held a queen, this time unconcealed and by another queen's pleasure. Whether it was Henry Scrope's pleasure to house her had not been considered. He'd had custody of Queen Mary at Carlisle, but Carlisle had been deemed insufficiently secure and she had been transferred, under the care of Sir Francis Knollys. Bolton Castle had but one entrance, and that well-guarded; it would be nearly impossible for her to escape, or be rescued, should an attempt be made.

Although Mary had been given Lord Scrope's apartments in the southwest tower, it was deemed he did not keep acceptable state for a royal personage. Tapestries, plate, and furnishings were borrowed from Barnard Castle and local houses to augment his possessions. The bundles so assiduously watched over by Dennis contained a selection of pewter vessels sent by the queen for Mary's use.

"Royal messenger," I said to the guard as he barred our path. "Letters for the Scottish queen, Lord Scrope, and Sir Francis Knollys."

He nodded, stepping back. "These are your people?"

"Yes. Behind me is James Welldon, sent by the principal secretary to scribe for the queen. The other is my manservant. He and I will be departing on the morrow, if I am permitted to have an interview with the Scottish queen by then."

"That will be his lordship's decision," the guard said and stepped back. "Go on through to the courtyard, someone will take your horses and the steward will see to you from there."

Dismounting, we shook the stiffness from our legs and looked around the courtyard. We stopped short as we saw Scrope's astronomical clock on the gabled wall overlooking the yard. No mere timepiece, it was a marvel worthy of a royal palace. Leaving Dennis to deal with the grooms, we crossed the yard and stared up at it. The clock's face, gilded by the afternoon light, was a tapestry of moving symbols. A golden sun, propelled by unseen mechanisms, traced an arc across a sky studded with tiny silver stars. The imagery was not only celestial: various human figures cavorted upon its face and, as the hand moved slowly to the hour, a trumpeter emerged, his silver horn heralding the time.

"Astonishing," Jamie murmured, rapt as a child as he watched the waxing and waning of a small crescent moon.

It was. The entire place was impressive. The wide courtyard where we now stood led to vast stables and storage areas, while the principal rooms were on the floor above. It was not Holyrood or Edinburgh Castle, but I thought that Mary might not be entirely discontented in this place, particularly if she were permitted to walk in the gardens or ride, under escort, in the beautiful nearby dales.

We were escorted indoors to the steward, who informed us that Lord Scrope was not at home, but that Sir Francis would see us after we had taken some time to refresh ourselves.

"A room has been set aside for Master Welldon in the east wing," he said, "as we were expecting him. If you would take a cup of wine in the hall, Master Hawkins, a chamber will be made ready for you."

A servant appeared to lead us away. Jamie turned back to the steward. "A separate room is unnecessary—Master Hawkins is a friend and will be departing after he delivers his letter to Queen Mary. He may lodge with me for the night."

"If Bolton Castle is capable of lodging a queen," the steward said solemnly, "it can provide a bed for a royal messenger. If you will follow me."


My meeting with Sir Francis Knollys done, and my letters to him and to Lord Scrope presented, all that was left was to deliver my letter to Her Majesty, Mary Stuart, Queen of Scotland. And of England, she liked to claim—a claim which in large part explained her secure housing in Yorkshire.

She would see me, I was told, in the evening, and so I ate supper in Bolton's small, formal hall with Knollys and the other retainers who lived in the castle. I asked after the Scottish queen's servants, having expected to see Jamie in the hall, but Sir Francis corrected my error.

"Her household keeps to itself," he said. "The queen is upset at her transfer from Carlisle, which she found more to her liking."

Mary, as I well knew, had no problems showing her distaste, whether it be for a place or a person. I did not envy Knollys; my employment was transitory, while he was stuck in this castle, far from his wife and children, guarding a queen who frequently behaved like a child deprived of a treat.

Chief among the courses was a dish of fish cooked with onions and ginger. Not the French cooking Mary would expect, but delicious all the same. "How has the castle handled the change?" I asked delicately. "Does it put a strain upon the kitchens?"

"The Scottish queen has her own cooks," he told me. "As well as a physician, an apothecary, an embroiderer... a veritable army of servants. We could fit but thirty men and six ladies-in-waiting in the castle, the rest are lodged in the town and come in each day to serve."

"Has it been difficult?" It was easy to sympathize with the fellow. At his age—over fifty, if I had to guess—he should be serving some quiet court appointment, arranging marriages for his children, and waiting for grandchildren. But instead, because of his strong Protestant faith and his history with Elizabeth and the king her brother, he was in Yorkshire, playing jailer to a queen.

"It is not easy." His tone was sober, but his mouth turned up at the corners. "I have given myself a project to make the time pass more quickly. I am determined she should learn English, and I will use my prayerbook to teach her."

I wished him all luck in his endeavors. Mary spoke French and Latin, and some Scots, but in the years since her return from France, she'd never seen fit to learn English. Margaery Lewis had attempted to teach her during her months at the Scottish court, to no avail.

Knollys and I were lingering at the table with wine when a man in Scots livery appeared in the doorway. "The queen is ready, Sir Francis."

"Good." He rose to his feet, leaning on the table to steady himself. "I will accompany you, Hawkins, but Cecil's letter said to give you several minutes alone with her." He gave a small shake of his head. "I assume they know what they're doing."

There were guards stationed along the corridor on the way to Mary's apartments, but they merely looked at me with Knollys; if I had his approval, it was no business of theirs. I filed that away, should I ever need to visit the queen without her captor's presence.

The doors opened and we entered Bolton's equivalent of a presence chamber, where Mary Stuart sat on a thronelike chair under a cloth of state. Her face lit up with recognition, but any personal happiness was quickly masked under a layer of hauteur and cosmetics. She looked pale and unfamiliar beneath an elaborate black wig.

"Your Majesty." I bowed and advanced until I reached her extended hand, bending my knee and brushing my lips over it. "I bring you greetings from Queen Elizabeth, along with the gifts which were earlier delivered to you."

"Monsieur Hawkins," she said in French, with a secret smile. "How good to see you again. Do you have a letter from my royal cousin, or only your own greetings?"

Angling so that my back was completely turned toward Knollys, I returned her smile. "My own greetings, Your Majesty, but"—I reached into my doublet and produced the queen's folded and sealed missive—"also this letter."

Taking it from me, she directed her gaze toward the door. "Sir Francois, must you remain here, eavesdropping on our conversation with our cousin's courier?"

"I..." He bowed and backed up. "I should not, but... for a moment, you understand."

Queen Mary pouted. "We shall walk in the gardens," she said, as if there were no question of permission. "You may follow behind, if you must."

She rose smoothly from her throne. Mary Seton hurried to straighten and arrange her skirts, while another woman offered a light shawl, which Mary refused.

Through the hall and out into the courtyard trailed the entire party, Mary at its head, escorted by Sir Francis. I followed close behind, my chest tight with the weight of everything which needed to be accomplished in this brief conversation. Once we reached the gardens, Sir Francis dropped back and I joined the queen at a respectful distance until she gestured for me to come closer, saying, "Monsieur Hawkins, we cannot imagine that very proper English gentleman will leave us alone for long."

"I think not." Looking around, I counted more than twenty people in the vicinity. "And we are far from alone, Your Majesty."

Dimples flickered in skin as smooth and pale as cream. "They are my people. They listen when they are told to listen."

I doubted that. In fact, I was almost certain that the fair-haired fellow studying the design of the knot garden was one of Cecil's men, though he'd been with Mary in France and returned with her to Scotland after she was widowed.

"In any case, Majesty, I will be brief." I pitched my voice for her ears alone. "I have taken a position as a courier for the English queen, which will enable me to visit without questions being asked."

A line appeared between her brows. "Could you not return to my service?"

"Your Majesty forgets that my heart and my birthright are at odds." I risked the tiniest of touches to her silver tissue sleeve. "I was always a member of the English court. If I had not agreed to this, I might not have been permitted to return at all. And that"— I gave her my best smile—"would have been tragic."

"Indeed." Elizabeth's letter flicked between her fingers like a card trick. "You will visit again?"

I kissed her hand once more. "I will. And if you have need of me—"

Her smile curled. "I will speak to that beautiful young man who arrived with you today, Monsieur Well-don of the long eyelashes." Her fingers rested lightly on my arm. "Sir Francois is closing in. Perhaps you should say your farewells and have some wine with your friend before you leave us."

"An excellent suggestion." I bowed, handing her off to Knollys. "God bless and keep Your Majesty."


My candle had not been blown out for more than five minutes when there came a scratching at my door. It was Dennis's habit to knock and enter, knowing he would not encounter me in a compromising position—though he would care little and tease me unmercifully if he did.

"Come," I called quietly, reaching under my pillow for my dagger.

The torchlight from the corridor leaked in as the door opened, showing the outline of a curving figure with its hand cupped around a candle. My visitor was a woman.

"William." A French accent with a faint burr of Scotland. Mary Seton.

"Mary." I put the dagger back in its hiding place. "Does the queen have a message—one she does not wish Sir Francis to know about?"

She approached in silence, moving her hand to reveal a light robe worn over a billowing nightdress of white silk. Her face, lit from below, was stark and determined. "I am not here on her behalf."

"No?" While Mary had been with the queen when I'd had my audience, I had avoided anything beyond the barest of greetings. After leaving Scotland without telling her, I had not expected a private meeting, nor did I particularly desire one.

She placed her candle on the small table at the bedside. Her unbound hair fell forward, covering her face, strands trailing over my chest. She smelled of musk and rosewater. My body responded to those remembered scents and the activities associated with them. I thought of my mission—of my father—and tried to control myself.

I had never liked the way desire made me feel. Since I was young, I had kept a tight rein on my emotions, but lust collapsed those lines and I would come to myself afterward, depleted and shamed and wondering why this part of me needed to exist at all.

"You should not be here," I said, hoping she would leave.

"Do you know what I do all day long, William?" Mary sat on the edge of the bed, her soft hip pressing against my knee. "I comb her hair. I brush her hair. I listen to her lament that she must wear wigs to cover its shortness. I brush and style her chosen wig until she is satisfied, and then she changes her mind and wishes to wear a different one." She clapped her hands softly over her face. "I am so bored! I think of throwing myself off a tower—and then you are here to save me."

Her hand drops with unerring aim to the bedcover. I sit bolt upright, trying to hide my reaction. "Mary, we are guests in this house."

"Do you wish me to go?" She stroked me through the thin cover, her hand warm and knowing.

She had been useful before, and likely would again. As the blood drained from my head, I thought that it would not do to alienate the queen of Scotland's chief waiting-woman.

"I worry that we will be found out," I said, shifting to make room for her. "No more than that."

Mary shed her robe and loosened the ties of her nightdress. Candlelight spilled golden across her skin, and I reached out to push the gown from her shoulders, exposing her breasts and the small silver pomander she wore on a cord around her neck.

"Do not worry," she murmured, throwing back the covers and pushing up my shirt. Her tongue flicked to her lips, and she lowered her head. "Your man is guarding the door."

# Chapter 10

Dennis entered whistling, carrying a basin of warm water. "Good morrow, master!" he sang out.

I was alone; at some point in the night, my guest had crept out as stealthily as she had come, doubtless requiring my man's escort back to her quarters and causing the grin that I turned away from. "Pack my things," I said brusquely, hoping to stave off further mockery. "We're leaving as soon as I've broken my fast."

Washing away Mary Seton's lingering scent did not assuage my discomfort about what had occurred the night before. The thing between us was not love—nor even a particular liking—but when we were in Scotland it had been convenient for both of us. If I returned to Bolton with any regularity, I would have to find a way to put her off, else I would not be able to live with myself.

After I had dressed, I found Jamie in the hall and took a seat beside him. "I may not be able to pass on your message to Mistress Rowan immediately," I said. "I have another trip I must make first."

It had come to me in the night, as Mary had slept with her head pillowed on my shoulder, where I needed to go next. While I yearned to see little Jane, I was too fragile in myself to submit to another meeting with my father quite yet. I needed someone who would answer my questions, not give me more.

When Dennis joined me in the courtyard, he looked at me and knew enough to ask, "Is it Hawkmoor or your sister's home?"

"Neither," I said shortly. "Whitby."

He sighed but remained silent, staying thus until we stopped for dinner when our hunger drew us to a roadside inn.

"Ten years since we've been there," he said. "A bit different this time."

"A bit." The first time I had visited Robin Lewis's house, I had come with near a dozen armed men to take him into custody. My second visit was years later, when I escorted his wife back from Edinburgh. I was welcome at Winterset any time, I had been told, but I had confined my relationship with Robin to an active correspondence.

Whitby was an easy two days' ride from Bolton. As the dales flattened into the moorland of my childhood, something opened in my chest, and I breathed easily for the first time since leaving Scotland.

On the first day, we stopped to rest a scant hour before dark. The sun set late in the summer, so it must have been near ten, but the pleasant innkeeper produced bread and cheese, along with ale, without having to be shown my messenger's credentials. I sat alone, trying to work out why seeing my friend was more important than visiting my family, when I had no clear idea if I would be returning to the north anytime soon.

Although Robin had children himself, he had never struck me as particularly fatherly. Yet he had taught me much in the years of our friendship: about taking the time to see things properly, learning what I could in every circumstance, and not jumping to judgment. His counsel was what I needed.

He had come from nothing—an orphan turned secretary to Thomas Cromwell, who had made a place for himself in Elizabeth's court alongside Ned, who had been his friend since the days of King Henry.

It was because of Ned, I understood, this gnawing need to speak with Robin.

In the years that I had been away from court, Cecil, and Ned along with him, had become far more serious about the business of spying on the Scottish queen and worrying over Catholic rebellions. That their concerns were valid, I did not doubt for an instant; what I doubted—deeply—was my involvement.

Robin had left court himself not long after my final departure for Edinburgh, so it was unclear to me what, beyond a desire for his isolated house and its library, and the wish to spend time with his family, had driven him to leave. Had he experienced similar qualms? Did the work of protecting the realm sometimes also make him feel desperately in need of a bath?

Mary Seton had shared more with me than her body; she had given me insight into the queen's desperation. Her sole wish was to return to Scotland and wrest the crown away from the men who had given it to her son. She clearly expected that Elizabeth would assist her in these undertakings. If Elizabeth did not, Mary told me, there were assurances of help from other quarters. She would not tell me who, leaving me to wonder if Cecil's suspicions regarding Norfolk were correct.

An eruption of giggles made me look up from my musings. Dennis was flirting with the tavern girl, and from her sparkling eyes and the hand resting on his shoulder, I understood I would be alone in my room that night. It was just as well. My thoughts did not require company.


Dennis came in before dawn, his boots in one hand. "You can make a light," I said. "I'm awake."

"Thank Christ," he responded. "My head needs all the help it can get."

Dropping his jerkin on the chair, he pulled his shirt over his head, exposing an uneven line of purple-red bite marks that extended partway around his neck. He reeked powerfully of ale and sex.

"Did you not leave her time to complete your necklace?"

"She found better things to do with her mouth." His hand went to his throat, and he plunged his face into the bowl of water intended for my washing, then shook himself like a dog. I dodged the spray, laughing. "Shall I tell you the tale?"

"Please don't." I rolled out of bed, twisting to stretch my low back, which complained at our endless riding. "When you're done splashing, I'd appreciate a fresh basin."

"Yes, sir!" He sketched a bow and pulled on a new shirt, wrinkling his nose at the state of his discarded one. "Wherever we fetch up next, I'll pay my regards to the laundry maid."

"You are a disgrace," I told him, but the words were said fondly. As a boy in my father's service, Dennis had always chased girls. As he aged, so did his paramours.

"Why do you not judge me as severely as you judge your father?" he asked, gathering up my dirty shirt with his.

I raised my eyebrows. "I may deplore your behavior, Dennis, but your women come to you freely."

"Do you think your father has been committing rape all these years? I've watched the man." He spread his hands, mimicking the feeding of birds. "He casts his crumbs upon the water, and they flock to him."

It was pointless to argue with him before breakfast, and anyway, I knew what my father was. "The basin," I reminded him. "I'd like to get downstairs before the food is gone."

Dennis paused at the door. "I'll make sure that Joanie saves a plate for you. It's the least she can do, after last night."


We reached Whitby in the late morning, having started at dawn. The village had expanded since my last visit, but the hulking remains of the Benedictine abbey looming above were the same, or close enough. Passing through the village, resisting the dizzying aroma of the pie shops, we guided our mounts along the uneven coast road.

The sky was dull, but the Yorkshire coast had always looked its best under gray skies. The water to our right was a deep charcoal, fading until the two colors merged at the horizon. Far out to sea, three tiny sails: a vessel on its way to the Low Countries.

"It was snowing, remember?" Dennis said. An early November storm, starting with fine snow as we approached the house and turning to sleet overnight, the area becoming a sea of ice-crusted mud that made our departure impossible for two days.

"I remember." That week had changed my life. Robin was a man, no better and no worse than me, but I believed we both emerged from that strange journey as different people. And so it was to Winterset that we rode today, a house I had once invaded with armed men. Now I returned as a friend, visiting my mentor, a man in need of his sage advice.

Dennis nudged his horse forward. "I thought you were mad when you joined him."

"I know."

"I also thought you joining the court meant we'd stop riding all over creation." He snorted. "I was wrong."

We had reached the turning; from there, the road led to the limestone gate which marked Winterset's boundary. I slowed my horse to look ahead, and said to Dennis, in as offhand a tone as I could manage, "You don't have to come along, you know. If you don't want to."

He snorted again. "What, and have you riding hither and yon with your shirt-tails flapping, looking like who-knows-what?" He gave me a sidelong glance. "The Scottish queen's lady might never look at you again."

"That would be no bad thing." I touched the horse with my heels, and he moved off obligingly. Dennis followed.

"I know you're funny about all that," he said, whipping off his cap and pushing his hair back. "But there aren't many who'd be upset to have a French tart sneak into their bed."

"She's not a tart," I said. "She's lonely. I'm a diversion."

Dennis hooted. "And there are no others to divert her in your absence? She's been pining, according to the Bolton servants." He slapped my shoulder with his cap before jamming it back on his head. "And now we know for who."

We cantered through the gate and into the courtyard. "Be silent or I will send you to Hawkmoor to await my return."

"Anything but that!" He jumped down as a boy ran from the stables to see to the horses. "Not your father!"

I dismounted more slowly, disturbed, as always, by mention of my sire. By the time my boots were planted on the cobbles, the round-topped door had swung open, and Robin and his wife stood framed on the threshold.

"Will!" Margaery Lewis advanced first, planting kisses on both cheeks and dragging me by the arm into the house. "What are you doing here? Why did you not send word?"

I struggled to free myself from her grasp. "I was tasked with delivering a message to Bolton Castle and thought to see you both before returning to London."

"You are always welcome here." Robin embraced me, though with less enthusiasm than his wife. He was thinner and leaned heavily on a stick. "How long will you stay?"

"Two or three days, no more." We moved inside as Dennis carried in my things. "Ned expects me back."

Something dark crossed Robin's face. "I would speak to you about him, while you are here."

A knot of worry loosened in my gut. "As I would to you," I said. "Ned is the reason for my visit, although he believes me to be with my sister, Elizabeth."

"Liz was here two weeks ago with her children," Margaery told me. "I'm sorry you missed them."

Robin broke away. "If you'll excuse me," he said, "I've got work to do." He smiled at Margaery with an affection I'd never thought to see in such a closed-off man. "Will you entertain our guest over dinner, wife, while I finish?"

"Of course." She pushed him gently in the direction of his library. After the door closed, she said, "Nothing yet gets in the way of his books. Not even the children."

It was comforting that he hadn't changed. "Where are they?"

"Ralph is out in the fields. For all that he's seven, he thinks himself a man grown. Margaret is three, and with her nursemaid." A private smile, and she laid a hand on the flat front of her gown. "There will be another by the new year."

"Congratulations." Her fecundity, and her obvious happiness, made me awkward. I directed my gaze at the painted wall-hanging so as not to look at her.

Mary Seton's chestnut curls and talented mouth could never touch what I felt for Margaery Lewis. Robin had asked me to watch over her in Scotland, and I took my duties a little too seriously. She was out of my reach, but I had reached once, kissing her in a secluded corridor of Holyrood Palace. She struck me a blow that rattled my brain back into its proper moorings and the next day, kindly told the queen's ladies my black eye was due to defending her virtue, not assaulting it.

I tried not to think about her after that.

But I did. Endlessly over the years since, as she grew happier in her marriage and more beautiful in her happiness. I thought about her when she attended my sister's wedding and the birth of Nell's two babes. I thought about her when her children were born, and she retired to the country to care for them—which took her out of my reach.

"Let me take you up to Anselm's chamber," she said. "You can wash and change. Come down when you're ready to eat. I'll tell Mistress Dunham to hold dinner."

Anselm's chamber was the room I had slept in when I'd come to arrest Robin. The old monk, an important part of Robin's past, had ridden through the same storm to send word to Ned; we met at Hatfield after Elizabeth had been proclaimed queen.

"Where is Anselm?"

"He died in April." Margaery's brown eyes glistened with tears. "It's been very hard for Robin."

"I'm sure." Anselm had been a brother in the monastery where Robin was raised, but they had not met again until years later, when a group of monks sought shelter at Winterset. The others left the country, but Anselm stayed on. The story given out was that he was Robin's uncle, and they were in truth closer than many blood relations.

"He rests on our land," she confided, brightening. "Robin wouldn't allow him to be buried in the churchyard. Fowler found a priest to come at the last, and he stayed for the burial."

That was dangerous but entirely Robin's way: he appeared unemotional, but he did what was necessary for those he cared about.

"I'm sorry for your loss." The words seemed inadequate. "How is Robin bearing up?"

"He is in his library more than ever." She directed me through an open door, where Dennis was already unpacking my things. "Your visit will do him good—it will bring him out of himself."

I wasn't so sure, considering what I had come to speak with him about, but I did not wish to cause her any worry and let her leave with an assurance that I would be with her shortly.

When I joined her in the hall, my face and hands scrubbed clean and wearing a fresh shirt, Margaery had our dinner brought out, while a maid took a tray into the library.

"I'm sorry about this." She nodded at the bowls of pottage. "Robin likes his food plain, and so do the children."

"It's fine." The pottage smelled delicious—there was bacon in with the peas and barley. "Traveling, I've learned to eat what's put in front of me and enjoy it."

We ate and we talked desultorily of my travels and their children and Robin's project—a history of the dissolution and his speculations on what was lost—and after the table was cleared, Margaery fetched me into her private parlor, where she took up a bit of embroidery and settled in for a proper chat.

"So... is there anyone in your life? Any woman?" She looked down at the cloth, but I did not have to see her face to know her expression.

"No." Where was Robin? As often as I dreamed of being alone with her, the reality was never what I expected.

She continued to work, silent for once, but only because she was thinking. "You know, even if you don't want a wife, you could come to a tidy arrangement with someone. It would be good for you."

My face throbbed with heat. "Why would I do that?"

There had been women in my life, but Margaery was suggesting something akin to my father's relationship with Lady Rose. My infrequent encounters with Mary Seton were entanglement enough.

The cloth dropped and she grasped my wrist with a surprisingly strong hand. "Because I don't want you to be like Robin. It damages a man, to be without companionship. Especially when solitude is not forced upon him but chosen from fear of intimacy."

"There is companionship in my life." I enjoyed the chance to touch her even as I peeled her fingers away, one by one. She was plain-spoken, and somehow always brought out the side of me that balked at pleasure.

She shook her head and retrieved her abandoned stitching. "Men don't count, Will. Not in your case, anyway."

This was an oblique reference to my feelings for her and an acknowledgement of the rumors about her husband's past. How could she know about those? I knew more than most, and I was uncomfortable with that knowledge.

"I can manage my life." I tried to inject more warmth into my tone. "I thank you for your care, but it is unnecessary."

"Fine." It was never good when a woman said that; I had learned that in my dealings with them. "But I think Lord Kelton has been remiss. If you won't find a wife, he should find one for you."

"He has no time for matchmaking. He is too wrapped up in Jane's care."

Margaery laughed. "Lord Kelton is a man of many parts. I'm sure he could find the time."

He could if he chose; he'd found an heiress for Harry—who did not require one, as he was due to inherit a good portion of Yorkshire should the current lord ever choose to shuffle off to a warmer clime. It might be a long time. Father was a dozen years older than the man I had come to visit, but energetic and frequently angry—the secret, I thought, to his continued vitality. He would not die until Death ceased to be frightened by him.

## CHAPTER 11

IT WAS LATE AFTERNOON before I was summoned to Robin's library. I had gone for a walk along the cliff, declining Margaery's offer to accompany me, and let the stiff breeze blow away the inappropriate thoughts she inspired. When the door closed with her on the other side, I sighed with relief. Robin glanced up with a frown; he knew both my affection for and frustration with his wife.

"I'm not disturbing you?"

"No, it's not you." He folded a letter and set it aside. "Just an annoying correspondent."

"Who?" It wasn't like him to sound so short-tempered. Abrupt, certainly, but Robin didn't care enough about most people to let them annoy him.

He smiled, the disruption forgotten. "Bjorn. Someone I met in Amsterdam while avoiding the late queen." Glancing again at the letter, he said, "He started writing to me a few years ago. I didn't respond at first—he feels tied up somehow with everything that happened back then—but he was persistent." He reached for his empty glass. "Fetch the bottle, will you? And pour some for yourself."

The food at Winterset might be plain, but the wine was always excellent and the glassware in Robin's library was fine-blown and Venetian.

"Will you respond?" I took a sip and closed my eyes with pleasure. Exposure to his tastes had made me learn to appreciate wine. "To this Bjorn fellow?"

"Eventually," he said with a shrug. "The more he asks, the slower I become. I blame age, but he brings it on himself—though he does know an uncommon amount about the monasteries and has, more than once, given me an insight into this project of mine."

"What's he like?" I continued to ask questions because I didn't know how to bring up the topic I wanted to discuss.

He cracked his knuckles. "Other than annoying? Good looking fellow, I suppose. Blond, one of those Viking types. Fancied himself a bit."

I thought back on the past Robin had so carefully related. He was a lover of men as well as women, although he had never shown interest in me that way. I was both glad and occasionally disappointed—yet one more person for whom I held no appeal. "Were you close?"

"Aren't you tactful?" Robin smothered a laugh. "No, we were not close. And I had Sebastian with me, so even if the question had arisen, nothing would have come of it."

"You would have put off your pleasures for Sebastian's comfort?" I didn't understand him, all these years later.

"I would have done anything for Sebastian." His gaze went distant for a moment, remembering his lost servant, a dark-skinned African whom he had treated like a son. "It would have been but a passing moment, and truthfully, we didn't have the sort of intellectual connection that brings about attraction for me."

I did not know how to respond to that and wanted to keep him from dwelling on Seb. Nodding at his desk, adrift in paper covered with his close, italic hand, I asked, "Your work is going well?"

"Margaery told you what I'm doing?" He put his glass to one side and cleaned his quill, then flexed and shook his hands.

"She did." It sounded quite an undertaking, but the breaking up of the monasteries had been a deep wound for Robin, and perhaps this was a part of its healing. "I'm glad of it. It's a tale that needs to be told."

He tipped his head back, staring at the ceiling. Through the open window came the faint sound of seabirds. At night, the waves themselves were audible in the house. "Perhaps not at this time," he said. "I would be accused of papist sympathies and you know it." One corner of his mouth turned up. "When once I was accused of heresy by those same papists."

We lived in a ridiculous world. He knew it better than anyone. I shook my head and placed my palms flat on the desk. "About the reason for my visit..."

"Yes, do tell." Robin seemed relieved at the change of topic. "Are you out of Scotland for good?"

"I believe so, now that the queen is in England." I explained that Mary believed she'd sent me to London to plead her case. "Now I've been made a royal messenger, so I can be of more broad use—in and out of houses in England, across to France. Whatever is needed."

He nodded, his expression troubled. "Was this at Ned's suggestion?"

"Ned or Cecil." A high-pitched squeal reached us from the other side of the door, followed by Margaery's lower tones as she attempted to calm the children. "They are one and the same."

"They are not," Robin said precisely. "Cecil lives for God and Elizabeth Tudor, not always in that order. Ned's first loyalty is to himself. You must be wary of him, Will. He is not always what he appears."

I had learned that over the years, but I was surprised Robin would speak openly against a man who was a close friend. "What do you mean?"

He considered the question, rubbing at his sparsely bearded chin. "It's not that Ned doesn't believe in whatever he's doing. When we worked for Cromwell, he was fiercely against the monasteries."

"He's still anti-Catholic."

"No," Robin told me. "This was different. He took joy in plundering the monasteries, mistreating the men, because it was his job." His eyes drifted closed, as if exhausted, and I wondered again at his thinness. "Having it be his work gives him the excuse of doing more, perhaps, than he otherwise would." When I did not respond, he continued. "I know for a fact that he read my letters when we worked together, and I introduced him to my friends to save him the trouble of investigating them himself."

"But he trusts you. Why would he—"

"It's what he does," came Margaery's crisp voice from the doorway. I hadn't heard the door open and wondered how long she'd been there.

"He listens and he plans and he plots." She smiled at Robin, her eyes soft with affection. "I'm not criticizing him any more than you are, husband. My chief complaint about Ned over the years was that he was no respecter of bedtimes."

The purpose of my visit accomplished, I could have left the next morning. Instead, I extended my stay for several days, enjoying Winterset's easy hospitality. I found young Ralph Lewis, their firstborn, to be an engaging child. At his mother's urging, I took him behind the stables, where butts were set up for the men to practice archery and gave him instruction on his small bow.

Margaery wandered down after an hour to see how we were doing. "What do you say, will he make an archer?"

Most of the boy's arrows had gone wide, but he had good form and a strong focus once he understood the basics.

"I would not send him off to war yet, but he shows great promise." I tousled his flaming curls. "That is enough for now, Ralph. We will try again tomorrow morning, before I leave."

The boy's lip came out. "I don't want you to leave."

As my comings and goings frequently failed to register with anyone save those in London, his words warmed me. "I'll come again," I promised, "when I am next in Yorkshire."

CHAPTER 12

WE MADE GOOD TIME coming back from Yorkshire. The blazing heat and clear skies meant the roads were good, or as good as the roads ever were. In the countryside, however, and even the small cities through which we passed, the people were grim. There was talk of failing crops. Priests prayed for deliverance, and rain.

A drought was a fearsome thing, causing more than empty bellies in winter. A hungry populace might quickly become discontented in their search for someone to blame for their misfortunes. Add in the problem of religion, particularly in the north, and the country was rapidly becoming a powder keg.

Listening as we went, Dennis and I compared notes later and found little difference in what we'd heard. The poor and the servant class grumbled less than their betters, but with more reason. I stored it all up to tell Ned when we reached London, only to find him off to Surrey for his yearly visit to his family.

The city was at its worst in August. The heat and the thick damp rising from the river exaggerated all the already unpleasant smells. Ned was not the sole absentee: along with the queen, many of the courtiers had abandoned the city for the countryside, but the business of government went on at Whitehall. The place buzzed like a hive from morning until night.

Waiting for Ned's return, I spent my days visiting the book stalls at St. Paul's to choose a gift for Robin and Margaery, and judicious evenings at The Minstrel's Arms, making sure to leave while I could sit a horse. I would give Dennis no opportunity for mockery.

Harry never mentioned my last visit. When Jenny breezed through the crowded room, her smile told me that my shame had not been forgotten, but she was as tactful as her brother and said nothing.

Having recovered from her ailment of earlier in the season, their mother sang for the crowd each night, accompanied by her husband. I sat apart, listening to them, turning over in my mind the knowledge that she had been my father's mistress in the days before his marriage. Robin had shared that shocking fact during our long-ago ride toward his execution.

In her sixties now, Bess was thick-waisted and near-blind, but her voice was that of a much younger woman. To my surprise, she navigated the crowded tavern as surely as the maid who delivered ale to my table, with a merry word for everyone who spoke to her. It was clear that, even when young, her appeal had come more from her warmth than any beauty she might have had.

As I watched her sing, her husband watched her no less closely, fingers on his lute and a private smile upon his lips. Harry said his parents had a long road before they were wed, but they had set such an example that he could not wait to find a woman of his own and make for his children the same happy life they'd given him. People who spoke thus about their parents were alien to me; even had I not disliked my father, my feelings would have extended no further than respect and fear. Growing up, most of the boys I knew felt the same. There was little open affection in their families; certainly, I had never seen my father look upon my mother with the open, loving expression of Thomas Minstrel.

The song ended and Bess rose, one hand reaching out as her husband's steadying arm appeared. She curtsied to her customers and the pair disappeared into the tavern's back room.

"Let's to Whitehall," I called to Dennis, draining my cup and pushing back the bench. "They expect Ned on the morrow."

"Aye, you'll need your rest for that." He blew a kiss to the tavern maid and followed me out into the dark street.

The minuscule window in my chamber managed to keep all the air out while letting most of the noise in. I turned over and punched my pillow, trying to get comfortable. Trying to cool off. When we returned from the tavern, I'd washed away the smells of smoke and ale, the water drying almost instantly on my hot skin. Now, as I lay naked on the lumpy mattress, praying for a breeze, those cold Scottish winters felt like a fever dream. I had always been this hot, this uncomfortable, and I always would be.

"Go to sleep, would you?" Dennis said from the antechamber, where he set up his pallet. "It's bad enough without hearing you thrashing."

I didn't bother to reprimand him. What was the point? He was equally miserable.

Getting up as quietly as I could, I leaned on the sill and looked out at the night sky. My chamber was over an inner courtyard, so there was little to see except other windows. Most were dark, though some showed light as the occupants read or drank or distracted themselves with everything from card games to bed sport.

If only distraction came that easily. I had not been able to let go of Robin's warning about Ned, as it reinforced my suspicions. But I couldn't walk away from their plans with the flimsy excuse that their games of intrigue made me uncomfortable.

*You have the standards of a fainting maid.* My father's voice echoed in my brain. Was I being womanish to want to stand apart from all this? What would he have done in my situation?

He wouldn't have left The Minstrel's Arms without having kissed the tavern maid. He'd have had her against the alley wall and come back whistling to pay a call on whichever mistress he had stashed nearby.

Did it make me a fainting maid that I found his behavior repellent? I had never enjoyed lightness with women, not even when I was in Paris, when I had nightly trawled the streets with Matthew and the other students in search of amusement. We found many, from drinking houses to entertainments to brothels, but I never let on my discomfort when we frequented the latter establishments. To my companions, buying an hour with a woman was the high point of a long and studious week; to me it was a reminder of my father's careless infidelities.

Each time I found myself in the arms of a woman, I froze, fearing this would be the encounter that would turn me into my father, a man whose appetites knew no bounds of honor or family.

I did not return from France in a virgin state, but I came home with my heart untouched.

Until Cecily.

I turned from the window. When I could not sleep, regret came easily, and tonight, for some reason, I thought of Cecily. We would be fifteen years wed, if things had been different. I would have an unimaginably different life, but for my father.

When I left my uncle's house for Cambridge, Cecily had been no more than a pretty child, fast friends with my female cousins. The two years difference in age was less noticeable when I returned for the summer. By the time I left for Paris, she was seventeen, with a peach bloom on her cheeks and smooth hair the color of ink.

God, I had wanted her. And she wanted me. Or so I thought.

The Christmas after my return, we reached agreement on our feelings in a remarkably short time, and stole a moment alone during the festivities, huddling under the grand staircase of her father's house. Her small hands slid around my neck and her lips were soft and yielding. I had no more than kissed her twice when my father's voice echoed in the hall.

"William!"

We broke apart and I stepped out of the darkness. "Yes, sir?"

"Where the hell have you been hiding yourself? Your mother—" He broke off, his glare fading when Cecily emerged from the shadows. "Mistress Cecily, I do hope my son wasn't making a nuisance of himself." Holding out his arm, he said, "The dancing has begun, and I thought I would ask the prettiest girl to stand up with me."

Not looking at me, she took his arm, blushing until her cheeks matched her gown. "And yet you are here, sir."

One dark brow slanted upward. "Indeed. I would ask you to dance—unless you've already promised yourself to my boy here."

The top of my head could have lifted off with the force of my jealousy. How dare he flirt with her like she was one of his whores?

"Not at all, Lord Kelton." She giggled and lifted her face to his. "I would be honored to dance with you."

They passed through the arch and disappeared from view. I held tight to the stair rail until I could breathe properly. He had asked Cecily to dance to prove his power over me. Surely, he knew, when she followed me from beneath the stairs, what we had been about. What sort of man would take a girl from his son?

The sort of man who had sired me, I concluded, sick in my guts and yet unable to keep myself from watching them. Cecily stared up into his face the way she had recently looked into mine. Every touch of his hand registered in as a caress.

I found my way to my mother, sitting to one side with the other ladies. She had recently lost a babe, and this was the first time she had ventured out since leaving her bed. "How are you?"

"I'm fine, darling." She smiled sweetly, watching my father. "It's so kind of him to dance with Cecily, don't you think?"

I made a noncommittal noise. Could she not see what was in front of her? "Are you certain you won't dance?"

"I'm not up to it yet, Will." She ran her hand down my sleeve, patting me. "Don't spend the evening with your old mother. Find a maid to dance with."

As if I could, when the maid I wanted was making a display of herself with my father. When the music stopped, he bowed to Cecily and returned to my mother's side. I claimed her for the next dance but regretted it almost immediately as all her conversation was of him.

"Lord Kelton is so very kind." She placed her hand on mine, but all I could see was her hand in his. "He must have known I was scared no one would ask me to dance."

I nearly tripped over my feet. "You knew I would ask," I said, my voice strained. "You should have known, considering—"

"Hush, Willie!" she squealed, and her color rose again. "People can't know what we were about, they'd think I was common." Her black lashes fanned her cheek. "Even your father said I should be wary of being seen in dark corners with young men."

"As if he hasn't done the same, or worse," I said roughly, a years-old picture coming unbidden to my mind. "He is no saint, my father."

Cecily looked at me with something like pity. "Lord Kelton is a great gentleman, Willie, and you should take care to learn from him."

It was no use.

I struck a flint and lit my candle, closing the door so as not to interrupt Dennis's sleep. I might need rest before my conversation with Ned, but there was none to be had. My one hope was that he would put off our meeting for another day, but I doubted that would happen.

My luck did not run that way.

## CHAPTER 13

WALTER STARLING HAD BEEN a royal messenger since the days of King Edward and was looking forward to a well-earned retirement in a small patch of Devon purchased with the salary he'd had no opportunity to spend. His last assignment was to see that I became an adequate replacement.

"Nice little house," he confided as we shared a pitcher of ale in his rooms. "Going to call it Starling's Roost." He tipped back his cup and his strong throat worked as the ale flowed down. "And that's what I'm going to do, Hawkins. Roost, and about time, too."

"You've not been in England recently?" I was rather looking forward to learning the foreign routes. Anything to keep me away from Bolton and the varied complications within that castle.

Starling shook his head. "I've been in England constantly, just never for more than a day or two at a time." He refilled our cups. "Don't get me wrong, I get across to France and the Low Countries. Amsterdam twice. Once all the way to Rome, but I was young and seconded to someone else then."

I'd never imagined going as far as Rome. It reminded me of Robin and his desire for a world outside of England—which had led him, in the end, to a very small corner of England.

"Tell me about Rome." I took a sip, trying to give the appearance of keeping up with him.

He slid out of his chair and paced, a stocky man with a horseman's powerful legs. "Strange," he said at last. "The past is so in evidence that I wanted to fetch my schoolboy Latin and try speaking it to the statues."

I liked Starling. He seemed a straightforward fellow, with a sense of humor and a capacity for drink that would make him an agreeable traveling companion. We had been speaking for nearly an hour and he had not yet brought up women or brothels—which was more than could be said for Ned, who had arrived straight from the arms of his loving wife and proposed a trip to a whorehouse to clear his head.

I went along but remained downstairs with a drink rather than choose a woman. The madam earned her coin anyway by telling him I'd come down the stairs ahead of him, but Ned suspected the truth.

"You don't know how to have fun, Hawkins," he said, scratching himself and giving a bleary smile. "Annabelle there would set you to rights."

Annabelle, red-haired and older than her paint let on, winked at me over his shoulder. "I'd do my best, sir."

I raised my cup to her. "Another time, lady."

"Sir Edward told me about you." Starling's voice cut through my reverie.

"What did he say?" I wasn't sure I wanted to know what struck Ned as important enough to tell others.

He dropped back into his chair. "Most of us who get into this either have no family—that's me—or are younger sons of good family, trying to make their way." Starling met my gaze steadily. "He says you're both, a second son who has no contact with his people."

"My father and I aren't on the best of terms," I said. "But I do speak with the rest of my family. I would have visited them on my return from Bolton Castle, but there wasn't time."

There had been time enough to visit Winterset, but no one needed to know that.

"You saw the queen?" His eyebrows, thick and brown like his beard, lifted with interest. "I haven't had that pleasure. What's the lady like?"

I thought of all the things that could be said about Scottish Mary and began with the easiest. "She's tall," I said. "Almost mannishly tall, but pretty enough that you don't notice. She can't speak English worth a damn, but she's charming in three other languages." I thought of Cecil and Ned and all their worries. "And she's not as Catholic as they fear, though she could turn that way if mishandled."

"You'll not likely be seeing her again for some time." Starling grinned at me. "I'll be going south and across to France next. Sir Edward said that's where they want to start you."

I listened as he explained the route: the Tilbury ferry from the London dock to Gravesend, down the south side of the Thames estuary. From there, we would pick up horses to ride down into Kent and on to Dover to take ship across to France. It was difficult to keep track of the inns he mentioned, and other places where the best horses could be rented—with or without our messengers' identification.

"There are times," he said, "when it's safer to travel as a man than a messenger."

That was understandable enough; the queen's business could be dangerous.

A final brief meeting with Ned. He looked up, his pretense of busyness falling away at the sight of me. "Hawkins!"

I wondered when he'd lost the use of my given name; he hadn't called me Will since I'd returned from Scotland. Perhaps they had gotten so used to seeing me as a chess piece that my humanity had fallen away.

"All ready?" he asked, a jovial smile splitting his face. "I think you'll do well with Starling."

"I think so." Everything I had learned about the man so far led me to believe we would get along.

"Say." Ned stopped, his palms pressed to his desk. "We spoke of Bolton, but I never inquired as to how you got on with your family."

"Fine." I smiled tightly. "You know how it is with us. But I saw my niece and my sister, which was my intention."

Ned came around the desk and clapped me on the back. "You should have taken extra time and gone to Whitby."

Despite the heat, my skin prickled as if I'd touched ice. He could not possibly know where I had been. Before I left the north, I'd sent a letter by post to my sister, asking that if inquiries were made, she should say I had spent three days with her and Jane.

"I was told to return promptly," I said. "And so I did." Though Ned had been in Surrey, I gave a report of my meeting with Mary to Cecil himself. "Have you heard from Lewis?"

"A letter in June," he said. "I haven't answered yet. I love the man like a brother, but he talks about nothing but books."

"He is set in his ways." And all the safer for it, I hoped.

"Aren't we all?" Ned slung an arm around my shoulders. "Starling has everything you'll need for the journey. He's waiting for you in the yard."

I bid him farewell, escaping from the principal secretary's offices with all possible speed.

Starling, his man, and Dennis were waiting by the stable block, looking up at the clear sky. I hurried to meet them. As our horses were led out, harnesses clinking, a warm breeze blew through the courtyard. It seemed an auspicious beginning to this new phase of my life, and I swung up on the back of my mount with optimism in my heart, determined to put Ned's worrying comments behind me and focus on the journey ahead.

# PART II
## 1569

## CHAPTER 14

STARLING SPRAWLED ON THE bench, his back against the wall, legs extended toward the fire. A jug of ale was on the table between us. He wore a happy and slightly blurred expression, as it was our second jug in as many hours and would likely be followed by more.

"You think we'll be able to leave tomorrow?" I asked idly, aiming my feet toward the flames. "Before we drink them dry?"

"Likely," he grunted. "But we could try praying for more rain."

It had been raining for the better part of ten days; if it rained any more, I thought I would grow mold. But our message had been delivered and there was no rush to return. In such weather, any delay could be blamed on a rough crossing.

"I'm not much of a praying man." The divide between Catholic and Protestant as I was growing up made me retreat from both, even as I'd wanted to please my mother by assuming her faith.

"Nor me." Starling belched and tipped his head back to look at the shadowy ceiling beams. "Though I'd make exception for a warm body in my bed tonight." He grinned at me through whiskers grown bushy against the cold. "Nothing against you, Will, but you snore, and you don't cuddle."

Although there were scarcely more than a dozen years between us, I had come to think of Starling almost as a father figure: he taught me much and mocked me not at all, which I believed was what a healthy father-son relationship should be. My initial liking for him had not flagged, even as he had taken advantage of the occasional offers made by

servants and strumpets on our various journeys. He never insisted on
company for his adventures, though Dennis often went with him while
I stayed behind with our host or the innkeeper, content to be alone.

Messengering was more enjoyable than I had expected. I liked the
constant travel, even when inconveniences such as weather or a lame
horse or chasing a message's recipient from town to town made our days
longer. I liked being away from the expectations of Ned Pickering and
William Cecil, and of Francis Walsingham, whom I did not know but
who was the latest member of the cabinet to involve himself in the matter
of the two queens.

We had returned to London a half dozen times in the nine months I'd
been with Starling, and that was our eventual destination on this trip—if
the rain ever stopped. Outside the pleasant inn where we drank was a
mud-soaked village in northern France, not far from where Margaery
Lewis had a house once owned by her grandparents.

I'd not been able to visit Whitby since setting off in August, but
Robin's letters, circumspect and informational, arrived at Whitehall on
a regular basis. They appeared intact when I received them, but I never
assumed they hadn't been read and re-sealed. Like my sister, Robin knew
to address important letters to Harry Minstrel's care.

"You know," Starling said, tipping the last of the ale into his cup, "we'll
be separated after we return. You've enough knowledge to take on your
own second now, and I'm overdue for my roost."

"I hope you find a warm body to share it with," I said, touching
the rim of my cup to his. I would miss him. He was good company, and
more importantly, I trusted him. He wasn't reporting back to Ned
about my conversation or any letters I posted while in England. Starling
cared about his job, but more important was adequate ale each day and
anticipation of his new life in Devon while he was young enough to enjoy
it.

"I will," he said with enviable assurance. "Pretty maids bloom like
roses on the south coast. I'll pick one and set up housekeeping. Might
have some young ones before I'm old enough to be their grandfather."

I couldn't imagine thinking so plainly about such a fraught subject.
My parents' marriage had been happy in its way, but I never viewed it
as an exemplar of what I wanted. Nor had I seen other happy marriages,

until Robin and Margaery, and their relationship would not be easily duplicated.

"If we are able to leave tomorrow," I ventured, "would you mind another brief stop? I promised a friend I would look in on her house if I passed this way."

Starling sat upright. "What's that, Will? A lady with a house? Have you been keeping secrets?"

"No." I hid my shameful blush by turning to the fire. "She is the wife of a good friend. When they married, she left France, but she has a house here."

He shrugged extravagantly and raised a hand for more ale. "It matters not. We'll meet our men in Honfleur. Dennis will have found us a ship."

We had sent them ahead several days ago to scout for passage to England. Howland, Starling's manservant, was less sharp at these matters than Dennis, who had shown an aptitude for the travails of messengering beyond my own.

"And he'll no doubt be settled in some portside brothel." Dennis rewarded himself amply for his labors.

"Perhaps you should sample his follies before you pass judgment," Starling said, wrapping a meaty arm around the maid as she delivered a fresh pitcher. The first two times she had pushed him away, but this time she allowed him, with a giggle, to pull her onto his knee. He said something to her in growling French, and her giggles multiplied. She settled herself, squirming, and my companion broke into a wide grin. "You may be sleeping alone, after all," he said, and shoved the pitcher across the table.

Starling woke me in the morning with his stumbling arrival. The rain had stopped overnight, though the dawn sky was pale and watery.

I sat up. "I take it you had an enjoyable night."

"I did, I did." He sat heavily and fell back across the bed, and my legs. "Lovely lass. If she spoke a word of English, I'd take her home with me."

"She'd hardly handle the ride," I objected, pulling my limbs from beneath his bulk and getting up.

Starling made an obscene gesture. "She rode my pony just fine, Will." He sighed happily. "Just fine indeed."

I washed and dressed and left him to his reverie, looking for all the world like a man who'd staggered away from a feast. "I'll be below," I called over my shoulder. "I need food, after drinking all the ale you left me with."

An inn breakfast was the same no matter the country: bread, ale, and some sort of pottage with added grain to stave off hunger. Cheese if a man was lucky. I was as fortunate in my meal as Starling was in his bedmate—who blushingly served me and looked around for my companion.

"Il dort," I said, wondering if he had fallen back to sleep. "Ou rêve de vous."

She giggled and ran her fingers along the back of my neck, sending a chill down my spine. I wouldn't mention to Starling that his devoted rider was willing to share her delights.

I mopped my trencher with the last of the bread and stood, stretching. Where was the man? Had he worn himself out so badly? I called her over and asked if she would hurry him along.

"And no more of that!" She giggled again and disappeared up the twisting steps in a flutter of drab skirts. "We need to leave before the morning is gone," I muttered. "Damned man *should* retire if an evening's revelry is going to do him in."

A shrill scream echoed down the stairs, and I bolted toward the sound. Arriving in the doorway of our chamber, I collided with the maid, still shrieking, her apron over her face.

Walter Starling lay on the bed, stark naked, a smile on his face and his cock in his hand.

He was quite dead.

## CHAPTER 15

THE PRIEST WAS CALLED, and I paid what was necessary to give Starling a decent burial and took my leave, bearing his scant possessions with me in the event Ned could find some relation. It was a sad business that someone like Walter Starling should have such an end. He was a man of appetites, but not dissolute; if his habits were fatal, Dennis would have succumbed decades ago.

As I rode, I missed his jovial presence. It had been years since I was alone on the roads, other than short distances. A solitary rider is rarely safe, and in times like these, a man could easily go missing. After a period of quiet, the wars of religion had flared again in March. Violence could break out at any time, and a foreigner, even one with excellent French, would be a target. I stuck to the roads I knew best, even when cutting across country would speed my journey. There were risks enough; in less populated areas, cutthroats and highwaymen could conceal themselves behind every shrub. I had no intention of dying before I reached England.

When an unseen animal crashed through the brush, scattering birds across my path and startling my horse, I was nearly unseated. At that moment, I was very glad to be alone, because my companions would never have allowed me to live it down.

At Honfleur, I would take the first ship bound for England—no matter the destination. I'd had enough of traveling. Now, if I could get those in London to agree.

Starling's death unsettled me. Not just its suddenness, but the man himself, and the sheer waste of it all. He had stayed with the messenger service for years to be able to afford his small spot in Devon, and then died just short of achieving that happiness.

I did not wish my life to end in the same fashion.

Starling had had his dream: a quiet home and a plump lass. What, then, was my dream? I had lived my whole life longing for unattainable things—love, respect, a sense of my worth. Things no one could give me, and that I could not seem to find on my own.

In our brief acquaintance, Starling had become one of the people to whom I was closest. For a man my age, I had an embarrassing lack of close friends. I also had few close relations, but that was by choice.

My lack of attachment stemmed from my feelings for my father. It was difficult to imagine a traditional future for myself, with a wife, children, and a happy household, and not think of his petty kingdom, his high-handedness, his casual infidelity. What if that was dormant in me? What if I got myself a wife and became my father's son?

I could have reached my destination that night with hard riding, but prudence made me stop at the next inn. I would be no good to anyone if I were robbed and left for dead on a dark road. As I slid from my horse, staggering a bit, a fair-haired boy slouched from the stable to take the reins. He grinned at me vacantly, pretending not to understand when I gave instructions for his care.

I pushed open the weathered oak door to be met with a murmur of conversation and the welcome smell of food. The inn's main room was dimly lit and shabby, no larger than Robin's library at Winterset. Ceiling beams, black with age, hovered no more than a foot above my head. The hearth radiated a gentle heat, but the chimney smoked, causing me to pass a hand over my tired eyes.

"Monsieur?"

I blinked. The voice belonged to a buxom, pretty maid of perhaps twenty-five, blond curls springing from beneath a plain white cap.

"Food," I said. "And a bed for the night."

Her face fell. "There is but one chamber, monsieur, and it is already occupied." Seeing my expression, she apologized. "It is late. Perhaps I could..."

"It is not necessary," I interrupted, before she could offer me a place in her bed. "I will sleep by the fire."

A small knot of young men—apprentices by their youthful look and level of drunkenness—glanced curiously at me and made room at the end of the table. I eased onto the bench, my low back and seat protesting. Riding alone gave no distraction from my intrusive thoughts nor from the aches and pains resulting from hours in the saddle. Enough ale and I would not even mind a fireside bed.

A bowl, a half loaf, and a brimming pitcher were placed before me. "You may have our bed, monsieur," the maid said, nodding toward an older, thick-set man speaking with the apprentices. I could not make out his words, but his gestures were wide and encompassing. "We will sleep in the barn."

She was the innkeeper's wife; I had assumed her to be a trollop of the sort beloved by Dennis and Starling. "The fire suits me well enough, madame."

"As you choose." She bobbed, her skirts brushing my leg, and circled the room to reach her husband. Ducking her head, she whispered my refusal in his ear. He stopped speaking and looked at me, brows raised in surprise. I nodded and he returned to his conversation, but not before pulling his wife close and blowing on the curls at the nape of her neck.

Her happy laughter cut through the other sounds in the room, slicing open the pleasant fog of exhaustion and laying my heart bare.

As I ate, I watched the innkeeper. What had made this lovely young woman choose such an ordinary man over what had surely been a cavalcade of admirers at her father's door? She seemed content, teasing the apprentices as she delivered their drinks, skipping away from their straying hands, slapping one who was brave enough to make contact.

"Are you English?" It was one of the young men.

"Yes." A new face in a small village elicited curiosity from the locals, and young men were always in need of distraction. "Riding for Honfleur to join the rest of my party."

"How did you come to this place?" Another young man looked up from his cup. "You could have ridden straight through."

What sort of group had I intruded upon? There was a Catholic church in the village, but now I wondered if I'd stumbled into a meeting of Huguenots.

"My horse was lame yesterday," I said. "He seemed better this morning, but I decided not to strain him and let the others ride ahead." I smiled disingenuously. "Will I make Honfleur by midday, do you think?"

They nodded and returned to their discussion. I hoped I had been judged as non-threatening. There were six of them, plus the innkeeper; if they decided I posed some sort of threat, I could not fight them all.

The innkeeper's wife came through again and began to collect their dishes. "It is past your bedtime, boys!"

They protested, grabbing at their cups, but she swatted them away. The smile never left her face. I did not see how she could be so pleasant when her day was so long.

My bowl was empty, but there was ale left in the jug. I refilled my cup, hoping to dull the pain in my back and my growing uneasiness.

The room emptied, the apprentices departing with a flurry of farewells and rude jests directed at the innkeeper. He stood and stretched, gesturing to two men seated in an alcove—the occupants of my longed-for bedchamber. Their presence in the corner had been eclipsed by the rowdy boys, but I wondered whether those travelers had been similarly questioned.

A log split with a shower of sparks and the innkeeper's wife moved to tend it, her husband having gone up with the other men.

"You are well, monsieur?" She stopped by my bench, one work-reddened hand resting on the table. A clear hint that it was time I retired.

"Well enough." I drank the last of the ale and offered her the empty cup. She took it but lingered, leaning a hip against the table.

"You are not, I think." Her voice was soft, the French words circling me like a wisp of silk.

Unaccustomed to feminine kindness, I responded to the warmth in her voice. "I am not," I agreed. "A friend is dead. But that is not your affair. You may go to your rest, madame, with my thanks."

"Should you not check on your horse?" she inquired, her expression turning serious. "My son is good with them, but he is young."

The fat-faced stable boy was at least twelve; I said she did not look old enough to have such a hulking lad.

Her cheeks flushed, making her look even younger. "My husband took me in when my parents died. I was fourteen when Jacques was born."

Took her in and took advantage, I thought. Fourteen!

"Your horse," she prompted. "You should see to him."

I shook my head, thick with exhaustion and sorrow. "I'm sure your boy has done his job."

"Were you never a boy?" Her fingers closed around my wrist. "Look to your horse."

Her strange urgency disturbed me, and I got to my feet. "If you believe it to be necessary, madame."

"Félicité." She gave me a candle to light my way.

Happiness. How odd, to find happiness in this bleak place.

The night air was cool and damp, silent but for the buzzing of insects in the grass and the low hoot of an owl out hunting for his supper. Once I turned the corner of the building, the darkness was absolute but for the small, brave light in my cupped hand. I reached the stable and opened the door, placing the candle on the handy shelf just inside. It was quiet, the horses asleep. At the sound of my footfall on the straw, one woke and nickered.

"Shh," I murmured. I made my way along the stalls in the faint light. My horse stood at rest, one foot cocked, the picture of a well-cared for beast.

The innkeeper's wife had sent me on a fool's errand. My breath stopped as I thought of those drunken boys and their questions. Were they concealed in one of the stalls, waiting to leap out at me?

I eased my dagger from its sheath and stepped quietly along the row. The boxes were either empty or occupied with sleeping animals. No blackguards loomed, no drunken Huguenots awaited me with knives drawn. I turned, intending to march back inside and confront her, and slammed into her instead. A hiss of breath. Her face was in shadow, but her white cap was as luminous as mermaid's light on the water.

"My horse is fine." I sheathed my blade and made to pass her. "You worry overmuch."

"I worry not at all," she said placidly, and put her hand on my chest. "I wanted to speak to you."

"We could speak indoors."

"Do not go back inside." Her voice had changed, its silk gone sharp-edged. "Please."

Whatever this was, it was not over. Perhaps there was someone in the loft or outside the door. My hand drifted to my hip and encountered another hand, smaller—hers—attempting to undo the points attaching my hose to my jacket.

"Madame, desist!" My throat was dry with the import of her action, as well as fear that her husband or son would come into the stable. That would be worse than any attack by the apprentices because their violence would be justified.

"Félicité," she reminded. She peeled back my codpiece with a sound of satisfaction and cupped me, her fingertips as rough as their touch was tender. Despite my horror, I grew hard almost immediately. I tried to back away, but it was impossible to escape her grip and equally impossible to wish to be released.

"Your friend is dead," she said in my ear. "But you are alive."

Her warm breath made me shiver. "Madame, you are married."

"My husband uses me like a whore." Her grip tightened and I gasped. "I choose who I want."

I shook my head, wanting nothing more than to drive away the filthy thoughts flooding my brain, but something in her words stopped me.

"You looked happy in there," I said, and gasped again as she ran her nails up the length of my cock. "You... laughed when he touched you."

"As I must." Félicité knelt before me, the white smudge of her cap hovering at my waist. "I am a good wife."

I could not allow her to do such a thing to me—no matter how her husband treated her, this woman was no whore. I raised her up and tried to set her away, but she caught at my collar and drew my face down to hers. Her tongue in my mouth made me forget my desire for hard floors and penance; all I wanted now was softness and the chance at life she offered.

"Félicité..." My voice was ragged.

"Come." She backed into an empty stall, pulling me with her. We kissed again, pressing against the wall. Félicité dragged her skirts up to her waist and shoved them behind her as a cushion. Taking my hand, she guided it between her legs. When my fingers slipped into her wetness, I moaned against her mouth.

"Now." She closed her legs around my hand. "Now."
I thought how that tightness would feel locked around me. How I could lose myself, just for a while. I ran my hand down her thigh to the garter and drew her knee upward. Bracing one hand on the wall to steady myself, I pushed slowly into the hot center of her. There was a momentary resistance and then a deepening as she opened to me. It felt as though I were being drawn in, held, then spun into the darkness.

The stable, with its scents of hay and horse, retreated, and my waking mind along with it. There was nothing left but her mouth and her wetness and the frenzied rhythm of our bodies and the almighty surprise of it all. I surrendered my tight-held control and buried my cry in her neck as her nails scored my buttocks.

We separated slowly, wetly. The air was cold on my exposed skin. Now that my vision had adjusted to the darkness, I could see her pale thighs and the darker gray of her stockings below. Seeing where my eyes drifted, she dropped her skirts and came away from the wall.

Her cap was askew. I tucked a curl beneath the crisp fabric, wondering that I could feel so gentle towards her when moments before we were tearing at each other like animals.

"See to yourself," she said, laughter in her voice.

I restored my clothing to its former order and reached for her, but she evaded my grasp.

"I must bar the door," she said matter-of-factly and picked up the candle.

The fire had burned low. I rolled my cloak around my small pack to make a pillow and settled myself before it. "God's rest, Félicité," I said, watching from the floor as she rested the heavy bar in its brackets.

"Bon nuit, monsieur," she said softly. "Fais de beaux rêves."

My dreams would have been sweetly filled with her—if I'd been able to sleep. I listened to her move about above my head. Quiet voices reached me through the ceiling, and I smiled, remembering her mouth, her other parts. I began to drift off until another sound pierced my consciousness.

A squeak. Then another. Then an insistent thumping. The same voices, no longer a murmur, in rhythm with the thumping.

The innkeeper had decided to have his wife before they slept, and he made more of a leisurely business of it than I had.

I awakened before dawn to the sound of footsteps. The stable boy squatted beside my head. "Breakfast, monsieur?"

"Yes."

My head ached and I was sick with shame. I struggled to my feet and went outside in the light drizzle to piss, thinking again of the rattling bed and the innkeeper's loud grunt of completion. He was her husband—she had no choice—but how could she have let him, after what we had done?

When I came in, shaking the damp from my clothes, Félicité was carrying in a tray with bowls for me and the other guests. They retreated again to the alcove while I sat by the window and stared out at the rain.

"You will ride in this?" she asked, pouring my drink.

"I have ridden in worse." I caught a bit of her skirt as she turned away, and thought of Starling, who would approve. "Would you come with me?"

"With you?" she repeated in a whisper. "Where?"

"To England," I said recklessly, unable to rid myself of the vile thoughts that he had taken her fresh from me, somehow spoiling the gift I'd been given.

"You are mad." Her blue eyes were wide with shock, as if some other woman had lured me into the stables and given herself to me. "My life is here. My son. My husband—"

"He does not suspect what we have done?" I had no appetite but tore off a piece of bread to have something to do with my hands.

"He does not think me capable," she said, her lips twitching. The toe of her shoe caressed my leg. "He wants another son, but he drinks and can't always finish what he starts."

My head was filled with the buzzing of a thousand insects. I stared at her through air grown thick with meaning. "Then you will not come? I would protect you—"

"I need no protection." She pushed my breakfast toward me. "If you put a baby in my belly, he will leave me in peace until it is weaned."

"And if not?"

Félicité shrugged. "I will try again with another stranger."

Several hours later, filled with a fierce self-loathing, I located Dennis and Howland in a portside tavern, relatively sober and full of excessive but sincere regret at my news.

THE SON IN SHADOW

"There was no foul play," I assured Starling's man. "It appears that his heart gave out."

Howland's narrow face pinched. "He was so close to going home."

"He spoke of it frequently." We raised our cups in his honor.

"What of his body?" Howland put down his drink.

"Buried in the churchyard," I told him. "I'm sorry if that's not what he would have wished. I knew not what else to do, and the priest was there."

"He followed the old ways," Starling's man said. "He didn't speak of it, but he was a papist."

I hadn't wanted him buried according to rites to which he did not ascribe, but I was surprised—after so long together, I thought I would have known of his Catholicism. People were a mystery. I closed my eyes, said a prayer for the repose of his soul, and then turned to the business at hand.

"Have you found a ship?"

"Two," Dennis said. "I was waiting for you before booking our passage. One sails tomorrow, and the other early next week. I thought you wanted to visit Mistress Lewis's house."

"We'll leave tomorrow," I said, pushing away from the table. "Lead me to the captain. I have had enough of being out of England."

## CHAPTER 16

THE SHIP PUT IN at King's Lynn in the first week of May. We could have made London in five days, but my malaise persisted, and I could not bring myself to hurry. By the time I learned the court was not in London, Walter Starling had been dead for some two weeks.

It was too early for a progress, so they had followed the queen to either Hampton Court or Greenwich, those being her preferred palaces in the warmer months. We were fortunate to encounter a messenger who pointed us in the direction of Greenwich and I sent Dennis on to Whitehall and rode five miles further to present myself to Ned.

"That's a sad state of affairs," he said, accepting the news and Starling's credentials but shrugging off responsibility for his belongings. "I'd worked up a new route for him, as he complained of being weary of the French."

I shifted uncomfortably in my seat. "He'd planned on leaving the service after this trip," I reminded Ned. "He had a place in Devon…"

"That old tale," he scoffed, pushing back his chair and gesturing for me to follow him. "Starling would have been miserable."

I looked at Ned, wondering what plan he had in mind for me next. "We'll never know for sure."

We passed through the hall. The doors stood open to the air from the river. Ladies clustered together, vivid as bouquets of flowers, their voices rising in competition with the birdsong in the trees outside. Men in equally lavish attire danced attendance on them. The riot of color was interrupted by the occasional black of ladies-in-waiting and white of the queen's maids-of-honor. From as far back as her coronation, the queen wanted her women to be a neutral backdrop for her splendor.

"Where are we going?"

Ned turned to answer, but his attention was caught by the sight of a splendid black horse beyond the doors. "Leicester."

His naming of the man was unnecessary, as I was not so long from court that I would fail to recognize the queen's favorite. Robert Dudley was Elizabeth Tudor's childhood friend and, despite all attempts to marry her off, likely the one man she would consider. The unfortunate death of Dudley's wife made the match impossible. Unable to have him herself, Elizabeth promoted his marriage to Mary Stuart, but unsurprisingly, both parties objected.

Leicester loved the queen, but he was not a faithful lover. He slid gracefully from his horse and landed lightly on the gravel path, then turned to assist his companion from her mount. She leaned forward, and his hands circled her waist as he lifted her down. There was intimate laughter, and a sidelong glance from beneath black lashes.

"Hoo," Ned breathed beside me. "He's getting careless."

"Who is that?" Her pink and white complexion and abundant, red-tinged brown hair reminded me of Margaery Lewis when I'd first met her.

"Douglas Sheffield." He looked from them to me, his eyes creasing with humor. "John Sheffield died in December. For safety's sake, Leicester should carry on with married women, not widows. His luck cannot hold forever."

There was something gleeful in his tone, as if the thought of Leicester's inamorata falling pregnant would be an excellent diversion for a dull day.

I faulted his choice of lady for the same reason Ned bestowed his schoolboy grin upon their coupling, but I could not blame him. He was, after all, a single man. With a dead wife and no children—and a royal mistress who barred him from her bed—he was in an uncomfortable position with no prospect of improvement. Most men in a similar situation would catch at happiness with both hands.

"What have you next for me?" I shoved away thoughts of happiness. Félicité. "I have been gone nearly a year."

He swung around, having seen his fill of the lovely Douglas. "In a hurry to be off?" he asked. "I've a mind to keep you with me for the summer. Walsingham and I—have you met him?— are working on several plans having to do with the Scottish bitch. You might come in useful."

I bit my lip. The idea of spending the summer at court was more punishment than reward, and it might well have been one. I didn't know how Ned felt about me; he was all bluff goodwill, but he had worn that mask for years and it covered a variety of faces.

"A problem?" His head cocked. "Most men would jump at the chance to spend the warm months surrounded by maids in need of a tumble." He broke off, his grin wide but unpleasant. "But that's not you. I forgot. Brother William, monk and messenger, looking for his purpose."

"I am not so bad," I muttered, my fingers curling into fists at my sides. I tried not to think of maids or tumbling; I was sickened by the stupid sentimentality of trying to rescue a woman who did not wish to be rescued. Félicité had sensed a weakness, a malleability that caused her to choose me over the apprentices or other travelers. I would not make the same mistake again.

"Untrue!" Ned hooted. "You're thinking of smashing my face in because of how right I am." He put a hand on my sleeve. A ruby glinted on his first finger like a drop of blood. "I should not tease. You take it no better than Robin."

Robin had either a thicker skin or he'd simply learned to disregard the worst of Ned over the years. Still, I remembered his warning to be wary and mustered a smile.

"I'm not myself. Starling's death was a blow." I paused, wondering if I could use the same excuse a second time. "I wonder... while you and Walsingham are working on your plans, would I be permitted"—I changed course mid-sentence—"to ride north and visit the Lewises?"

Ned guided me from the doors and the people lingering nearby. "No visit to the family this time?"

The back of my neck prickled again.

"I'd prefer to spend time with people I like. Perhaps I'll visit my niece on the way back, if I can arrange to have her brought to my sister's." Elizabeth and her useless husband lived halfway between Winterset and Hawkmoor; I would send a message by post before I left London and hope for the best.

"Give me a few weeks," Ned said genially, then looked at me with distaste. "Do you have aught but traveling clothes?"

"The rest of my things are being brought from Whitehall." I had a perfectly serviceable doublet with me; I simply hadn't bothered to change before finding him. "I'll be more presentable the next time you see me."

"Good." A shoulder slap, hard enough to rock me on my feet. "Come to the presence chamber at seven, Hawkins, prepared to dance. The ladies will be happy to see a fresh face."


Dennis did not appear with my things until nearly seven.

"Where were you?" I asked, stripping off my clothes. "I am due in the privy apartments. I shall be late."

He drew out my best doublet and hose and made a great show of brushing them, though they appeared perfectly clean. "I took time to have a drink with Harry Minstrel, if you must know."

"Have you not drunk enough on my time?" I was filled with sudden rage. "You were required here."

"Calm yourself." He caught the shirt I threw at him. "I wanted to see if there were any letters."

My head emerged from the neck of my clean shirt. "And were there?"

He produced two folded and sealed missives from an inside pocket and tossed them on the bed. "Am I forgiven, master?"

I scanned them quickly—one was in my sister's hand and the other was from Robin. I left Elizabeth's letter on the bed; should anyone have reason to check my chamber, they would find something. The other was tucked into my doublet for later reading.

"Possibly," I said. "But you are more good than bad. It will take more than delivering two letters to cleanse you of your sins."

"I like my sins." He shrugged cheerfully. "They keep me company when you are gone." Tying on a starched and embroidered ruff he must have borrowed from another servant, he added, "I'm not the one who will be dancing all evening with the queen's ladies."

"Don't remind me." I sat on the bed to put on my shoes. After so long in boots, they felt strange and insubstantial, whereas the layers of cambric and brocade and velvet were as uncomfortable as a suit of armor. "I am out of practice at being a gentleman."

"You've never had much talent at it." Dennis found his jest so funny that he clung to the bed post. "Why change now?"

As I descended the stairs, others passed me by: men in garb far more elaborate than my doublet and fitted hose; ladies in wide skirts and farthingales. All broke into a hurried walk when they reached the open doors to the presence chamber.

The sound of the queen's minstrels, in their gallery above, met me at the doors. The dance floor was already crowded, although it appeared that Elizabeth herself had yet to arrive. Making my way into the chamber, I took up a place on the far wall, content to watch from a safe distance. I would not be fortunate enough to be left undisturbed. Ned would find me, or someone else, and I would be forced to dance or talk or agree to another year of riding around in the rain.

I wanted to be left alone to read my letters.

I wanted to be left alone.

"Hawkins, isn't it?" The Earl of Leicester stopped beside me, his eyes glinting with mischief. "I thought you were in Scotland with the woman I refused to marry."

"That was last year." As a member of the privy council, he should know that.

Leicester struck his forehead in mock dismay. "Now I remember. Pickering says you've been a busy fellow."

"I just returned." I chose a few pointed words to test his reaction. "I was speaking with him in the hall today when you and your lady came back from your ride."

"Not my lady." His smile fell away. "Lady Sheffield has needed a friend to lean on since her husband's unfortunate death."

"Ah." Scanning the room, I saw her near the doors with some of the queen's ladies. She was watching us. "She is beautiful."

"Don't let Her Majesty hear you say that—she permits no other women to be beautiful in her presence." He laughed, then turned to me consideringly. "Come, I'll introduce you—it would do me no end of good if you could step in if the queen happens to see me speaking with her."

I raised my eyebrows. "I thought you were old friends. Is friendship not permitted, either?"

"Not all friendships are the same."

We sidestepped the dancers, taking the long way around until we reached Douglas Sheffield. Leicester reached up to smooth his hair before speaking her name, and I understood that it was more than friendship on his part.

"Lady Sheffield," he said deferentially.

She turned, her face glowing. Not one-sided, then. "Lord Leicester."

He drew me forward. "I wish to present William Hawkins. He's from an old northern family, but these days he's with the principal secretary."

I bowed to her and kissed her hand, which was soft and smelled of roses. "Lady Sheffield."

"Why have I not seen you before?" Her words were directed at me, but her gaze was on Leicester, who was devouring her with his eyes. "Do you have family keeping you from court?"

"I have been traveling," I told her. "But I am here for the next month." I stepped between them. "Would it be impertinent to ask for a dance?"

Trumpets blared. The chamber fell silent as Elizabeth entered, followed by the rest of her women. She blazed in a gown of silver tissue, diamonds sparkling at her neck and in her ears. As I rose from my bow, I saw her beckon imperiously to Leicester. He scurried to her side.

"I should love to dance," Douglas Sheffield said resignedly. "Thank you, Master Hawkins."

It was very late when I returned to my room—staggering with tiredness, but sober. I did not wake Dennis, but when I tripped over him, he got up, swearing, and helped me to undress.

I handed over my doublet, which was now stiff with sweat, and shucked the rest of my clothes, going to stand naked in front of the small window.

"A good evening?" He picked my things up from the floor. "Shall I light a candle, or can your letters hold until morning?"

My letters! I reached for my doublet, and he tossed me the letter he'd retrieved from its pocket. "A light, please, Dennis."

Standing so the candle shed its light on the page, I read Elizabeth's letter first. It was full of news of her family, of my niece and my father and her hopes that I would visit soon. Nothing important enough to warrant sending to the tavern, I thought, but perhaps she did not want her letter to chase me all over England as the court moved about.

"How is the lady?" Dennis asked. He liked my sister, and I believed he also had an affection for one of the women in her household.

"Very well," I told him, putting the letter aside. "She is expecting and hopes it will be a girl. My niece was with her for two months after Christmastide and is getting on well with her studies."

I moved the candle to the bedside table. Robin's letter would require my full attention. Cracking the seal, I unfolded it and saw only three sentences.

*Recall the warning which I gave to you. I have further information which may not be committed to paper. If you cannot yourself visit, send a trusted courier at the earliest opportunity. R.*

## CHAPTER 17

"I HAVE HAD A letter from my sister," I told Ned the next day. "Has any decision been made about when I might leave London? I would like to visit her."

He looked up from his papers as if surprised to find me standing before him. "Is something wrong?"

"I am not sure," I said. "She is with child and understandably nervous at her age."

"My Joan had our last at forty." Ned stretched and cracked his knuckles. The sound was so loud in the quiet room that I flinched. "We'll get you moving by the beginning of June. Will that do?"

It would have to.

"That gives me time to write back and ask to have my niece brought from Hawkmoor at the same time." I made it sound as though he had done me a favor.

"Good." He turned his ring, staring off over my shoulder. "How is the child? Her education going well?"

"Very." Something in his tone nagged at me. I would have to make certain to either burn Robin's letter or keep it on my body.

"It's admirable, taking an interest in your sister's child," he said. "Since you don't have any yourself."

I had always had a fondness for little Jane; her mother was one of the few members of my family who had seen me as something other than a disappointment. After her marriage to Richard Curtis, I had returned to Scotland, and although my presence could have done nothing to save her, I reproached myself for not being in London when she died.

"Perhaps that's why."

To someone who wished to be there, three weeks at Greenwich would be but a moment. For me, they stretched endlessly. I had no real interest in the riding and dancing and other entertainments of the early summer season. Nevertheless, I rode and danced as required, bantering and flirting and returning each night to my bed exhausted—and alone.

Douglas Sheffield took a liking to me. As the queen required most of Leicester's waking hours, I served as a frequent dancing partner.

"I do thank you," she confided, as we glided through another mind-numbing pavane. "My situation is... difficult, you understand."

Did she mean to acknowledge their liaison? "Many situations are difficult here," I said carefully. "I am happy to be of service."

I was as glad to be of service to Leicester as to her—he was a powerful man, and it never hurt to have his gratitude in my pocket.

Her cheeks turned pink, and I thought again how flowerlike she was. "You may speak plainly to me, Master Hawkins. Dissembling does us no good service. I think you understand my relationship with Robert."

"I have suspected."

She circled gracefully around me. "So long as the queen does not suspect," she said. "I do not wish to be exiled to the countryside."

"I would consider exile a reward, not a punishment." I looked over her shoulder. Leicester was dancing with Elizabeth, but his eyes were on us whenever she was not looking at him. "I am not skilled in the courtly arts, as you may have noticed, Lady Sheffield."

"You are perfectly charming," she said. "And please, call me Douglas when no one is listening."

"Then you must call me Will," I returned. "We will be informal in secret."

The music stopped and we retired to the side of the room. Douglas's face was flushed, beads of moisture glittering along her hairline. I wanted to suggest a breath of air, but rumors spread like fire. It was easier to remain indoors until the late evening fireworks, when we could stand together in the dark without being noticed.

"It will be a long summer." She played with the pearls edging her square neckline. "Robert's rooms adjoin Her Majesty's. If she sends for him in the night, he cannot be found missing."

From my sister's tales, I knew the queen was a restless sleeper. She would wake her ladies and make them play music or call for Leicester to sit at the foot of her bed and talk until she slept again. It would not do for him to be absent—or occupied—when a royal summons came.

"What do you intend?" I asked. "She cannot marry him, but she will not release him. You are young—"

"We may yet marry." Her eyes glittered with unshed tears. "He has promised me."

Leicester should not make promises he would never be permitted to keep. I wanted to advise her to find another object for her affections, but she would not listen, not so soon. Their affair would drag on, with Douglas risking pregnancy after every encounter, while no harm would come to the Earl of Leicester if she fell. The queen would be upset for days or even weeks, but she always forgave him, and she always would. Douglas Sheffield would be exiled from court, as Amy Robsart had been, but without the protection of marriage.

"Could you perhaps visit a relation during the summer?" I suggested. "That would get you away from court when you are unable to be with the earl. It would be better than my poor companionship."

"I will have other companionship very soon." Douglas brightened. "My cousin is coming to stay. She is recently widowed, as well—her second husband—and I summoned her so we can be sad widows together." She gave me a sidelong glance. "Perhaps I can find her a third husband. She is a bit older than you, but very beautiful. She would be a good match."

I held up both hands in protest. "I seek no match, lady."

"What a shame." She pouted. "Will you promise to dance with her while she is here and pay her the same attentions you give to me?"

"Until my departure at the end of the month," I promised, "I put myself at your disposal."

At one side of the presence chamber stood a small crowd of women. A flash of red-brown curls told me Douglas was among them. I made my way over to claim a dance.

"Lady Sheffield."

At the sound of my voice, she turned, her face alight in a way I had previously seen directed only at Leicester. "Master Hawkins! I am so glad to see you." She laid a light hand on my arm. "My cousin has arrived, you see—you must dance with her, for she is my guest."

"I will do that," I said with a smile, "but perhaps you might first introduce me to the lady."

Her laughter tumbled over itself. "Master Hawkins, this is my cousin, Lady Isabel Ferren. Isabel, allow me to present Master William Hawkins, my favorite dancing partner."

"Master Hawkins." Douglas's cousin dropped into a graceful spread of unadorned black satin.

I did not need to see her face; her voice was enough. "Lady Isabel," I said stiffly. "I'm very pleased to make your acquaintance."

Rising, she met my eyes. I saw recognition there, and something else. Fear? Defiance?

"The pleasure is mine." Her smile was serene—she was a woman accustomed to wearing masks. "My cousin has said many kind things about you."

"Lady Sheffield overspeaks." I could not look into her face, focusing instead on the gleaming strand of pearls down the center parting of her smooth black hair, which terminated in a small pendant drop at her forehead. "I am no more than any other man."

Douglas took us each by an arm. "You must dance," she insisted. "Isabel, he has done me a world of good. Let him be the cheer you need."

There seemed no way to escape Douglas Sheffield's good intentions, but I could not—could not—dance with that woman.

"Please forgive me," I said, my voice strangled. "I am late to an appointment in the principal secretary's office."

I fled like a boy, without looking back.


Near the end of King Henry's reign, I came to court for a period with my uncle and aunt. While they settled into their apartments at Greenwich,

Aunt Hannah directing the placement of furniture and baggage like a fury, I was sent along to my father's rooms to see if he was available to dine.

"Why not send a servant?" I asked. "I could be of more use here."

Uncle Henry looked down his beaked nose at me. "You can't avoid him forever, boy," he said kindly. "Get it over with."

Alone in the corridor with directions to my father's lodgings, I took a deep breath and straightened my doublet. No point in giving him more reason to criticize. I pursed my lips and whistled a tune, trying to convince myself my guts weren't in knots. As I went on, the corridors widened and became grander. I looked around. Was this how my father lived when he was not with us?

"Lord Kelton's apartments?" I asked a passing boy in neat green livery.

"Right there, sir." He pointed to a wide carved door.

I thanked him, marveled at the novelty of being called 'sir', and thumped the door with my fist. My father's man did not answer. I waited a moment longer and tried the handle. It turned easily and I pushed the door open.

The chamber had been recently vacated. Silver cups with the dregs of wine remained on the table, and my father's dark brown cloak was hung untidily over a chest. He was a fastidious man; he must have been called away and taken Terrence with him.

Should I wait? There was a cross-framed chair by the fire, cushioned in blue velvet and adorned with a pillow embroidered by my mother. I hovered over it, but curiosity won out: I wanted to see the inner chamber and Father would never think to show it to me.

The door opened soundlessly, and at first, all I saw was the corner of an enormous bed, curtained in dark blue velvet. Moving further into the room, I was met with a sight that sent me stumbling back against the plastered wall. The bed curtains framed a tableau from some nightmarish mystery play. My father lay sprawled across the velvet coverlet, his big hands firm on the narrow waist of a woman who rode him as energetically as if he were a stallion. She made a noise somewhere between panting and gasping, and her hair, long and black, swept back and forth above the dimpled pink rump that held my horrified gaze.

I made a strangled sound, and the girl sprang off him and dove behind the bed curtain, using it to cover her breasts. They were as round and pink as her buttocks, and I tore my eyes away reluctantly.

"Christ, is Henry here already?" My father pushed himself up on one elbow, pulling a crumpled bit of linen from beneath his body and tossing it to the girl. "Get dressed, sweetheart," he said. "This is my son, here to spoil our pleasure."

She hastily pulled the shift over her head. "Is this your eldest, sir?" She looked between us, wondering, like most people, at our lack of resemblance.

"God, no." My father strode naked across the chamber and bent to retrieve his discarded shirt. "This is William."

The girl curtsied, her arms filled with an abundance of pale blue cloth. "Sir, would you lace me up?"

Busy with his dressing, Father barely looked at her. "Family obligations call. I'll send Terrence in. He won't mind."

She ducked her head, her cheeks reddening, and I spared a thought for her even as I stifled the urge to scream and cry and be sick, all at once. Most of all, I wanted the strength to knock my father down and pummel him until the blood flowed from his nose.

"How could you?" I pitched my voice low so the girl couldn't hear. "You are a married man."

He buttoned his russet velvet doublet and plucked his shirt neatly through the slashes. "What has that to do with anything?" he asked.

The girl was quiet, listening as she attempted to dress herself. Her gown was quality fabric; this was no trollop brought in from outside the palace to slake his appetite.

"She trusts you." My voice trembled, and I wiped my damp palms against my hose.

Disgust rippled across his face. "Have you ever seen me with a woman at home?"

"No..."

"Nor would you see any here, should your mother decide to leave her children and come to court." Father jerked his head in the girl's direction. "Pretty Isabel would sleep in her own bed and Lady Elinor would be none the wiser."

THE SON IN SHADOW 115

Terrence was in the outer room, tidying the detritus of my father's seduction. He brushed past as we left the bedchamber. "Let's get you put together," I heard him say before the door closed.

"How could you?" His previous answers made no sense. Did he have a separate life when away from his family? Had he ever loved Mother? And what about pretty Isabel? Was she his mistress or an unfortunate snared by his charm?

There had been, in their coupling, evidence of familiarity as well as pleasure. Despite her youth, this was a relationship of some duration. Whose daughter had he despoiled with his lust, and what would happen when her father or brother wanted justice for her lost maidenhead?

"Christ, William!" His hand closed on my shoulder. "I like a woman in my bed. Am I supposed to do without because your mother prefers taking care of sniveling brats to being with her husband?"

"Don't you dare blame her." I tore myself free. "If you hadn't given her so many children—"

He laughed harshly. "Given her? Elinor milked me like a bull for every last one of you. She wanted babies from the moment we were wed. I have no doubt your brother was conceived on our wedding night."

I didn't want to hear these details. My mother had devoted her life to keeping his houses and raising his children, doing everything in her power to make him happy and comfortable—and he repaid her with infidelity.

"This would kill her." I imagined her expression when she realized his betrayal.

"That's why you won't tell her." His hand came down again on my shoulder, harder this time. "It would hurt her, and to what end?" His brown eyes regarded me warily. "If you hurt her, I'll hurt you. Do you understand?"

Father's voice was quiet, and that I understood: when he sounded like that, he meant business. "Yes."

"Yes, what?"

"Yes, sir." I hated him. I hated that he could make me cower like a child in fear of his temper. He was the adulterer; he was the one in the wrong. How, by finding him out, was I at fault?

He slowed his pace. "Look, William," he said, trying for patience. "This is the world we live in. You'll be a man soon enough. You need to understand. If you act like a shrinking virgin every time you are presented with something you don't approve of, you'll be a figure of ridicule."

It hurt to breathe. "So?"

"I won't have my sons laughed at," he said. "Not even you."

When we appeared, Uncle Henry gave me a keen look, but we were unable to speak privately until the next day. Riding together into the city to visit his lawyer—something about a transfer of property—he glanced at me as I slumped on the back of my horse.

"You came back yesterday looking as if you'd seen a phantom." He gave me a half smile. "Your father's not the easiest of men, Will, but you must learn to accept him."

"I'm getting tired of being told what I must learn to accept," I said violently, then subsided, appalled. Uncle Henry was my mother's brother; I couldn't reveal my father's shame to him.

We rode through the stinking streets, our mounts up to their fetlocks in filth.

"Your father lives a different life in London," my uncle said, choosing his words with care. "Your mother doesn't know. She mustn't know."

Did my uncle truly understand what Father had done? I felt sick, and it wasn't from the contents of the chamber pot which had just sluiced past our heads. "But—"

Uncle touched his hat and smiled at a gentleman passing opposite. "He will not change, and what he does here harms your mother very little. She has what she wants: a good marriage, healthy children, and a circle of friends in both Yorkshire and Hertfordshire. She never did care for court."

"But it's dishonest!" The memory of the girl Isabel's smoothly circling hips, and those *sounds*, had dogged me all the night before, keeping me from sleep. Father raised us to be honest and yet he lied to our mother about their most basic relationship.

Uncle Henry guided his horse to the side of the street. "He's not lying to her," he said simply, swinging down and handing me the reins. "And she'd never be unwise enough to ask. Mind the beasts, there's a good lad."

"What about Aunt Hannah?" I couldn't imagine her not asking.

"Your aunt does not allow me to come to court alone, for that very reason."

The rest of our visit dragged. Time spent with my father made me uncomfortable, and now I was filled with a loathing that was difficult to conceal. Seeing him pass through the great hall like a carefree boy made my head pound with fury, but I said nothing, for my uncle made it clear he would tolerate no scenes.

I resented keeping secrets from my stiff-necked aunt, as on our last night she unbent herself sufficiently to dance a pavane with my father. I lingered at the side of the great chamber, having been presented earlier in the evening to the old king.

Raised on vivid stories of the eighth Henry's exploits, the man to whom I'd made my bow and addressed a few stumbling words was not what I'd expected. Mother had been lady-in-waiting to his third wife, Queen Jane, but she'd retired from court after that. The king looked old and ill, with one tightly bandaged leg propped up on a stool. It smelled of rot and no doubt explained his peevish expression.

They'd been young men together, according to the tales I'd heard. While my father had gray in his thick black hair, and the lines on his tanned face never relaxed, he wasn't old. Not yet. Not like that.

A flash of green passed before my eyes, and I looked away from my giddy aunt to find my father's paramour at my side. Dressed in full court garb of silken gown and a pearl-trimmed hood with lappets, her glorious hair mostly hidden, she was nevertheless delectable. I pushed down a heady response to her beauty.

"Mistress."

"Master William." She sketched a curtsy. "Pray forgive my forwardness in speaking to you."

I fixed my eyes on Aunt Hannah again. She was blinking coquettishly, her sallow cheeks flushed with my father's unconscionable power.

"I would consider *that* to be your forwardness," I said.

"He said you were hard." Her hands clasped at her midsection; she wore several rings, one of which resembled my mother's favorite, but with a green stone instead of a sapphire. "Don't blame him."

I did not wish to be seen speaking with her and stepped to one side, to put some space between us. "Are you then to blame?"

"Oh, why must there be blame?" she cried softly. "I love him, that's the truth of it."

How could she possibly love him? I was disgusted by what I had seen, but I couldn't entirely blame her—how could I when, all my life, I'd watched females turn themselves inside out for his favor? Not just my mother, but my sisters too. Nell, the youngest, was five, but already she'd learned to smile and coo and raise her arms to be lifted into his orbit.

This girl was no different. Even my aunt, who I had never seen look at Uncle Henry that way, was embarrassing herself over my father.

"And what will this love get you?" I asked, not looking at her. "Besides pretty rings and the risk of a child?"

She gasped, a different sound than the one she'd made in the bedchamber. My stomach tightened in response. When she spoke again, her voice was steady. "Do you see that man over there, near the king? The one in the black gown with the jewel on his cap?"

I noted the gentleman; he was in better health than the king only in that he was upright. The expensive black gown covered a figure of similar bulk, and his sagging skin was mottled with age. "I see him. What of it?"

"That," Isabel said, "is my husband-to-be. In two weeks' time, I'll be his third wife, and hopefully his last. Forgive me for wanting to know a bit of pleasure before being yoked to that human pustule until one of us perishes."

She swept away before I could speak, and in truth, what was there to say? It was, as my father said, the world we lived in.

CHAPTER 18

LONDON WAS AN EASY journey by river from Greenwich. The next day I joined a party heading into the city. I wanted to send letters to both Robin and my sister, and to get away from the stifling atmosphere of the court for a few days.

Without Dennis, my visit to the Minstrel's Arms was less prolonged than usual. Harry brought me to the family quarters upstairs to compose my letters. Once they were finished and sealed, Jenny delivered bread and cheese and a pitcher of ale, and I spent a pleasant hour with Bess and Tom while she and her brother handled the customers below.

Tom spoke knowledgeably of the political situation and the conspiracies and rumors abroad in London. Being Robin's friend, he must surely know of my employment, and his son would have told him that I used his tavern to send and receive confidential letters.

"What about the Scottish queen?" The question was my own curiosity, not on Ned's behalf. "What do the people say about her?"

"Many speak against her imprisonment." I wondered if Tom was one of them. "They ask if a queen has the right to judge another queen."

"A good question," I agreed. "If Elizabeth believed Mary had no designs on her crown, I think she would be more lenient."

"What of Mary's husband?" Bess asked. "The assassin."

Her bluntness made me smile. "Unconvicted assassin," I said. "But he is exiled and not likely to return, knowing what would await him in Scotland."

"Could she marry again?" Tom looked out the window, his cup slowly revolving in his hands. "There are rumors of the Duke of Norfolk..."

Those rumors had never faded, but he could come no closer to achieving his goal until Mary's union with Bothwell was annulled. "I don't believe it would be permitted—" I began.

The sound of wheels in the street below made them both turn. "I should help Harry," Tom said, pushing silver-blond hair from his eyes.

"Be careful." Bess put a hand on his arm. "Your back is not as young as your intentions."

"Yes, my sweet." He bent down and kissed her with a boy's transparent affection. It struck me that they were, somehow, childlike in their care for each other. It made my chest hurt to know I would never experience that kind of love.

Something went out of the room with his departure. Bess sat with her hands folded in her lap, diffused light from the window falling across her cheek and slanting over her shoulder.

"How is your father?"

I took a breath. "He is himself."

Her lips formed into a reminiscent smile. "He always was."

"Would you like more ale?" If we were to speak of my father, it would ease the conversation.

"I can do it." She reached out surely and moved our cups to the right of her other hand, then grasped the pitcher by the handle. I watched as she filled both cups, stopping before they overflowed. Harry had told me her sight was greatly diminished, but I would not have guessed the severity of her impairment by her actions.

"I can hear you thinking," she said, amused. "I don't just sing now, I do tricks."

"Can you see at all?" I took a sip.

Bess picked up her cup. "Light and shadow, mostly. On overcast days like this it is easier because the shadows are not so harsh."

I had cursed the cloudy skies on my way into the city, fearing it would rain and delay my journey back.

"Don't you mind?" Her direct manner encouraged an equal response.

"You sounded like him then." Her face tilted up, wide brown eyes turning in my direction without any sign of seeing me. "I mind, of course, but there is naught to be done. It does not stop me from playing or singing." There was a patience in her smile that I thought was hard-won. "I've seen kings and queens, Will. I've seen my babies born, and their babies. I will never have to watch my husband grow old."

We lapsed into silence—comfortable on her part, uneasy on mine.

"May I ask a question?"

"If you like."

I swallowed, my throat working with the enormity of the words which struggled to break free. "Why did you choose your husband over my father?"

Her laughter was kind. "There was no true choice," she said. "I had loved Tom since we were children."

"But my father—" I broke off at the sound of footsteps, but they continued past the door.

"I had loved him just as long," she said with a sigh. "He was such a beautiful man."

"He is not kind." I hated the pettishness in my voice.

She reached out, and I slid my hands forward so that she could clasp them. "Nick is not unkind," she said gently. "He never lied or pretended to be someone he was not. He never led me to believe I could be anything more than his mistress. It was not enough for me."

It was surprising to hear her call him by his given name; he was Lord Kelton or sir to nearly everyone.

"You speak fondly of him still."

"What harm he has done is long past, and he has done good to make up for it." Bess took a breath, a decision evident on her face. "Even Tom does not know this, but your father paid our way when we left London during Anne Boleyn's fall."

Robin had told me, but I didn't know she'd been aware of it. "Why do you think he did that?"

She squeezed my fingers once, then let go. "Because he loved me once, and he is not a monster."

I could not avoid Isabel Ferren forever. The evening of my return, I took extra care over my appearance, nagging at Dennis until he trimmed my hair and gave me a close shave. He polished the new silver buttons on my blue doublet and told me I looked as pretty as a lady-in-waiting.

Isabel was standing with several of the queen's ladies, her widow's garb blending with their sober gowns. Taking a deep breath, I walked up and bowed to the group, and directed my next words at Isabel. "I must apologize for my hasty departure the other evening. I had truly forgotten that I should have been elsewhere, and then business called me to London."

"Considering our history," she said quietly, "I would not expect you to dance attendance upon me."

"I would ask for a dance, though, Lady Isabel." I held out my hand. After a moment, she placed hers on top and we took our places as the musicians struck up a fast tempo.

I felt a stab of dismay. It was not a galliard, but a volta—a dance for lovers, not two uncomfortable people paired from a sense of misplaced obligation. Wordlessly, we followed the initial movements, the hop, the skipping steps. Together, apart, stepping and circling with the other couples.

Finally, she said, "You have changed since our first meeting."

"Not so much in my behavior." Older, perhaps, but my opinions were the same as they had always been. "I am sorry for that—and for your loss."

An indrawn breath. I looked to see her lip caught between her teeth. "At least I cared for Lord Ferren." she said. "Unlike my first husband."

The music swept on, and we followed, executing the swift turns that made the dance scandalous, because a lady could become dizzy and fall against her partner.

I recalled the grotesque man she had pointed out. "How long was your first marriage?"

"Six years," she said with a wry glance. "Six years, three months, and twelve days."

"You kept track." When she turned, I took in her delicate profile; she reminded me of Lady Rose—the same black hair and dark eyes. The same, too, as Bess Minstrel, who'd been his lover before either of them.

"I had plenty of time." As we proceeded, she sketched a brief description of her marriage: trapped in a remote estate with her husband and a handful of servants for company and a son whose wardship had gone to the crown upon Lord Griscom's death.

"Do you not see him?" It seemed hard, making a woman give up her child; men loved their children, but they understood there was nothing personal in such matters.

"Not since he was taken," she said, and then, "Oh, look at Douglas!"

I glanced over my shoulder. Leicester had taken to the floor with Douglas Sheffield. He was holding her far too closely, his gaze ardent. She threw her head back and laughed, staggering comically against him as he spun her faster and faster. They were mad, the pair of them, to play such a dangerous game.

"Perhaps you could warn your cousin that the queen mislikes competition in the sport of love."

Isabel shook her head. "Douglas will not listen to me."

I turned my back on the spectacle of Leicester and his ladylove to complete the most difficult part of the dance: the lift, where the combined efforts of Isabel's hand on my shoulder, my hand on her waist, and my left thigh supporting her bottom were supposed to deftly raise her into the air.

"I cannot do it." I was awkward after a year of travel, and I'd had no instruction in the volta. "I will drop you."

"Put both hands on my waist," she said quickly. "No one will notice, they are all watching them."

I did as she directed, turning and lifting her again and again as she pushed off my shoulder with one hand and held tight to her skirts with the other—the risk of accidental exposure being another scandalous aspect of the dance.

"Cease this frivolity!" Elizabeth's voice cut like a blade through music and chatter alike. Everyone froze. The chamber fell silent but for the fading echo of a drum.

While the other dancers fell back, Leicester and Douglas remained at the center of the floor. His hand was under the hard edge of her bodice, which allowed him to lift her higher, while hers rested not on his shoulder but inside his collar, her fingers on his neck.

"Your Majesty." Leicester bent into an elegant bow. Beside him, Douglas almost disappeared into a puddle of skirts. Everyone followed suit, though plenty of eyes were surreptitiously raised to watch the queen's face.

"My lord Leicester," she said, her tone icy. "We called for you, and when you could not be found, we were afraid that something ill had befallen you. We see now that you were too pleasantly occupied to obey a summons from your sovereign."

The humor drained from his face. He moved away from Douglas to fall upon his knees. "Your Majesty," he said, "I did not know you wished to see me. We were"—he looked around as if for support—"simply amusing ourselves until you joined us."

Elizabeth's chin lifted. "We do not see that we were missed at all in this happy gathering." Her eyes raked the chamber. "Our head hurts and music makes it worse. You will all leave immediately."

"Yes, Your Majesty," we murmured as a group.

"Not everyone." She paused. "I will have my ladies to care for me."

A half dozen women in black came forward. Douglas was among them.

"Not you." Elizabeth held up a glittering hand. "You are pale, Lady Sheffield, and you are sweating most unattractively. If you cannot dance without appearing sickly, you should stay off the floor."

Douglas curtsied and backed away, unable to resist a quick glance at Leicester, who was the very picture of a man torn. His state was noted by the queen. She smiled and said, "You, Leicester, may sit with us and tell us the story of how you spend your days." She paused. "Perhaps if you have so little to occupy your time. I should send you to France."

"That is unnecessary, Your Majesty—" His words trailed off as he sprinted after her.

Isabel sighed. "I must go to my cousin," she said. "She will cry herself to sleep tonight."

"So will my lord of Leicester, if he is permitted to leave the queen's presence." I bowed to her. "I thank you for the dance, Lady Isabel, and for the opportunity to make up for my appalling behavior."

"For a moment, I felt almost a normal woman again." Her lashes fluttered. "I thank you for not holding my youthful actions against me."

"I am trying to judge less as I age." My sigh equaled hers. "If you do not judge what I said then, I can hardly judge what you did—though I do often judge my father." I debated mentioning my plans. "I intend to go north before the summer," I continued. "I will most likely see him if I wish to visit my niece."

She ducked her chin, her cheeks turning a pretty pink. "He was good to me at a very painful time in my life. If it is not too much to ask, I wish you would give him my regards."

"I will do my best." Unsurprisingly, Bess had asked me to do the same.

CHAPTER 19

ACCORDING TO ROBIN, THOMAS Cromwell had collected promising young men. As the month wore on and I spent more time in the principal secretary's office, agitating for permission to leave, I saw that Cecil did the same. There were men who scribed, who transcribed, who translated; men who made and broke ciphers; men who worked for foreign ambassadors while also accepting a stipend from the English court for information and partial loyalty.

Then there were the outright spies, men planted in distant courts or English households, trained to worm their way into a place—or a family—and report back on all they had witnessed. It was a dirty business. I had dipped a toe in it while in Scotland. Ned would say that I had too many scruples for the work of spiery, but I saw that as no bad thing, to have reached the age of thirty-six with some scruples intact.

They were challenged daily and by stronger forces than any Ned could muster. I rode each morning with Isabel Ferren and Douglas Sheffield, who had been permitted to remain at court only after Leicester promised to avoid her company. Douglas spent the ride either lamenting the earl's lack of contact or complaining about the queen's dislike of her, while Isabel and I trotted behind, speaking whenever she stopped for breath.

"I shall miss you when you're gone," Isabel said one morning as we waited in Douglas's antechamber. She was late every day as she changed her riding costume in the hopes that Leicester would escape the queen's clutches. "You make these morning forays bearable."

She wore a tight-fitting black jacket with a collar of deep purple velvet, a concession to the months since her husband's death. Instead of looking drawn by the lack of color, she appeared absolutely blooming.

"I find them quite endurable myself," I confided. "It gives me something to think about in the afternoons when I am trapped with Cecil's men."

"What do they have you doing?" She raised a hand to her lips. "Perhaps I shouldn't ask."

"Perhaps you shouldn't." I did not want her involved in that part of my life. Because of her relationship with my father, I should not want Isabel involved in any part of my life, but I had grown fond of her and thought she showed me a side he had never seen, or which hadn't existed when she was younger. Despite Douglas's clear encouragement, I did not wish to marry her, but I enjoyed her company.

"I'll be right there!" Douglas sang through the open door. "Just my jewels."

"Including some given to her by the earl," Isabel said under her breath. "Which she should take care wearing in public."

"But she will not." Douglas in love was incredibly stubborn.

"No." She stood, shaking out her skirts. "Are you... is that something you want to do? Work with those people?"

"Ready!" Douglas spun through the door in a swirl of green, looking like a woodland sprite from my nurse's tales. Her hair was a mass of curls—some artificial, if I was not mistaken—on top of which a tiny hat rode like a ridiculous ship. At her breast was an initial jewel made of interlocking Ds, for Douglas and Dudley.

She pulled on embroidered green leather gloves and glanced between us. "I keep hoping that I will discover you in his arms, Is."

"I am more discreet than that." Isabel shook her head. "My cousin is in desperate need of fresh air, William. Her thoughts are disordered."

"They are not!" Douglas protested. "I want everyone to be happy."

That afternoon, I had a lucky encounter with Charles Mannion. We'd spent time together during our years in Scotland, but he'd never been a companion of choice. It was fair to say he likely felt the same about me. In my discontented state, though, seeing him was like meeting an old friend. We thumped each other on the back and made plans to meet that night.

Though in a different wing of the palace, his rooms were no better than mine. His man ushered me inside a sparsely furnished chamber, where I was presented with a spread of cold meats and cheese on a table, along with two brimming pitchers; though not extravagant, it would be no short visit.

"Good of you to come, Will," Charles said, coming from the inner chamber. "I am glad to see a familiar face."

"As am I." I took a seat, and he dismissed his man for the evening. "You've just come to Greenwich, you said?"

"That's right." He took the other chair, gesturing at the food. "Help yourself."

I cut a slice of beef and layered it with bread, smearing on a bit of mustard sauce from a crock. "I've been here almost a month," I said with my mouth full.

"The place is full of ladies in need of amusement," he said. "It can't be too bad."

"It's been endless." He wouldn't understand; Charles was content to hunt and dance and drink, as were most men. *I* was the strange one.

"And before you came here?" He tipped back a cup of ale. "Have you been up to Tutbury since she was relocated?"

*She* was the Scottish queen, and the move had happened in January: we'd heard in France she had been given over into the Earl of Shrewsbury's care and moved further from the border. Supposedly it was for her safety, but more than likely it was for Cecil's peace of mind, as Lady Scrope was sister to the Duke of Norfolk.

"I've not seen her since Bolton," I said. "I've been playing at messenger for months, all over France and back again."

"I've done the same," Charles said with a laugh, "but in England and up to Scotland. You'd think that without her the confederate lords would be in better order."

"They're still Scots." For all that they were a small country, they were abnormally troublesome. "What did you hear of Moray and the queen's letters?"

News of Mary's letters to Bothwell had reached us, though the letters had apparently been in Cecil's possession prior to my leaving London.

Starling and I had debated whether they were genuine or forged and had never come to a conclusion that pleased us. Whatever they were, they fatally discredited Mary's already tainted reputation.

"Hear of them?" he asked. "I've *seen* them. Ask Sir Edward—the originals returned to Edinburgh with Moray, but copies were made." He cut a hunk of cheese and chewed it thoughtfully. "They came in a silver jewel casket, a frilly thing that looked like something she'd have."

I'd been in Mary's privy chambers but rarely, but I could see it in my mind's eye: a narrow, footed chest, ornamented all over with silver gilt scrollwork and a crown. Mary Seton said it had belonged to her first husband, the young French king. It was of a size for correspondence, though a small thing to contain the destruction of a woman's reputation.

Mary's fate was litigated at a tribunal in York. At first, the Earl of Moray had not openly accused her of murder, fearful perhaps that he could not prove his case. Even if she were found guilty, there was no guarantee England would recognize his regency on behalf of his nephew. Squeamish at the prosecution of a fellow queen and fearing for her cousin's safety, Elizabeth refused to allow Mary to be dealt with by her lords, and when Moray asked that she not be returned to Scotland as queen, he did not receive even that.

"What do you think?" I asked. "Were the letters in her hand?"

"Who's to say?" He shrugged. "She claimed they were not hers, or not all hers, or not directed to Bothwell—and anyway, that her hand is easily copied." Charles rolled his eyes. "My daughter tells lies with a better face."

When things began to go wrong at the tribunal, Cecil had it adjourned and moved to Westminster, adding himself and his brother-in-law to the panel of judges. Only then, when Moray saw the outcome would go his way, was Mary accused of complicity in Darnley's murder.

The Scottish queen had not expected that, and impulsively ordered her counsel to withdraw. A day later, Moray produced the original letters and her advocates, being gone, had no right to view them or dispute their authenticity. Mary then demanded to address the tribunal in person. When her request was denied, she said she would not speak through an advocate, only to Elizabeth herself.

It was too late. The tribunal ended with no decision being reached. Moray's regency was confirmed, and Mary stayed at Bolton until her move to Tutbury.

"I heard you took Jamie Welldon to serve her." Charles refilled our cups. "Is he yet there? He must be a happy boy."

"As far as I know." Tutbury was nearer London than Yorkshire, but I would try to find a way to stop there on my way back from Whitby—that is, if I was ever able to get away from Greenwich.

The next day, after the midday meal, I reported to the principal secretary's rooms. Although more cramped than his quarters at Whitehall, they were, as usual, a hive of activity. While Whitehall was more spacious, Greenwich was far more pleasant. Casements could be propped open without the chambers being filled with the stench of the tanneries and other works on the city's edge, and the loudest noises aside from the shuffling of paper were birdsong and the laughter of courtiers disporting themselves outdoors.

Upon my arrival, one of the eager young men told me, "The principal secretary will see you at three."

"Why?"

"I tell you only what I am told." He shrugged and pointed to a stack of papers on a table. "Sir Edward asked that you read these while you wait."

The pages were reports received from various agents regarding the continued religious turmoil in France. I thought Ned gave them to me as a reminder of my cousin's sympathy for the Catholic cause. Matt's name had not been mentioned, however, and the one letter I received from Anne, via Harry, said Matthew was being attentive. I took that to mean she was keeping him close to home and out of trouble.

The situation in France was dire. The weak French king and his far more powerful mother, Catherine de Medici, were firmly against Protestantism of any kind, and the latest attempt at peace, represented by the Edict of Longjumeau, required the Huguenots to lay down their arms while permitting the practice of their religion in limited areas. The Huguenots' actions were no better than those of their Catholic brethren, and men, as Robin Lewis had drummed into me, did stupid things in the name of religion.

The report I held in my hand was a few days old. It read that Gaspard de Coligny, the Admiral of France, had fully recovered from the injuries he'd sustained at Jarnac and was again in charge of the Huguenot forces, but his brother was dead—a death, correctly or not, attributed to poison. That would only make the situation worse.

I rubbed my eyes and hauled myself upright, my head aching with all the information it had been fed. I pushed my chair back, muttering, "Jakes," to the man beside me, and ducked out.

Down a narrow service passage and behind a door was the men's garderobe. It too was on the small side, the bench having but ten holes instead of the usual twenty. The last hole, nearest the window, was occupied by a gentleman with his face hidden behind a pamphlet whose cover bore a grotesque parody of the Scottish queen offering her hand to the Duke of Norfolk.

I did what I came to do and escaped; the miasma in any house of easement was the same. I would rather piss in the open air or in a chamber pot than hold my breath and conduct my business side-by-side with my fellows.

By the time the bells told me I should present myself at Cecil's door, I had been back in my seat, turning the pages of another report, for some minutes.

Cecil was seated behind his desk, half-hidden by folios and documents. A figure at the window cast a long shadow across his desk. At first glance, I thought impossibly that it was Robin—the man was tall and thin, wearing unrelieved black—but then I saw that his hair and beard were dark as well.

"Hawkins," Cecil said. "Are you acquainted with Francis Walsingham?"

"I have not yet had the pleasure."

On first hearing his name mentioned, I asked about Walsingham and was told he'd been brought into the principal secretary's employ the previous summer. Fluent in French and Italian, with a wide acquaintance across all classes, he was asked to handle a threat to the queen sponsored by the Cardinal of Lorraine.

By the time the threat was dealt with, Walsingham had organized a circle of informants so extensive that he was less likely than me to ever be freed from royal service. Unlike me, he appeared to have no desire for freedom, standing at ease in Cecil's office with ink-stains on his fingertips like any junior clerk.

Walsingham inclined his head. He was swarthy, and the cut of his short beard struck me as Spanish, but when he spoke, he was clearly English. "I have heard of you, as well, Hawkins. You have done good service over this past year."

"I am gratified that you think so." Where was all this headed? Cecil and Ned were enough, but now this fellow looked ready to put his hands all over my life. "I am happy to be back in England."

Cecil made a noncommittal noise. "I wanted to get you into this conversation, Hawkins, because Walsingham has been extremely helpful in the gathering of information. With your messengering background, I thought you might have some ideas of how his work could be improved."

I said something I hoped sounded intelligent and sat next to Walsingham. They proceeded to outline for me the lengths to which they had gone and were prepared to continue to go to keep Elizabeth and the realm safe from Catholic plots, as well as increasing their knowledge of the actions and habits of every noble household in England besides.

"There are men of ours—footmen or grooms—in any Catholic house of size," Walsingham said. "Some holdouts haven't taken on anyone new, but my men are courting maids in those households as we speak. Soon they shall be installed—or the maids will threaten to quit, which no noble lady will allow."

"What of the maids themselves?" I asked. "Why do you not use them, instead of sending men to interfere?"

It seemed an altogether less complicated solution, although there was certainly an attachment among well-born women to their maids.

"Women are a last resort," Walsingham said with an expression of distaste. "Their humors are inconsistent, and they often sympathize with those they consider to be at a disadvantage."

The women of my acquaintance, though not numerous, were as clear-eyed and logical as their male counterparts. Often it seemed unfair that they were considered less than capable but, in this instance, they would benefit from being kept out of the schemes of these men.

"I saw someone earlier," I said, "reading a pamphlet against the Duke of Norfolk. Is he still—"

Cecil smiled with delight, the most human expression I had ever seen on his dour face. "That is Walsingham's work," he said. "A most excellent piece of writing. Norfolk has not given up his ambitions for the Scottish queen."

Besides being England's sole remaining duke, he was the wealthiest man in Europe who was not a prince of the blood. That problem could be solved by marrying a queen, if such a marriage were permitted.

Walsingham smirked. "For all that he claimed he would not be able to sleep upon a safe pillow lying next to so wicked a woman, that is certainly his intention."

"In his eyes, I suppose the reward is worth the risk." I couldn't see it, myself, but then, I had never fallen under the spell of Mary Stuart. "Stronger men have been led to believe themselves the objects of her affections."

"And yet," Cecil said drily, "we have been blessed by the fact that she continually chooses men weaker than herself."

It was true: how much of a threat would she be, married to someone not swayed by her charm? Little to none if she'd but come home and married a Protestant Scot. But she'd had to have Darnley, a drunken, vicious boy whose appeal had faded faster than his beauty, and who was so uncooperative he could not be blown up in his bed, but had to be strangled, and thus implicate his wife.

"You are intent upon visiting your family in the north?" Cecil asked abruptly.

"I am." I waited for him to refuse permission; I did not want to resort to begging, but if I did not get away from Greenwich soon, I would throw myself in the river.

"You shall make a trip to Howard House first," he said. "You are known to the duke as having been in Mary's employ. He will understand you have been useful to us in the last year, but because of your previous loyalty, he will trust you. Ask if he has any commission for you to carry to Tutbury." He leaned forward over his folded hands. "Once that is complete, and any response returned to us by messenger, you may go to Yorkshire."

CHAPTER 20

A VISIT TO HOWARD House was unnecessary as Norfolk's barge tied up at the landing the next morning. The man himself disembarked, followed by a small party and a dozen retainers, their voices carrying over the still air. I paused to watch and listen, allowing the other riders to go around me.

What was he doing at Greenwich? Ever since his proposal, earlier in the spring, that the Scottish queen might be given liberty if she married an English lord, he had been persona non grata with both queen and counsel. It seemed unlikely he would be summoned after that, but as a member of the nobility, an invitation was not required unless he had been specifically sent from court. Which he had not, because it was easier for Cecil to observe him if he was nearby.

A horse blew softly at my side. I turned away from the spectacle of Thomas Howard. Isabel sat easily on her gray mare, the skirt of her black habit fluttering gently in the breeze from the river.

"Must you go back?" she asked. "It is our last ride."

"No." I continued to watch until Norfolk's party disappeared inside. "I'll come along now."

We trotted to catch up with the others, and I turned over in my mind what Howard's presence meant and whether I should ask him if he had a message for Mary. Best to check with Cecil or Ned; I did not want to ruffle their fur and delay my departure.

"He might be here to see the Earl of Leicester," Isabel said quietly. "Douglas says they are frequent correspondents."

"Really?" I hadn't expected that; Leicester had never shown a particular regard for Norfolk. But his antipathy with Cecil was of long standing, and aligning himself with the duke might be an interesting way to work against the only other man whose advice Elizabeth ever considered.

She slowed her horse. "I do not know what is between them, William, but if it would help you—make you less beholden to those men—I could try to find out."

"You put me in a hard place," I said with a smile. "I want to know, but nothing will get me away from those men, as you call them. Leicester and Norfolk are no better, only different. Titled, and with ambitions for power above all else."

"What are your ambitions?" Isabel reached out and put her gloved hand on my wrist. "I worry about you."

Touched, I put my hand over hers, unable to remember the last time anyone had shown concern for my wellbeing. "I am flattered, Isabel, but your worry is unwarranted."

She slid her fingers from beneath mine. "I do not believe you."

"You must," I said, "for it is the truth."

The other members of our party came into sight. Douglas was watching us, a hopeful smile on her pretty face.

"We are making my cousin very happy," Isabel said. "She refuses to believe that you are leaving."

"I think Lady Sheffield is deaf to any news she does not wish to hear."

"That is very true." Isabel ducked her chin, looking up at me. "I do not wish to hear it, either," she said, "but I am more accustomed to disappointment."

Her words warmed me. "I will return, Isabel, before the summer is over."

"By then, Douglas will have found me a husband and I will be moldering away in a house in Sussex or Devon or Surrey and you'll forget I exist."

"In twenty years, I've never forgotten you." The sight of her naked body would be one of the last memories to fade from my mind.

Her face flamed. "And I will never forget your reaction. During that first year, when I couldn't let go of my misery, I thought about you as often as Lord Kelton."

"Why?" I couldn't imagine how an angry fourteen-year-old boy had made any impression at all.

We reached the others but stayed slightly apart to continue our conversation. Douglas lingered at the rear of the group, but Isabel made a sharp motion with her hand and her cousin kicked her horse into a trot. "You seemed so shocked. So... lost." She smoothed a tendril of hair from her forehead, and I could feel her silken skin beneath my fingers. "And he was terrible to you, but I was so in love with him that I couldn't see it at the time."

I held my breath listening to her, realizing that on one of the worst days of my life, she had seen me in a way few people ever had.

"I hope Douglas finds you a good man," I said. "She will have me to deal with if she matches you with anyone less than what you deserve."

"Douglas wants me to marry you." Her expression showed she found little humor in her cousin's plans. "I have told her to search elsewhere, that we are friends, but she claims it is impossible for men and women to be friends."

"And yet here we are." Had it not been for our shared past, I would have found it easy to love her, but I could not bring myself to love where my father had come before. Isabel understood and did not press me.

"Here we are." Her hand came out again, then withdrew. "Should I write, if I learn anything of interest?"

I thought of Walsingham's disdain for female agents. He did not understand what a rich resource they could be.

"Only if you write of yourself. I want a correspondent, not an informant." I told her that Harry's tavern would hold my letters. "Now, should we join the others before they call a priest to marry us off?"


Ned was intrigued to learn of Norfolk's presence at Greenwich. I failed to mention his correspondence with Leicester; it seemed well to keep that in reserve, should it be necessary.

"I don't know what game he's playing at," he said. "But it'll save you a trip into London. Send word that you'd like to see him and report back with his response."

"And any written message he might give me." Even inside the palace walls, I was a messenger.

"I'm going to miss you while you're gone, Hawkins." Ned folded his hands on his stomach and smiled expansively.

Norfolk waited a solid two hours before acknowledging my message, then after summoning me, I was left fidgeting in his antechamber for a further hour. When a liveried servant finally opened the door, I was offered neither a seat nor any refreshment. The duke stood at the window—overlooking the Thames, not a courtyard—and sipped thoughtfully from a gold and enamel goblet while continuing to ignore me.

I shifted from foot to foot. When that did not make him look over, I cleared my throat loudly. "My lord."

"What—oh, yes, Hawkins, isn't it?" He didn't bother to assume a civil expression.

"That was the name on my message," I said. "Did you not read it?"

Norfolk put down the goblet, looking at me for the first time. "What are you about, saying you could do something for me?"

He spoke as if someone in my lowly position could not possibly do anything for him.

"We met last year." I waited for a sign of recognition. "I carried a letter from Scotland."

"Ah." He remembered now, though he didn't see fit to admit it. "What of it? If you're here for your coin, you've left it a bit late."

My jaw hurt from biting back words. Mary *would* choose such a man for her intrigues; he was no better than her previous husbands.

"I have come today, my lord, because I am sent to Tutbury. I thought you might wish me to carry a personal message to the lady."

He had the grace to look abashed, but it did not last. "I have my own messengers," he said brusquely. "As well as Queen Mary's commissioners. I need send nothing by the queen's courier."

"It is as you say." I paused, letting him think over the implications of his words. "But it is known that you use your messengers. Whereas if I am acting on behalf of the queen, there would be no assumption that I carried messages for anyone else."

Norfolk crossed the chamber with the suddenness of a cornered beast and stared into my face. "And why would I trust you?"

"The lady trusts me," I said simply. "Whether you trust me is immaterial."

He inhaled sharply. "When do you depart?"

"Early on the morrow," I said. "But the message will have to reach me tonight. I receive my orders at first light, and any meetings after that would be suspect."

"You will hear from me." He snapped his fingers, and the servant appeared to usher me out.

I waited until I was well away from his apartments before directing a page to Ned with news that our ruse had worked, and that I would deliver whatever missive I received into his hands first thing in the morning.

I had been asleep for several hours when a bleary-eyed Dennis appeared at my bedside and shook me awake. "The duke's man delivered this." He thrust a folded and sealed letter in my face. "Said it was important."

"It is." I sat up, striking a light as he grumbled back off to his pallet.

Ned would want to see this immediately, but I didn't relish hunting him down at this hour, nor did I wish to be seen leaving my room should Norfolk's servant be lingering outside.

The wax was still warm. Holding it close to the light, I debated opening it, but there was no point. Norfolk was vain and arrogant and possibly traitorous, but he wasn't entirely stupid. Any message for the Scottish queen would not be visible to the naked eye. I put it under my pillow, blew out the candle, and called to Dennis, "Wake me before sunup. I'll need to go to Sir Edward as soon as it's light."

There was a muffled sound of frustration, and he turned over loudly. "Yes, sir. Should I also make the flowers bloom and Lady Isabel weep for your departure?"

I punched my pillow, wishing it was his head. "That is enough."

It had not rung six when I arrived in Ned's office, but several clerks were there ahead of me. Another young man slept on a mat in the corner.

"Are you always here so early?" I asked, taking a seat and rubbing the last of the sleep from my eyes.

"Sir Edward told us we might be required early." His name was Pettigrew, I remembered. "It is easier to sleep here in such cases."

The man on the floor sat up, scrambling to his feet at the sight of me.

"Bestir yourself, Crispin," Pettigrew said. "Sir Edward will not be long now."

The clerk stumbled out, yawning, and I hid my open mouth behind my hand. I had slept no more after the letter's delivery: curiosity about its contents kept me wakeful.

Within minutes, Ned arrived. He appeared no more awake than his clerks and about as cheerful as Dennis.

"Is that it?" He jerked his head at the folded letter on the table before me. "Did you read it?"

"It's not my place." I showed him the intact red seal and pushed it toward him. "And it's not likely I'd have been able to read it anyway."

"True enough." Ned scratched himself and yawned widely. "I don't keep clerks' hours, haven't done since Robin and I were with Cromwell."

Crispin returned from the jakes looking wide awake compared to the rest of us. "Is that the letter, sir?"

"It is." Ned handed it to him. "Go gently with the seal, unless we have its duplicate."

"We do," Pettigrew said. He had fetched over pen and ink and a sheet of rough parchment which, by the look of it, had been scrubbed of previous writing. "And I am ready to take down a copy, sir, should you intend the original to be sent on."

"Not likely." Crispin took the letter from Pettigrew and opened it, holding it under his nose. "He's used verjuice. We'll have to heat it."

"You can tell?" I tried to keep away from these shadowy chambers, preferring to be on horseback in the open air, but some aspects of the work fascinated me.

"Crispin can smell a mouse fart," Pettigrew said solemnly. Though the day was growing brighter, he lit a candle.

"I can smell yours, certainly." Crispin spoke without looking up.

"Let me see." Ned cast a quick glance over the scant lines on the page. "Christ, I hope his secret words are more interesting than this."

I looked over his shoulder. The letter, written in French, contained no more than an anodyne greeting and wishes for Mary's continued good health with a sprawling signature at the bottom.

"I pray you keep in fine spirits and that God bless you with health and strength and all manner of good things." I read the closing. "That is hardly worth the sending."

"But the rest will be," Ned said savagely. "If not this letter, then the next. He will surrender himself into our hands yet."

The letter was passed back to Crispin, who took it and gently waved it over the candle flame, keeping an eye on the surface.

"It's coming now," he said, continuing his deliberate motion. "It's a bit light—I wonder if he's used a different preparation."

"What else might be used?" Verjuice was easily had, but I'd heard of orange or lemon juice being used on the continent, where the fruits were easier to come by.

"Milk," Pettigrew volunteered. "Though that doesn't take heat to develop, but charcoal brushed over it. And there's sympathetic ink, which is alum and vinegar."

"Don't forget my favorite." Crispin wrinkled his sensitive nose. "I am thankful the duke chose not to perfume his letter in that way." He smiled wryly and handed the paper to Ned. "Piss also requires heat before you can see it."

"Not very romantic." I turned to Ned, trying to make out the pale brown letters which appeared in between the lines of the original. "Is it worthwhile?"

"Very much so." He snatched it up before I could read it. "Go on to the hall and break your fast, Hawkins. By the time you're done, we'll have something for you."

## Chapter 21

WE HAD BEEN RIDING hard since daybreak. As our horses crested a small rise, I raised a hand and we paused. It gave me an opportunity to observe Mary Stuart's latest prison before I was too close to see it properly.

It was an old-style castle situated high on a wooded slope overlooking the winding River Dove, with commanding views of the distant Derbyshire hills. The surrounding plain was green and dotted with trees flush with springtime. It would be a pretty location but for the marshland that surrounded it. In winter, its elevated position meant it would be buffeted by every wind.

Mary hated the cold.

George Talbot, the Earl of Shrewsbury, had been appointed royal jailer after it was decided that Francis Knollys was ineffective and overly sympathetic to his royal captive. While being selected could be seen as an honor, it was Shrewsbury's bad luck that he had sufficient houses in the heart of England and fortune enough to keep a high-profile prisoner for the foreseeable future.

Tutbury was one of the lesser Shrewsbury properties, and it looked it. As the stench of the middens reached us, well ahead of the gatehouse, I remarked to Dennis, "Not a fit place for a queen, is it?"

"A queen?" He curled his lip. "What about us? I'd sooner stay in the village than this shithole."

"We might have to," I told him. "I don't know how much space has been allotted to Mary's household."

Neither of us were happy with the prospect of spending time at Tutbury. The trip from London had been pleasant, with blue skies and sun and no rain to speak of, but our destination made the days feel gray and close. Still, I could not remember a journey with better weather from start to finish and hoped our good fortune would hold when we continued on to Yorkshire.

"You're not part of her household, remember?" Dennis clucked to his horse. "You belong to Her Majesty Queen Elizabeth, body and soul, no matter what this daft Frenchwoman believes."

"Keep a civil tongue," I warned. "We walk both sides of this line and must keep in good favor with both."

He scoffed. "You'll be in good favor—and in possession of a soft bed—unless Mary Seton's had the sense to run back to Scotland."

I had tried to work out, all the way from Greenwich, a way to guarantee uninterrupted sleep and discourage any future overtures from Mary Seton. I had come up with nothing beyond the blunt truth that I did not want her. Though I had been led to believe women wanted men to speak plainly, telling this particular woman she was no longer welcome in my bed would not be easy.

"If she knocks on my door this time, don't let her in." I would think of something to tell her, but it would be more difficult in the dark, when my defenses were down and my clothes already off.

"Trust you to make your life more difficult than it is already." Dennis shook his head. "You should never turn down what's freely offered."

Piles of debris rested against the walls outside the gates and the sound of hammers rang out from nearby; despite Mary's presence—or because of it—building work was going on. I presented my credentials to the head of the guard, of whom there were a surprising number.

"Ride on up to the courtyard," he said, checking my papers and handing them back. "Your horses will be dealt with, and you shall be presented to the earl in due course."

"He is in residence?" I looked down the road to the castle, which, for all its moat, was more like an oversized hunting lodge in a defensive position.

"And the countess," he replied with a laugh. "Though I am told she is here against her will."

Tutbury was also unlike Bolton in that I was not assigned a chamber, but summarily told that I would share with one of Mary's household. Though insulted, I did not object as the arrangement would prevent unwelcome visitors, and I was pleased to discover that the chamber's regular occupant was Jamie Welldon.

In Edinburgh, we had made fun of his wide-eyed innocence and his obvious infatuation with the queen, but despite his earnest Catholicism, he would be far superior to the company I'd been keeping in London. I looked forward to hearing about his year with Mary, and any details he might let slip, or that I could inveigle him into revealing.

His chamber was on the top floor, a small closet with nothing more than a bed, a stool, and pegs on which to hang clothes—little better than a servant's room. Dennis grumbled about our accommodations, dealing quickly with my things as I washed the road dust from my face and hands and made ready to be presented to Mary.

I was kept waiting for several hours in an antechamber outside her rooms. Whether the delay was of her making, or whether Shrewsbury, whom I had met in passing as I handed over the message from London, controlled access, I did not know. The time was lightened by Jamie's arrival in the hall, and we took ourselves outside, beyond the reeking moat, to exchange news.

I told him of my travels and saw envy on his face. "Has it been difficult, being penned up for the last year?"

"No," he said slowly, but there was a sadness in his eyes for all that he was missing. "It is my honor to serve the queen, for as long as they will allow me to remain."

"How large is Her Majesty's household now?" There had been mention in London of their numbers being reduced.

"About... two hundred?" he hazarded. "Some have left, and Shrewsbury sent others away. She is reduced now to ten ladies."

Two hundred was a more than respectable number—an extreme number for a prisoner, though not for a queen. Elizabeth would not be able to get through the day with so few attendants.

"Is her hairdresser with her?"

"Mistress Seton?" His expression was open; she had not chosen to alleviate her boredom with him, thank heaven. "Yes, I think she will never leave her mistress."

I shook my head. Mary's loyalty was admirable, but it would also keep her locked in a prison for crimes of which she was not guilty.

When the door at last opened for me, Mary Stuart's head lifted from her embroidery. She appeared at first to be annoyed at the interruption, but when she recognized me, her smile was genuine.

"Monsieur Hawkins!" Her changed circumstances had not altered her wardrobe; she wore an elaborate scarlet taffeta gown trimmed with pearls, and her sleeves were heavy with goldwork. "How wonderful to have you with us again."

"Your Majesty," I said quietly, coming to stand before her abbreviated canopy of state and bowing over her hand. "I regret not being able to visit before now."

An airy wave drew me upright. "We understand you have been doing your best for us, monsieur."

Did she have any idea how I had been occupied? It would be difficult to explain my work as having been on her behalf, but kings and queens tended to believe themselves at the center of all, so it was possible.

"I am sorry you are held in this place." As prisons were concerned, Tutbury wasn't bad, but this prisoner had grown up in the French court, where nothing had been denied her.

Better that the tribunal had gone against her, I thought, and sent her back to Scotland to face punishment than she be forced to live in fetters in this place, which smelled of damp plaster and had guards on every door. Even in Edinburgh, she had refused to be constrained by something as simple as the weather; walls and doors and locks would drive her mad.

"Your queen, our cousin Elizabeth, when will she come to see us?" Mary demanded. "I thought perhaps upon our arrival in England, but—" She stopped, staring through the rippling glass window at the green hills beyond the castle walls. "And now I am in this place, which is worse than Bolton."

Over the years since Mary's return to Scotland, each queen had evinced curiosity about the other, but I could not imagine a circumstance where Elizabeth would willingly meet Mary, nor one where Cecil would allow it.

"In time, I am certain that a meeting will be arranged." I tried for a conciliatory tone. "I come bearing a message from the queen, and"—I lowered my voice—"one from the Duke of Norfolk, who recommends himself to you most heartily and hopes you will accept his letter."

"Ah, the duke is most kind." Mary glowed with attention even as the letter disappeared into her sleeve. She was not so different from her cousin, only less careful and without men like Cecil and Walsingham to guide and protect her.

A movement caught my attention. Mary Seton was hovering nearby. I gave her a brief nod and returned my attention to the queen, who continued to bemoan the conditions of her imprisonment.

"The smells," she said, rolling her eyes. "There are drains beneath all our windows. The beds are lumpy. We ache in every joint! And the food, Monsieur Hawkins—we have our own cook, but the food they are given is terrible. How are we to survive such treatment?"

"That may be English food, Your Majesty." I tried to make light of the situation, in the hope of distracting her.

"Your Majesty, we will be moving to Wingfield Manor soon enough." Mary Seton bent to speak in her royal mistress's ear. "I have been told it is a more comfortable place."

"It could be no worse," she said bitterly, and turned her face away. "We shall see you again this evening, Monsieur Hawkins. Do you play?"

I squinted at her, not understanding. Did she mean cards or music? "Play, your Majesty?"

"An instrument." She picked fractiously at her sleeve. "We know every one of Marie's songs by heart."

"I have no musical ability." It was part of why I enjoyed visiting Harry Minstrel, to listen to his parents perform. "You would not wish to hear me sing."

Mary Seton's hand fluttered to her heart. "I shall request that the earl have new music sent for you immediately."

The queen flung herself back on her throne with a wail of frustration. "Why are you the only Marie we have left?"

When Mary Stuart had traveled to France as a child to be raised alongside the dauphin, her eventual husband, four young girls of good family, all named Mary, were chosen to accompany her. They were educated in the palace and became her ladies-in-waiting; when she returned from

France, they came with her. Only Mary Seton remained after the flight from Scotland.

"Madame, they have husbands and families," she said. "Whereas I have no one but you."

The queen looked up, tears overflowing her lovely hazel eyes. "Then we are both sad cases." She began to weep, and Mary Seton gestured that I should leave.

I dined with the Shrewsbury household that afternoon, a meal of many courses but little conversation. George and Elizabeth Talbot were married the year before—his second marriage and her fourth—in a triple ceremony with four of their children. I wondered if responsibility for the Scottish queen, with all its attendant risks and expenses, would put an undue strain on their new union.

George Talbot was in his late forties, a long-faced man with a scraggly, gray-streaked beard, unprepossessing for all his titles and power. His manner was listless, as if recovering from an illness, and so what speech occurred at table came from his wife, Elizabeth, who had vitality enough for them both.

"How did you find our guest, Master Hawkins?" she inquired, her voice acid. "Still singing her complaints like a caged lark?"

I blotted my lips with my napkin and returned it to my shoulder. "She is accustomed to gentle living, my lady. It is an adjustment."

"As am I." She snorted. "This location is no more to my liking than hers, and until more things are sent from London, her rooms are furnished with all my best pieces from Sheffield. Even if I could escape this dreary place, my home would be empty."

"Hardly empty, Bess," the earl said, gazing at her with affection. "Sheffield is well-appointed and has every comfort available for you."

Her plucked brows rose. Skin pale and smooth as milk was topped by tightly curled red hair in the style of Queen Elizabeth, whose lady of the bedchamber she had been until her latest marriage. "My lord, if you attempt to convince me one more time that my rooms are at all habitable without my best tapestries—and my bed, which she calls lumpy!—I will leave this chamber and you will have to make my excuses to Master Hawkins and the others."

He inclined his head, spearing a piece of meat with his knife. "It is as you say, Bess."

I ate quietly after that, speaking when spoken to—occasional questions from Talbot about Leicester and several of the queen's other gentlemen—and sighing with relief when the earl wiped his mouth and threw his napkin on the table.

Pitying my situation, Talbot offered access to his library which, despite the size of the chamber, boasted a collection of books smaller and less varied than those owned by Robin Lewis. He apologized, explaining that the library at Sheffield was superior and hoped they would remove there soon so he did not have to transport his books cross-country. Nevertheless, I found a copy of Erasmus's *In Praise of Folly*, which I remembered seeing on Robin's shelves. When I visited, we would have something new to discuss besides the sad state of the world.

While my education was appropriate to my upbringing, after leaving university I rarely thought to open a book. Robin's love of reading, and the lengths he went to in acquiring books for his library, made me reconsider. Since joining Elizabeth's court, I had become known as a man who was more often to be found reading than dancing or shooting at targets. It was yet another way that knowing him had changed me.

I retreated to my chamber, half-hoping Jamie would be there for further conversation, but I was alone. I stripped off my formal clothes and sat by the window, planning to read until summoned to Mary's apartments in the evening.

The book held my attention better than expected; it was more than a religious treatise. Erasmus had been Catholic, but he criticized his faith with clear eyes. No one was safe from his mockery: women were foolish for trying to please men and be beautiful, while men were targeted in that something as unimportant as physical beauty could make them behave like fools.

It was clever and well written, and I looked forward to hearing Robin's thoughts and seeing how well they matched mine.

A knock on the door startled me from my reading.

"Come!" I called.

A boy's head came around the door. "The Scottish lady will see you now, sir."

I thanked him and rose, stretching my stiff muscles and hunting out a clean shirt. Where had Dennis gone that he couldn't be here to see to my preparations? There was little enough to be done—resuming my breeches and doublet, running a comb through my hair, jamming on my cap. I hoped that the windows in Mary's chambers would be open, so we did not stick to our clothes before being dismissed for the night.

The staircase was grand in design but sparse in decoration. I ran lightly down, stopping short at the sight of Mary Seton lingering in a shadowed alcove.

"William." She advanced with outstretched hands. "Her Majesty is not ready to receive you."

"But I was told—"

She smiled. "You were told that the Scottish lady would see you. I *am* a Scottish lady."

"Ah." I brushed my lips over her knuckles. "It is good to see you, Mary."

She took my arm. "We have a few minutes. I am permitted to leave the house, although not unaccompanied, for fear that I will pass messages. Will you walk with me?"

The air was soft; the sun had lost its daytime brilliance, but there were hours until sunset. Hedge sparrows and thrushes sang in the nearby trees and an unfamiliar bird cheeped insistently from somewhere on the castle roof.

"How is it for you?" I asked, as we paced the graveled paths of the neglected grounds, trying to avoid the moat. "Are you well?"

"As well as I can be." She twitched her full skirts away from a shrub that encroached onto the path. "But I worry about Her Majesty. The damp here will destroy her health. She looks hardy but she gets a chest in bad air."

She spoke as if I hadn't spent years observing her mistress. "I must ask," I said, recalling another story I had heard. "It is being said in London that you were involved in her escape attempt at Bolton. Is that true?"

"Of course," she replied, as if it were a given. "The same as I did at Lochleven." She had worn Mary's clothes while the queen crept out of the castle and was taken away on a boat. "There are few choices, as you know, when your life belongs to another."

I understood that well enough. "Have you never thought of leaving her?"

Mary sat on a bench in a billow of silver-gray silk. "I could not," she said, "and what would I do if I left? I have been with her for over twenty years. I know nothing else."

"But Beaton, Livingston, and Fleming were with her as long, and they left."

She shrugged. "Beaton, Livingston, and Fleming all found husbands. That is impossible for me."

"It is hardly impossible." I perched beside her on the small portion of the bench not covered by her spreading skirts.

"What would you have me do?" She raised her eyes to mine; the bleakness I saw there was chilling. "Marry one of the earl's gentlemen, who gaze at me like something from a menagerie? Hope for an emissary from Edinburgh or Paris to fall quickly and fatally in love?" Mary laughed. "I do not inspire those feelings, while the queen has but to show her face to have gentlemen swearing their love. Any man who would have me would have to be blind, or without any sense at all."

Mary Stuart's magnetism was similar to that possessed by my father; it was difficult to be seen beyond its warming circle. Commiserating would help nothing, so I said simply, "No one would judge you if you chose to leave."

She went very still, and I saw that she *had* thought about leaving and hated herself for it.

"I would judge myself." Her hand sought mine, and she trailed her fingernails over the inside of my wrist. "It is more difficult for me to move freely here. Perhaps you could find a way to come to me tonight..."

"I do not see how," I interrupted, pretending that I felt nothing at her touch. "I do not have a chamber to myself, and you know how well the queen's apartments are guarded. I cannot smile and say I'm paying a call on one of her ladies and expect to be allowed in."

She bit her lip. "You must think of something, William, else I will surely go mad."

"Surely not." I laughed to soften my words. "No one has ever died from lack of my presence, Mary. You shall not, either."

"You do not care!" She rose gracefully, but her voice was choked with fury. "And we must now go in, for it is time for your audience."

I stood, brushing off my hose, disappointed that I had not stopped her before she offered herself again. "Mary, it is not that I don't—it is not proper for me, serving as I do."

"We both serve," she said harshly. "And we will likely do so until we die. Why should we not take our pleasures where we find them?"

## Chapter 22

Once my audience was ended, I returned to my chamber to resume my conversation with Erasmus. Jamie appeared not long after and we talked into the night, burning Shrewsbury's candles and drinking his ale, keeping up such a constant conversation that Dennis huffed and groaned and finally took himself off to sleep elsewhere.

Jamie was not the font of information I had hoped; either Mary used other secretaries for her confidential correspondence, or my young friend had developed a talent for dissembling. I did not wish to believe that was the case. He appeared to be the same open-hearted romantic he had been since arriving at Mary's court.

"Your man has little respect," he said without judgment, as the door banged behind Dennis. "Is he always thus?"

"Always." I leaned back, propping my bare feet on the windowsill, safe in the knowledge that I would have no female visitors. "You surely remember he complained all the way to Bolton last year."

"I remember little of that journey," he admitted. "My thoughts were occupied with the young lady whose acquaintance I made at Matthew Darcy's home."

Father's little governess, to whom I had failed to pass on Jamie's message when I could not bring myself to visit Hawkmoor.

"You still think on her?"

"Occasionally." He shook his head, bemused. "There are few enough distractions here. Some of the queen's ladies are pretty enough, but it is not a situation that invites courtship."

"No, I suppose not." I tipped down the last of the ale. "Do you wish
to stay here, Jamie? I could perhaps speak to someone in London—"

He sat upright so quickly that the legs of his stool thudded on the
floor. "It is not that I don't appreciate your offer," he said, "or wouldn't
like the change of scenery, but I feel I should stay with Her Majesty until
Queen Elizabeth recognizes her rights."

The breeze shifted, bringing a waft from the moat so foul that I
reached over and slammed the window shut.

"That will not happen," I told him. "The privy council will never
allow Mary to resume the throne, nor will they devote men and treasure
to that end, not when Catholics all over England and beyond are flocking
to her cause."

Jamie stared, his mouth open in surprise. I had never spoken so baldly
before about Mary's prospects.

"These are not necessarily my feelings," I added. "You know I have no
issue with Catholics, so long as they pose no risk to the crown. But Mary
is a magnet for intriguers. I do not wish you caught up in it."

It was enough that my cousin had been caught up in them. Perhaps I
could check on Matthew before I returned to London—or would that
take too long?

"We should sleep." He pressed his lips together. "And I am caught up
in nothing, Will. The queen has asked nothing of me that I would fear
to admit before the privy council."

"Then she has others besides you to do her bidding." I blew out the
nearest candle. "For there are letters coming in and out of this place,
whether you are involved or not."

He rubbed his face with one hand, then pinched out the second
candle. "I truly hope you are wrong about that."

I wanted to be wrong, but I knew Mary too well to believe it to be
possible.


Two days later, we left Tutbury. It was a damp, gray morning, but I was
eager to start for Yorkshire and refused with little regret the steward's
offer to remain until the weather cleared. The Talbots were acceptable
hosts, but their castle was more disheartening than anything the skies had

to offer, and I was happy to set out with Dennis and take our chances with the weather.

"You're going to get us rained on," he said as we passed through the gates, nodding farewell to the men lounging inside the guard house.

I looked back at the castle with its unhappy occupants and reeking moat. "I don't care. We've been wet before."

We took a different path and passed through a village. It was as shabby as the castle that loomed over it, but market stalls filled the small square. I swung down from my horse to take a quick look to see if I could find gifts for Robin and Margaery. There were no books in this place, and I could hardly appear with ribbons and trinkets for the lady of the house without also buying something for her husband. I looked at selections of fruits, dried and fresh; vegetables; live poultry and rabbits; leather goods; and bolts of wool before following my nose to a spice seller. Judging by their prosperous stall, they did a brisk trade with the Talbot and Stuart kitchens, and I increased their profit by purchasing ground ginger and saffron to contribute to the Winterset larder.

No gift could adequately convey how special the Lewises were to me, but this would serve. Robin was a plain man, and Margaery would not spend on expensive spices if they would not be noticed.

I returned to where I had left Dennis. He was drinking a tankard of ale and teasing a black-haired wench with a pitcher held between her ample breasts.

"That was lovely," he said, handing back his empty tankard upon seeing me. "But my fun is over, lass."

She scurried away. He watched her go, a smile spreading across his face. "We should have stayed here."

"If we return, you may do so," I said, feeling generous. The girl was pretty, and Dennis had been less annoying than usual. "Though I don't know when that might be."

"The queen had no response to the duke's letter?" He held the reins while I mounted.

I did not bother to ask how he knew; if Ned had any sense at all, he would hire my servant and leave me in peace.

"No," I said shortly. "I even asked her at our final audience."

"She has another way of reaching him, then." He nodded slowly, thinking. "I don't envy his lordship on the hill there, having to be responsible for her."

"Nor do I." The market was breaking up and I nudged the horse into the flow of carts and riders heading toward the road. As we turned north, hooves thudded behind us. I slowed, a hand on my dagger, but quickly recognized the young page who fetched me for my audiences with Mary.

He stopped his horse, threw down the reins, and jumped off. "I carry a message."

"Let's have it, then." I held out my hand. "Is it from Queen Mary?"

He shook his head. "The other lady, sir."

I curled my fingers around the tightly folded paper, almost wishing the boy hadn't found us. Whatever Mary Seton had to say, I wanted no part of it. Flipping him a coin, I tucked the message into an inside pocket for later perusal. We would stop eventually. I would read it then.

Pushing the horses a bit, we made Winterset in four days. I refused to change at any of the usual stops—this was a personal trip and I wanted none of the queen's beasts, with the expectation they would be returned within a certain period, nor did I want it noted where and when I had passed through. I would return to London when I was ready and damn the consequences.

Needing to put some distance between myself and the events at Tutbury, I did not open Mary's letter until the next day. It was no more than I had expected: regret that we had not spent more time together and well wishes for the journey. At the end, she appended something I could pass on to London. "The queen is allowed by the earl to have a priest to hear her confession and celebrate mass. He also carries letters."

I had seen no priest during my visit, but Cecil's men could discover his identity easily enough and place someone in his household or have him replaced with a tame Catholic in their employ. It bothered me that I hadn't met him; work left undone.

Should I respond? I didn't want to open a correspondence with her for fear it would also open a door that was better closed. I decided I would tell Ned that I had responded. Because of their disdain for female agents, it was unlikely there was anyone among the women to say whether Mary Seton received letters or not.

The rain had been near constant since we left Tutbury, but by the time we reached the coast, it had ceased. Whitby looked as unlike our last visit as was possible, with brilliant skies, streaks of pale cloud, and a sapphire sea. As usual, I stopped at the turning of the road to look out over the water and then at Winterset, set snug against its backdrop of trees. Even on my first visit, during a driving storm, I had admired the place. It seemed more perfect to me now because of the people who lived there.

In a lifetime of going unnoticed, Robin Lewis had always seen me. Despite what passed between us, he welcomed me into his home, watched me play with his children, shared food and drink and the contents of his library and his mind, all while knowing my desperate love for his wife. Margaery, knowing too well where my affections lay, smiled at me with indulgent patience.

"Are we to stay long?" Dennis fractured my reverie with a question. "I feel like we've been on horseback for a week."

"We have been." I would have done murder for a hot bath and clean clothes, and my back was in knots from hours in the saddle. "Or have you not noticed?"

"I was trying not to." He shifted in the saddle and groaned. "We are too old to be kiting around the country like boys."


Margaery waited at the open door. "Robin is out with Ralph, riding over the estate." She stepped back to let me in, shifting her sleeping baby to her shoulder so she could take my hand. "He will be sorry to have missed your arrival."

"I apologize for the lack of notice." I didn't mind his absence; it gave me a chance to bask in her presence. She and Robin observed very little formality in the privacy of their home, and her rich brown hair was bundled into a thick braid down her back. She wore nothing on her head. "I am surprised that he still rides," I said. "It seemed, at my last visit, that his knee was worse."

"Oh, it is," she assured me. "He does not ride as often, but we go out once a week, up to the old tower, and he tries to go as often with Ralph."

She shook her head. "He will be back when it pains him too much to stay on, and he will swear and limp for days after, but I can't stop him."

"Nor do you want to." They had always ridden together; it was as much a part of their union as their love and their sparring conversations.

"Nor do I want to." She folded back the wrap from the baby's face. "Meet young Sebastian. I dare not wake him. He is not so easy as Ralph and Margaret were."

I peered at the child, seeing a smooth, round cheek with a fringe of dark lashes like his mother's. "He is a fine boy."

"We think so." She handed him gently to her maid. "Would you give him to Susan, Alice? We will be in my parlor until they return."

Alice smiled pleasantly at me. "And I shall see that your chamber is made up directly, Master Hawkins."

Despite being my age and the mother of three, Margaery was as attractive as ever. I had to remind myself that she was as impossible a target for my affections as Isabel Ferren. "I brought something for you," I said, to drive away those distracting thoughts. Dropping my bag on the hall table, I dug into it and produced the packet of spices.

Margaery held it to her nose and smiled delightedly. "Ginger?"

"And saffron."

She sniffed again. "We shall feast like Queen Elizabeth before your departure!"

A feast was unnecessary; I had come to see them, not to be treated like a foreign ambassador. "Robin sent word that he wanted to speak with me. Do you know what it is about?"

Her brow wrinkled. "I believe so, but I'll not speak out of turn. He'll be back soon enough and then I won't see the pair of you until he is near starvation." She extended her hand. "Come and sit with me. We get very little company out here."

That was exactly why Robin loved Winterset; he was happiest with his books and his small family. It had always surprised me that he had worked at court for most of his life.

"How did he manage?" I asked, taking the offered seat. "All those years with Ned."

"It was hard." She called for wine through the open door. "It goes against his nature, being so involved in the world, but he wanted to do what he could to stop the same mistakes being made in the future."

"Mistakes are still being made."

"That's because people don't change." She smiled wryly. "Except for Robin, who has learned he is not an island."

We continued our conversation over wine and a hearty loaf, spread with soft cheese which she said proudly was a new sheep's milk cheese she had been experimenting with.

"It's far better than any I've had recently." I contrasted this proud goodwife with the sleek lady-in-waiting she had once been and knew this was her true self. "I've come from Tutbury. Their cook is not so good as yours."

"Tutbury!" Her expression softened. "How is the queen?"

"Discontented." I explained Mary's living situation, her pleasant rooms divided into presence and privy chambers, her large household, and the grim, disordered castle with its foul drains and numerous guards. "It is not as she would have it."

"She is not free."


"You must have wondered at my summons." Wincing, Robin eased into his chair. As predicted, his leg hurt from riding. Margaery would not allow him to retreat to the library until he was adequately dosed with willow bark.

"I did," I said, "though I need no summons to visit."

His mouth tightened into a line, and he shifted again in his seat. "I heard something recently that might be of interest to you."

Though Robin had retired from royal service, Ned was far from his only correspondent among his former colleagues.

"What have you heard?" It would do no good to inquire as to his source; he would either tell me or not. In his way, he was as infuriating as his wife.

"Have you been to Hawkmoor lately?"

"Not in two years or so," I admitted. "I thought to see the Fremantles on my way back, but I had not intended to visit my father."

Robin's brow furrowed. "Have you ever met your niece's governess?"

"In passing." There was some complicated story as to why my father had taken her on, but I could not recall it. "Why?"

He shuffled some papers on his desk and produced a letter. I did not recognize the hand. Not Ned, then.

"Her name is Katherine Rowan," he said. "I can't tell you much at this point, but she has come to Cecil's attention and that is never good. Particularly since she is in your father's household."

"You don't think Father—" I had little regard for the man, but I didn't believe him capable of interfering with his granddaughter's governess.

"Whatever the interest is," he said with a shake of his head, "it stems from the girl. Your family is not involved."

I closed my eyes, trying to bring Mistress Rowan's face to mind, but my clearest memory was Jamie's infatuation and his undelivered message.

"What do you suggest?" I would follow his guidance; his instincts were generally correct.

"You must pay a visit to your father," he said blandly, knowing how I relished that prospect. "Inquire—discreetly—what he knows of her background, what reason there might be for interest from those parts."

I was curious why Robin cared. He liked my father no more than I, and should something affect Lord Kelton, it would not touch me; everyone, including Cecil, knew we were estranged.

"What purpose is there?" I asked when he said no more. "He will not tell me freely. You know how it is with us."

"He cares about young Jane. Frame your concern in terms of the girl." Robin rubbed his chin. "Have you learned nothing from our acquaintance?"

"Not enough, apparently," I said. "Do you mind if I ask a question?"

"Ask away." He put the letter into a drawer. "I know nothing more of this matter, though."

"I am done with this matter," I said. "It is only... why did you tell me your story on the road?" I had always wondered, as he was not the most forthcoming of men, and yet he had doled out his life to me over that week, leaving me constantly hungry for more.

"Aside from trying to prolong our trip, so you wouldn't kill me?" His eyes crinkled with laughter. "Seb asked that, too. I think I wanted someone to see me before I died. No one ever has, not completely, other than you."

I was stunned, as his words so closely echoed my thoughts. "What about Margaery?"

His eyes were distant. "She knows most of it by now, but not in the same detail. Before you ask, she does know of Salvatore—though not his name or the more intimate details."

I sat with that idea, that Margaery knew her husband had been in love with a man. "She is, as you always said, exceptional."

"Indeed." Robin leaned forward, resting his elbows on his desk. "Now, tell me, what have you been reading?"

## CHAPTER 23

IN THE END, I agreed to visit Hawkmoor, but I was able to put it off for a fortnight because Margaery insisted that I stay for a proper visit. Even though she made me damned uncomfortable, I enjoyed her company, as well as Robin's, and the experience of a happy house was a wonderment after my childhood.

My other reason was young Ralph, who had shouted with joy upon seeing me. He was excited to have an active man to ride with him and showed me over the estate in every detail, acquainting me with all the livestock, naming each horse in the stables and every ewe in the sheep-fold. The lambs he did not name, he said, because they would be sold or slaughtered. We even visited the dovecote and the chickens, miring our boots to the ankles in muddy straw, which made Dennis roll his eyes and snatch them from me at the back door.

Margaery got her way regarding the feast, as well, retiring to the kitchen for two full days with her cook, the maid Alice, and another young woman brought up from the village. Appetizing smells floated out to the hall, but Robin and I received nothing but pottage, bread, and cheese during that time—the better to sharpen our appetites, she said, daring us to complain.

When the afternoon arrived, there were no complaints. The table was full—not only was their household casual in matters of dress, but on special occasions, servants were deemed part of the family. In addition to ourselves were Dennis, on his best behavior; Colin, the steward; Jasper Fowler, his predecessor, retired to a cottage on the estate; Margaery's maid, Alice; two pale girls from the village, who Margaery said did the cleaning and laundry; and Susan, the nursery maid. Small Sebastian, in his swaddling frame, was propped against the wall within easy reach, and a smaller table, set to one side, held Ralph and Margaret and four other young ones who belonged to Susan.

"Did you not invite the cook?" From my place at Robin's side, I looked around at the odd assortment of people, none of whom seemed to find anything unusual in being present at an event like this.

"Mistress Dunham keeps to the old ways," Robin said easily. "She eats in the kitchen."

Margaery leaned forward. "Sarah," she said, nodding at one of the girls, "will take her a plate of everything she cannot serve herself."

The first course was a pottage of barley with bacon and dried peas, followed by spiced small pies made with local fish. Stewed greens and turnips were served alongside. The table fell silent as everyone began to eat. Robin and Margaery drank wine. Everyone else wanted ale and I joined them, as the estate's ale was excellent.

When little remained on the serving platters, the two girls took them up and went to the kitchen, returning wreathed in smiles and carrying the main courses. A general shout went up at the sight of them, and I was glad Margaery had insisted on an elaborate meal.

A lamb roast was placed at the head of the table and a long wooden platter with at least ten mackerel in a sauce smelling strongly of ground ginger was set at the other end. The centerpiece was a large and fragrant pie made of dried quinces, flavored liberally with ginger, cinnamon, and other spices. The crust had been turned yellow with saffron, and instead of a plain top, the fruit was covered over with a lattice and trimmed with leaves and flowers made of pastry.

There was a chorus of squeals from the children's table at the sight. It was a remarkable achievement, worthy of the queen's kitchens and I said so.

Margaery smiled proudly. "I will give Mistress Dunham your compliments. We have been practicing the ornamentation, but the labor was all hers."

When the final course—plum tart, cherries conserved in jelly, and fresh fruit—was consumed, the servants excused themselves to continue the revels elsewhere, leaving me alone with my host and hostess as Ralph and Margaret abandoned us for more interesting pursuits.

"That was delicious," Robin said, draining his wine. "Will, can I pour you a glass, or are you happy with your ale?"

"I am content." I shifted so I could lean against the edge of the fireplace. "I have not eaten so well in weeks."

"That doesn't say much for George Talbot's kitchens." Margaery preened. "I'm sorry that Queen Mary does not eat so well as we do."

I did not want to discuss queens. I wanted to enjoy my pleasantly full stomach and sit and talk with them until bedtime, listening to the strains of music and shouting from the servants' party outdoors. But the sun would not set for several hours, so that was unlikely.

Robin folded and unfolded his hands, looking over his shoulder toward his library. "Would anyone mind if—"

"Go along," she said fondly. "I can keep Will company."

He looked abashed but stood up so hastily that he almost overturned his chair. "Give me an hour or so," he said. "I'm sorry."

"I'll manage." I smiled at him, fuzzy with ale and goodwill. "Come back before your wife bakes me into a pie."

"I make no promises." The door closed gently behind him, leaving me alone with Margaery and the littered table.

"Would you sit outside?" she asked. "The light is good, and I can take my embroidery with me so there's no risk of dicing you up for a pie filling."

There was a sturdy bench outside the front door, on the opposite side from the closed windows of the library, so neither our speech nor the music would disturb him. Margaery settled herself, arranging her embroidery on her lap and giving me a spool of black thread to hold in case of need.

"Now, tell me truly," she said. "Have you no one in your life?"

Other than Mary Seton, the innkeeper's wife, and shameful thoughts of my father's former mistress? "No."

"I don't believe you." She picked up the thin white cloth, stabbing it with a black-threaded needle. "Ladies have always sought your eye."

"But I don't want them," I said. "Not for the reasons they seek me."

"Ah." She took a breath, forming her next words carefully. "I think you are as great a romantic as Nell ever was. But your sister believed the universe would deliver love to her, and you are... not so trusting."

"Nell was in love every other day." I could smile now, but during her brief year at court she had worried me frantic.

Margaery nodded. "Why is it so different for you?"

Why couldn't Robin forgo his library on this, my last evening, when I needed his support? Barring that, I prayed one of the children would come crying to their mother. Margaery was like a dog with a bone when she got started, and I did not wish my romantic life examined by a woman who had played a large part in that life, if only in my imagination.

"My husband can't save you," she said placidly. "He will emerge when the words no longer speak to him and not a moment before."

"It is not polite to leave a guest unattended." I looked around the courtyard, hoping again for one of the children, but they were around the back of the house, singing lustily along to a poorly played lute.

"You are hardly unattended. You have been well fed and watered, and you have the full attention of your hostess." I chose to believe there was kindness behind her mockery. "I know from Robin that you work with Ned. And I know enough about Ned to find that worrisome." Another few stitches and a small flower bloomed under her fingers. "Have you been... put into situations not of your choosing?"

I laughed in spite of myself. "By God, that's tactful for you."

She grinned, looking more like little Margaret than a woman in her thirties. "I don't often choose tact, but it is a weapon I can wield, if necessary. And you didn't answer me."

How could I answer that question? A man did not tell a woman—his friend's wife and someone whom he had loved—that he had bedded women for information or out of desperate loneliness. I had overreacted to Félicité's advances, I suddenly understood, for the same reason Mary Seton clung to me. It was an uncomfortable realization.

"I will say no more than that some of my choices have not been in my best interests." My tone was stiff, and I suspected she could read every thought behind it.

Her work dropped to her lap, and she reached across to grasp my wrist. "Be kind to yourself, Will," she said. "There are women who will want you for yourself—not for what you can give or take from them, or because of who your father is." Her voice lowered. "As I once told you, had I not already had my most excellent husband, I could have loved you."

My face heated, remembering the time in Edinburgh when I had stupidly kissed her, and then our rushed journey to her grandmother's deathbed, when she sought to make me feel better about my guilt by offering to kiss me in return. It felt like one of the few genuine caresses I had received since my youthful fumblings with Cecily.

"Well, that is a fine thing to remind me." I tried to make light of her words, stifling the feelings that rose up at the thought of the life we might have had—if my very dear friend had not married her first.

"We cannot change the past," she said blithely, "and I for one have never gained anything from dwelling upon it." Her mouth tipped up at the corners. "If you are taking advice, I think you compare yourself too much to someone else. That does not serve, either."

"You are full of advice today." I let sarcasm creep into my voice. "Is there anything else I'm doing wrong?"

She pursed her lips, shaking her head slowly at my refusal to listen. "I meant you should keep yourself open, and not let yourself be taken advantage of."

Was that all? It appeared whenever I left myself open, bad things happened, whether by design or my own naïveté.

"I will do my best," I told her.

"I will not hold my breath waiting," she said in return.

My final evening was spent with Robin, once he invited me into the library. Early the next morning, I went riding with Ralph, and bade farewell to the entire family in the hall while Dennis waited outside with the horses.

"When I next get to France, I promise to visit your house," I told Margaery.

She squeezed my hands. "It is of no matter," she said. "Did you notice that Leon is no longer with us?"

"No…" I could not remember a servant named Leon.

"You knew him, briefly," she said. "He is married to Susan, our nurse-maid, but he grew homesick for France. This spring he took over the property as steward."

Learning this, Dennis's lingering conversations with Susan made more sense. I hoped he had done nothing to embarrass us—though I wasn't sure he was capable of embarrassment.

"I am glad of it," I said. "I felt bad that I wasn't able to get there."

They walked me through the door, Margaery still talking. "You've been a tonic. And I cannot thank you enough for the spices—we have plenty left to save for our Christmas feast."

The thought of Christmas in this warm and happy house made me smile. "I wish I could be here."

"You should come back," little Margaret said, hanging off my hand. "I like you."

I smoothed her curls away from her face. "I like you, too, Mistress Margaret. And I will see what I can do."

Robin clasped my arm. "You are welcome any time, you know that."

It was a compliment of the highest order, coming from him; so deep was he in his writing that he would not notice for a full day if his wife and children disappeared entirely.

"I will do my best," I promised. "But for now, I have a less pleasant destination in mind."

Margaery failed to hide her smile. "He is just a man, Will."

"To you, perhaps." Upon meeting my father for the first time, she blushed and stammered and then somehow *blossomed* under his gaze. "It is not so easy for me."

"It is as easy as you allow it to be," she said firmly. "Say farewell, children."

"Thank you for riding with me, sir." Ralph stuck out his hand and I shook it. "I would that you could stay."

I said with genuine regret, "So do I, but I'm off to visit Jane."

"You remember Jane." Margaery squatted down, straightening Ralph's coat. "You were friends when you were small."

"She's a girl," he said, with all the scorn of a boy his age. "I've got a sister if I want girls."

Margaery shook her head, tendrils of brown hair springing loose at her temples. "Elizabeth used to bring her to visit," she said. "Your father keeps her close now."

I dropped a hand to Ralph's head. "I'll see if I can change that."

## CHAPTER 24

TWO LITTLE BOYS WAVED from the hill, disappearing as I trotted along the road. My sister's boys, I assumed. Despite my best intentions, I had not seen them for several years, but they seemed the right ages.

Within minutes we had passed through the wide gate and Elizabeth met me at the door, the boys and two older girls behind her. We embraced and she made me welcome in a way that would have felt special had I not come from Winterset. When she offered a bed for the night without asking how long I would stay, I accepted with gratitude.

It had come to me as I rode: how to blunt the discomfort of meeting my father. I would persuade Elizabeth to accompany me, and to bring her children. Father liked the house full, so he could play lord of the manor. If I could not avoid him entirely, perhaps I could lose myself in the crowd.

"I was hoping you could be convinced to come with me," I said, as we settled into a small, charmingly decorated room at the back of the house. "I aim to visit Hawkmoor on my way back to London."

Her eyes widened. "You are visiting Father because you... want to?"

"I am visiting Father's *house* because I want to see Jane," I corrected. "And I carry greetings from the Lewises, who miss her. I promised to try to convince him to allow her to visit."

"Bonne chance," my sister said, smiling wryly. "Better they come to her. Father does not like Jane out from under his eye. I have told him myself she would benefit from the company of other children, but he scarcely permits her to play with mine."

That sounded like Father; his way was the only correct way.

"How is it with you, Liz?" I nodded discreetly toward her midsection. I was no connoisseur of ladies' fashion, but the front of her dark green gown looked surprisingly flat to conceal what must be a six months' pregnancy.

Her face clouded.

"Oh, Liz, I am sorry." I opened my arms and she leaned against me, shuddering with sobs more alarming for their silence. Finally, she stopped and wiped her eyes with her sleeve.

"Don't cry for me, Willie." She sounded tired but at peace. "Bearing at my age might kill me, and while I mourn the babe with all my heart, I do not wish to die and leave my children in their father's care."

I had never considered my brother-in-law to be a good husband, but until now I'd had no ill opinion of him as a father. "Surely he is not so bad."

"A barn cat cares more about its young," she said simply. "He likes the getting of them, but he barely knows his sons. And as for the girls—"

Our father had pampered and petted his daughters, in no small part because they adored and made much of him in return.

"He does not do right by them?" Tom Fremantle was often in London, a minor gentleman perennially at the fringes, never welcomed into any one group for long. He could be sent from court at a word from me, but I was not sure if my sister would welcome his presence any more than his absence.

She sighed and gestured for me to follow her outside. Once we reached the gardens—small, but as charmingly arranged as her parlor—she turned and said, "He ignores them, which is for the best. His attentions are not worth the earning, and they have learned not to try."

I felt bad for my nieces, and for devoting my energies to Jane, when Elizabeth's children needed me even more.

"If I am ever at court full time," I said, "I could take a house and you and the girls could live with me until they marry. And perhaps the boys, as well, though they might do better in the country."

She looked up, tears wetting her lashes again. "That is very sweet, Willie. But Martha will be married later this year."

Were my nieces old enough to marry? I soon found out they were—at table, seventeen-year-old Martha was a gay hostess, and Ellen, thirteen, had her mother's seriousness along with her dark hair and eyes.

"May we please visit Grandfather and Jane?" Ellen bounced in her seat.

Elizabeth blotted her lips with her napkin and gazed calmly at her younger daughter. "Not if you act no older than Jane." She turned to Martha. "What about you? Would you like to visit Hawkmoor?"

"I should like to see Kit," she said, smiling so that dimples appeared in her cheeks. "It has been too long."

I reached for more bread. "Who is Kit?" I asked.

"Jane's governess. Her name is Katherine, but the girls call her Kit."

The governess again. After a year, Jamie Welldon was still starry-eyed over her, though it was unlikely they would meet again; he would not abandon Mary and the girl was not likely to leave my father's employ before Jane was old enough to go to court or marry.

It took another day before Elizabeth's household was organized enough to travel. I had forgotten the labor involved in transporting a family, even a short distance. When we were children, we traveled between Hawkmoor and Kelton, my father's smaller estate in Hertfordshire, several times a year. It was an unusual occurrence when my mother did not dissolve into tears of frustration, even though we had an abundance of servants—far more than Elizabeth had—to lighten her burden.

Unsupervised, the boys needled Ellen into forgetting her adolescent dignity so that she shrieked at them like a costermonger. Martha stepped in to comfort her sister and then distract the boys. Elizabeth would miss her help when she was gone. I resolved to investigate the possibility of a house in the city. A change of scene would do Liz good, even if she chose to share the place with her husband.

As it took so much effort to ready a family of five, plus servants, my sister decided to make their visit of some duration. The servants and the cart with the family's belongings left before dawn, and we were up and breakfasted not long after. I helped to load the few things that would travel in the coach with them—Elizabeth's jewel case and a book; Martha's embroidery; a badly-knitted stocking and yarn for Ellen. I stowed my few things under the seat to lighten my horse's load and set Dennis to collecting the boys.

At last, all was in order, Elizabeth and the girls settled in the coach, while Nick and Tommy planned to ride their ponies under my watchful eye. There was room in the conveyance should they tire, but the boys argued this suggestion so loudly that I grew impatient and threatened to make them take the ride in turns if they could not behave. They quieted almost immediately, and Elizabeth gave me an approving nod.

With a rumble of wheels upon stone and a jangle of tack, we set off. It was not long after six; barring any trouble with the roads, we would arrive at Hawkmoor in twelve hours without undue strain. My horse tossed his head and we fell in behind the coach so I could judge for myself how well the boys acquitted themselves before leading them off the road for a proper canter.

There were frequent stops, another complication to traveling with women and children. The moors offered little privacy, so we spent a good amount of time with our backs tactfully turned so the ladies could relieve themselves behind clumps of rushes along the ditch. Then there were clamors at noon that starvation was imminent, and the coach stopped on a stretch of flat road and baskets of food were unloaded and spread on the grass.

"Surely there is an inn between here and Hawkmoor," I murmured to Elizabeth as I accepted a hunk of cheese wrapped in a napkin. "It would be easier than this."

"That shows you do not have children," she said, slapping Tommy's hand away when he tried to use her knife. "They would scatter like jackstones, and it would take until dark to round them up again."

We spent a half hour over the meal, which put us no further behind than if we'd stopped at an inn. At the end the boys were yawning, their full bellies making them sleepy, and they piled into the coach without protest.

"I'll lead the ponies." Dennis looped their reins over his saddle. "That way you can ride alongside and talk to Mistress Fremantle."

He liked children, and I appreciated his help—though of similar age, Nick and Tommy were more trouble than Ralph Lewis. "I'll remember this the next time I catch you with a kitchen maid."

"Or a nursemaid?" He winked, and I wondered if I would be receiving a letter from Robin in nine months' time, telling me that my manservant was about to be a father.

Lichen dusted the glaring stone hawks on the gate posts. I paid them no mind, riding through the gate and along the graveled road leading to the house. A wide expanse of grass, dotted with precisely trimmed conical hedges, stretched on either side. To the left was my mother's knot garden, to the right, a small tiltyard built by my grandfather so the sons of Hawkmoor could learn knightly skills as soon as they could sit a pony. I had never found jousting enjoyable, nor had I shown any skill at it.

Once a mere hall, solar, and buttery, Hawkmoor had grown two new wings when my grandfather acquired it from the family of an executed Yorkist supporter, and my father had carried out his own improvements. When the time came for him to take charge, I was certain my brother would do the same.

Made of stone in an unwelcoming shade of gray, crenellated towers loomed on either side of the great entry, the door to which was a massive, studded affair relocated from a demolished monastery. It was in truth more castle than manor house. I was grateful my forebears had resisted digging a moat around the place.

The stones rang under our horses' hooves, and a boy sprinted across the courtyard to take the reins from me. "Master Hawkins, sir. Welcome back."

I slid down, wiping white foam from the beast's flank. "Feed him well, once he's cooled down," I said. "He's had a hard ride."

"Yes, sir."

"Is there anyone here who can ride out?" I glanced around the quiet yard. "The Fremantle coach is not five miles down the road. They need a fresh horse—one of theirs has gone lame."

I had been riding alongside, telling young Ellen about the queen of Scots when I noticed one of the grays bobbing its head in an odd fashion.

"Stop the coach," I called to the driver, riding forward and looking at the horse. "The one on the right is favoring a leg."

The driver jumped down. "We're nearly there, sir. I think he'll be fine."

Behind us, the door opened, and Elizabeth climbed out. "What is it?"
"You've got a lame horse." I squatted and ran my hand over its right
front leg. Although I felt nothing out of the ordinary, the horse blew
and shifted its weight at my touch. "He might make Hawkmoor without
injury, but I wouldn't risk it."

She nodded agreement, and the driver moved to unhitch the gray from
the coach. "Will you ride ahead and have them send a replacement?"

Looking up at the towers, I swallowed my discomfort and headed
toward the door. Behind me, Dennis was dealing with our things, and
shouting pointlessly at the boy, who knew his duties. No one touched
horseflesh in my father's world without sure and certain knowledge of
their task.

The door swung open at my approach and a manservant wearing my
father's damnable hawk badge bowed to me. "Master Hawkins, welcome
back."

It's been a long time, the fellow seemed to say. Once in a decade was
too often for me, but it was difficult to face a man like Robin and say,
"Sorry, but I don't like my father," when he suggested that I pay a visit.

"Uncle Will! I didn't know you were coming!"

A pattering of footsteps across the marble-floored entry and a sprite
in a pink dress hurled herself at my midsection, barreling headfirst into
me and taking my breath. I staggered and swung her up into my arms.

"Hello, Jane!" I held her so we were nose to nose. It was unnerving,
seeing my dead sister's brilliant eyes in her pointed face.

Jane kissed me loudly on both cheeks and shouted, "Kit, come meet
my uncle!"

Another light step and a young woman stood in the doorway. My
breath caught in my throat, and it suddenly seemed that the cage of my
ribs was not large enough to hold my beating heart. I took her all in at
once: honey hair, wide-set blue eyes, a faint sprinkling of freckles across
a tilted nose. There was an agonizing moment before she spoke.

"Jane, you must stop charging at people." Her voice was soft, with a
hint of laughter in its depths. I thought she was what I had missed my
entire life. "Master Hawkins, I apologize for your niece's enthusiasm. She
saw you from the window and escaped my grasp."

I put Jane gently down and bowed to the slight figure before me. She wore a sober gown of good gray broadcloth with an embroidered partlet. Her head barely reached my shoulder.

"I am uninjured," I said gravely, "but I thank you for your concern, Mistress—?"

"Rowan," she said, in the voice I would hear later that night, when I could not sleep for thinking about her. "Katherine Rowan. I am Jane's governess."

"Mistress Rowan." How had I not *seen* her when we were introduced? Between my cousin's stubbornness and my father's mere existence, I had been in a welter of emotions, but it was impossible she had made no impression. I could not say the same of our second meeting—my blood fairly boiled in my veins at the sight of her.

"Are you well?" A faint line appeared between her brows.

My mouth was slightly open, and I shut it, thinking I no doubt looked like an idiot. How could this angel reside under my father's roof? A better question—how had this angel come to the attention of a man like William Cecil?

"Quite," I stammered. "I am—"

"What a charming tableau." My father stared down at us from the landing, wearing the same expression as the lichen-encrusted birds at the gate. "To what do we owe the honor, William? A second meeting before we've had opportunity to forget the first."

Bowing, I said, "Business has carried me north, and I thought to visit Jane." I explained Elizabeth's situation, then turned back to my niece, the better to look at her governess. "I also bring greetings from Robin and Margaery Lewis."

He did not bother to hide his flicker of distaste. I had never yet heard the entirety of his long history with Robin. "You've been to Whitby, eh?"

"Among other places." I allowed myself to be distracted by Mistress Rowan leading Jane away. The child followed meekly but clung to her hand, looking back at us. "I thought to stay for a few days and better acquaint myself with my niece if you do not object. Elizabeth plans a longer visit."

What would I do—how would I be able to speak to Mistress
Rowan—if he refused? And how was I supposed to follow Robin's
suggestion now that I'd seen the girl?

Father descended the final steps, escorted by four greyhounds, two
white and two black. He carried a silver-headed cane—a hawk, of course.
It seemed to be more of an ornament than Robin's. "Does Liz have her
litter with her?"

"She does indeed," I said. "And one of your grooms has taken a horse
out to meet her coach."

He shook his head, looking like one of the lions at the Tower rather
than a bird of prey. "Terrence!" When the steward appeared, he nodded
at me. "This one's come to stay, and Mistress Fremantle and her children
will be here within the hour." He crossed the floor more quickly than a
man his age should have managed. "I'll ride out myself and bring them
in."

## CHAPTER 25

I COULDN'T ALLOW THE lord of the manor to ride off alone to rescue his defenseless daughter—though all I wanted was to run up the stairs to the nursery, find Mistress Rowan, fall to my knees, and stare at her lovely face until I'd mapped her freckles like an astronomer mapped the stars in the night sky. It was both ridiculous and unrealistic. She would slap me, or laugh, or flee, thinking me insane. And she would not be wrong.

Shaking my head at the muddle, I called for a horse and caught my father's surprised glance. "Should I not go, sir?"

"You are unnecessary." He approached a well-muscled black gelding and raised a booted foot to the stirrup.

The stable boy approached with a gleaming chestnut, and I took the reins. "We are both unnecessary," I pointed out. "Your people are capable of whatever is needed."

"Do as you wish," he snapped, landing in the saddle with less than his usual grace. He kicked the horse into motion, swerving through the gates and leaving me in the dust.

As expected, the grooms had already arrived and set to work. One was buckling the new horse into harness, while another walked the lame one slowly up and down, carefully observing his gait. Elizabeth, Martha, and Ellen watched from the verge as Nick and Tommy raced their ponies on the empty road.

At the sound of our horses, Elizabeth turned. "Father!" she cried. "You needn't have ridden all this way."

"It is nothing." He dismounted heavily. "You look well, daughter."

Elizabeth curtsied, then stretched up to kiss his cheek. "I am well. This is nothing but an inconvenience, to make the anticipation of seeing you and Jane all the sweeter."

She knew how to handle him; all my sisters did. My brother Harry, having all our father's worst qualities and none of our mother's softening influence, got along well with him so long as they were not in the same house for more than a week. He was arrogant and dictatorial, like our father and, according to my sisters, just as handsome.

Second sons can be a disappointment, but I was born third, advancing to my sorry position upon the death of my brother Francis. He had been destined for the church, another future I refused.

"William, you will bring my horse," he ordered. "I shall ride with Eliza and hear her news."

I led both horses and boys to the house. Rooms had been made ready in our absence and I gratefully handed Nick and Tommy over to their nursemaid and took myself off to wash and change before the light evening meal.

There was no Winterset informality in this house; proper clothing was required by Father's decree, and all table etiquette maintained, which meant I was seated at his right whether we liked it or not. As we were but a small party, Liz would be on his left, and then Martha and Ellen. The boys were in the nursery with Jane.

Mistress Rowan was seated on my right. She wore pearl-gray sarcenet and her hair, covered by a simple white lace cap, was braided in a complicated manner that did not detract from her fresh-faced beauty. She was delicious, there was no other word for it. My palms grew damp at the prospect of spending an entire meal beside her and having to make conversation, as it was unlikely that my father would address a word to me while Liz and the girls were present.

"Jane has permitted you to join us," I ventured at last, surprised that my voice worked.

"She is distracted by her cousins," she said.

"Mistress Katherine, you cannot allow Jane to run your life." My father gazed at her benevolently, his mouth twisted in what could only be interpreted as a smile.

"No, sir." She looked down at the table and then up again, her eyes sparkling. "That is your province."

How did she dare? I watched with my heart in my throat. This girl appeared untouched by my father's fearsome magic. She treated him as she would Jane, and her tone, had she been one of his children, would have brought a swift reprimand followed by icy silence. Instead, he shook his head and turned back to his conversation with my sister, his mood unchanged.

I was in awe. Behavior such as this could only stem from an upbringing entirely unlike mine. Mistress Rowan's childhood had clearly been filled with affection. She had never sweated over how to please her parents. And she—astonishingly—did not fear my father, but instead found him *amusing*.

From that moment, I was lost.

As I expected, my father spoke exclusively with Elizabeth and her girls, so unless I was willing to interrupt their conversation, I was left with Mistress Rowan. I could not imagine calling her Kit. Although I tried to appear interested in her words, I wasn't sure how often my interest devolved into staring at her, moon-eyed, and then grasping for the correct response when she fell silent.

"I apologize, Master Hawkins," she said at one point. "I occupy too much of your attention. You must wish to speak with your father."

"God, no," I said hastily and in all truth. "Nor does he care to speak to me."

"What's that, William?" came his lazy drawl. "Are you bothering Mistress Katherine?"

"Not at all, sir," she said. "Do not distract yourself on my account."

I followed with, "She thought I would prefer to speak with you, and I was assuring her of the wrongness of that sentiment."

Father put down his heavy goblet, looking at me in the way that had turned me to jelly since I was a boy. "You are, in that regard, correct." His eyes shifted to her, warming as they did so. "If you do not mind his prattle, then I withdraw my concern."

He turned back to Elizabeth before Mistress Rowan could even respond, and she raised her eyebrows at me. "Are you always so cold with each other, Master Hawkins?"

"Ever since I can remember." I cut a hunk of bread and passed it to her. "Are you on good terms with your parents?"

"Very much so," she said, "except for their recent disappointment in me."

"How could you have disappointed them?" I carried a bit of beef to my mouth, thinking it would be impossible for a woman so young and lovely to disappoint anyone.

She ducked her head. "They wish for me to marry."

"And you do not?" My father would have roared if any of my sisters had dared to refuse a match. That was, I thought, why my mother insisted her girls be permitted to marry for love, because her father had married her off to keep himself safe. Though she had been fortunate in loving my father, it was not always the case.

"No." She looked down at her plate. I strained to see more than her profile. "The man who offered was not to my liking."

"I believe a woman should have a say in who she marries," I told her. "Life is long. It would seem far longer with the wrong person."

"Exactly!" Her eyes glinted and it warmed me that I had been able to elicit such a response. "You are unwed, Master Hawkins?"

"I am." I lowered my voice. "It is not a topic for discussion at this table."

Father rose before the conversation could go any further. "The children should be abed." He snapped his fingers. The greyhounds burst from beneath the table in a scrabble of claws. "Mistress Rowan, you have amused my son long enough."

Flushing, she pushed back her chair and made her excuses. "Mistress Fremantle, may I settle your boys, or would you prefer to come up yourself?"

"They are in their nursemaid's charge." My sister didn't bother to conceal a yawn. "It has been an exhausting day. If they are not asleep already, they will be shortly. As will I."

Elizabeth and Martha went to their chambers, as worn out as the boys, while I took a short walk through the knot garden with Ellen.

"You are pleased to be here," I noted, as she skipped along beside me. "Doesn't your grandfather frighten you?"

She laughed aloud. "He is all sweetness beneath his bluster, uncle."

My female relatives saw a different man; it had always been thus.

"You were happier, I think, to see Mistress Rowan." Ellen could be more easily guided than my sister, who would sniff out my intentions if I questioned her about the governess. "You like her?"

"Oh, yes!" Ellen bounced along, twitching her skirts away from the low privet hedge bordering the gardens. "She is so sweet—and unlike Martha, she is not fixed on marriage and having *babies*."

"Your time will come," I assured her.

She looked up in horror. "I hope not! I am no Catholic, uncle, but I find the idea of a nunnery strangely attractive."

I squeezed her to me, this strange, quicksilver child who was so unlike any of my sisters except her mother. "Is it the peace you want?" I asked. "Or the lack of gentlemen?"

"You are an acceptable gentleman," she said with a grin, "but you must admit Father is no example. I fear for my brothers with only him to guide them."

We came to the end of the path. I took her elbow and turned us before she kept going and we ended up at The Bower. "I spoke to your mother," I told her. "I thought to take a small house in London in the next year. She could keep it for me, and you and your brothers could live there."

Ellen trailed her fingers over a bushy lavender plant and the smell, sharp and astringent and sweet, reached my nose. "And what of my father? He already has a small house in London. Wouldn't it be strange to live with you rather than him?"

"I suppose it would," I agreed. "Only you do not live with him there, and you would be welcome to live with me."

She stopped, her vital face going blank. "Grandfather is right, Uncle William. You do not know how to talk to ladies," she said with a choke in her voice. "You do not know at all."

Hawkmoor had space aplenty for servants, which meant I was alone in my bedchamber for the first time in months. That being the case, I very nearly called for Dennis, because his flippant chatter would keep me from obsessing over Mistress Rowan all night. After the long ride, the shock of our meeting, and the strain of dealing with my father, I should have been exhausted. Instead, my eyes were wide open and fixed on the ceiling, thinking about the utter miracle of her and the corresponding unholy mess of her presence in my father's house.

It was impossible—was it not?—to fall in love simply upon seeing someone for the first time? It reminded me of Nell, who had been in love every other week. How shallow was I that the very first sight of my niece's governess made me want to wrap my arms around her and protect her from all harm? She needed no protection; she was under my father's care, as well as having a father of her own. Nothing I could offer would improve her life.

I had been in love before, or so I thought. Cecily, Margaery. In a way, Isabel. But this lightning strike was different. My reaction to Katherine Rowan had changed me in some essential aspect, as if the mere act of seeing her turned me into a different person.

The problem was that I was no different. William Hawkins, as he was, was not worthy of this girl—even Ellen objected to my manners. And what could I offer her, besides myself? No home, no fortune, an uncomfortable relationship with my family. A job that took me all over, with little warning. What woman would choose regular abandonment, or to compete for her husband's attention with not one but two queens?

These reasons were sufficient without delving into the flaws in my character, which were legion.

And though she seemed untouched by his charm, her proximity to my father was troubling. I kept what little feminine companionship I had far away from him; the wounds left by Cecily Farr no longer pained, but his presence kept the memory sharp-edged. Being Mistress Rowan's employer did not mean he would never interfere with her.

Perhaps that was the service I could render. My original plan had been to discover what Cecil found interesting about Mistress Rowan, but Father might be convinced to keep his distance if he knew of their interest. That would be my new plan: to spend some time in her company, find out what I could—tormenting myself in the bargain—and warn him off.

Satisfied, I rolled over and attempted to sleep, but everything was against me. I saw her face in the dark and tried to remember the exact location of the freckle at the corner of her eye. Her partlet—were the embroidered flowers roses or pansies? It might do well to compliment her handwork; mayhap she was susceptible to flattery.

The breeze touched my bare skin, a lover's fingertips trailing over my body. I hauled myself up and shut the window; if I kept thinking like that, I would never sleep.

## CHAPTER 26

IN THE MORNING, I slipped downstairs before the servants were up and let myself out the front door. The stable boys were awake, but they were happy to let me saddle my own horse and take him out across the moors.

The night lingered at the edges of my mind in the same way the unknown made itself felt after excessive drink; a lingering sense of dread and a fear of having embarrassed myself without remembering what I had done. Being in my father's house always did that to me, and now, having unmanned myself by falling instantly in love with the one person whom I should not even look at—for myriad reasons—I was more untethered than usual.

I rode almost all the way to The Bower, stopping when I was in sight of the tree. Once there, I slid from the saddle, dropping the reins, and letting the horse graze while I paced back and forth on the grass and rehearsed aloud all the words that I could not say to Mistress Rowan, ranting at the sky until my head was empty.

I did not return to Hawkmoor until the sun was high and the house's inhabitants were guaranteed to be awake and scattered.

The midday table consisted of my father, my sister, and my nieces. "Where is Mistress Rowan?" I asked, as Martha sat beside me.

"With Jane and the boys," my father said. "She dines downstairs only in the evenings."

Still a servant, then, despite her beauty and his obvious affection for her. I found that comforting, though her absence meant I could not avoid being drawn into the general conversation.

I distracted Father by mentioning the fine gelding he'd ridden the day before. That started him off on the bloodlines of the horses in his stables, a topic which could last through the day and into the evening. Across the table, Elizabeth screwed up her face at me, but I nodded and made noises of agreement as he went on; it passed as civil conversation and I needed to remain on his good side if we were to at some point speak about Cecil's interest in his governess.

The table had been cleared when Jane, Nick, and Tommy streaked down the stairs, Mistress Rowan in their wake. "Ellen!" Jane shouted. "Come see my pony!"

My niece rose agreeably and allowed herself to be dragged out to the stables. Father stalked alongside to harass the grooms and make sure his grandsons did not get underfoot.

My sister and Martha surrounded Mistress Rowan, their vivid gowns making her look like a sparrow in a flock of bright tropical birds. Martha took her arm, and Elizabeth smiled fondly at them.

"Play for us, Kit?" she asked. "Did you know, Will, she is giving Jane lessons on the virginals."

"How do you keep her still?" My niece was like a bit of fluff carried on the breeze.

"Bribery," she said, looking up at me. I took an involuntary step back at the power of her gaze. "No pony until she's practiced."

"Then how is it she is with her pony now?"

"Do hush," Elizabeth said as we climbed the stairs. "If you're not going to listen, go away."

I lingered in the doorway of the upstairs parlor, where the beautifully painted virginals, which had not existed in the house prior to Jane's arrival, sat between two tall windows. Mistress Rowan settled herself before the instrument while Martha sorted through a stack of music. Choosing something at last, she placed it on the rack and leaned against the edge of the windowsill.

Mistress Rowan placed her hands over the keys and a cascade of notes filled the air. Her playing was skillful—Jane was in good hands—and the lilting tune she played was new to me. It was not unfamiliar to Martha, for she began to sing, and gestured for Mistress Rowan to join her. When she did, I retreated hastily to the landing, understanding I could not both watch and listen to her.

From there, I could get my breathing under control while simply enjoying her voice. She had none of Bess's training, but her tone was clear and extremely pleasing, and my niece sounded better for singing with her. I stayed through two songs, realizing then that their musical occupation would allow me to venture upstairs without being missed. What could be gleaned about Mistress Rowan by visiting the nursery?

The schoolroom and the attached nursery occupied the top floor of the house's east wing. It had been both a sanctuary and a place of torment for me and my siblings, for my father kept a steady succession of masters and governesses in terror, and they were accordingly strict with us. Did he follow the same policies of child-rearing for his beloved granddaughter or had losing Nell changed him? And what influence did Mistress Rowan have on Jane's upbringing?

She had plenty, I discovered. It was already apparent that Katherine Rowan had been cherished by her parents, for she treated Jane with a patience and kindness wholly unfamiliar to any child raised under Hawkmoor's roof. Her touch was apparent in the serenity and order of the schoolroom. The books in the low-ceilinged chamber where she and Jane spent their days were not all lightness; this angel of my heart had a quick mind and a respect for learning which would be passed on to her charge. A paper set out on the table showed Latin verse in a steady, adult hand, with the sheet beside it a fair copy in younger, rounder letters.

A quick peek into the adjoining chamber—where my sisters had shared a bed—showed a childhood far different from theirs in other aspects. The room was furnished for a miniature lady, with a tall bed draped in rose-colored hangings and a round mirror over a chest, whose lid was scattered with childish trinkets. An array of slippers littered the floor and a blue ribbon peeked from beneath the pillow.

There was a closed door beyond which I dared not open. Despite my curiosity, I would not intrude upon her privacy. I left, closing the schoolroom door quietly, and returned to my former position on the stairs. Elizabeth had joined in the singing now. She'd always had a pretty voice, though little reason to use it. They sang one more song before the instrument fell silent. I remained where I was, not ready to rejoin them.

"I wish I could play like you," Martha said. "We were never taught."
I could hear Elizabeth sigh from where I stood. "Your father does not
appreciate music the way we do, daughter. Perhaps your husband will
feel otherwise."

Martha moaned dramatically. "I wouldn't know, would I? I've scarcely
said ten words to the man."

Thomas Fremantle had matched his elder daughter with a wealthy
neighboring landowner. He was pleasant enough, Elizabeth told me, and
wanted Martha primarily as a stepmother to his two young children.

"He wrote a very nice letter," Mistress Rowan said diplomatically. "Is
that not enough?"

A thud told me that my niece had disposed herself on the cushions
of the window alcove. "I would like to be courted," she said. "Not
contracted. You shall see, Kit—wait until you marry."

As I awaited her response, my heart seemed to pause in its beating.
They were doing me a favor by plumbing Mistress Rowan's feelings on
marriage, but her response could doom my future before it was begun.

"You think we all should be similarly blessed," she said, her voice
teasing, "because you shall be wed at Christmas. That is not what fate
has in store for me, my friend. I must work for my keep."

"Martha is right," my sister said. "Father be dashed, one day a fine
gentleman will ride through these gates, and you will leave gladly."

From my sister's lips to God's ears, I thought—but did I have the
temerity to proclaim myself such a man, and could I offer anything
worth leaving this pleasant situation? I shifted position as they moved
further into the room, praying no servant would come along and catch
me eavesdropping like a child.

"I shall not," she said calmly. There was a thump, which I recognized
as the sound of the balky casement being struck with a closed fist. "I have
promised Lord Kelton to remain with Jane until her twelfth birthday."

Five years! It was both an eternity and not nearly enough time for me
to sort out my life and become worthy of her.

My niece's quick step crossed the room and the window screeched as
it was forced open. "Have you no suitors now?" she asked. "Jane says you
receive letters from a gentleman..."

My ears pricked up and I eased down another two steps.

"Martha, you mustn't plague her!" Elizabeth chided. "Kit will tell us if she wants us to know."

"Not a suitor," she said after a long silence. "Not precisely. He is more a correspondent."

"Really?" Liz drew out the word, her curiosity as great as my own.

"His name is James Welldon," she confessed. "We met last year at your cousin's home when Lord Kelton escorted me here."

My hands lost all sensation, tingling as if I'd slept upon my arm. *Jamie?*

They were at the window now; I had crept far enough down the stairs to see their rippling reflections in the glass on the other side of the alcove.

"Is he a young man?" Elizabeth asked. "What is his family situation?"

"Is he handsome?" Martha wanted to know.

"He is fairer of face than I, for a start," Mistress Rowan said with a laugh. "We are of similar age. I know very little of him, despite his letters."

How *many* letters, and why had Jamie not mentioned them when we spoke at Tutbury? If he failed to mention writing to a young woman living in my father's house, what else might he have neglected to tell me?

"Why ever not?" Once she decided to interfere, Elizabeth had no patience with not knowing all the details of a situation.

"He is in the household of the Scottish queen," she said. "He writes of her, and his work, and includes in each letter some small verse."

Verse! My foot skidded, striking the newel post, and they stopped speaking. I shook my head, clearing thoughts of Jamie in his small room, chewing his quill, and penning sentimental poems to the woman *I* loved.

Jamie had loved her first. Ever since that meeting at Matthew's home, he had spoken of her with increasing interest. I cursed myself for a fool: if I had delivered his message last year, I would have met her sooner.

As they had heard me, I continued down past the turning and looked in the door. "Don't linger indoors if you are not going to sing," I said. "It is a very fine afternoon. Can I entice you to walk in the gardens before supper?"

My niece went ahead with Mistress Rowan, while I set a more sedate pace with my sister. "I intend to stay but a few days more," I said. "You will have no problems getting home without me?"

"Father will send two of his men to ride alongside," she said. "If he doesn't come himself in the coach. He did that last time—we rode in his coach and the girls rode in mine."

It struck me as odd, the day before, that he had chosen to ride back with Liz, and I remembered his arrival at Matthew's house, in the coach with Mistress Rowan. "He likes the coach more than he used to," I said. "It is not like him."

"He has an ache in his hip," Elizabeth told me. "An old jousting injury, apparently, but the damp makes it worse. As does getting on and off a horse."

Like Robin's bad knee. "That's why he uses the coach?"

Elizabeth smiled. "He has to keep his riding to a minimum, or he will walk like an ancient for a week."

This was a new aspect to my father's vanity. I had always wondered how many seductions had taken place in that shining black vehicle, and for certes a good many had, but knowing he chose to forego riding so as not to appear an old man made me feel some sympathy for him.

After our walk, we came through the entry and into the great hall. It was the only part of Hawkmoor which had survived my father's frenzy of improvements to remain in its medieval glory, with a gallery overlooking scrubbed stone flags and a table long enough to seat twenty. There was a vast fireplace and a series of five hunting tapestries, faded by smoke and time but impressive still. The lofty ceiling was hammer-beamed; as a child, I pretended it was a ship floating upside-down above our heads.

"Here I must leave you." I paused at the door leading to my father's study. "There is a matter which must be addressed."

"Good luck," Elizabeth said in a loud whisper. "I will pray for you."

Mistress Rowan alone gave me a kind smile before they disappeared up the staircase with a rustle of skirts.

I knocked on the solid panel and listened for a response. When none came, I knocked again and opened the door.

In Robin Lewis's cozy library, the walls were lined with shelves, and more books covered every surface. Here, expensive linenfold paneling covered walls with no ornamentation beyond framed portraits of my parents on either side of the window—together but separate, as befitted their marriage. They had been painted by Master Holbein before he became King Henry's court painter, when he was just another German artist looking to make a living. He had done himself proud, but then, his subjects required no flattery.

Lord and Lady Kelton faced each other, my father in profile, with his aquiline nose and strong chin, a stubborn curl of black hair escaping from a plumed tawny hat. My mother was in three-quarter view, a private smile on her lips, her pale hair mostly hidden beneath a sleek French hood. Her eyes were wide and guileless and as blue as the sapphires she wore.

My father's painted face held the same arrogance as his living one. Someone who did not know him might interpret the heavy brow and full lips as confirmation of his physical superiority, but I could not see those features without hearing the hectoring voice that had dogged my unhappy childhood.

He sat behind the heavy wooden desk, facing the open window. A wide leatherbound book was pushed aside and his booted feet were propped on the cleared surface. His head, cushioned by the chair's high back, lolled to one side. He was asleep.

Waking him would incur his wrath, scorching me and leaving a lingering taint over the rest of a day which had, thus far, been extremely pleasant. I took a step back, then stopped. I could not remember ever having seen him sleep. His features, always animated by some strong passion, were slack; his lips parted, a faint snore issuing from between them. His age was somehow *more* noticeable when the harsh creases around his mouth were relaxed, but nothing smoothed the lines on his forehead or the deep groove between his still-black brows.

His white shirt was open at the neck, revealing a shadow of dark hair at his throat. A pulse beat faintly beneath his skin.

Suddenly it felt wrong to be standing there. Seeing him vulnerable was worse than seeing him naked. A picture of Isabel flashed through my mind: if I had bedded her, as I had dreamed of doing, I would have, in a sense, uncovered my father's nakedness, as she had once belonged to him.

The thought made me laugh; just a breath of air through my nose, but it was enough. His brown eyes snapped open and stared back at me, none too pleased at being caught napping.

"How is it you are always in the wrong place?" He swung his feet down and swiveled to face me.

"It is a talent of which I am very proud." I sat, unbidden, on the chair reserved for the steward; none of his children had ever been invited into this chamber. "I wish to speak to you."

"You *are* speaking to me." His hand went to his neck; his dishevelment discomfited him, but he was too proud to adjust his dress. "If you must be here, make yourself useful and pour the wine."

A narrow side table, draped with a small rug, held a tray, jug, and two chased metal cups. I did his bidding, filling the second cup for myself without being invited to partake.

"I should tell you," I said, handing him the drink, "in addition to the Lewises, I have recently met others of your past acquaintance."

"Really?" One brow arched upward. "Who have you been speaking to?"

"Isabel Ferren and Bess Minstrel." I watched for any reaction. "They both send fond regards."

If their names meant anything beyond the memory of past bedmates, it did not show on his face.

"Is that how you occupy yourself in London, then?" he asked. "Hunting up my former mistresses in some pathetic attempt to embarrass me?"

"No, sir, that is not how I *occupy* myself. And it is hardly embarrassing—they speak more highly of you than I ever have."

"Do they?" A momentary flicker of curiosity, squelched. "I never treated them badly." He took a mouthful of wine and reached for the leatherbound estate book. "Get on with what you have to say, William. I have work to do."

I allowed myself a disrespectful grin. "Yes, I could see how hard you were working when I came in." That was not the way to begin a successful conversation with him. In a warmer tone, I said, "Jane seems to be thriving."

"Of course, she is." As if anything else could occur under his care. "She has the best of her mother, but with better guidance."

Was that a criticism of my mother or the army of harried women who helped bring us up—or perhaps himself? "She seems very attached to Mistress Rowan."

His eyes narrowed. "Why the sudden interest in Jane's governess?"

I couldn't tell him I was in love, as thoroughly stunned as if I'd been struck over the head like a beast. That would bring out his worst qualities while admitting my weakness. He was a dislikable man but not a dishonorable one. I could sketch the barest framework of the situation and leave him to imagine the rest, especially since I did not know it all myself.

"It is not my interest alone." I reached for my cup. "I'm here in an official capacity."

Something in his face changed; I saw it but could not register its meaning before he became his usual sardonic self. "Ah, so you're still involved with the little men who think they run the world."

Another sip of wine, until I could moderate my words. "Not everyone can be a courtier, Father. Nor is everyone fortunate enough to be beloved of their monarch."

He laughed harshly. "Being beloved of Elizabeth got Leicester an earl-dom, but he'll never achieve the woman."

"No," I said with some regret, for I genuinely liked him. "But perhaps that's to his benefit."

My father put his feet up on the fender, toasting them at a non-existent fire. "But what about Mistress Katherine?"

Her freckles were a wonder, like a sprinkling of some exotic spice across her pale skin. And her eyes—

"I don't know the whole of the story," I admitted, banishing thoughts of her eyes so I could think clearly. "But there is official interest in her, for some reason. Since she is part of your household, I wanted to better understand their interest, should it become something more."

"She's a child herself."

"How old is she?" Did I need to know this or was it because I wanted to know everything about her? She felt very young—though there were almost thirty years between Robin and his wife, and they managed well enough. But I was no Robin Lewis.

He shrugged. "Twenty or thereabouts? Young enough to recover from her current foolishness."

"She strikes me as level-headed." Mild disagreement was better than begging for information.

Tilting his cup, he drank deeply. "She refuses to marry," he said. "Arthur Rowan found another match—a more acceptable one, this time—but the fellow insisted on a substantial dowry and Katherine refused." His hand, heavily veined and thick about the knuckles, reached again for the jug. "She's not theirs, you see. They took her in as an infant and she won't allow them to dower her because it isn't their responsibility."

"But they must be willing—"

"They are willing," Father said. "She is not. She claims she will marry only if the man takes her for herself alone." He shook his head. "The first man was rich and wanted her for her face. This latest one is like Martha's intended, a widower with children. Both wanted a dowry."

I would marry her for herself. I would marry *any* woman I loved for herself. Perhaps that was pride. Though Father and I did not get on, I was never short of funds, and while Harry would inherit Hawkmoor and his title, I would not be left penniless.

"Shall I keep you apprised?" I asked, hoping that my feelings did not show on my face. "Of anything I might hear concerning Mistress Rowan?"

"You had better." He opened the book, dismissing me. "She is under my roof, and my care. I will not allow them to trifle with what is mine."

## CHAPTER 27

AFTER THAT CONVERSATION WITH my father, I had no reason to stay but found myself unable to leave. That evening, as we sat at supper, I said as much to Mistress Rowan. "I should be getting back to London, but I am enjoying this break."

"What do you do there?" she asked. "Lord Kelton has never said."

I shook my head. "That's because Lord Kelton neither understands nor respects my work." Nor did he respect me, but I would not say anything so self-pitying in her company.

"What is your work, Master Hawkins?" She put down her knife, choosing to ignore the criticism of my father.

"I am a royal messenger." An errand boy, he would have said.

"You work for the queen?" Her eyes widened. "Have you ever seen her?"

Could she be so easily impressed?

"I have," I said, "though not often in the last year, as I've been mostly in France. When she first came to the throne, I saw her frequently. I even danced with her once. Jane's mother was one of her maids of honor."

"It must be exciting," she said, "to go to court and see all the people, to see the queen."

"To dress in your most uncomfortable clothes and bow and fawn over people with brains like fleas." My father cut in, stating—in harsher terms—what I would have said myself. "You are better in Yorkshire, Mistress Katherine. You need none of that polish to shine."

Across the table, Elizabeth's and her daughters' heads turned as if watching a tennis match. Ellen was fascinated with the court; Martha would be if her mind was not taken up with her upcoming nuptials, while Elizabeth had attended only twice during the early years of her marriage.

"You were at court for years, sir," I said. "Was it such a terrible experience?"

He steepled his fingers under his chin, considering. "It took me away from my home and my children."

"Was that a bad thing?" Certainly, he could not have mistresses at home, and if he spent too long with Mother, she ended up with child. He'd always hated the sound of a crying baby.

"Family life did become wearing after the first two or three children," he agreed.

As his fourth child, I took the comment in the spirit in which it was intended and turned back to Mistress Rowan. "Would you permit me to disrupt the discipline of the schoolroom tomorrow?" I wondered at my daring. "I would ask that you and Jane ride with me in the morning."

"I think that may be arranged." She tilted her head to one side, a smile playing on her lips. "An occasional disruption serves to refocus her attention. Might we ride to The Bower?"

"You know Lady Rose?" I had not expected her to be acquainted with my father's mistress.

"We met not long after my arrival. Jane and I were riding one afternoon, and it began to rain. We were huddled under a tree when a coach came along and the woman inside told us to get in. She dried us before the fire, gave us bread and warm cider, and sent word to Lord Kelton that she would keep us overnight."

That sounded like Lady Rose. She took in stray dogs and children with equal affection. "Do you see her often?"

"Not so often as I would like," she said. "Jane keeps me busy. But she is a very special lady."

"I found my way to her often as a boy." Until I went off to Uncle Henry, and then to court, and realized what she was to my father—and that he was not even faithful to her. "I had not seen her for a long time," I concluded. "Until a brief visit last year."

"She told me." Her hands lay at rest on the table; I had never seen someone with her capacity for stillness. "She said it was because of your difficult relationship with Lord Kelton."

I licked my lips, my mouth dry with fear of what she thought of me. Which was ridiculous—I was fifteen years her senior. Her opinion was irrelevant; I would not marry, and she would never consider a man like me anyway.

"She told you that?" What else had she said?

"Lady Rose can be indiscreet." She leaned toward me, and a loose strand of hair caught the light. I longed to smooth it away from her face. "Don't worry," she said, laughing at my expression, "it was nothing shocking."

"That's good." She had some respect for Mistress Rowan's virgin state, if not for my reputation.

"It would please Jane to see her, and I am as fond of Lady Rose as any member of your family."

"You don't know that many of us."

Her eyes narrowed. "I met your brother last Christmas and all your sisters at Kelton in the spring, as well as the Darcy family. Are there many more?"

I had not seen Barbara and Agnes for a decade, and Harry in perhaps half that time, nor had I felt their lack. But it unsettled me that while I had not thought of them, they had continued living without me, and this young woman knew and felt affection for all of them.

"Then perhaps you do not need my company." I hated the stiffness in my voice, but I didn't know how to absorb the feeling that I had missed something. I was perfectly content without family. Wasn't I?

Her face altered. "Have I said something wrong?" She looked down at her lap. "I would be very happy if you escorted us."

"Very well, then." My tone was sullen, but my heart was racing—she had minded my about-face and still wished for me to go with them. Perhaps it was her agreeable nature and not any true feeling for me, but I would accept that. At least I had not damaged her regard with my stupid hurt feelings.

We started out soon after breaking our fast, Jane on her gray pony and I on my chestnut gelding. Mistress Rowan was a picture in a dark blue riding costume that clung to her slender form, sitting capably on a brown mare with the stamp of my father's taste upon her. I was surprised, as we started out, how easy it felt to be in her company. When she was not asking me questions about London, she and Jane teased like sisters, giggling as though they were the same age. Adding Lady Rose to the mix would be almost fatally feminine.

I looked forward to it.

"A good friend's wife rides astride," I told her, thinking of Margaery and how shocked I had been when she and Mary Stuart dressed in male clothing to go into Edinburgh town and visit a tavern.

"Does she?" It was said with no judgment. "I've never tried that."

"Grandfather would never allow it!" Jane piped up. "He says ladies ride sidesaddle."

"Most ladies do," I told her. "I'm speaking of Mistress Lewis, Ralph's mother."

Her eyes lit up. "I remember her!"

"She would like to see you again," I said. "If your grandfather invites her, I'm certain she would bring Ralph to visit. She also has a little girl named Margaret and a baby called Sebastian."

"Are these the friends you were visiting before coming here?" Mistress Rowan asked. "Lord Kelton said they worked for the court."

That he had spoken of me was surprising; that he mentioned Robin and Margaery was completely unexpected.

"Robert Lewis worked for Lord Cecil—he is, in fact, the reason I came to work for the principal secretary. His wife was a lady-in-waiting until their son was born. She wanted to return to their estate near Whitby, but it took some time before he could leave the queen's service."

I had been in Scotland and returned to London to find my friends gone. Robin left a letter explaining that Margaery was expecting again, and that he'd had enough of courts, and the men who populated them, to last a lifetime. I understood, but his counsel was sorely missed.

"That must have been quite a change for them." She smoothed the mare's neck with a gloved hand. "I have never been to London."

"It is very different," I said. "Their house is on a cliff overlooking the sea, very isolated."

It was *too* isolated for my tastes, but I understood why Robin loved it, as well as Margaery. Winterset and the surrounding land and farms had been in her family for generations; it was she who worked with the steward and managed the estate, not Robin.

"Sometimes I feel trapped at Hawkmoor," she confided. "It is one reason I like to visit Lady Rose."

"How did you come to governessing?" I wanted to hear her story—and I wanted her to stop talking about Lady Rose, whose very existence brought memories that throbbed like a sore tooth. "How did you come to Hawkmoor?"

She did not appear to mind my questions. "My father is a physician," she said. "He had no sons, and I was educated as if I were a boy." Her brows knitted. "Father was acquainted with Lord Kelton when they were younger and when my circumstances changed, he—"

"That's right," I said before I thought. "A broken engagement."

"Yes." Her lips pressed tight.

"I'm sorry." Her proximity caused me to lose control of my tongue as well as my thoughts. "You need not say more if it is too personal."

"I do not mind," she said, then called ahead to Jane, "Not so fast, darling!"

"Her mother was fearless." I had vivid memories of chasing Nell across the countryside at every one of the queen's palaces, making sure she did not break her neck. "Jane takes after her."

"You said that I broke an engagement, but I have refused two marriages, not one." She took a deep breath and straightened her spine. "To marry properly, a young woman must have a dowry."

"And did your parents not offer one?" I would not speak of what I had learned by way of my father.

"I will not allow it. They have done enough."

"But it is their place—" I began.

"It is not." Her voice was steely. "My mother died in childbed, you see." She turned toward me, her blue eyes shadowed with sadness. "Doctor Rowan treated my mother, and after her death, my father already being dead, he took me in."

To have suffered such tragedy before being old enough to understand, to remember neither the man nor woman who created her. No wonder she was attached to the people who had raised her, educated her, even offered to provide the dowry which she would not accept.

"Were you much in society, living with your parents?" When my father left the court, he seemed to want no company other than those he chose to be with—his family, the men with whom he hunted and rode. His mistress, just over the hill.

"Not very," she said. "There were several families nearby with whom we dined, and my father trained me to help him prepare medicines. Occasionally he would bring me along to visit his patients. If he was called to a birthing, I would sit with the woman while she labored."

That was very progressive behavior and explained her manner with Jane and perhaps with my father. "Did you enjoy that?"

"Very much." Her smile was genuine. "I like being of assistance."

I imagined what a comfort she would be to someone in pain. I imagined what a comfort she would be to *me*.

"There's the tree!" Jane halted her pony and pointed to the hill. "May I ride ahead, Kit?"

Mistress Rowan paused. "Not too fast, Jane. And let one of the grooms help you down." Turning back to me, she said, "It is too beautiful a day to rush, if you are not Jane. Don't you agree?"

I could have spent all the hours until sunset trading casual conversation and easy silence with this miraculous young woman. But Jane had reached the stables and was being lifted down from her pony. Her shrill voice carried down the hill. Within moments, Lady Rose would be outside. Once she had seen us, there would be no escape.

"I could leave and come back later," I offered, suddenly wishing not to be confined in The Bower, even in her company.

"Why?" Her pretty face was puzzled. "Lady Rose speaks so highly of you—between her and what your father has said, I could scarcely wait to meet you."

I nearly choked. "When has my father ever said anything that would recommend me?"

For a moment, she tipped her head back to look at the sky. "I don't think you are able to see each other clearly. Lord Kelton does not know how to speak to those who fail to respond to his charm."

"He barks louder than Lady Rose's dogs, and everyone jumps to do his bidding," I said drily, thinking of the years of shouting I had endured with varying levels of obedience.

"He does not mean it," she said. "He is short-tempered, but he feels deeply for you and all your siblings."

Defending my father was a sure way to work herself out of my affections.

"He has a strange way of showing it." I tightened my grip and my mount pranced, feeling my agitation through the reins. "I have not felt welcome in his house since I was a boy."

"And yet you are there," she said with a sidelong glance. "It is too late now, Master Hawkins—look, there is Lady Rose with Jane. She is waving to us."

Lady Rose greeted us as if she had not had visitors in decades. She held out her hands. "Kit! My dear, you are glowing!"

Mistress Rowan leaned over Jane, who was wrapped around the older woman's legs, nearly smothered in her skirts. "As are you, Lady Rose. Jane, let go so your uncle can approach."

"Is it the fresh air or this young man's attentions?" Lady Rose beckoned to me as I handed off the horses. "Give me a kiss, William. It has been too long."

I obeyed, touching my lips to her soft and fragrant cheek, and wondered if it was too late to refute her words or if I would sound stupid, as they had been addressed to Mistress Rowan. I stole a glance at her; her color was high, but that could be from exertion as much as Lady Rose's teasing.

"Come in, come in!" She drew us after her through the door beneath the arch of green leaves, where a fair number of roses bloomed. "I'll have Tippett bring cider, and there are some sweets for you, Mistress Jane."

The hall was as welcoming as ever, the windows on either side of the door open to the sweet air. LeRoi and two other dogs sprang to their feet at our entry, barking excitedly. Jane flung herself down on the hearth, allowing the beasts to tip her over and lick her face.

"Get up, Jane," I said. "You'll get filthy."

She looked up at me innocently, her blonde curls tumbling free. "They're not filthy, uncle."

"They are not," Lady Rose agreed. "Your uncle is silly."

I turned to Mistress Rowan, lowering my voice. "I should have let you come alone."

"I heard that, William." She grasped my arm and drew me to the table. "You sit here, at the head, and Kit and I will dispose ourselves and listen breathlessly to your every word."

"Have you always talked nonsense?" I took my seat, and when Tippett arrived with a tray, helped myself to a cup of cider made from apples grown on the estate. It was simultaneously sweet and tart, with a richness that told me it had been fermented for some time.

"Only around you and your father," she twittered. "Kit, have you noticed that our William has the same effect on you as Lord Kelton?" She pressed a hand to her breast, clad this day in shimmering blue satin. "Such charm! It is a very good thing that I am an old woman."

"You are far from old," Mistress Rowan assured her. "And while I highly esteem Lord Kelton, I perhaps do not respond to him as strongly as you do." She did not say what response I inspired, and I wished to know that more than anything.

Apparently, so did Lady Rose, for she said, "That says nothing at all. Do you find William charming or do you not?"

"Enough," I said firmly before she embarrassed the poor girl to death. "It is enough that Mistress Rowan does not flutter her eyes and fall at my father's feet, as every woman has ever done."

"Grandfather says it's because he is so handsome." Jane licked a froth of cider from her upper lip. "Lady Rose, may I go upstairs and look at your jewels?"

"Yes, poppet." She pushed herself up using her stick and dropped a hand on my shoulder. There were rings on almost every finger. "Why don't you two take your drinks and wait for us in my parlor?" She smiled sweetly at me. "There will be fewer dogs."

"That is reason enough." That, and the opportunity to be alone with Katherine Rowan. Lady Rose always knew what I needed.

## CHAPTER 28

IN WINTER, LADY ROSE's parlor was snug, dominated by a crackling fire, but now warm air streamed through open windows, bringing with it the scent of roses. It was an intimate chamber—a private place for private meetings—and it felt both wrong and utterly right to be alone with Katherine Rowan in such a space.

Although all I wanted was to gaze at her until I was sated, I felt that I should talk, and did so, stupidly. "Do you know what Lady Rose was to my father?"

Her brow wrinkled. "I believe so."

"And it does not make you think less of her?"

She was quiet a moment, then said, "Lady Rose's business is her own. I do not judge her choices any more than I judge yours. And as for a man having mistresses, I may be unmarried, but I do know some of the world. Your father is a handsome man, and he likes his way."

Having her acknowledge his looks sent a breath-robbing rush of blood to my face. "And is a fair face and a fortune enough to turn a woman's head?"

"Not mine." She laughed softly, pricking the bladder of my pride. "If I have turned down two acceptable proposals, I am unlikely to enter into the risks of a union with none of its benefits."

Her pragmatism was surprising. There were no blushes, no false modesty, only a clear-eyed acceptance of a woman's place in society, for good or ill.

"You are more accepting than I." Footsteps moved overhead, and now, instead of wishing for our hostess to return, I wanted Jane to keep her up there for all the hours until dark.

"What do you mean?" She shifted from her original hard chair to Lady Rose's cushioned one, which brought us closer together.

I sighed. "Surely you've noticed how I dislike talking about myself."

"I assume it is because of your upbringing," she said. "A harsh father, I think, harms his sons even more than his daughters."

That was it exactly, but I could not agree because I found myself embarrassingly near tears. Was this why people opened themselves to others, to be seen and understood in this way? I would feel less exposed if I stripped off my clothes.

"I'm right, aren't I?" She reached out and laid her fingers, light as a butterfly's wing, upon my wrist. "I am sorry to make you think about it. It must be hard to be in his house if you were so unhappy there."

Her fingers were gone as quickly as they came, but her touch lingered. I swallowed, and said, "It is not so painful, with you there."

She could say nothing to that, and we lapsed into a comfortable silence. This room had always made me feel safe; in its colors, its softness, its luxury, it could have belonged to no one else. It was a room made to soothe, to cosset. A room where, for all I knew, she had received my father. But I would not think about that now, not with Katherine Rowan inches away, sitting in front of the Flemish tapestry of Queen Esther.

"I have always loved this little chamber," she said unexpectedly. "If I ever have a home of my own, I want it to be a place like this, that will make me feel protected."

"You will have that home," I assured her, thinking for the first time since Cecily what a fine thing it would be to have a house and a family. "When I was a small boy, and upset, I would run to Lady Rose, and she would bring me into this room and feed me sweets until I stopped crying."

"She has done that for me and for Jane," she said. "At separate times."

"What caused your tears?" Jane was a child, and prone to upsets, but Mistress Rowan seemed so serene.

"Fear." Biting her lip, she looked at me through her lashes. "Once my parents are dead, I will be alone and perhaps too old to have the life I have refused. Jane will not require me forever."

I leaned forward. "And you do want that life?"

She blinked. "I do. But I will not show my gratitude to my parents for all they have done by turning my back on them."

"If you marry a man of substance, he will take care of your parents, as well as you." The sort of people who raised her could not possibly be a burden.

"Not all husbands are so good," she said with a smile. "Or they are good, in the beginning, but they do not wear well. I think your sister, Mistress Fremantle, would agree with me there."

"Elizabeth knew what she was getting," I said. "Perhaps it has been worse in the long run than she expected, but she married for freedom, not for love."

That stopped her. She smoothed her dark blue skirt and said, "I'd never thought of it that way. I would hope to find love in marriage, though perhaps not from the start. Affection, certainly, and respect. But she speaks of her husband as if she does not care for him at all, and on the two occasions where he has come to Hawkmoor, he has been almost... contemptuous of her."

I had not known it was so bad. Liz wouldn't tell me, though her husband's lack of attention certainly showed in their boys' behavior. A few short days under my father's roof had done wonders for them. I thought again of my offer of a London house, and her reasons for refusing. They were valid; she could hardly keep to a different house in a city where her husband also resided.

The stairs creaked under Lady Rose's step, then Jane pounded past her, diving through the door of the parlor and spinning like a top. She was draped all over in our hostess's jewels. "Look at me! I'm a princess!"

"Don't bellow, Jane," Mistress Rowan said. "You're not being chased by wild Scotsmen."

Jane wore a heavy sapphire collar that nearly touched her chin. A double strand of pearls swung past her waist and her hands were curled tight to keep a clutch of rings on her fingers. Her hair had been braided with jewels and her round babyish face was liberally touched with cosmetics.

"You cannot go home like that," I said, even as I jumped to my feet to offer her my deepest bow. "You would give your grandfather an attack."

"Grandfather thinks I'm beautiful," she said, giving a low but unsteady curtsy. "And some of these are from him, Lady Rose says."

Mistress Rowan met my eyes over the child's head. "Nevertheless, you'll wash your face before we leave." She sniffed suddenly. "Are you wearing perfume?"

Jane straightened and one of her rings flew off, bouncing across the floor. "It's only Hungary water."

Mistress Rowan knelt and retrieved the ring from beneath the table, handing it to me. "Little girls don't wear perfume."

"They do in my house." Lady Rose stood in the doorway, a fond smile on her face. She gestured with her stick for me to follow her. "Come out, William, so Kit can lecture the child in peace."

We returned to the hall. The dogs lurched upright, surrounding her in a wiggling pack.

"You are a bad influence," I told her, shoving one of the dogs aside as it tried to push between my legs. "Can't you train these beasts?"

"You," she said with evident delight, "are besotted. It's all over you like Jane's perfume."

"What are you talking about?" She was a witch. There was no way she could suspect my feelings for Mistress Rowan; I'd been careful not to show anything.

She poked my chest with a finger that looked bony without its customary adornments. "You're in love with that girl."

I sat without waiting to be asked. "I am not. We have just met."

"You are." She sat next to me and leaned her head on my shoulder. "Don't deny yourself happiness, my boy. It doesn't come along that often."

"She works for my father," I said, swallowing the lump in my throat. "And I am in no position to take a wife."

"Who said anything about marriage?" she asked. "Don't look like that—I wasn't suggesting you set the girl up as your mistress. I'm saying there's no law against love."

"I return to London tomorrow." There was no place in my life for a woman, even if she could be convinced to leave Jane. "And anyway, Liz told me she is being courted by someone."

Lady Rose stretched her neck toward the parlor door, where Jane and her governess were bickering. "Do you mean the men she refused or her young correspondent?"

"The correspondent." I hated myself for manipulating her into revealing information. "Is it serious?"

"It is on his end." She raised her eyebrows. "Kit doesn't know what to make of him. They exchanged no more than an hour's conversation, but he seems as smitten as you are."

"He is." I told her I knew Jamie, although not well. "And he is no better suited to pay court to her than I am. Though"—I spoke without real thought—"I believe he is also involved with one of the Scottish queen's maids."

Why had I assigned Jamie my situation? Perhaps Lady Rose wouldn't tell her, but it was far more likely she would. Jamie was in no position to marry, but their exchange of letters no doubt heartened him in his royal semi-captivity.

"Well, that's interesting. I'm glad to know it." She raised her voice. "That's enough now, you two. Jane, let Kit take you up to my chamber so you can remove all my finery."

There was a wail of protest, but they emerged and marched up the stairs, Mistress Rowan's hands on Jane's shoulders. The child's cupped hands were filled with glinting gems and her hair fell about her face.

"I didn't realize you were such a jackdaw," I said, hoping to distract her.

"I like pretty things," she said with a shrug. Her smile widened, catlike. "Kit is very pretty."

"She is," I agreed. "That does not mean I am in love. There are many pretty women in the world. You, for example."

"Flatterer." Lady Rose slapped me lightly on the arm. "I am too old, William, and you would never accept a woman who'd been in your father's bed. Which eliminates a great many women." She clicked her tongue. "This is perhaps indelicate of me, but you have no worry about Kit on that front."

"I would hope not." Was my father a stag who would rut until he died?

"Not because of his age," she said hastily, as they descended the stairs. "The Bower *is* but a short ride over the hill."

Jane was quiet on the trip back, worn out with dressing up and too many sweets. Mistress Rowan and I kept our conversation to a minimum; I could not bear to speak after what Lady Rose had said, for fear she would comprehend my feelings and make light of them.

"You are leaving tomorrow?" she said as Hawkmoor came into sight.

"I must. If I don't return soon, they will send someone to find me." I would not put it past Ned, particularly if Cecil had some new assignment in mind.

"Don't you ever wish your life was your own?"

"About as often as you do," I told her. "And it is even less likely to happen."

She nodded, and cast her gaze at my niece, riding slumped in the saddle between us. "Jane will miss you."

I gathered my courage and said, "I hope she will not be the only one."

## CHAPTER 29

MARTHA SLID IN NEXT to me at supper with an apologetic smile. "Mistress Rowan sends her regrets."

"Where is she?" I had rested after our return and was ready to resume our gentle flirtation.

"Her head aches," my niece said. "She says she will stay in her chamber."

"I am sorry to hear it." She had seemed herself when we came in; perhaps Jane had been wearing on her.

Ellen spoke from across the table. "It came on suddenly. She wishes to be left in peace until tomorrow. Our nursemaid has taken charge of Jane for the night."

"But I am leaving in the morning." My appetite gone, I placed my knife across the plate. "Would she object to a farewell visit?"

"Don't be a pest, William," my father said. "You're the reason the girl's head hurts to begin with."

"Father!" Liz's expression was more tolerant than her tone. "Will and Kit have become good friends this week. You mustn't be unkind."

"Why should he change now?" I excused myself and went to my chamber. It was evident from the mess that Dennis had begun packing, but the man himself was blissfully absent. I'd hardly seen him all week, other than to close my eyes while he shaved me and listen to him complain about the state of my boots. It was no matter. On the morrow, our partnership would resume and continue unabated until London. The prospect gave me no pleasure.

I threw myself on the bed. Was Father correct? Had I unwittingly done something to cause her withdrawal? Thinking that it was my fault was unendurable.

Robin had given me a book upon parting. I dug it from my satchel and pulled a chair close to the window, determined to read and think no more on women, for they brought me nothing but grief.

The house grew quiet as I turned page after page, and the gnawing inside me faded with steady application of the words of William Baldwin. Robin told me that the book, *Beware the Cat*, had been suppressed during Mary's reign as anti-Catholic, very few copies ever having seen the light of day. Being Robin, he had located one. The moral of the tale, he said, buried under layers of fable, was that cats could see what occurred behind closed doors.

Did he mean to call me a cat?

Dennis appeared to see if I required anything. I sent him away, lighting a candle and continuing to read. What did it matter that Mistress Rowan did not wish to see me? I was not likely to soon return to my father's house, nor was I in any position to plan a future for myself with her—or any woman, for that matter.

The candle had burned down to a stub. My eyes were gritty, but if I attempted to sleep, I would simply lie there, the book and my problems mixing together into an unappealing stew. I put my head out the window and saw that the sky had changed from black to darkest blue. The birds would soon wake, but for the moment, it was still, even the insects silent.

I put on my shoes and stealthily descended the staircase to the front door. Sliding back the bar, I stepped into the cool darkness, closing my eyes and breathing deeply.

It would be all right. She was just another girl for whom I had developed—far too quickly—feelings inappropriate to the situation. In the distraction of work, she would be forgotten. I almost looked forward to whatever Ned would throw at me next.

We were days from the full moon; away from the house's shadows, there was no difficulty in following the path to the garden. I always paid my respects to my mother in this place before leaving. She had devoted long winters of my childhood to its creation and embellishment and spent much of her time there.

The smells of rosemary and lavender, used for edging inside the privet border, hung heavy in the air. I entered by the corner path and made my way to the center, where a small fountain—my father's contribution, deemed unnecessary by my mother but installed nonetheless—plashed quietly. A trio of carved wooden benches circled the shallow bowl. I sat on the nearest one, sliding down and crossing my arms behind my head. If I was going to stare into the darkness without sleeping, I might as well stare at the stars.

I had nearly drifted off when the crunch of gravel made me open my eyes. A figment—a ghost—paused at the fountain's edge.

"I did not expect anyone to be here." Mistress Rowan wore a loose gown over what appeared to be her nightdress.

"Did you not see the door was unlatched?" I sat up hastily, trying to look more presentable.

"I came by way of the back stairs." She plunged her hands into the cold water, bathing her wrists. "I could not sleep."

"Do you feel better?"

She turned questioning eyes on me. "Oh—my headache. Yes, it has faded. I took some willow bark."

Her hair was uncovered, twisted into a thick braid that reached her waist. The moonlight silvered everything, but I knew already it was the color of sun-struck honey. What would it feel like under my hands? Her gown was gray, or perhaps lavender, flowing without interruption from her shoulders to her shockingly bare feet.

"Don't the stones bother you?"

She sat on the other end of the bench, tucking her feet beneath her gown. "I ran barefoot through most of my childhood."

My mental picture of a placid child adjusted to a laughing, barefoot girl. Her nightclothes made her seem insubstantial and yet also more real. She was both a phantom and the most solidly human woman I had ever been close to.

"You must wish to be alone," she said, hesitation in her voice. "I will go. I should not be out here"—she waved a vague hand—"like this."

"I promise not to notice, if you promise not to leave," I said. "I was very sorry you didn't come to supper. I did not wish to leave in the morning without saying goodbye."

A faint smile touched her lips. "Have you enjoyed your visit, Master Hawkins?"

"You could call me William," I said. "I would like that."

"Then you may call me Katherine," she said. "Or Kit, as you choose. Have you enjoyed your visit, William?"

I savored the sound of her voice saying my name, but I could not bring myself to call her Kit—not out loud. "More than I had expected, Katherine, and for several reasons."

"You do not visit often." Her hands lay at rest on the smooth fabric over her thigh. I imagined what that limb must look like: smooth and pale, the shadowed bending of her knee...

"I do not. If you are close friends with Lady Rose, she has told you more about my relationship with my father than ever I could." Thoughts of my past did not hurt so much with her close by. If I were brave, or stupid, I could reach out and take her hand.

As I sat, thinking thoughts that would get me slapped, or worse, Katherine Rowan moved close enough that I could smell her faint floral scent. The air grew thick with my wanting. Her hand rested on the smooth oak seat. I put mine beside it so there was a scant inch between our little fingers.

"It is not my place," she said softly, "but I believe he would welcome you if you came more often. He has reached an age where he realizes his children see him from duty, not from affection."

What did she see, standing quietly by? The man she described was not the father I knew, but I also could not declare she was wrong. Liz had already disabused me of some of my illusions; I did not know the man he had become, only the man I had loathed all my life.

"Duty was what was drilled into us," I told her. "Duty and fear. He has never said a kind word to me."

Katherine leaned down and plucked a sprig of rosemary, crushing it between her fingers. "Lady Elinor must have been an exceptional woman, then, because you do not strike me as a man who was treated unkindly."

"She was." Would I think of her every time I smelled rosemary? I hoped so. I shifted my hand until I could feel the warmth emanating from hers.

"You resemble your mother."

My chin came up. "In what way?"

"Your eyes," she said. "I have seen the portraits in Lord Kelton's study. You have her eyes and her kindness. But there is something of your father in you, though you do not see it."

"I am nothing like him." How easily the stiffness and hurt returned to my voice. "Why would you say that?"

"There." She dropped the rosemary on the ground and turned so our hands touched. "Your quickness in taking offense is very like him. And Lady Rose was not wrong—there are other similarities."

"I'll thank you to keep your misguided opinions to yourself, Mistress Rowan." For a moment, I'd felt her touch in my very core, but when she spoke of my father, my love flamed up and burned to cinders. How dare she compare us?

"I'm sorry"—she recoiled as if I'd raised a threatening hand—"I thought we were speaking as friends."

"We are not friends." Each word dropped like a stone. "You are my father's servant. My niece's governess. You have no idea what it was like to grow up in this house."

She scrambled to her feet, her breath unsteady. "And you, Master Hawkins, are everything you claim to find disdainful in him. Someone has taught Jane manners, but I cannot say the same for you."

Whirling in a flash of twilight silk, she disappeared. I remained on the bench until dawn pinked the sky, wondering how something so promising had suddenly turned to ash.

# PART III
## 1570

## CHAPTER 30

ONCE AGAIN IN LONDON, I was informed that this season of my career would be different. I was being sent to the ambassador's residence in the French capital. "We like to keep two or three men on hand," Ned said casually, "in case of need. But Hallett has returned unexpectedly—some malady, I don't know—and a trustworthy man must be sent n the next ship. Damned inconvenient."

It was an honor—or perhaps a punishment—that my assignment would keep me shuttling between London and Paris, with no perceived opportunities to see Katherine Rowan or Robin or anyone besides Dennis, innkeepers, ostlers, and ships' captains—and Ned.

"What does the job entail?" I didn't truly care. The journey from Yorkshire to London had passed in a fog of regret; not even Dennis's antics could bring me out of it.

"You'll live in the ambassador's residence," he said. "Do whatever Norris asks of you—it may be errands in the city or carrying messages to London or something else entirely. Between the queen's marriage negotiations and their damned religious wars, there will always be occupation."

I did not need occupation. I needed rest. When I swung down from my horse outside of Whitehall, I was tired in my bones. Too much had happened in a short time, from the torment of visiting my father to the discovery and ruination of my hopes for Katherine Rowan. The reason for Cecil's interest in her remained a mystery.

Ned was still talking, his arms expanding and contracting as he described the unrest in France and Henry Norris, the ambassador, a particular friend of the queen as his father had been executed on suspicion of adultery with Anne Boleyn.

"You don't look enthusiastic." He gazed at me across the desk with dissatisfaction. "Is the post not to your liking?"

"The post is fine," I said. "I have spent time with my family, that is all."

He bellowed with laughter. "How is Lord Kelton? Still a thorn in your side and a siren to the ladies?"

"I hope he has aged beyond such matters." I did not want to discuss my father. Our relationship had always been complicated, and while Katherine and Liz insisted he had mellowed, I saw no proof of such a miraculous occurrence.

"I doubt it. Once a boar, always a boar." He paused. "And how is our friend, Lewis?"

Why did the sound of Robin's name in his mouth make the hair stand on the back of my neck?

"He is fine," I said carefully. "In his library, as always. Mistress Lewis runs the estate and the children and everything else, so far as I can tell."

"She must like that." His lip jutted out. "She never seemed to appreciate my affection for Robin."

I thought of something I could repeat that would divert him from his questions. "The worst thing I have heard her say was that you did not respect their bedtime."

Ned laughed again, tears leaking from the corners of his eyes. "That is true," he wheezed. "Rob and I would stay up, drinking and talking, and the damned woman was always *there*, wanting to go to bed."

"How domestic." My longstanding fantasies aside, what man in his right mind would not choose going to bed with Margaery over sitting up with Ned?

"They're better off in the country," he grumbled. "Best place for them—and the little ones."

Ned had at least five children with his very patient and absent wife. "How is your family?"

"Fine, fine," he said. "Would you believe I have grandchildren?"

"Did you hear the Lewises had another baby?" I asked. "They named him Sebastian."

Ned's face did something strange, then smoothed itself blank as a sheet of paper. "Sentimental fools, the pair of them."

I settled with Dennis into the ambassador's residence on the rue des Bernardins. Despite the size of the house, I was put in with two other messengers. As we were rarely there at the same time, the chamber was never crowded, but I resented the others—Geoffrey Barnard and, surprisingly, Peter Sturgis, one of the brothers in whose company I had left Scotland—simply for existing when I wished to be alone.

"Separated from your brother, are you?" I asked as I stowed my few things in a chest allotted to my use. "I thought that was impossible."

"With Master Cecil, all things are possible." Peter rolled his eyes. "You've landed on your feet. This isn't the worst assignment you could get, and you'll get home in one piece unless you do something stupid, like Hallett."

Hallett was the man whom I had replaced. "What happened to him?" I asked. "I was told no more than that he returned unexpectedly."

Peter sprawled back on the bed. "Once he recovered."

"Recovered?"

"He was stupid enough to interfere in a confrontation on the street and got himself sliced up for his gallantry." He related a tale of a Huguenot woman being tormented by a group of young Catholic men, and Hallett staggering through the door of the residence with a knife sticking out of his stomach. "She ran away, so it got him nothing in the end!"

I suppose he had the satisfaction of shielding a woman from abuse, but what I wondered was that Ned had not bothered to tell me of Hallett's reason for returning to England. These things happened; I didn't anticipate getting into the same situation, so there was no reason to keep it from me. But the workings of Ned's mind were a mystery best put aside for another day.

From my travels with Starling, I thought I knew France, but we had not gone often into Paris, dealing instead with agents who came to us in various locations. For the first weeks, Peter Sturgis was my guide, showing me the common destinations and the best ways to get to them through the twisting, medieval streets.

Some parts of Paris had not changed since my student days. Other areas were more modern than London, with grand houses any English lord would be proud to claim, but they were cheek-by-jowl with the falling-down houses of the poor, a stark contrast that the nobility seemed able to ignore.

As I became reacquainted with the city, I tried to convince myself that I was done with England for good. There would be things I missed, of course—roast mutton, properly cooked. Good English ale. Robin. Katherine Rowan.

Kit.

What a fool I had been.

I turned over and over our fateful encounter in the garden. How differently it might have gone, had I been a different man, or had a different father. What sort of man found himself alone in the moonlight with a woman in her nightclothes and picked a fight when he could have kissed her instead?

There could be no doubt that she hated me—unless I was too unimportant to inspire any emotion at all. Jane would keep my name in her ears, so it was impossible that she would forget me or my hurtful words. I certainly would not. Why had I flared at her when she likened me to my father? It was an insult, but could I not have corrected her gently or asked why she would compare me to a man she knew I despised?

Happiness had been within my reach, and I had thrown it away.

I was filled with a howling emptiness for someone who was not mine, had never been mine, and who never would be mine, because I was too craven to speak my heart and too untrusting of my emotions to keep from hurting her. The certainty that I would never improve deadened me to thoughts of other women, which was, perhaps, for the best given my circumstances. Before departing England, I had attended the wedding of Isabel Ferren—arranged by her indefatigable cousin Douglas—to an acceptable gentleman, kissed her smooth and fragrant cheek, and felt absolutely nothing.

Deep in the night, when Sturgis and Barnard snored around me, I fixed my eyes on the ceiling and summoned Kit's face. Why had I believed I'd had any chance with her to begin with? She said plainly she would not marry; she had promised my father she would not leave Jane for five years. Why, then, did I believe I could have built with her a life such as Robin and Margaery had—a life not to everyone's tastes, but which would make us both content?

In the times in which I found myself, thinking of her was a grave distraction. Instead, I forced myself into the city, learning its ways and building the kind of acquaintance that might prove useful to a man in my line of work. The plays and music and shops which might have proved diverting after my time in the French countryside no longer felt safe in a city on the verge of war.

When I was a student, one of the few destinations on which Matt and I could agree was Notre Dame—not from any religious fervor on my part, but because the lofty space quieted my mind and induced a serenity that made my studies easier. Now the air was heavy with fear of what might come and encountering more than a handful of people there made me anxious. Not every churchgoer was peaceable; I had witnessed fights break out in markets and taverns, so why not in church? Although I'd thought what happened to Hallett could not happen to me, it could, and quite easily.

Despite my growing awareness of the situation between religious factions, I preferred the streets to the court. Norris attended regularly, but after two trips, I allowed the others first opportunity to accompany him. I had never been comfortable in Elizabeth's court, but the French equivalent seemed to be made entirely of spun sugar, with dark and noxious undertones, like an open sewer on the other side of a walled flower garden. Whatever was rotten in France was rotten at the very core.

Paris was not only Paris; it was also London. Laid over the city like a web was a network of Cecil's men: servants in the ambassador's residence, but also in the houses of both Catholic and Huguenot French, in taverns and churches and shops. If eyes and ears were required, they were there, and reports presented with regularity, though through irregular channels, to Henry Norris, his assistant, and occasionally to me or Sturgis when our superiors were absent, as both of us had long been in Cecil's employ.

Our heads were filled with information that could be something or nothing; names of men who might be plotting or simply bedding the wrong man's wife; letters stolen from purses or pockets or chests, which might or might not be in cipher.

It was exhausting, looking at everything through a filter of what it could mean for Elizabeth's England, but the sheer amount of intelligence that flowed through the ambassador's house made it impossible to ignore; not all of it could be false, or misdirection.

On a dull, rainy afternoon in early February, one such bit of information presented itself. I had been in France for seven months, long enough that it had begun to feel familiar, but not so long that it felt like home. I'd slept badly the night before, dreams of Kit causing me to wake hard as a tree and covered in shame. Consequently, I had little patience for the man sitting across the table from me.

He reeked of damp wool. He was also nervous, staring down at his chapped and reddened hands, nose twitching like a rabbit's as he tried unsuccessfully to stifle a sneeze. An enormous kerchief was whipped from a pocket, and he disappeared momentarily behind it.

"You were saying?" I asked when he reappeared.

"I don't know for certain," he said, for the third time. "But the man who rents a room from my sister, he is English, although he says he is Scottish." His eyes narrowed scornfully. "A Frenchman can tell the difference."

"And this Englishman—Scotsman—is suspicious for what reason?"

His head came up sharply, cap sliding on greasy black hair. "He's not who he says he is," he sputtered. "Isn't that enough?"

"Not really." I rubbed at the tightness in my neck, knowing it would not ease until the fellow was gone. "Many people are not who they claim to be. There's no crime in that." If pretending to be someone else had been a criminal offense, I would have been thrown into Ludgate jail years ago. "What has he *done*?"

"He claims he's a student," the man said, scratching himself vigorously. "A bit old, if you ask me."

"Students are not all boys." When I studied in Paris, there were in our group men aged fifteen to forty.

"No," he said consideringly. "But she's let to students before. They drink or they sleep. This one, he is never drunk, and he has many visitors. Often, they come after Mariette has barred the door for the night."

That *was* unusual. Most of the students I'd known had spent their time out of classes either drunk or sleeping off their excesses. Any socializing that took place at night was unlikely to happen in a lodging house.

"What sort of visitors?" I firmly pushed dream-Kit to one side. Last week Sturgis had uncovered a fellow carrying letters from Rome directed to several Catholic nobles, including the Duke of Norfolk. If I could discover something similar, perhaps Cecil would show his appreciation by allowing me to return to England. "Other English? Scots?"

He shook his head. "One was Italian. He spoke English but it didn't sound right."

Slowly he told me of visitors noted down by his sister—the Italian, if that's what he was; a Frenchman who might be Catholic—he and his sister were Catholic but not *that* sort; and a priest whose English was rougher than the so-called student's.

Not the usual crowd with whom a student would spend his free hours. I took down the location of the lodging house and descriptions of the student and his visitors.

"I thank you, monsieur," I said. "We will look into the matter. Does your sister have a bed available, should we wish to observe the student at close hand?"

He sat back, considering what an ambassador's man might be willing to pay. "She could make one available. She has eight children," he explained. "Difficult to fit them all in one bed."

"I imagine." I folded away my notes. "If we decide to look into this fellow—"

"Thorpe," he interrupted.

"This fellow, Thorpe, someone will contact your sister and ask for a bed for a week."

"Very good, sir." He bounded out of the chair and left the room before I could complete my farewells.

I let him go. The dream had decided me—on one hand, I might have ruined any chance with Kit Rowan, but on the other, the intervening months could have faded the effects of my appalling behavior. I sprinted up the stairs to my chamber, set on writing a letter to a living girl whose reality far exceeded my dream.

*Dear Mistress Rowan,*

*I hope this letter finds you well and in good spirits, and not excessively vexed by my niece.*

*At our last meeting, you accused me of having worse
manners than Jane. You were correct. I accept your rebuke
and hope I may someday earn your praise in its stead.*

*Considering my boorish behavior of last summer, I would
understand if you chose not to answer this letter,
but it is my hope you will forgive my errant ways and
understand that my words were the result of excessive
emotion at the thought of parting on bad terms.*

*If it might affect your decision, please know that I am in
Paris and unlike to visit for another half year. France has
become a second home, which is strange as I do not feel
as though I have a first home.*

*Why is it that I can say such things to you, when all my
life I have been uncomfortable with people knowing me?
I have felt, since we first met, that you did know me and
it is for this reason that I hope you will write.*

*Your obedient servant,
William Hawkins*

The next day, Sturgis departed for London. I gave him the letter,
asking him to see it privately sent north. "Not with any court messages,
you understand," I said, "unless you take them yourself."

"A lady, eh?" He grinned at me. "Well, you deserve some privacy from
Sir Edward, I'll not say otherwise."

## CHAPTER 31

AMBASSADOR NORRIS THOUGHT THE matter of the false student worth looking into. He leaned forward in his chair until it creaked, tugging at his full, reddish-brown beard. "But you won't suit at all," he said, "and Sturgis won't be back from London for weeks."

Travel during the winter months being neither pleasant nor rapid, I imagined my colleague waiting impatiently at the port for a captain willing to set sail before April.

"What about Barnard?" It struck me as strange that he never appeared to be given the extra duties occasioned by our position.

Norris shook his head. "He's too well known and knows too little." At my confused glance, he elaborated. "Barnard has been messenger to the last three ambassadors. He's never been involved in that... other business."

I understood his distaste. The ambassador already had to walk a fine line between the feuding courts; subterfuge must have seemed, on occasion, too much to ask.

"We could use my servant." Dennis had been alternating, of late, between pestering me about my lovelorn condition and lecturing me for roaming Paris alone. A week or two apart would do us good.

"An excellent proposition," Norris said. "Send him to me so I can explain the task."

Dennis came to me for further details after he met with the ambassador, knowing Ned and Cecil might be looking for something different. He went off, with no little grumbling, to lodge in the house and attempt to befriend Thorpe. If he could not manage that, he should observe him closely and report back with information regarding the subject.

Three days later, he appeared as the bells chimed noon. He wore a collection of cast-off clothing borrowed from the other servants, as I apparently permitted him to dress too well to pass as a merchant's son.

"Have you left him alone?" I ushered him inside.

Dennis gave me a heavy-browed look. "Scarcely since we've met," he said. "That's a man who needs a friend. I walked with him to meet his tutor and I'll see him at Madame Mariette's table later."

We sat at the upstairs window so I could watch the comings and goings of the house across the street. "What are your opinions?" I asked. "Is our informant correct? Is this Thorpe involved in something?"

"It's early to tell. But he's got secrets." Cocking his head, he added, "But what man of reasonable age does not?"


Two weeks later, while Dennis continued his pursuit of Thorpe's confidences, I journeyed to London. Sturgis had not yet returned, but Norris's latest report to Cecil could not wait and so I set out alone.

Spring had begun to show itself, but the Narrow Sea believed it was still winter. I spent the better part of two days being blown in the wrong direction, pitched up and down until my stomach, generally not afflicted by seasickness, gave up its contents and sent me to my bunk to think violent thoughts about the effects of Dennis's absence on my overall comfort.

He had been with me since we were children, a servant-companion even before I was sent to live with Uncle Henry. He was somehow related to Terrence, Father's steward—a cousin, perhaps—and was living on the grounds of Hawkmoor when he was plucked up and given to me.

Though not a particularly happy child, I had a solid sense of my own importance, and Dennis had an equally solid instinct for how to bring me down to earth when I was high-handed with him or anyone else. We argued frequently, even coming to blows over the years, but I was closer to him than my brother and thought he would say the same of me.

Traveling without him was not only inconvenient but lonely.

It continued cold once I reached England. Upon finally arriving at Whitehall, I delivered Norris's report into Cecil's hands and then slept like the dead until late afternoon. When it appeared that my presence would not be required, I took myself off to Cheapside. If I was lucky, perhaps I could wallow in ale and sentiment while Bess sang her husband's love songs. At the very least, I could pick up my letters and have a drink with Harry.

It was too soon to expect a response to my letter to Kit, if she would even respond. There was no reason to waste time or ink on a man who had behaved like a petulant child, especially if she was being courted by Jamie Welldon. In addition to being extremely handsome, he was more articulate than I could ever be.

The Minstrel's Arms was bustling when I arrived. I made my way through the crowded room to the back door, where Harry and his son had just brought in a fresh barrel of ale.

"Some of that, please." I shouted over the din, and nodded to indicate his father, alone on the small stage with his lute. "Is your mother not well?"

"She has a bad throat," he shouted back. "Go up the stairs—she'll give you a drink and your letters."

*Letters!* My heart lifted even as I knew it was unrealistic to hope.

Faint music filled the dark stairwell. I hung on the rope that served as a rail until I got to the chamber above. It was no brighter; Bess did not require light.

"Mistress."

The music stopped. A movement from a chair by the window and she appeared, setting a small harp upon the table. "Is it William?" She came forward, her hands outstretched. "Light a candle and I'll fetch you a cup of ale."

I took her hands, kissing her on both cheeks. "Harry says you're not well."

"I'm better," she said, though her voice said otherwise. "I caught a chill. My menfolk are fussing over me."

"As they should." I struck a light and moved the candle to the table where she'd been sitting. "Do not strain your voice by speaking. Harry said there are letters for me. I'll take them and be on my way."

"You will not." She handed me a cup and gestured that I should sit. "You will read them here and tell me what you have seen and done since our last meeting."

"Mistress—"

Bess ran her fingertips along the wall until she reached a tall chest. Opening a drawer, she felt under several layers of bed linens and produced a small packet.

"You will stay for a while," she said, "and talk to me. If we leave the door open, we will hear Tom play."

I could not resist such inducement and subsided with my drink and my letters. The sound of the lute reached us beneath the murmur of the crowd. We sat together, listening, and Bess sang along under her breath.

"You were to be quiet," I reminded her when there was a pause.

Beneath her white cap, her expression was merry. "You want to be alone with your love letters," she teased. "I'm going down. Stay as long as you like. The jug is on the chest if you want more."

Her footsteps had not faded before I spread the letters on the table. There were three, each tightly folded and sealed. I scrutinized the writing on each and chose the one which appeared to have made the longest journey.

It was a note from Anne Darcy, two scrawled lines that chilled my blood.

*Matthew has strange visitors and tells me nothing. Please*
*see to his safety for he will not hear me. I am fearful.*

I crumpled the letter in frustration, then smoothed it again. Oh, Matthew. I could not imagine how I would be able to fulfill Anne's request and maintain my schedule. Perhaps if Sturgis was yet in London, he would cover for me. I took a gulp of ale and considered my options.

The second letter, from Robin, was no more cheering.

*The matter which we discussed has again reached my ears.*
*There is little I can do from here. You may have to speak to*
*Lord Kelton. A longer letter from Margaery awaits you at*
*Whitehall.*

The combination of Matthew misbehaving and Robin's suggestion of speaking to my father sent me back to the ale jug and made me wish I could go back to France without dealing with either of them.

I returned to my seat, cocking my head as the music began again from downstairs. Tom's playing softened something inside me, and made me wish, more than ever, for a pairing like his with Bess or Robin's with Margaery.

The final letter was badly folded, sealed with a blob of dark wax over roughly knotted string. I cracked the seal and my heart turned over in my chest at the sight of a feminine hand, familiar to me from the papers in the Hawkmoor schoolroom.

*Dear William,*

*Thank you for your letter. It did much to cheer me as this morning I am to depart Hawkmoor against my will.*

*Your hasty words have been forgiven many times over. I should apologize for my own speech, knowing any comparison with Lord Kelton would be unwelcome.*

*How very exciting that you are in Paris. Being ignorant of London, I cannot imagine the sights you will see and the things you will experience. If it would please you to write again, learning of those experiences would make me very happy.*

*I do not know where I am bound. Please direct any future letters to Hawkmoor. Whatever his faults, Lord Kelton will see that they are delivered.*

*Jane is sorely distressed and would benefit by a letter from her favorite uncle, so you would not be writing strictly to ask his indulgence.*

*Hearing from you has made this painful time brighter. I will close now, as they are calling, and seal this letter.*

*Katherine*

I scrambled from my seat and down the stairs, burning my hand on the prickly rope. "I must go!" I called to Harry and ran into the night. The rush of joy at receiving her letter had been rapidly replaced with questions. Why was she no longer at Hawkmoor? Who had taken her against her will—and why? And where?

Robin was correct. I would have to speak to my father.

I flung myself off my horse and strode inside, intending to track down Ned Pickering and shake answers out of him, if necessary.

"Master Hawkins!" One of the liveried pages who wandered the halls of the palace caught my attention. "I did not know you were back."

"Only this morning," I told him. "Is Sir Edward Pickering here?"

"I believe so." He looked over his shoulder. "You have letters, sir. Should I bring them to your rooms?"

I shook my head. "Get them now. I'll wait."

Robin said to expect a letter from Margaery, but I had no idea who else would write to me at the palace. For that matter, how had Kit known to write to me in care of Harry? Only my sister had that address, in case of need. They must have spoken even before Kit received my letter.

The boy returned and thrust the messages into my hands. "And sir," he said as I turned away, "I asked for you—Sir Edward has gone home for the night."

Margaery's letter was easily recognized. I tucked it into my doublet to read later. The other message was brief, scrawled in thick black ink that stood off the page.

*I am in London. Kelton.*

I would not have to travel to speak to my father. He had come to me.

CHAPTER 32

ACCORDING TO WHAT I'D learned before leaving Whitehall, my father was in residence with a small retinue, but Kelton House was lit as if for a party. I made my appearance at eight and Terrence led me upstairs to my father's chamber.

He sat before the fire, a bottle and glass by his side, one foot propped on a padded stool. His expression showed something more than his usual distaste for London; was he perhaps in pain?

"Father." I bowed and approached, waiting to see if he would offer me a chair.

"Sit, William." He waved a hand. "Drink if you wish."

I poured a glass for myself and sat, letting the fire's welcome warmth seep into my chilled bones. "Your message sounded urgent."

He snorted. "Would I be in London if it were anything else?"

"No. Nor would you have written to me if anyone else could render aid. What is it?"

For a moment, I thought he would disagree, but then he sank back into the chair and folded his hands across his middle. It was a posture frequently employed by Ned, but in my father's case, he appeared to be thinking, not plotting.

"It's Katherine Rowan," he said. "She's gone."

"Gone!" I started up from my seat, wine sloshing. It was worse than I thought. "What happened?"

"Sit, boy." He narrowed his eyes. "Not gone as in disappeared. Gone as in *extracted from my household*. One of those creatures"—the word was said with loathing—"in Cecil's employ came to Hawkmoor with Arthur Rowan. Apparently, the fat one is a friend of yours."

"Not a friend," I said through gritted teeth. *Ned.* "Rowan was with Sir Edward Pickering?"

"I would say not willingly. They arrived mid-afternoon. I was... elsewhere. By the time I returned, Katherine's things were packed, and she and Jane were sobbing in each other's arms in the hall."

My chest was tight. I resisted slipping my fingers inside my collar; it would not help me to breathe. "They did not ask your permission?"

"They did not." He emptied the glass. "I refused to let them leave until the fat one told me what was happening."

Despite the seriousness of his tale, it amused me to hear Ned called 'the fat one' over and over; he preened and strutted as if his size had not grown with his importance. "And?"

Father's mouth twisted in disgust. "He sat in my study and told me Katherine's presence was required in the Earl of Shrewsbury's household, and that Arthur had given his permission."

The Earl of Shrewsbury! That put her in the same house as the Queen of Scots—as well as Mary Seton and Jamie Welldon. The tightness dropped to my stomach, and everything I had eaten in the past twelve hours swirled rapidly in my gut.

"What had her father to say?" I asked when it became clear that Ned had given him no more than those few details.

"Almost nothing." He rubbed his temples, where the silver hairs seemed to have multiplied. "The man allowed the girl to put off two perfectly acceptable matches. He would never force her serve the Scottish queen."

I did not know Arthur Rowan, but I did not believe anyone who had raised such a daughter would be capable of that, either. "I am going to speak to Edward Pickering," I said, "and find out his purpose in doing this. And then, if you are willing, I think we should ride to wherever Arthur Rowan lives and find out what he knows."

"You may ride." My father nodded toward his elevated foot. "Wrenched my ankle two weeks ago and it hasn't healed properly."

Was it truly a new injury, or had he invented a story to cover for the persistent ache in his hip? "Mayhap your physician friend can give you something for the pain when we reach him."

I followed Ned across the city to the house on Lothbury Street, hammering on the front door until a yawning servant answered.

"Is he here?" I demanded, pushing my way in before the man could respond.

"What's all the noise?" Ned's voice floated down from the upper floor. "Hawkins—what in hell are you doing here? It's damned near the middle of the night."

I mounted the steps to his chamber door. "I would speak with you."

"Can it not wait until morning?" His fingers tightened on the door frame. "I was in my bed."

"This will not take long." I skirted around him into the chamber. The fire was smothered, and thick velvet curtains were drawn around the bed, with a narrow opening to allow for his exit. The air was thick with scent: smoke, ale, rose attar. "I have spoken with my father."

"Lord Kelton has come to London?" His surprise was feigned, I was certain. "I thought he seldom left the north."

"You seldom leave your offices in London," I countered, "and yet you traveled all the way to Yorkshire to remove a young woman from his home."

An unpleasant smile split his face. "Ah. Mistress Rowan. Must we have this conversation now, Hawkins? I'm tired."

"As am I." I sat in his chair and met his eyes. "I have arrived in London, been summoned by my father, and am now come to you. I would like to see my bed this night, but not until I have answers."

Ned pulled up another chair. "And what questions do you have?"

His flippant tone filled me with rage. I took a moment to calm myself before speaking. "Why she has been inserted into Shrewsbury's household. What you said to her father to make him agree to the scheme."

"Very simple questions," he said. "All with simple answers. We need someone there who can develop a relationship with the Scottish lady and keep us informed of what passes in her household." Ned no longer called her the queen, as he no longer used my given name. "Any unexpected visitors. Who her correspondents are, and how frequently they write."

"Do you not have Jamie Welldon there for that purpose?"

He crossed his arms. "Welldon is... less than satisfactory these days. I am considering a transfer."

"Why Mistress Rowan?" I asked. "Surely there are others you could have chosen. Cecil himself has said he does not like to use female agents, that they are undependable and too emotional."

A small sound intruded, and Ned moved his chair to cover it, looking over my shoulder at the bed. "Mistress Rowan is not an agent," he said. "She is a young lady in Elizabeth Talbot's household, one who will spend more and more time with the countess and her houseguest, until a rapport is established."

"You cannot *uproot* people to carry out your plans." How had Kit felt, to be informed by this insufferable man that her life was not her own?

Ned rolled his eyes. "Don't tell me you're going to be inconvenient."

"She is my niece's governess. A young woman in my father's employ."

"I thought you loathed the man?"

"I do," I said, though at that moment I loathed Ned more. "But I love my niece."

He shrugged. "Too bad for the child, but she'll form an attachment to Mistress Rowan's replacement." He looked straight in my face. "Is there going to be a problem, Hawkins?"

"No." I looked down at my clenched fists. I wanted to strike him, but that would not help anything. "No problem."

"Then you may go." He waved me toward the door. As it closed, his voice reached me. "I'm sorry, my dove—duty calls, even here."


At dawn, I left for Kelton House. A note waited on Ned's desk: I would be out of London for the foreseeable future. He should send my apologies to ambassador Norris. I left no regards to Ned; I had none to give.

The black coach was waiting outside the house with my father's trunk already strapped on the back. The driver lingered at the horses' heads, speaking softly to them. He looked up with a smile as I stopped and held out his hand for my reins. "He's just inside, Master Hawkins."

"I'll wait here," I said, not willing to go inside to fetch him.

The man nodded and jogged into the house. Within minutes, my father appeared, leaning heavily on his stick, Terrence speaking earnestly at his side.

"No!" I heard, and the servant tucked his head back at the force in his words. "I do not need a nursemaid."

"Not a nursemaid, sir." His voice was ingratiating. "My purpose is to make your life easier."

The stick swung wildly. Terrence ducked with the ease of long practice and put his hand under my father's arm. "Allow me to escort you to the coach, if I am not permitted to accompany you." He met my eyes across the expanse of packed sand covering the road. "I'm sure your son will be happy to aid you in any intimate matters."

Father stopped at the coach door. "Fine," he snarled. "But you ride with the coachman and say *nothing!*"

"It will be my pleasure, sir." Terrence handed him up and ran back to the house to speak to someone inside. He emerged with a bundle under his arm, which he shoved under the strap holding my father's trunk in place.

I walked my horse to the coach and leaned down. My father was on the upholstered velvet seat, his face drawn with pain. I straightened and knocked on the window, to allow him time to gather himself.

The window opened. "What?"

"Where are we going?" It was a topic not discussed the night before in my haste to get to Ned.

"Hertfordshire," he said. "Not far from Kelton. Did you speak to Pickering?"

"For what little it was worth." I related Ned's scant explanation of how Kit had been chosen.

"Shrewsbury," he repeated. "So, she's with the Scottish queen?"

"They want someone she might choose to confide in." I would have thought her a good choice myself, If I hadn't been in love with her and if she hadn't been Jane's governess. She was easy to talk to, with pretty manners and a pleasant way about her; Mary, I was certain, would take to her immediately.

My father swore vividly. "What was Arthur thinking, to allow her to be involved in all this?"

We would find out, though not as quickly as I would like. The coach creaked into motion, moving along the Strand at a walking pace. A half dozen outriders followed behind at a similar ladylike speed.

"We'll never get there at this rate," I said to Terrence. "Can he not ride at all?"

"Not with any comfort." He looked back over his shoulder, but the window was shut again. "He's well into his seventies, remember."

I did remember, when prompted; it was difficult to think of my father as old. There was silver in his hair as far back as when I broke my engagement to Cecily, but other than that, and a slowing of his movements, he'd never changed—or had not allowed himself to be seen as changed. It was an important difference, especially for a man like him.

The roads were kind and we got halfway to our destination by the time we lost the light. I rode ahead and secured a room at an inn. When the coach rumbled in an hour later, I nodded to the innkeeper, and he set his people scrambling to lay the table and assist with the baggage. I heard Father roaring at someone before I saw him, and then the door was flung open.

He surveyed the low-ceilinged room with its welcoming fire, found it lacking. "I see you have wasted no time in making yourself comfortable."

I smiled cheerfully, determined not to fight with him until the matter of Kit was resolved. "Only to assure those same comforts for you, sir. There is a room above for us to share, and food and ale will be out in a moment."

"Hmm." He looked disappointed not to have a reason to shout at me. Then he found one. "A room to share? Must I put up with your snoring all night long?"

I was no happier, but space was limited and the other guests—a large family traveling together—were unwilling to give up their shared room despite my offer of coin.

"I'm afraid so," I said. "But if you drink enough, you won't notice."

By the time the coachman and outriders came in and took seats at the other end of the table, we filled the main room. There was stew and crusty bread and enough ale to keep everyone in a civil mood. Terrence sat in his usual position, between us and the servants, fielding my father's comments and keeping up a running conversation with the other men.

"Rowan's home is near Kelton?" I asked.

"In the village," he responded. "He and Mistress Rowan bought the place perhaps ten years ago."

I had been so little near home in the last decade that, even if I had visited, it was unlikely I would have ever seen her. "But you knew him before?"

"For years." He leaned back against the stone fireplace and turned his legs to face the heat. "I met him through Charles Brandon, the old Duke of Suffolk. He attended his wife—the last one, the child bride—when she fell ill after her lying-in."

That child bride had been intended for one of his sons, yet Suffolk married her before his wife was long in her grave. My mother had been but sixteen when she was wed; how young had Katherine Brandon been on her wedding day for my father to speak in judgment?

I turned my cup in my hands, debating how many questions I could ask before he became suspicious that I had my own selfish reasons for this journey. "How old was Mistress Katherine when they adopted her?"

Father looked up sharply. "You're very interested in the girl all of a sudden." He broke into an unwilling smile. "And don't say again that it's all worry for Jane. I saw how you were with her during your visit. You looked like an ox on the way to slaughter."

My shoulders slumped. I didn't think he knew me well enough to see through me. "I am... fond of her."

"Fond." He could make the most innocuous word sound filthy.

"Fine." I slammed my cup on the table, making the outriders jerk around to look at us. "I would like to give her the opportunity to refuse *my* offer of marriage, if you must know."

He broke into hearty laughter. When he gained control of himself, he said, "That may be the smartest idea you've ever had."

## CHAPTER 33

TERRENCE LEFT AT DAWN, riding ahead to Kelton to ready the house
for its master. I asked one of the outriders to lead my horse and took
to the coach so my father and I could continue our conversation about
Arthur Rowan.

"I hear you've been in France?" He winced as the coach bounced. "I
thought you were with Cecil's little men?"

"I'm lodged in the ambassador's household in Paris." I ignored his discomfort, as I had ignored it the night before when Terrence had tried to
rub the ache from his leg and got his ears boxed for his efforts. I thought
of all the crossings to and from London, and the reasons for them, and
conceded, "There is some of what you are alluding to. Catholic plots
against the queen are everywhere, and the principal secretary must be
kept informed. It is a dangerous time."

"Religion!" he scoffed. "God had no intention that his followers
would be constantly at each other's throats."

Those same heretical sentiments had been voiced by Robin Lewis,
but I decided not to share that information. "I always believed you were
strong for reform. You certainly benefited from it."

Kelton had come to him upon his marriage to my mother, but he had
received monastery lands in both Yorkshire and Hertfordshire after the
dissolution.

"My faith is my business. If King Henry wanted to give me land as
a reward for faithful service, and for marrying a Catholic heiress and
keeping her family in the fold, I was not going to object."

Royal patronage was nearly impossible to turn down. "But you got yourself away from the court by the time the old king died."

My father shrugged. "I'd always hated the Seymour brothers. It was clear they would fight to the death to control Edward. And your mother wanted me at home more often."

"Ah, yes. She was always first in your thoughts." My tone was jaundiced; he was no more faithful a husband than Ned.

He struck the thick velvet upholstery with his fist. "Your mother never complained."

"She wouldn't," I pointed out. "And it would have done her no good if she had."

His face was red. "I know what you're referring to so delicately, and that part of my life was always kept far from Elinor."

"Lady Rose is just over the hill," I pointed out. "Do you think she didn't know?"

"You didn't know your mother as well as I did, William." There was pain as well as humor in his smile. "Do you know who she befriended when she first came to court? Bess Minstrel. She brought her to Kelton with us before Harry's birth. Made me live in the house with the pair of them."

I had never heard this story before. Bess had spoken kindly of my father, considering their history, but I'd had no idea she and my mother were acquainted, much less that she had spent time in our home. "Why did I never hear of this?"

"Their friendship faded as Elinor was less at court," he admitted, catching hold of the seat as the coach hit another rut. "And I don't believe Bess's husband approved of the relationship."

I raised my brows. "I can't imagine why."

Another silence fell. Father stared out the window at the landscape, gray and brown with occasional patches of green. Low afternoon sun shone through the trees. I watched him and re-examined some of my long-held beliefs about his behavior. It was an uncomfortable interlude.

A wave of small, dark birds flashed past the window. I squinted but they were gone before I could identify them.

"You mentioned keeping Mother's family in the fold," I said at last. "I heard from Anne Darcy recently. She thinks Matt is involved in something dangerous." My ability to see him depended on how long our visit with the Rowans lasted; despite my high-handed words to Ned, I couldn't be away from my post forever. "Could you speak to him? Impress upon him the importance of not risking his life for a cause that will succeed or fail without his help?"

His brown eyes snapped to mine. "That damned boy. Henry never could control him."

"Uncle Henry has been dead for years." But he was right; my uncle never could make Matt come to heel once he had an idea in his head.

"I'll speak to him," he said. "Put the fear of both our Gods—and me—into him."

It was dark when we arrived, the road barely discernible as we passed through the gates. Windows were lit on the house's lower level, giving it a welcoming aspect.

I'd always thought Kelton a more pleasant place than Hawkmoor. My father had expanded the kitchens and gardens upon being granted the place, but he left the manor alone beyond improvements to windows and adding a second story in place of the original gallery to create space for his numerous children.

And Bess Minstrel had once stayed there. What must that have been like for him—his new and pregnant wife and his former mistress, fast friends. For a moment, I felt a stab of pity for the man he had been, younger than I was now.

The moment the coach stopped on the gravel drive, any good feelings I'd begun to develop evaporated as he turned to me, snapping, "Are you waiting to be unloaded like baggage? Get out and go inside!"

I obeyed, leaving him with Terrence, and only realized, as a servant removed my cloak, that he hadn't wanted me to witness his difficulty in alighting from the coach. I took a breath, vowing to be more patient, and crossed the room to stand before the fire.

The sound of a tray sliding onto the table alerted me to the arrival of ale. Turning, I thanked the maid and took a cup, tipping it back and savoring the warmth it kindled in my belly.

Father and Terrence entered together. He shrugged the man off when he saw me and shed his outer garments. "Drinking already, William?"

I raised the cup. "It is your influence, Father."

"I shall join you." He sat heavily in his large chair at the head of the table and turned it slightly to face the fire. "Terrence—"

"I sent a boy down to the village upon my arrival," he said smoothly. "Arthur Rowan and his wife will be here in the morning. And before you ask, food will be brought out shortly."

He nodded curtly, eyes on his cup, but I smiled my thanks. With Terrence in charge, I would not have to share a bed with my father.

"Do you go back to France directly?" Father asked abruptly. "Or will you stay in England a while?"

I would like to stay in England indefinitely, but I could not manage that, not yet. "I will go back by way of London," I said. "But I cannot vanish from royal service. You must understand that."

Three servants entered and an array of dishes were set before us—beef and mutton, a thick barley pottage, stewed greens. The rich scents left me dizzy; I had not realized how hungry I was.

He sighed. "I regret allowing Henry Darcy to get you started in that place."

"It wasn't him," I said. "Harry got me the job for Queen Mary." Which led, more or less, to the job I had now.

His knife stopped midway through cutting a slice of beef. "I didn't know that. Damned interfering boy."

I was shocked to hear him refer to his son and heir with the same lack of respect he showed me. "It was after Cecily. He thought I needed occupation."

The beef made it to his plate but no further. "You would have been well occupied there. It took months to placate her people after you ran away."

"I'm sorry." I'd been so wrapped in misery, it had never occurred to me that her parents would have been upset. "But it was necessary."

"Why?" He placed his knife across the plate, apparently ready to listen. "She was a fine girl. Good family. You were besotted with her, until you weren't."

It came back in a sickening rush: her wide eyes following him across the hall; her hot mouth, which might have preferred his kisses to mine. "She favored someone else," I said shortly. "And I was afraid that if I married her, she would be unfaithful."

Father laughed harshly. "You could have beaten her to keep her faithful."

"Would you have beaten Mother?" I pushed my plate away, no longer hungry.

"If I'd had to." His chest swelled with pride. "She never looked at another man."

"Well, Cecily looked. And I saw." My pride would not have tolerated her feelings for him, even if he'd never looked at her. "I no longer wanted her after that."

He shook his head. "You never saw the girl but with family about. Who was she lusting for—your brother? Matthew?"

I swallowed hard and spit out the ugly truth. "You. And I could not trust you not to take what she might have offered."

The color bled from his face. I thought he had never been accused so directly and forced my body to relax so that the blow, when it came, would hurt less.

"You thought I would take your wife?"

"She was black-haired, dark-eyed. Beautiful. So was Isabel. And Lady Rose. And Bess Minstrel, for that matter." I shrugged, thinking of the oft-told Seymour family scandal—the goatish father caught with his son's wife. "It has happened in better families than ours."

## CHAPTER 34

BY THE TIME I came downstairs, the servants had cleaned up the detritus of my father's eruption, tidying away the shattered plates and carting off the chair with the broken leg to be mended by the woodwright. There remained in the air, like a whiff of sulfur, something of the hostilities of the evening before.

Terrence stood guard in the hall, watching the fire. He looked up at my approach. "What did you do?" he asked mildly. "He hasn't blown up like that in a decade."

"We were discussing past mistakes." I shrugged, hoping the stiffness in my shoulder would fade before I returned to London. For a man his age, Father had excellent aim.

"You got him to admit a mistake?" Terrence looked amazed. "No wonder he drank himself into a stupor."

After the chair caught me on the shoulder and broke on the hearth, I walked out, striding coatless down the road toward the village until I was chilled through. When I let myself in, hours later, the hall was shadowed and empty, a single candle burning on the table to guide me to bed.

"Is he well enough to come down?" I asked. "The Rowans will be here soon."

Terrence bent and picked up a minute shard of crockery. He held it between two fingers, examining it with a bemused smile.

"He's not coming," he said. "Told me to tell you to handle it yourself."

"But—" I swallowed my objections. Father would do what he would, and I would do my part and his. "Then keep him above stairs, Terrence.

I'll see the Rowans in his study." I thought how he would handle the meeting and deferred to the servant's greater experience. "Bring whatever he would normally ask for."

"Very good." He gave me a short bow. "If you don't mind, Master William—how is my nephew?"

"Your nephew?"

"Young Dennis," he said. "My sister's boy. He's still with you?"

"Yes." I had not recalled their precise relationship. "He is in Paris, working for the ambassador."

Terrence beamed. "He's a good lad. I'm sorry you and Lord Kelton see so little of each other, if only for that reason."

I took my bread and ale in the study and had been waiting but a short time when one of Terrence's underlings knocked on the door and announced, "Doctor and Mistress Rowan are here, sir."

"Show them in." I smoothed my hair and ran my palm over my cheek, wishing I had asked to be shaved that morning. Though I had no intention of telling Kit's parents that I was in love with her, I wished to make a good impression.

The door opened again, and a tall, stooped man entered, followed closely by a woman of nearly the same height. Both were dressed in plain clothes of good cut and excellent fabric, reminding me immediately of Kit and her gray governess dresses. They also shared her air of reserve. I liked them immediately.

"Doctor Rowan." I came from behind the desk. "And Mistress Rowan. Welcome. I am William Hawkins, Lord Kelton's son."

Arthur Rowan stopped short, inclining his head. "Will Lord Kelton be joining us?"

"I'm afraid not." I waited for them to sit and tipped my head to the servant to bring refreshments. "He is unwell this morning."

Rowan started. "Should I—"

"Please." I gestured for him to be seated again. "It is nothing serious."

"What is this about, Master Hawkins?" Mistress Rowan's hands were knotted together in her lap. "The note we received was very mysterious."

"I apologize." I smiled appeasingly. "The steward sent it on our behalf. He did not know to write anything else."

A maid entered with a trio of pewter cups filled with warm spiced wine and small plates of sliced gingerbread.

I waited until my guests had been served before continuing. "We wanted to speak to you about your daughter, Katherine."

Rowan pressed his lips together, drawing attention to the strong vertical lines bracketing his mouth. "Lord Kelton will find another governess," he said testily. "Katherine was needed elsewhere."

"Needed, or required?" I asked. "You came to Hawkmoor with Sir Edward Pickering. I was told that you spoke to your daughter before she was taken from the house. I need to know why."

"My daughter is none of your business." He unlatched his tight mouth and took a sip of wine.

"Why do you wish to know, Master Hawkins?" his wife asked, dabbing her lips with a napkin.

"I work for the queen's principal secretary." A slight exaggeration, but useful. "I am not in London at present, so I did not hear of Mistress Rowan's change of situation until after it had occurred. When I inquired, due to my family's involvement, I was given no explanation. My father is rightly concerned, both for your daughter and for his granddaughter, who is distressed by the loss of her friend." Beyond Mistress Rowan's shoulder, a shadow moved in the hall: Terrence, a servant, or my father? "Doctor Rowan, why did you permit your daughter to be removed from Hawkmoor?"

"That is none of your concern." His gaunt face was flushed but I could see that his quick retort was caused by fear, not anger.

I was glad, suddenly, that Father had kept to his chamber. If any ill temper remained in him after our clash last night, he would have already shouted at the doctor for his intransigence. But I was not my father.

"It is," I said quietly. "And I would help you, sir, if I but knew how. Has Sir Edward threatened you in some way?"

Rowan's mouth dropped open. His wife reached across and squeezed his hand. "I'll tell him if you won't, Arthur," she said.

He sagged in the chair, becoming somehow older as I watched. "Katherine doesn't know," he said hoarsely. "And she must not."

"You are wrong there," Mistress Rowan broke in. "Kit put herself into their hands to save you. She should know what information they possess. It's her life."

"And ours." He took another swallow of wine.

She straightened, primly brushing crumbs from her lap. "You are old, husband. So am I. Our daughter has her whole life ahead of her. She should not live it in service of our folly." Meeting my eyes, she said plainly, "The crime may belong to my husband, but the fault is mine."

"Go on, mistress." I resisted the urge to place my palms on my pounding temples. "Whatever you tell me will aid your daughter."

She took a deep breath. "You do know that Katherine is *not* our true daughter?"

"I do. She told me that you adopted her as an infant."

Another shadow in the hall, followed by a creaking floorboard.

"Not an infant," Rowan said, cutting a glance at his wife. "She was two years old when I brought her home."

That was still very young; it was unlikely that she remembered a time when these people were not her parents.

"We had been wed nearly twenty years," Mistress Rowan said. "With no children of our own." She sniffed and squeezed her eyes shut. "It was a great sorrow to me."

"To both of us." This time he reached for her hand. I liked him better for this softening.

Her chin lifted. "But you had your work. All I had was an empty house."

Chastened, he turned to face me. "My wife is correct. And yet it was my work that caused me to commit my crime." He launched into a description of his career, including his early meeting with my father. "It was while I served the Duke of Suffolk."

"What has that to do with your daughter?" His explanation had gone far afield. I tried to bring him back to the topic at hand.

"Not long after King Henry's death, the dowager queen married Thomas Seymour. She bore him a daughter and died of childbed fever almost immediately. Months later, Seymour was executed, and the wardship of the baby—Mary Seymour—was given to Suffolk's widow."

I knew this story already; Katherine Parr was a tragic figure. Twice widowed, she was being courted by Thomas Seymour when she caught the king's eye. Upon Henry's death, they had a second chance at happiness, but the dowager queen died before she could properly mother the babe it took four marriages to conceive.

"The child died, too, did she not?" There were no young Seymours about, and Katherine Brandon had remarried, living quietly in Lincolnshire with occasional visits to court.

"Ah. Well." Rowan cleared his throat, looking flummoxed. "Mistress Rowan and I were living in Bourne at the time, not far from Grimsthorpe. One day I received a summons from the duchess. I had waited upon her years before, after the birth of one of her sons. The Seymour child was sickly. Always coughing and crying, underweight, a drain on her resources. She was traveling to Cambridge to visit her sons and wanted me to see to Mary."

I began to get a sick feeling in the pit of my stomach. "And did you... see to her?"

"She was neglected," his wife burst out and he put a hand on her arm. "Not underweight but underfed, with bruises all over her sweet arms and legs."

"That is true," he said. "The duchess wanted no part of the child, for all that the late queen had been her true friend. The court was slow in paying Mary's upkeep. All her clothes were ragged and too small for her. She had not one decent cap to her name." His voice was filled with righteous anger. "The poor mite. I showed her a bit of care and demanded food for her, and she clung to me."

"He came home so distraught," Mistress Rowan said, wringing her hands. "The poor babe—that woman could have killed her."

"She is not dead?" I was afraid of their answer.

"She is not." He dropped his head into his hands. "She was improved by the time the duchess returned, but soon enough I was summoned again, and for the same reasons. I tried to tell her the child was suffering, but she would not hear me. She was readying to leave again—London this time—and told me to mend her—"

"As if she were a broken dish!" his wife cried. "That child needed more than mending."

"What did you do, Doctor Rowan?" I had my suspicions but needed him to say it. Only when I knew all could I find a way to rescue her.

"I took her," he said simply. "One of the villagers had a daughter who was dying of a wasting fever. She was of similar age. I paid the family and brought their child to Grimsthorpe, put her in Mary's bed and gave her a sleeping draught to ease her passing. I gave Mary a lighter dose of the same and carried her out in my cloak, telling the servants that the child upstairs was sleeping and not to be disturbed.

"I returned at first light, having given Mary into my wife's care, and found the child dead. I informed the steward, and a priest was called. The maids washed and dressed her. Small children don't look that different, especially when they're ill." He shook his head. "She was buried at St. John's, Spilsby, when the duchess next returned."

My head was spinning. "What did you do then?"

"I took my family south," he said, "and happened to encounter your father in St. Albans. He suggested that we take a house here in Kelton village. We've been here since."

"And the next year," Mistress Rowan said with a small smile, "the duchess's sons died of the sweat on the same day. Both of them."

I let that go, trying to wrap my mind around the fact that Kit Rowan was Mary Seymour, daughter of a queen, a child presumed dead for twenty years. Raised by my father's friend in a house in his village, and then going to work in his household. Father might not know her origins, but he was as wrapped up in her existence as the Rowans themselves.

"And Pickering suspects the truth?"

"He knows it," Rowan said. "Somehow. Perhaps one of the servants talked, though that seems strange after all these years."

Mistress Rowan sat forward. "That vile man accused Arthur of kidnapping a valuable heiress. He said when the queen was told, he would end his days in the Tower."

The duchess had been deprived all these years of the income for that heiress—though it was doubtful she would have been permitted to maintain the child, considering her Protestant faith had caused her to flee England and wander the continent until Elizabeth's accession.

"It does not matter how they know," I said. "For the moment, it serves them best that she does their bidding."

"She should have refused," Mistress Rowan whispered. "Kit loves young Jane."

Arthur Rowan sighed. The sound seemed to come from his very guts. "She would not," he said. "Always, she puts us first."

"And now it is too late for her," his wife said bitterly. "She will spend her life as a creature of these terrible men, spying on that poor woman—to protect us."

I folded my hands on the desk to hide their shaking. "I think it is commendable that she is willing to sacrifice her freedom for yours, especially without knowing the reason." Mistress Rowan began to protest, and I held up my hand. "It may take some time," I cautioned, "but I will do what I can to remove her from that unfortunate situation."

"Thank you." Her chin trembled. "She is all we have. I cannot bear her to be locked away from all of life because we were greedy for a child."

"She would not have lived long enough for them to use her," Rowan said roughly, but his eyes were moist. "I thank you, Master Hawkins, for your assistance. I do not understand, though, why you wish to help—she was not with your father's household for very long."

I could let them believe I was being a good son, defending their daughter on my father's behalf. I could tell them the high-handed behavior of the Cecil's men sickened me, even though I was one of them. Or I could tell them the truth.

"I wish to marry your daughter," I said. "I will take her without a dowry—without even a decent cap—if she will have me."

Mistress Rowan put her hands over her face. "Oh, now that is even worse," she sobbed. "She is locked away from the man she loves!"

"We have not come so far as that, mistress," I said. "I love your daughter, but her feelings for me are unknown. I will do what I can, notwithstanding. If, when we speak, do I have your permission to marry her if she accepts me?"

Rowan nodded. "It is her choice," he said solemnly. "She will tell you as much. But if you can earn her affection, you have our blessing."

Having spoken to Kit's parents and not being likely to speak again to my father, there was no reason to stay on. I gathered my few things and claimed my cloak in the hall.

Terrence lingered by the door. "If you would wait until tomorrow," he said, "I'm sure he'd be of a better mind to talk to you. He has always been bad-tempered, but these last years have been difficult. He is often in pain and will not show it."

I had noticed that: how offended he was by aging. It was more than the aches and pains of years; he had never been a respecter of elders, and the idea of becoming one must have appalled him.

"My time does not belong to him, nor even to me." I smiled to take the sting from my words. "I thank you for your help. Please remind him of his promise to speak to my cousin Matthew."

"Do not worry. I will make certain we call in on him on our way back to Yorkshire."

He handed me a packet of food and a flask of ale for the journey and stood by until my horse was brought out. I stowed my things and swung up into the saddle, looking back at the house one last time. Terrence stood in the doorway with his hand raised, and in the diamond-paned window above, my father did the same.

I saluted them both, turned my horse toward the gates, and rode away.

## CHAPTER 35

DENNIS WAS BACK WHEN I returned, sprawled in the messengers' chamber with his feet on the sill. "Saw you coming," he said. "You've been gone a long time."

"What happened with Thorpe?" I threw down my bag and manipulated my still-aching shoulder.

After a moment, he got up and began to pull clothing out of it, sniffing my worn shirts with an expression of disgust. "It was a woman," he said. "Not a queen. He enrolled himself at the university in the hopes of gaining her brother's friendship."

In other words, Thorpe was doing to someone else what Dennis had done to Thorpe. "What happened?"

"The brother liked him well enough until the sister's name was brought into it." Dennis put my packet of letters on the chest. "Then he beat him bloody and threw him in the Seine. I fished him out, took him back to Madame Mariette's, and he's gone home to England a wiser man."

That was that, then. "I'm glad you're back."

He grinned. "I'm sure you are. Your things are in a state and what you're wearing isn't any better."

"I've been on the road for a week." I grumbled but let him fetch a basin so I could strip down and wash the dirt of travel from my skin.

My mind was not so easily ordered. On the journey from England, I had kept to myself, vexed by my renewed worry over Matt and those strange moments of sympathy for my father, shattered as surely by my accusation as the dishes he'd broken. Nevertheless, he could be counted on to bring Matt to his senses; his feelings for me were separate from his responsibility to his family.

The issue of Kit was more complex. I hated that she had been taken from Hawkmoor to provide yet another pair of eyes in Mary Stuart's household, but she was safe there, so long as she did what was asked of her. And she would do what they asked, out of fear for her parents' safety.

Her care for them over herself was admirable and made me love her more. While I deplored Arthur Rowan's actions, I understood them. Now was not the time to place blame; it was Kit who was important, not the child she had been, nor the one she had replaced.

She was alone in a strange environment with heavy expectations upon her. Nothing could be done to relieve them—yet—but before I left England, I had written another letter and hired a private messenger to deliver it. "Whatever location the Scottish queen is in," I said, handing him more coin than strictly necessary. "It may be Wingfield or Chatsworth if she is not at Tutbury." I could have found out from Ned, but I did not feel secure enough in my temper to confront him and sent a message that I was returning to Paris.

The fact that she was not *entirely* alone nagged at me. Jamie Welldon, sweet writer of letters, was there to smooth her way and condole with her when things were difficult. What gains would he make in his courtship before I could even attempt to intervene? That her parents knew of my feelings was a comfort, but they were not the interfering sort. If she came to them and said she wished to marry Jamie, my name would not even enter the conversation.

I would have to find a way to visit her before her head was completely turned. Whether that visit would be sanctioned by my employer or whether I would take matters in my own hands remained to be seen. Generally, a messenger's assignment lasted a year or more; if I could pay one visit during my remaining time in Paris, then I could attempt to negotiate a return to England with a corresponding flexibility in my time.

All this was dependent upon Kit sharing even a scrap of my feelings. That she responded to my letter quickly, and with such kindness on a difficult day, gave me hope. But hope was nothing if she married Jamie Welldon.

"You going to stand there naked all day, sighing like a maiden?" Dennis's abrasive voice cut through my reverie. "Ooh," he said as I turned. "*Not* a maiden. Thinking about one?"

I threw the wet rag, and it made a satisfying slap as it struck him in the face. "Be careful," I said. "Mayhap there's more of my father in me than you realized. Next time it will be a boot."

In my absence, spring had come to Paris. The city itself was dirty and full of smells, as all cities were, but inside the walled gardens of the wealthy, the trees were in leaf, young and painfully green; flowers bloomed; people shed their heavy cloaks and ventured outdoors, albeit in high pattens to keep them clear of the mud.

The change in the weather affected me, as well, despite my continued worry for those I loved in England. When not occupied by work, I put my concern about the simmering unrest aside and went on with my explorations, going both further afield and deeper into the winding streets near the ambassador's residence.

Having just returned, I would not be sent to England again soon, but I nevertheless stockpiled gifts as if to present to the queen at New Year's. Perfumes for Margaery, Elizabeth, and Anne Darcy: muguet-de-bois, rose, and lavender. Ribbons for Jane, in all the colors of the rainbow. Small toys for the Darcy children. Books for Robin, which I intended to read before giving them to him. The queen paid a good wage and I'd had little enough opportunity to spend it before now, but a handsome leather-bound volume could be as expensive as a horse.

Dennis found a chest and I began to fill it with treasures, turning them over in the evenings and thinking of the happiness I would have in handing them over and the joy with which they would be received.

"Who are those for?" Dennis asked, handing me another book to slot into the chest.

"Who are what for?" I slid the package he was referring to beneath some other items.

"That sky-blue silk." He reached past me and pulled out the package, shaking from the wrappings a pair of sleeves that were, as he said, the color of the sky. "Pretty."

"They are a gift." At the best of times, Dennis tormented me like a brother, so I had not discussed my feelings with him. I said tentatively, "For Mistress Rowan, who was Jane's governess."

Dennis disregarded the fact that I had bought an expensive gift for my niece's governess and went straight to the meat of my words. "*Was?* Where is she now?"

"Transferred," I said, "by Ned Pickering to the household of the Scottish queen."

He made an interested sound, bending to pick up another book. "Will Mary Seton give over her place in your bed for such a young miss?"

Unlike London, where the bookshops were clustered in St. Paul's yard, in Paris there were individual shops all around the city, and I made it my business, as the spring dragged on without an excuse to return home, to visit each of them.

A tiny shop in the center, not far from Notre Dame, was filled with new books from all over. The scent of ink and leather bindings was dizzying. Another shop in the Marais, squeezed between a silversmith and a glover, was closed every time I went, though the glover, from whom I bought squirrel-lined kidskin mitts in anticipation of giving them someday to Kit, said my timing was wrong and the shop was often open in the evenings.

"The fellow keeps odd hours," he said. "But his customers come to him whenever he is open."

"Then I shall return later." Something about the shop reminded me of Robin's tales of Paris during his exile. I was determined to gain entry and find something for him.

Norris had asked me to look up one of his Protestant contacts, conveniently located in the same vicinity. Before doing so, I took myself off to a tavern and played cards with the locals, then walked the streets until the light faded. If the shop was open, I would need to hire a boat to get back to the residence after doing my other errand; only a fool would cross the city on foot at night.

The narrow street was dark but for the glow of a single lantern. The glover and silversmith had closed their shutters, but a lamp burned outside the bookshop and golden light issued through the window above its display of books.

I opened the door, expecting to hear the usual "bon soir" from the shopkeeper, but the place was silent.

It was, in its essentials, the same as the other shops I'd visited. While this one also smelled of ink and leather bindings, the scents were subtly different. Old leather, faded ink, paper softened by decades of being handled. There were books on every surface, including the floor. Prints and hand-drawn maps were tacked to the walls between shelves of dusty volumes. A chair drooped under the weight of a stack of Latin texts; a small table sagged under its burden of poetry and plays; an uneven pile tottered on the edge of the proprietor's desk, where a branched candleholder shed warm light over the room.

I took a deep breath, savoring the familiar smell of knowledge. Of potential. If only a Parisian perfumer could bottle that scent!

"Excuse me." A deep voice, coming from the back room. "I did not hear you enter. Bon soir, monsieur."

I turned to jest with the man whose inconsistent hours had prevented me from experiencing this wonderland sooner, and instead took in his dark skin and hazel eyes, his assured manner. The dawning recognition on his face.

The man before me had been as much a part of Robin Lewis as his red hair, his acerbic wit, his love of books. They had been together for more than two decades before Sebastian's death during the same plague that orphaned my niece.

And yet there he stood. Older, with rusty gray touching his hair at the temples, an unfamiliar scar marring his smooth brown forehead. But indubitably alive.

"Sebastian," I said as my mind sought the words to express my astonishment.

"Master Hawkins." He came around the desk and bowed, then offered his hand. "It is so very good to see you. What brings you to Paris?"

His words were calm, the matter-of-fact greeting of an acquaintance not seen in years but met unexpectedly in this place.

"How is it *you* are here?" I asked, finding my tongue.

"One must be somewhere," he said. "Are you looking for a particular volume?"

I turned quickly and struck the edge of the table with my hip, sending a cascade of books crashing to the floor. It was very loud in the quiet shop and the sound echoed in my head as I tried to process the impossibility that I was speaking to a dead man.

But Sebastian Black was alive. In Paris. And apparently not comprehending why I was nearly dead of surprise at the sight of him.

We knelt and picked up the books, straightening bent pages and placing them on the table.

"I'm sorry," I said. "It was the shock—"

"Yes, it's been a long time," Seb said. "How is Master Lewis? And his wife? And little Ralph?"

"Little Ralph is eight and would be the first to tell you he's a fine young man. He's got his father's hair and his mother's temperament." I studied his face. "But Robin—"

"Is he well?" he interrupted. "I have wondered why he never wrote to me, but Sir Edward assured me that he would when it was safe for him to do so."

I goggled at him. "Robin thinks you dead. He was like a ghost himself for nigh onto a year."

"Dead?" Seb repeated. "I am alive, as you can see."

"And what's this about Sir Edward?" I asked. "Pickering? What has he to do with this?"

"One moment." Seb opened the door and stepped out into the street. He closed and locked the shutters, then doused the lantern, bringing it inside and placing it carefully on the floor. Picking up the candleholder, he gestured that I should follow him.

"This, I fear, will require wine," he said.

He led me into a small chamber at the rear of the shop; there was a narrow bed with a crucifix above it on the wall, a table and two stools, a few pegs holding plain, serviceable garments. A bottle of wine stood on the table, with a cup beside it. Seb took a second one down from the shelf and filled them both before taking a seat.

"Now tell me," he said, "why is it that you think I am dead?"

"Because Robin told me so." I took a sip: a robust red. Seb had gotten his tastes from Robin, having entered his service when he was sixteen. "Margaery was also ill. He couldn't be with either of you to protect Ralph."

Seb's expression was difficult to interpret. He listened and drank, and in between folded his hands together so tightly that his knuckles showed pale. When I ran out of words, he told his story.

"I was never sick," he said. "I was out of London on an errand for Sir Edward. It was his idea to say I was ill, to give me time to go and come back."

"Go where?" How did Ned fit into all this? He'd been there for Robin during the long period of mourning, keeping him occupied at court when he couldn't bring himself to be with Margaery and their son. He had even paid for a memorial plaque in the nearby church, because the plague victims were buried in mass graves.

"To Kenwood, in Lincolnshire." He met my eyes. "Do you remember Jack Darlington?"

"I do." He was an old enemy of Robin's, a fact I'd neglected to comprehend on our journey toward the Tower. That laxity had nearly cost Robin his life.

"Sir Edward came to me that summer, during the queen's illness," he said. "I remember everyone was worried that she would die with no successor."

"She still has not named one," I put in, then shut my mouth and waited for him to continue.

"He was causing trouble again, Sir Edward told me. Making accusations that Master Lewis was involved in a Catholic plot." His mouth tightened. "As if my master would ever be that stupid. But Sir Edward had heard rumors, and he sent me, along with two of his men, to confront Darlington, to let him know that his plot would not succeed. That Master Lewis had powerful friends."

Seb passed a hand over his eyes. "To this day, I do not understand why he insisted I be there. Perhaps because of my loyalty—but the others were loyal to him, and the one who survived would have given a full report."

A chill crept over me. "What happened to the other man?"

"He died," Seb said. "Darlington was anticipating a fight. We were not." He paused, then said carefully, "I *believe* we were not. I cannot be certain, especially if what you are telling me is true."

"What happened to Darlington?" I was almost afraid to hear the answer.

"I killed him."

The world shattered around me like one of Robin's delicate Venetian goblets.

"May God forgive me," he said, "for I will not forgive myself, even though he was a man deserving of death." He rubbed the scar on his forehead. "He had several of his men with him—you remember them?"

"Yes." Darlington had a collection of unsavory fellows who had taken great delight in tormenting their unexpected guests.

"One killed Sir Edward's man almost straight away." He narrated tonelessly, as if watching the scene play out in his head. "When he fell, we realized it was a trap. Darlington went for me. He was laughing. He said he would tell everyone that Master Lewis had sent me to kill him. He said he would put me in a cage and exhibit me like a dangerous ape." Bitterness edged his voice. "I begged him not to hurt Master Lewis. He said it was either that or he would have the cage shipped to Spain, where I would be sold as a slave and live the rest of my days in chains." He stopped speaking and drained his cup. "I pulled my dagger and stabbed him."

The other man had given in, once Darlington was dead, but Ned's man had cut his throat so there would be no witnesses.

"We rode back to London," he said, "and presented ourselves to Sir Edward. He congratulated us on our work and handed his man a bag of coin. To me, he said word had reached London ahead of us that a man—a man like me—had been seen with Darlington before his murder."

"What did he suggest you do?" As far as I knew, Jack Darlington had died in the plague summer of 1563, so Ned's instruction to kill the witness had served. Why would Ned have sent such a recognizable figure to deal with Darlington? There were other black men in England, but they were not so common that he could not be traced back to Robin. Seb was lucky to have survived whatever Ned had planned.

"Leave England." He turned the empty cup in his hands but did not refill it. "He made all the arrangements himself, even purchased my passage."

"But Robin believes you to be dead." Ned's betrayal of his friend was astounding. I had been in Scotland that summer, but Margaery told me later of Robin's devastation and guilt that he had not been with Sebastian when he died. If all that suffering had been for naught, Margaery might attack Ned herself.

"That was the story Sir Edward put about. He assured me that Master Lewis knew the truth and I would be summoned home as soon as it was safe."

"Telling everyone you were dead would eliminate any possibility of you coming home," I pointed out. "Robin knew none of this, Sebastian, I swear to you. He has not been fully himself since you were lost. You must go back."

"No," Seb said, his eyes closing. "My life is here now. I do not think I could bear to see him again, knowing that my actions placed him at risk."

"He was never accused of anything," I said gently. "Ned protected him. But he also hurt him, by depriving him of you."

"Sir Edward is his closest friend." Seb picked up the bottle and refilled our cups. "If he thought it best for me to leave, it must have been in the master's best interests."

CHAPTER 36

"I saw no one," I said the next morning when Norris asked. "I saw no one."

He did not need to know that I had been shut up in the back of Seb's shop all that time. I was, I realized, peculiarly unsuited to my job. I loved the queen, but abstractly; I would trade her without question for the safety and happiness of any of the few people close to my heart.

For the next week, as I mechanically carried out my duties, part of my mind was always in the back room of Sebastian's bookshop, trying to find new ways to convince him to return to England. He clung stubbornly to his belief that Ned must have been acting in Robin's interests, even without his knowledge. Seb was good. Unlike me—or Robin, for that matter—he could not conceive that he had been torn from his life for reasons known but to one man.

"There was no threat to Robin," I said when I visited later that week. "He was concerned with Margaery's health and worried for his boy. The fact that he could have lost all of you nearly undid him."

Losing Seb did undo him, but I couldn't bring myself to tell him that our friend had been a lost soul for nearly a year, leaving his wife and child alone in Yorkshire because he could not bring himself to be with people who cared for him.

"There must have been." Seb moved smoothly between an open crate and an empty shelf that waited for the books he unpacked. "Darlington certainly acted as if there were."

"Seeing you may well have made *him* feel threatened." Darlington had hated Robin since they were young men working for Cromwell. But that was likely why Ned insisted on Seb's presence—recognizing him would push Darlington into rash action.

He looked doubtful but stopped his constant motion. "It may be as you say. But it has been seven years. What good would come of returning now?"

I wanted to shake him. "Having you return from the grave would do Robin a world of good."

"He has the mistress and his children." Seb rubbed the scar again. "I'm certain he is happy."

"Do you not miss him?"

"Every day," he said, irritation creeping into his voice. "But... we correspond, in a fashion."

"How does a dead man carry on correspondence?"

Seb ducked his head. "When I first left England, I traveled around, trying to find a place where I could bear to live. I spent some time in Amsterdam, thinking to visit someone we had met on our earlier travels, but he had recently died. I wrote to Master Lewis in the man's name, changing my hand and giving as explanation that I had taken on a secretary. We have exchanged letters these last four years about the book he is writing on the monasteries."

I remembered Robin mentioning a correspondent from Amsterdam; it made sense, considering Seb's devotion, that he would find a way to stay in touch with his master even behind a veil of anonymity.

"That is all well and good," I said, "but he needs *you*, not this made-up fellow."

"He does not need me."

"Robin has always needed you," I told him. "I do not ask you to stay in England, if it is not your wish, but pay him a visit."

Seb collapsed onto a stool and dropped his head into his hands. "I do not know the right course, Master Hawkins. I want to see him, but I do not wish to make trouble between him and Sir Edward."

I put a hand on his shoulder, feeling his tension through my fingers. "He has always known what Sir Edward is capable of. He can welcome you back without necessarily breaking that friendship."

The first part of my speech was true enough. Robin certainly understood Ned's fluid grasp of the truth and his capacity for manipulation, but I was not sure their relationship would survive the revelation of what had been done to Sebastian. Given the choice between the two men, I knew who Robin would choose.

"Do you remember Sebastian?" I asked Dennis that night. "Robin Lewis's man?"

He spread my doublet over the table, brushing energetically at the road dust that clung to the cloth. "The black fellow?"

"He is in Paris." I saw the same shock on his face that had been on mine. "He is not dead."

"How has he managed that?" Dennis held the garment close to the candle, then resumed his brushing. "I thought the plague carried him off."

"He is here by Ned Pickering's hand." I explained the whole tangled business, pausing while he disappeared to fetch the polish for my buttons and continuing as he wielded the cloth until they shone. "The question is, why?"

Dennis looked up. The light cast harsh shadows on his face, and now that I had been reminded, I could see his resemblance to Terrence. "The answer is Sir Edward Pickering is a snake who does what he pleases without anyone's by-your-leave. Sebastian likely got in the way of his influence over Master Lewis."

It was as good an explanation as any.

"I've been trying to talk him into going back," I said. "Do you think he remembers you kindly? Would he listen to you?"

"Servant to servant, you mean?" Dennis grinned. "He'll remember me. When you arrested his master, he spent most of that long ride trying to get information about you." At my startled glance, he added, "I was no more help than he would have been in my place, but I appreciated his effort."

"You didn't think to tell me?" Dennis shared every inconsequential thought in his head but kept something like that from me.

He lifted a shoulder. "You didn't need to know. You were doing well enough without my help."

"Be that as it may," I said with more patience than I felt, "I need to know these things."

"You do now." He buffed the hilt of my sword and stopped with the rag in his hand, searching for something else to shine. "Do you want me to talk to him or not?"

"If you would." I sat on the bed and removed my boots. "You can polish these, if you want occupation."

He looked down his nose. "This is *metal* polish." Picking up the boots, he headed for the door. "I'll do these and be off to bed. I'll see him tomorrow while you're with the ambassador."

"Tell me what he says," I called after him. "All of it!"

It was two days before I saw Dennis again, as the next morning I accompanied Norris to the French court and was sent out twice with messages which kept me from returning to the house. A marriage was being negotiated between the French princess, Marguerite, and Henry of Navarre, a Bourbon relation who also happened to be a Huguenot. Like the marriage negotiations for our queen—which were as ongoing as they were unlikely to succeed—they required the participation of a great many people, and the opinions of many more.

In theory, a marriage between the two families would settle the wars of religion, but few were naïve enough to believe that would ever happen. The French royal family, particularly the young king and his mother, were too invested to simply cease their agitation because a daughter of Valois might marry into the opposing faith.

Norris collected all this information for his next report to Cecil, of which I had been promised the delivery. Perhaps if Dennis were successful with Seb, we could travel together. I would not have him disembark in London; his return should not be public knowledge unless there was a reason to reveal it.

When I finally staggered in after ten at night, I was tired, stiff, and in a bad mood. Dennis took one look at me and vanished, returning with bread, cheese, and ale. I had already discarded most of my clothes and was leaning back against the pillows in my hose and shirt.

"Where is everyone?" I reached for a piece of bread. "I haven't seen Barnard and Sturgis in the better part of a week."

Dennis pulled the table up to the bedside and arranged everything within my reach. "Barnard has been recalled," he said. "And Sturgis took your place with the ambassador this afternoon. You must have passed on the road."

The news of Barnard's recall struck me hard; he had seemed completely contented in the ambassador's service, if not in his confidences the way Sturgis and I were. If my fellows left this place before me, I would never get away. I changed my opinion on Sturgis's French mistress, as she would make him less likely to wish for a permanent return to England, whereas that was all I could think of as I rode about on my duties.

"Did you speak to Sebastian?" I asked after I had eaten my fill. "What does he say?"

"Give me time to gather my thoughts." Dennis settled himself on the stool. "I went to the shop. It was closed, but I hammered on the door until he let me in."

I sighed, imagining the reaction of the glover and the other merchants. "And?"

"No." He shook his head. "Or not yet. He has a business to settle. He must find someone to run it while he is away."

That sounded promising. I wanted him to come with me, but it would be unfair to damage his livelihood simply because I wanted to spite Ned and force a reunion with Robin.

"How did you convince him?" I sank back against the pillow and rubbed my shoulder.

Shouts erupted from the street below and Dennis flew to the window, pushing it wide and thrusting half his body out. The voices—all male—increased in volume. I began to worry that the city's tenuous grip on peace had shattered on our very doorstep. Then a woman's shrill voice interceded, louder than theirs, and the quarrel faded, the men grumbling audibly as they dispersed.

"What did you want to know?" Dennis returned to the stool, filching a piece of cheese from the plate.

"How you talked him into it." I stretched forward over my legs. My low back had not appreciated two long days on horseback. Paris life was making me soft.

"I told him Master Lewis was getting old." He shrugged apologetically. "That the last time I saw him, he looked gaunt, and it would be a shame to finally go home only to visit his grave."

"Dennis!" I hadn't wanted to frighten him into cooperating.

"He's your friend," he said. "You don't look closely enough—or you're busy looking at his pretty wife. The man isn't well."

Robin had always been thin; often, when wrapped in his books, he forgot to eat. I plumbed my memory to check if Dennis's description matched what I had seen on my last visit. I couldn't be sure. But Robin was in his sixties, and unlike my father, he would not live forever.

If it got Sebastian to Winterset, I would forgive the lie.

"By the way," came Dennis's voice. He was at the window again, looking down. "There's a letter come for you."

My heart jolted on seeing it, as the paper bore my father's spiky hand. Once the seal was broken, I saw it was an outer wrapping only and another sealed letter, this one from Kit, was inside. I turned the outer sheet in my hands before opening her letter. There was no word from my father, only the passing on of a message received. It was sufficient.

Before I was able to crack the seal, the door opened and Sturgis entered. I slipped the letter under my pillow. A pleasure deferred.

"Is the ambassador with you?"

"We just got in." He dropped his clothes on the floor for his man to pick up in the morning. "Is that ale? Is there any left for me?"

In the morning, Norris called for me before I had even eaten. He was red-eyed and yawning, having stayed up all night to complete his report.

"I hope you're well rested," he said, pushing it across the desk. "This needs to get to London as quickly as possible."

The last days had been hard, but at least I hadn't been up all night condensing my thoughts into something for Cecil to read.

"Yes, sir."

The ambassador rose to his feet and stretched his arms above his head. "I'm for bed, then," he said, bending to pick up his discarded shoes. "And I pray this diabolical marriage will not haunt my dreams."

"Do you think it will come off?" The smell of food wafted in from the next room and my nose twitched. "The marriage?"

"It remains to be seen." He yawned again, showing me his back teeth. "Both sides want it until they believe it might benefit the other."

"What of the pearl of the Valois?" I was interested despite my hunger. The princess, famed for her beauty, was kept from public view after rumors of an illicit relationship with Henri of Guise. "Has she made her views known?"

"Our queen is the only royal female permitted opinions on the matter of marriage," Norris said. "Damn me, but that smells good. Come on, Hawkins, eat with me and then make ready."

Dennis packed while we ate. Once Norris was gone to his bed, I called him and we set off. The weather was fine, and the trip to Rouen was accomplished almost without my notice, for I had something else on which to focus my thoughts.

I had finally read my letter while our horses were being brought around, and Kit's words continued to swirl in my brain. I read it again standing at the rail of the merchant ship taking us across the Narrow Sea. A crisp spring breeze, tasting of salt, stirred my hair, reminding me that not all aspects of this job were unpleasant.

*Dear William,*

*How precisely should I thank you when I do not know what you have done? My father's letter, received but a few days ago, told of a mysterious meeting with you at Kelton. He did not repeat your conversation, only that you have eased his mind considerably regarding my situation.*

*My situation, at present, is tolerable. I miss Jane, and this house, for all its size and splendor, does not feel like a home. There is much shouting, but no one like your father.*

*Master James Welldon is here as a scribe for the queen. I t was good to see a familiar face. He sends his regards, and I send mine, along with the hope that we may meet when you next come to England.*

*Katherine*

Emotions warred within me: pleasure at her praise, and that she wished to see me, and a stab of fear at the mention of Jamie. The warmth of her feelings for me mattered for little when he was with her every day, performing small services or walking with her in the gardens in the evening. By the time I was with her again, he would be firm in her affections and my chance would be lost.

There must be a way to see her before I returned to France. Tucking the letter away, I turned from the rail, smiling to myself. After the interview I planned with Ned Pickering, he was not likely to object.

## CHAPTER 37

IN LONDON, I ATTEMPTED to speak to the principal secretary, only to be told that he was closeted with the queen and would remain so for several hours. I left Norris's letter with one of Cecil's assistants and went to my room to bathe and change my clothes. The inevitable summons came in the late afternoon, while I was in the gardens with Douglas Sheffield. She was full of news about her cousin and pouted when I told her I must go. I wanted to hear of Isabel's new life, but my future hinged upon this meeting with Cecil and a later conversation with Ned.

When I was at last admitted, Francis Walsingham was already there, lounging on an uncomfortable-looking chair as Cecil read to him from Norris's report.

"You sent for me, sir?" I stood in the doorway, unaccountably nervous.

"Hawkins, come in. Sit." He waved a hand. "You made good time. This news is not old yet."

I sat in a chair no more comfortable than the one occupied by Walsingham. "The roads were good," I said, "and the winds favorable."

Cecil resumed his study of the report, and the room grew uncomfortably quiet despite the open window and muted birdsong from outside. He turned over a page, nodding, then looked up. "We had some questions for you."

"Of course." They would want my opinions on the temperature of the city, perhaps, or French court gossip.

"Your father had a woman in his employ," Walsingham said. "A Mistress Katherine Rowan."

"He did." *Kit!* I heard Jane's piping voice. "She was my niece's governess and is now with the Earl of Shrewsbury's household."

Walsingham's thin fingers caressed his chin, his beard making a crisp, scratching sound. "You've been writing to her."

I tried not to show my surprise; were they watching me or her? "I have," I admitted. "I am very fond of Mistress Rowan."

"That is inconvenient," Cecil said. "But she will remain where she is, you understand." His mouth formed a smile, but there was no pleasantry in it. "For as long as we require her to be there."

Despite my feelings, I responded first to the implied threat in his words. "And how long will that be?"

Walsingham shifted in his chair. "For as long as we see fit, Hawkins. The girl understands her assignment, as it has been explained to her. She will stay without complaint, because she honors her father and does not wish him to be punished for his past deeds."

"I know what Rowan did," I told them. "But if he had not taken her, she would have died and the loss to the crown would have been the same."

Sharp laughter outside the door made us all turn our heads. Two of the young men were disputing about something. Another shout of laughter and they moved on.

"It would not," Cecil said. "He could have treated the girl and kept her alive until she was older. As it is, he has deprived the queen of a valuable ward, the daughter of her favored stepmother."

Very nearly a lost princess. Queen of my heart, serving the Countess of Shrewsbury, and intended to ingratiate herself into the affections of another queen.

"I thought you did not use female agents."

The principal secretary looked up, met my eyes briefly. There was understanding in his gaze, quickly disguised. "We do not *like* using them," he said. "Too emotional. Undependable, for the most part. But in this case, necessary."

"Why?" There had to be something I could do to get her clear of the grasp of these men. "She is not at all suitable."

A barking laugh. "Because you care for her?" Walsingham asked. "Or because she worked for your father? She's working for the crown now, and gladly."

"But why must she be the one?" I persisted. "There must be other women willing to undertake such a mission."

Walsingham sighed. "We don't need to explain our plans to you, Hawkins, but I will, because your cooperation will help this to go smoothly. We need someone in Mary Stuart's world who could not possibly be believed to be our creature." He raised an inky brow. "You are our creature, after all, even if she does not know it."

Swallowing my pride, I bowed my head and made a final request. "I will cease petitioning you," I said. "But I would visit her when I am in England, to see that she is well and to foster such a relationship as may be had under the circumstances."

"Hmm." Cecil curled his long beard around his finger and looked up at the ceiling. "You will carry a letter to Shrewsbury from me, in which I tell him she is your distant cousin. You have our permission to see her twice a year, and to continue to exchange letters."

Twice a year! It was not enough, but it would do—and might do very well. As her cousin I would be able to speak with her alone, which was a freedom unlikely to be granted to a man merely come courting.

"Thank you," I said. "That is acceptable."

"I'm glad it meets with your approval," Walsingham said drily. "But remember, the girl stays with the Scottish woman's household for as long as it suits us, not you. Of course"—his eyes brightened—"it could be no time at all, if that damned woman ruins herself with her constant intriguing."

I took that to mean that the Duke of Norfolk still contended for her hand. No doubt there were others. "She will achieve her own downfall."

"Papists." Walsingham hated Catholics even more than Cecil. "They come out of the paneling to support that woman. The saints know why, for I do not believe the French would stand with her if it came to a fight."

Nor did I. They had enough to contend with in France without supporting a distant relation, even if she was the current king's sister-in-law. His mother would never allow it.

I went from Cecil and Walsingham directly to Ned, pushing my way through clots of young men in the corridor, desperate to get to him before any of our conversation reached his ears. When I leaned in the door to his office, he had a young man backed up against the desk and was berating him quietly and with great vehemence.

"Do you have a moment?" I gazed with sympathy at the fellow, no more than twenty by the look of him, with ink-stained fingers and spots on his face. He appeared ready to cry as Ned loomed over him.

Ned paused, glancing indecisively between me and his terrified junior. "You'll know better next time or you're out," he said. "Hawkins, come in." He thumped into his seat and pushed a jug of ale across the desk. "I heard you were back."

I ignored the offered drink and sat, propping one foot on my knee. "I am, and I've been looking forward to speaking with you."

Ned filled his cup so that it sloshed over the edge and onto his embroidered cuff. "I'm glad you found me here instead of ruining my bedtime fun."

I smiled thinly. "Sorry about that," I said, not sorry at all. "That wouldn't wait, and neither will this."

The untidy room was lit only by a clutch of candles in one corner. How did he work here? Was it a better atmosphere for intimidating his underlings? He peered shortsightedly at me.

"Not again," he said. "Does your father want his governess back, or is it something else this time?"

"*I* want her back. Not for Jane, not for my father, but for me." I leaned forward so he could see my face in the gloom. "And I understand that right now she must serve the queen, but that service will end, whether with Mary Stuart's death or her escape. I want your guarantee that she will be released then."

"You have no grounds to make demands," he said, inflating with the same rage he had shown earlier. "You're a servant—a nothing—the same as she is."

"And I will continue to serve," I said. "I have no issue with serving the queen. It is Cecil and Walsingham's other interests that I object to."

Ned stared at me, his expression inscrutable. "They also serve the queen."

"And that is why I will continue with them, so long as Katherine Rowan is released."

"Into your care, I assume," he scoffed, but his hands twisted on the blotter.

"My care or her father's," I countered. "Whichever she chooses. I have already spoken to the principal secretary."

"That is not your place!" Ale spattered the papers strewn on his desk. "You speak through me."

"Today I speak for myself." I reached for the jug, poured a cup, and raised it to him. "From this day, Mistress Rowan is to be known as my cousin. I have permission to both visit and write to her. Walsingham thinks it a clever way to ease her further into Mary's graces, as she already trusts me."

Hearing of his superior's approval, Ned tipped his chair back and considered. "It's not a bad scheme," he said grudgingly. "But your family seems to believe it can make its own rules. You need to think again—"

"I have thought long and hard these last weeks," I told him. "About what I would say to you when we met."

"I'm flattered."

"You shouldn't be." Leaning forward, I placed the cup on the desk and pushed my chair back. "I encountered an old friend in Paris."

"Yes?" He turned his focus to his damp cuff, smoothing the black-bordered white lawn. "Who was that?"

"Sebastian Black." I waited, one hand on the door, for him to look up. When he did, my smile showed every bit of the loathing I felt. "He told me everything, Ned. All of it."

He started out of his chair, his eyes wide. "You don't know what you're talking about! Darlington was a threat—"

"A threat worthy of killing?" I asked. "You have the resources of the queen's government at your disposal, yet you used Sebastian. Was it worth it to separate him from our friend?"

In the golden glow of the candles, Ned was pale. His pupils were wide and black, his lips moving without sound.

"It was necessary," he said at last. "And who better to defend Robin?"

I debated resuming my seat but leaned against the door instead, to prevent him from fleeing. "Perhaps someone not so recognizable? You know how bad it was for Robin after he lost Seb. How could you?"

"It was necessary," he repeated. Something had changed in his voice. There was steel in it now: he was not ready to give up.

I didn't care.

"You will support me in this matter." I leaned into his shock. Rage flooded my veins so that my very skin tingled like the air before a storm. "My contacts with her. Her release when it is time. Whatever I ask. Or I will tell Robin what you have done, and he will never forgive you."

## CHAPTER 38

THE SCOTTISH QUEEN WAS permitted to vacate Tutbury for another Shrewsbury property for the summer. Nearby Chatsworth belonged not to the earl but to his wife, Elizabeth Talbot, having come to her at the death of her second husband. The house was reputed to be palatial in size; I assumed that both captive and captors were as comfortable as could be expected.

I also hoped that the size of the house would mean a chamber to myself rather than sharing with Jamie Welldon or another servant.

During the long days of our journey from London, I spent a lot of thought on what to do about Jamie: he would be there, in the same household, and he was in love with Kit. She was a different problem, confined to the house with not one but two lovelorn suitors.

I thought that even if she did not choose me, I would be content so long as she did not choose Jamie, but that wasn't true. Not at all.

"Dennis, I'll need a favor while we're here." We cantered the last distance toward Chatsworth. I could see it in the distance, an enormous pile of turreted golden stone, set against a backdrop of rolling hills. "Do you remember Jamie?"

"The pretty boy?" He laughed, nudging his horse ahead of mine. "When he kneels at night, do you think he prays to God or Mary Stuart?"

"You heretic!" I caught up easily. "Do what you do best and speak to the servants about him." I was uneasy asking him to investigate someone I considered a friend. "We were well acquainted in Scotland, but the situation is different now."

Dennis nodded acceptance of the task. "And why would that be?"
He could never resist asking one more question; it was what made
him so good at the jobs he was given. "Because he's in love with Mistress
Rowan, if you must know."

His laughter echoed through the vale, turning the heads of the men
gathered on the bank of the Derwent, waiting to cross. "And he's getting
in your way!"


The west front of Chatsworth was embellished with four towers and
what looked like a hundred glinting windows. We rode up the winding
road to the entrance and were swarmed by guards before we had even
reached the courtyard. Our identities proven, we were permitted to pass
through the gate and into the hands of the grooms. My things were given
over and I entered alone, Dennis following with our baggage.

I presented my royal warrant to the steward and asked to see the earl.

"He is with her ladyship at the moment, sir, if you'll take a drink in the
hall while you're waiting."

"My cousin is among the countess's ladies. I would like to speak with
her if it is possible." I wanted to explain our new relationship before
it was brought out publicly; she was quick, but gaining a new family
member might be cause for surprise.

The man eyed me curiously. "Which lady would that be, sir?"

"Katherine Rowan," I said. "Would I be able to speak to her?"

"I'll send a page," he said. "Please wait here."

I drank the excellent ale and glanced with interest around the hall.
The enormous hearth was swept clean on this bright day, but it was large
enough to roast an ox. That seemed unlikely as it was faced with beautifully carved stone and a heavy wood mantel. Vast hunting tapestries
stirred in the breeze from the wide doors, and the space was filled with
light from the many windows.

So distracted was I that I didn't hear her step until she was before me.
I leaped from my seat, nearly tumbling over as I bowed to her.

"I apologize for the state of myself," I said by way of greeting, realizing
how I must look. "We have been six days on the road."

"Master Hawkins." Kit ignored my flood of words and dropped a neat
curtsy. She no longer wore the sober garb of a governess but was instead

clad in a gown of deep amber. It set off her coloring and would look well paired with the silk sleeves tucked into my bag. "I was told that my *cousin* was in the hall."

Where was the more familiar *William* of her letters? "Mistress Rowan," I said stiffly, abandoning the name I had anticipated using. "About that." Looking around for eavesdroppers, I rapidly explained that my arrangement with Cecil required us to be known as cousins for the matter to succeed. "I thought, being in a strange place, you might like to have an occasional visitor."

She sank down, hiding her face in her hands. "Oh, William, you have no idea how much that means."

My heart rose into my throat, making speech impossible. Finally, I choked out, "Is it so bad, being here?"

"Not so bad." Her hands fell away and while I saw no tears on her face, her eyes were troubled. "But it is lonely. I loved Hawkmoor, teaching Jane and being part of Lord Kelton's household. This"—she gestured around us—"is too large to be a home, and contains far too many people to feel like a family."

"You have a friend here, do you not?" I asked, twisting the knife in my wound before anyone else could do it. "James Welldon?"

Kit's head tipped back for a moment, as if in frustration. "I do, but it is not the same." Her fingers darted out to touch my sleeve. "I am glad you are here."

The steward entered, clearing his throat to catch my attention. "He is ready for you, sir."

I rose, placing a hand on her shoulder. "I must speak with the earl," I said, "and I would like to pay my regards to Lady Mary, if it is permitted. If you would like to speak further, we could meet again later."

"I would like that very much." Her face brightened like a flower turned to the sun. "After dinner, her ladyship likes us to sit with her, but I will ask to be excused."

The responsibility of the past months had worn on George Talbot. He looked tired and not completely well. He accepted both Cecil's letter and my fabrication of a familial relationship and bade me to stay a week if I was able, to better spend time with my cousin.

"Lady Elizabeth says she is settling in," he said in the tones of a man who had no clear idea what occurred on the feminine side of the house. "But as I understand from Sir Edward Pickering, she is not here solely to wait upon my lady wife. I imagine such a situation would be a strain upon a young lady. It is good she has you to see to her."

I murmured assent, thinking no one under this roof—save Dennis, perhaps—knew that I wanted to see to her every need. She was safe in this place; so long as she kept her eyes and ears open and reported what she knew, nothing evil would befall her. And I would make certain, when we spoke later, that she understood this.

"Would it be possible to speak to the queen?" I asked. "As you remember, I was part of her household in Edinburgh. Perhaps it would divert her to see me."

He rose, shaking his head. "Divert her, please, before she drives us to distraction. Lady Elizabeth has taken to sitting with her in the afternoons. They are both keen needlewomen and it passes the time."

"My young cousin might be an appropriate addition to their endeavors," I suggested, remembering the embroidered hem of the robe she had worn that night in the garden. "She has always been skilled with a needle."

"I'll mention it." We walked together to the door. "I'll deliver you to her myself," he said. "She's got the entire top floor—might as well be keeping state, the way they permit her to live."

He did not exaggerate. Though her household had been reduced, there was no evidence of similarly reduced circumstances in the tapestry-hung chamber where Mary sat beneath her velvet cloth of estate, surrounded by her women. My eyes passed over Mary Seton; she was another problem to be dealt with before my departure.

"Your Majesty," I said quietly, after the door closed behind Talbot. "I am happy to see you in good health."

"Good health, perhaps, but not good spirits." Her voice was as low as mine. The carefree woman who had ridden through Edinburgh dressed as a young gallant was nowhere to be seen in the drawn face turned upon me. "How have you come to be in this backwater prison?"

I made my bow and approached. "I am here to pay a visit upon my cousin, Katherine, who recently joined the household as waiting woman to the Lady Elizabeth—but I am also here to pay my respects to you."

Her brows raised. "Your cousin serves our jailor's wife?"

"We go where we are bidden," I said, letting her believe what she would. "You will, I think, find her agreeable should she be so fortunate as to be in your company."

Mary Stuart crossed to the window and her women followed at a respectful distance. Her dress was as elaborate as ever—a dark rose day gown liberally trimmed with silver tinsel—but her gait was slower, as if lack of exercise had aged her. With a flick of her hand, she ordered me to join her.

"Is she sympathetique, your cousin?"

I inclined my head, looking out at the nearly empty courtyard. "She is, indeed, Your Majesty, though she—like so many of us—plays the heretic in public to save her neck. She has elderly parents for whom she worries."

"I understand." Mary smiled with a hint of her old liveliness. "You had best refer to me as Lady Mary in this house, Monsieur Hawkins. There are ears at every knothole. Lord Cecil may have spies behind the tapestries."

"Let us hope not," I murmured, though I would not have been at all surprised. "Have you been at Chatsworth long, my lady?"

"A few weeks." She turned from the uninteresting view. "It is good country for riding, if that man would only permit it."

I'd heard she was given some freedom in the more isolated houses. "He does not?"

She sank back onto her padded chair and a young, flaxen-haired woman darted forward to offer a fan. "He has allowed to me to accompany him hawking *once*."

If they had been in residence but a short time, that did not seem unreasonable; Talbot was still setting things to rights, both in his household and regarding the cares placed upon him by his royal prisoner and the queen's men.

"I do not believe he will listen to me," I said, "but I will suggest another venture, nonetheless."

Mary nodded graciously. "We would appreciate that, Monsieur Hawkins." She waved the fan unevenly. "We will rest now, Mary—"

Her women rose as one, Mary Seton and another coming to take her arms, while two more skimmed over the polished floor to open the privy chamber door.

I put my hand over my heart. "Until next time, Lady Mary," I said, and backed from the room.

Dinner was a drawn-out affair of many courses, during which I squirmed in my chair like an impatient schoolboy. Kit was seated entirely too far away down the long table. As a guest and the son of a lord, I was placed near my host, with only two men between us.

One of them, I was interested to learn, was John Lesley, the Scottish bishop of Ross and a former member of Mary's council. A Catholic bishop at his lordship's table! That would be a scrap rich enough to sate even Francis Walsingham. I bent myself to my meal and kept my ears open to their conversation, but it was conducted in low tones. To make it worse, the man's dense burr rendered his words almost unintelligible, which was frustrating as I had lived in Scotland for years and had an ear for languages besides.

The men on either side made polite conversation about the weather and the state of the roads—the same dinner conversation Englishmen had been having for centuries and would go on having until we were all dust. I commented on the number of mills along the Derwent, while they inquired about London and whether the queen had gone on progress this summer.

I answered as best I could, asked about their plans and businesses and families, their relationship with our host, and discreetly plumbed their opinions about the earl's unwilling guest. To a man, they seemed firm for Elizabeth—with the exception of Bishop Lesley, who looked down his long nose when we were introduced and never addressed another word to me.

It seemed a year before the earl rose from his seat, gesturing for the men to follow him. I made my excuses, extracting myself from the knot of those bent on drinking away the afternoon and joined the ladies, greeting Elizabeth Talbot and her women, and holding out my arm to Kit.

"My cousin promised to show me the gardens," I said, acknowledging the countess again. "I appreciate that you have permitted her to join me."

"Not at all." The Countess of Shrewsbury was another pale-skinned redhead with piercing eyes; she could have been Elizabeth Tudor's cousin. "She is at your disposal for the remainder of your visit, except for her attendance on me in the mornings and when I retire."

We murmured our thanks and stepped through the doors into the air. Chatsworth was built around a central courtyard—the lackluster view enjoyed by Mary Stuart—but the exterior doors gave way to lavish gardens with rolling wooded hills beyond.

"Where shall we go?" I could have walked in circles without noticing; the pressure of her small hand on my arm was enough.

"What about the rose garden?" She turned us in that direction, and we trod the gravel path, passing several other couples, until we reached a low stone wall, beyond which was a riot of pink and white and red blooms. "It is one of my favorite places."

"I can see why. Shall we sit?"

There were benches set at angles beneath trained arches of blossoms. I chose a seat over which drooped a multitude of pink roses. They reminded me of the ones covering The Bower, and I wondered if Kit would think so, too.

"How has it been for you?" I sat so there was space between us. "Your... situation."

"I should not have made it sound so bad." Her voice was steady. "I was distressed at leaving Jane."

My niece was a safe subject. "She misses you. As does my father."

"Do I sense the smallest rapprochement?" she asked teasingly. "I believe you and Lord Kelton have become friends."

"You are mistaken." I leaned back, appalled at the very idea. "Oh. You were joking."

She sat at ease, her straight back not touching the bench, her hands in her lap. Her skin was lightly tanned, as if she spent a good deal of time in these gardens. With whom?

"William, I think you have some made-up version of me in your head," she said with an impish smile. "You should get to know me—you might not like me nearly as much."

Or I would like her more, which was terrifying.

"Do you not mind what they ask of you?" Her serenity baffled me.

"Of course." A flicker of something in her blue eyes. "But I am a woman. My life will always belong to someone else." She smiled again. "Even a queen may lose control of her life."

"You do not object to her faith?" I asked.

She lifted her gaze to mine. "I am Catholic, William. I thought you knew."

"I did not," I said slowly. It was one more thing she had in common with Jamie. "I assumed, because of your position with my father, that you shared his beliefs."

"So long as I did not interfere with Jane's religious education, he said the state of my soul was in my own hands." She shrugged. "I attended church with the family and said my own prayers. I would not be a recusant in his home."

Recusants paid a fee to the crown to avoid attending the state church, but as their religion was discouraged, there were few other options for worship. It was a practical solution, and I liked her for it, and for not complicating my father's life.

"I'm glad you've come," she said after a moment. "I wasn't certain you would even answer my letter."

As if that had ever been an option. "I was afraid you would not answer mine."

She looked down at her hands. "I should have been brave enough to speak to you before you left that morning. The man I believed you to be would not have spoken so harshly."

"Perhaps you have your own version of me," I said. "I do not wish to be that man, but he is part of me. I'm sure Lady Rose has told you about my dealings with my father." I thought of how he had looked to me to handle the matter of her parents, and that perhaps—finally—something might be changing between us. "I should not have taken it out on you. Being angry was easier than being truthful."

It was difficult to sit with her and speak of such weighty matters, especially now that I was certain of my feelings. I sprang up as if poked with a pin and went to stand across the path. Seeing her throat, the pulse beating below the curve of her jaw, the sprinkling of freckles visible through the narrow opening of her partlet... my dreams would be filled with these details for weeks to come. It was almost too much.

"What is the truth?" Kit leaned forward, as if intending to stand, but I pinned her with my eyes. "Will you tell me that?" Her gaze shifted and she sagged. "Oh, not now!"

"Hawkins! Will!" I turned and looked past her to a familiar figure at the garden entrance. Waving his hat, Jamie Welldon sprinted down the path and skidded to a stop before us, his fair skin flushed, chest rising and falling from the effort of interrupting my long-awaited meeting. He bowed to Kit and clapped me on the back hard enough to make me stagger.

"Jamie." I tried to sound glad. "How are you?"

"I'm well." He grinned at me in apparent delight. "I saw your man in the hall. He told me where you were." Looking past me, he said, "Mistress Katherine, Lady Elizabeth has asked for you."

Her face fell. "She agreed William and I could spend the afternoon together."

As my heart leaped at her use of my name, Jamie's pleasant expression underwent a transformation. "She sends her apologies," he said, "but she is with Queen Mary, and the queen has requested your presence."

"Not the queen," I reminded him, torn between disappointment at losing Kit and pleasure that Mary had so quickly acted on my words and invited my cousin into her chambers. "Lady Mary."

Jamie straightened. "She is my queen. I will call her by no other title."

He had always worshipped Mary, but something new in his tone gave me pause; most English Catholics had disregarded the pope's bull of excommunication against Elizabeth, much less his encouragement to depose her, but Jamie was young. Young men were easily led to anger, easily driven to action. Ready pawns for a lost cause.

Ned had spoken of recalling him to London, and I would give my opinion that it was the best course; he could get himself into trouble in this place. I had enough worries with Matthew. I couldn't watch over Jamie, as well.

He folded easily onto the bench beside her. "I was so pleased to see Mistress Katherine when she arrived. I have made it my duty to see that she lacks for no small service that I can provide."

"How kind of you." It physically hurt to see him next to her. He spoke to me, but he watched Kit—Kit whom he saw every day and yet could not look away from.

"And have you requested many small services, mistress?"

Her cheeks flushed. "I have told Master Welldon repeatedly that I am well-contented and require nothing beyond correspondence with my friends." She met my eyes, as if to convince me that his enthusiasm was not her concern. "And as you can see, *William*, it is a most pleasant situation."

He looked between us. "Have I interrupted something?"

Dropping a heavy hand on his back, I shifted my weight slightly and watched as he drew away. I was not the largest of men, but I knew how to intimidate. "As I said, this is the first opportunity we have had to speak—but if Lady Mary calls, we cannot ignore her." I looked down at Kit, who observed us warily. "Perhaps we might attempt to meet again this evening?"

"Perhaps," she said, rising smoothly and shaking out her skirts. "I shall go in on my own."

Jamie jogged after her. "Is your head better, Mistress Katherine?"

"It is fine." Her voice was crisp. "Please, Master Welldon, stay and talk to William. I must attend my lady."

We watched her walk away, our conversation stilled. "What was that about her head?" I asked when he showed no sign of leaving.

"It ached." He gave me a sideways smile. "We went walking yesterday and she complained of it."

I was supposed to react to the thought of them together and so I did not. But my chest flooded with heat, and I seriously considered battering a man I had once thought of as a friend.

## Chapter 39

THERE WAS MUSIC IN the hall that evening; a page came to my chamber with an invitation. I sent him to Kit with a request that we meet there. If we could not escape, we could listen together. Before I went down, I tucked the small parcel containing her silk sleeves into my best deep green doublet and looked at my reflection in the window, straightening the small ruff at my neck.

"Not so fair as Master Welldon," came Dennis's impudent voice, "but you'll do."

"I hope so." I could not even be annoyed with him, as it was unlikely that Jamie, a member of Mary's household, would be permitted to witness the entertainment. "I hope you can find amusement for yourself while I am gone."

"I am certain I will." He bowed elaborately and opened the door. "And on you go into the night, Master Cupid. May all your arrows be true!"

People had already begun gathering in the hall, but the one whom I wished to see was nowhere to be found. I lingered near the stairs, pretending to admire the ornate carving, in the hopes that Kit would soon appear. Then I heard my name and saw Bishop Lesley bearing down on me.

"Hawkins, isn't it?" he asked, as if we had not been introduced hours earlier.

"Yes." I gritted my teeth in annoyance. He was going to make me miss her arrival with something which could have been said earlier. "May I be of assistance, your grace?"

"Talbot told me you work with the principal secretary," he said. "Is that correct?"

"It is." Feminine voices floated down; I strained to hear if hers was among them. "I am here to visit to my cousin and will likely leave at the end of the week."

The bishop looked around, as if not wishing to be seen speaking with me. "That means, I assume, that you know Sir Edward Pickering?"

Even as my impatience reached its boiling point, I could not but wonder how he knew Ned's name. "Yes, I do—ah, there she is." I nodded toward Kit, coming down the grand staircase with three other young women. "My cousin, Mistress Rowan. Lady Elizabeth introduced her to Lady Mary this afternoon."

His hooded eyes narrowed as he took her in. She wore the same amber gown she had worn earlier in the day, but the white partlet was gone and simple jewels sparkled at her neck. Her smooth hair was uncovered and had pearls woven through it.

She was so far above me in her loveliness that I could not believe my aspirations.

"Your cousin, eh?" He smiled at her as she approached. "Fine girl."

"I agree, your grace." I turned to Kit, lifting her hand to my lips. "You look very beautiful."

Her cheeks pinked but her eyes met mine frankly. "It is the very same thing I had on earlier."

"You looked very beautiful then, as well." I offered my arm. "Do you wish to listen to the music, or should we attempt another walk?"

She shook her head. "It has begun to rain. Did you not notice?"

"Why would I?" I took a deep breath. "I've thought of nothing but seeing you again."

She stopped, and the others flowed around us to find spaces near the gallery where the musicians would play. Later, there would be dancing. I yearned to partner her, to touch her hand and perhaps even her waist—but I also wished for us to be alone.

"Come," she said, leading me behind the stairs. "There is a private chamber here where we can talk. We can always join them later."

I followed eagerly but questioned whether she would get into trouble for missing the gathering.

"Lady Elizabeth was sorry to intrude on our time earlier." She paused before a door which I hastened to open. "She has given me leave to spend whatever time I wish while you are here—unless the lady calls for me again."

I shut the door behind us. The breeze of its closing caused the flames on the nearby candles to flicker and stretch tall. "Perhaps I will pay a call on the lady tomorrow morning and beg her indulgence for the remainder of my visit."

Kit edged past and took a seat on a wide padded bench by the window. "Do you know her well, William?"

"I was part of an embassy to Scotland when she returned from France," I explained. "With the exception of a few trips south, my life was there until she fled to England three years ago."

"Causing you to flee." It didn't sound like a question, and she proved it with her next words. "Or simply to return? Are you one of those men like the ones who sent me here?"

I lowered myself to the cushion beside her. "I am more like you than them," I admitted. "My work now is mostly for the ambassador in Paris. Occasionally I am asked to follow leads when threats against the queen are discovered."

"Are there many?" She picked at the edge of the cushion, separating its threads with her nails. "Threats?"

I tipped my head back, noting for the first time the light patter of rain against the glass. "More than I can count. French plots, Scottish plots, Catholic plots—" I stopped, remembering her recently proclaimed faith and not wanting her to think that I was criticizing her. Would she wish our children to be raised Catholic? "Too many plots," I finished lamely. "But I am not here to talk about the queen. Either of them, for that matter."

"Why are you here?" Her chin was lowered, her lashes dark against her blooming cheek.

There were so many things I could say: that I wanted to save her from Cecil and the rest; that I had discovered I could not live without her; that I would be content in her presence, if that was all she would grant me.

"I met your parents several months ago," I said at last. "As you have heard."

"Yes." One hand fluttered up, as if to touch me. "I was very glad to hear it—you lightened my father's burden."

My hands were clasped firmly on my knee, to keep from reaching for her. "I would that I could have lightened his burden entirely by releasing you from this scheme, but I could not make them agree."

"You tried." Her voice trembled. "That is enough."

"Are you not troubled by all this?" I asked. "You were, as you said, happy at Hawkmoor. To be pulled away with no explanation must have been very upsetting."

She twisted to look out the window and I watched her reflection in the glass. "It was to keep my parents safe," she said quietly. "That is all the explanation I need."

"Do you not wish to know why you were chosen? Why your father agreed?" Most young women would be railing against their fate, but this great disruption seemed barely to ripple the waters of her calm.

"I do not." Her voice was steady. "I have been schooled to docility, William, but it is not my nature. I would run through this great house shrieking insults like a fishwife or saddle a horse, ride into London and spit in Sir Edward Pickering's fat red face, if I dared." She punched the cushion. "Instead, I am small and meek, and no one thinks me capable of anything."

I stopped her before she assaulted the cushion again. "I know you are capable of a great many things."

She blinked away tears. "I believed my father when he said it was necessary. My esteem and affection for him would be untouched, no matter what he did."

Would she defend him so mightily if she knew she'd been stolen—that a dying child had been put in her bed while she was carried out under cover of darkness? Would she be upset to know she was the daughter of a queen and an executed traitor? Life as she knew it would never be the same. I vowed, like her father, to keep that knowledge from her. She should never know anything but peace and happiness.

"May I ask you something?"

"Of course."

Kit smoothed her skirts with nervous hands; it was the third time her emotions had broken through. "Before Master Welldon interrupted, you said being angry with me was easier than being truthful. What did you mean?"

Of all the questions she could ask, she had chosen the one that, if I were honest, would force me to tell the truth. Did I dare? Was I brave enough? I chewed my lip and wished I had something to do with my hands to disguise their shaking.

"The truth is," I said, my voice low, "I fell in love with you the first moment we spoke, and I have lived in terror ever since."

Her mouth opened, her full lower lip trembling. I thought of crushing those lips with mine and turned away, disgusted with myself. She deserved far better than my lustful imaginings.

"Why in terror?" She leaned forward, staying seated as if by force of will.

My fingers tightened on the window frame. "Because you deserve better," I said. "I knew Jamie Welldon was writing to you, and now that you were in the same household, there is nothing to keep you apart."

"Nothing," Kit said, "but the fact that I am not in love with him." At my startled expression, she went on, "And I have told him so, though he does not wish to believe it."

"Why would you not love him?" I knew little of Jamie's birth, but status would not matter to Kit, who had already turned down two acceptable men. He was young, handsome, well-spoken—far more than I was.

"Because I'm in love with you, William Hawkins." Her face broke into a merry grin, her eyes crinkling. For a moment, she reminded me of Margaery. "You great oaf."

My body left the window even as my brain attempted to process those fantastical words. Standing before her, I looked down, focusing my gaze on her skirts, which flowed smoothly over her knees and puddled on the wide plank floor.

It was not possible. My skull felt as if it had been put into one of Walsingham's torture devices, suddenly too small for the brain throbbing inside it. "You love *me*."

"Yes," she said, as if it were the simplest thing in the world to have fallen in love with the world's largest, blindest fool.

Why had she not told me sooner? I could have taken her from my father's house and saved her from all this. That was impossible, my brain

returned rationally. Even if I had known of her feelings—and had the
courage to tell her of mine—I had a job to do. I could not simply walk
away from the queen's service. Nor would Kit abandon her task, for fear
of what might befall her father. Having little filial sentiment, I would
walk away from my entire life if it meant I could have her.

"Well, that is good," I stammered, backing away again. "I am glad to
know it, but—"

"Don't you want to... touch me?" She had resumed her perfect posture, hands calmly in her lap. To an observer, she would appear relaxed, but now that I knew her better, I could feel the emotion coursing
through her veins. Feel it and recognize it as my own.

"God, yes," I said in hoarse astonishment. "But you are a lady." I
clenched my fists. "And I am a gentleman, though I do not always feel
that way in your presence."

Kit pushed up from the bench and came to stand in front of me.
"There seems a solution to that, William."

She was so close that I could feel the heat of her body. My hands raised
of their own volition, then dropped again.

"I can't."

"Well, it's not my place," she said. "Lady Rose told me such matters
should be spoken of only to convince a gentleman it was his idea after
something happened."

That sounded so much like Lady Rose that I had to laugh. "You've
spoken to her about me?"

"Many times." She cocked her head. "Would you have had me speak
to your sister? Or your father?"

"No!" Given those options, Lady Rose was the obvious choice. "But
why—"

She sighed, and it seemed to deflate her. "I don't understand everything that I feel." Her chin tilted up and she met my eyes. "Lady Rose
was very helpful in that regard."

"I'm sure she was." Going to my father's mistress for advice!

Kit placed her palms slowly and deliberately on my chest. "Not the
physical aspect," she said. "Her conversation had more to do with desire
than specifics."

"Even so." Was it possible that her hands were burning through my
shirt? I wanted to remove them—to remove my shirt, along with all her

complicated clothing—to kiss her so she would stop saying words that made me burn with shame.

"You are your father's son, she said, for good or ill." There was a glint of humor in her eyes, a reminder of my overreaction to her previous comparison. "She said that a man of passion would pass along that quality to his sons."

I was gratified by Lady Rose's faith in me, and her confidence that my performance would be adequate to Kit's needs.

"Did she have any opinion on my mother's contribution to my character?" I brought one of her hands to my lips, then the other. They were soft and smooth, and when I released them, instead of returning to my chest, they twined around my neck.

"No, but I do," she said with a shake of her head. "I believe her gentleness balances Lord Kelton's stronger qualities." One finger slowly stroked the back of my neck and I retreated so she wouldn't feel my shameful reaction. "And you have her beautiful eyes."

"You should stop," I said, my breathing ragged.

Confusion clouded *her* beautiful eyes. "Did I do something wrong?"

"No." I led her back to the bench, sitting so close that our thighs touched through layers of fabric. That was the most I could bear at the moment. "You did everything right, Katherine. Kit. Everything."

"Then why—?"

"Because it is not so easy." I cupped her cheek in my hand and leaned in, brushing her lips with mine. Her quick gasp nearly stole the breath from my lungs. I kissed her again, still lightly. Her hand came to the side of my face, mimicking my touch.

"It feels easy," she murmured, her mouth against mine. "What happens next?"

"We can continue kissing as long as you like," I said, though I was not sure how long I could restrain myself. "After that, there is touching."

Kit leaned against my chest, offering her lips until I took the invitation. I led her slowly from closed mouth to open, from open to a slow sweep of the tongue to a near frantic exploration that left us both breathless. I lost all awareness of the room around us. With my eyes closed, we were surrounded by a pulsing velvet darkness. I heard nothing but the beating of my heart and, strangely, a few plangent notes on a lute.

"Oh!" She fell back, her lips swollen but smiling. "I think I love you even more. If kissing feels like this, how good is touching?"

"Have pity," I said honestly. "If I touched you right now, I might burst into flames."

## Chapter 40

In the morning, I met Kit as arranged and we made our way to the Scottish queen's apartments. Although she had been presented to Mary the day before, I wanted to introduce her properly as my cousin and make Mary understand I would prefer to have her to myself until my departure.

Her hand on my arm sent a chill through me, and I looked down to meet her knowing smile. "Are you certain you want to spend so much time together?"

"God, yes." I was in disbelief that she wanted to be alone with me—I had hardly slept the night before thinking about my good fortune and had jumped from my bed to make ready before Dennis was even awake.

One thing slowed my feet on the stairs. *Mary Seton.*

I paused on the landing, making a show of looking out over the hall. "When you were with Lady Elizabeth yesterday, did you meet any of Lady Mary's women?"

"Five or six of them." She ticked them off on her fingers. "Another Elizabeth, Lettice, Mary, Grace. I don't remember them all. There were so many people there."

I understood her confusion. Mary might be confined but she hardly lacked companionship.

"One of her women," I began. "Mary Seton."

"The woman with the brown hair?" she asked. "She looks after Lady Mary like a mother, though they are of an age."

Pressure built in my head until I was forced to speak. "I knew Mary Seton in Scotland. Perhaps better than I knew the queen."

She turned from the view below and tilted her head to one side. Her gaze was trusting. "What are you trying to say, William?"

"That I was once involved with her." The words came out muffled as I hung my head. "Intimately involved."

I held my breath as she remained silent, finally opening my eyes to see conflict on her face.

"You were not a nun," she said slowly. "As I am not, but women have less opportunity and far less information." She tucked her hand through my arm again. "When I think of all I learned last night!"

She had learned no more than the pleasures and frustrations of kissing; we left our private chamber before the music ended, afraid of being discovered. On my part, it was also the strain of holding myself together in her presence, for even the lightest touch of her hand or lips brought me to a precipice of feeling that was frightening and unfamiliar, and yet irresistible. I could not wait to be alone with her again to suffer anew.

"You are an apt pupil," I said softly, as we presented ourselves at the doors to Mary's apartments. "Would you like to go riding after this, or take a walk by the river?"

Kit pulled a face, looking down at her pale gray dress, ornamented by the blue sleeves which I had given her before we parted. She looked positively angelic and not at all suited to riding. "I'll dress for a ride tomorrow."

Mary was again seated under her canopy, surrounded by women. Bishop Lesley was off to one side, talking with Jamie and another man. I acknowledged them with a glance and bowed low before the Scottish queen.

"Monsieur Hawkins," she said in halting English—a souvenir of her time with Francis Knollys?—and waved her hand for us to approach. "You honor us by visiting again so soon. And you bring the charming Mademoiselle Rowan."

Kit curtsied in a swirl of cloth, murmuring a greeting. "Lady Mary."

"This is my cousin of whom we spoke yesterday." I lowered my voice. "I would beg Your Majesty's indulgence with regard to how her time is spent over the next several days."

Mary sat back, her arched brows raising slightly. "For what reason, may we ask?"

I glanced at Kit for permission, then turned back to the queen to reveal my heart. "Because I would hope that someday this cousin will be my wife, and I would like to spend more time with her before I depart."

It was not how I had intended to propose, nor had I planned to reveal my innermost feelings before a chamber full of people including a former bedmate and a man in love with the woman I wished to marry, but Mary Stuart's warm brown eyes drew the truth from me as surely as a thorn was drawn from flesh.

"That is wonderful." She clapped and bounced in her chair, diverted as only a true romantic could be by the love of others. "Ladies! Bishop Lesley! Did you hear? Monsieur Hawkins is to marry the lovely Mademoiselle Rowan!" Her hands clasped. "May we be the first to offer our blessings."

Mary's announcement made me look to the corner where Jamie and the bishop had been huddled. Only the prelate remained, smiling benignly in our direction.

"Thank you, my lady." I took Kit's hand and we bowed and curtsied again. "Then you will allow me to borrow her until my departure on Sunday?"

A flick of her hand raised us up. Over the queen's shoulder, Mary Seton glared at me, spots of color burning high on her cheeks. That our relations had been curtailed, she understood; that she had been replaced was another matter entirely.

I would have to warn Kit.

After a round of congratulatory sentiments in French and English, we were able to make our withdrawal. As we skimmed down the stairs to the freedom of a perfect June morning, I said, "I hope you don't mind what I said back there."

She caught my hand. "About marrying me? I do not mind at all—so long as you ask me again properly when we are alone."

We walked down the gentle slope from Chatsworth House toward the river, our fingers touching. The air was heavy with the smell of newly shorn grass. Behind it were the rich scents of river mud and damp greenery from the thick woods on the other side. Small boats dotted the water, which reflected the cloudless blue sky. High-pitched pipits sang in the trees and skylarks soared above our heads.

It was perfect, as far from London and its dark intrigues as I could imagine.

"Shall we sit?" I asked when we reached a flat area a short distance from the bank. The rains of the night before were gone, and the lush grass was dry enough that it wouldn't mar her skirts.

She stopped, neatly lowering herself to the ground. "This should be far enough."

"What do you mean?" I sat beside her.

"We can see them coming," she said, "and perhaps you could hail a boat to carry us across before they have a chance to interrupt."

It was a shame to risk the ruination of a brilliant day, but I forced myself to say, "Mary Seton did not look pleased for us."

"And why should she?" Kit sobered. "Losing you is no doubt painful."

"What of Jamie?" I hated to even bring his name into our happiness. "He disappeared before we were even finished speaking."

She sighed, folding her hands in her lap. "Leave him to me. It was only ever one-sided. He will have to accept that."

I thought she was optimistic but did not wish to spoil the mood by saying so. Instead, I said, "Your sleeves look very well with that gown, but I have another gift for you."

"Another?" Her face lit with pleasure. "You needn't have done that, William. You are enough."

Warmth kindled in me that had nothing to do with desire. For years, I had watched people, how they were with each other, or when they were alone, trying to understand how to live my life. I had learned the most from Robin, who seemed to simultaneously take things as they came while also having prepared for every conceivable eventuality. Still, his life was not mine. When had I ever been enough? Perhaps for my mother when I was yet in swaddling bands, but I had never experienced the feeling as an adult.

"It is not as pretty." I removed a small parcel wrapped in a white linen kerchief from my doublet. "But it will keep us close."

She undid the wrapping and put it aside, turning this latest gift over in her hands and opening it. "A prayerbook?" Disappointment clouded her eyes. "You wish me to convert before we marry?"

I had purchased the book before I knew her beliefs, or that she would even consider me as a husband and hastened to explain. "Not at all. My father and mother were of different faiths, and if their union had its imperfections, they did not stem from religion." I took her hand. "Katherine, you know the work I do, and which you have been drawn into."

"Yes?" She did not see where I was heading.

"I bought the same book for myself. They are identical in every aspect." She continued to look puzzled. "I thought to teach you a simple code so we may write to each other without our words being open to all."

Kit drew away, dropping the prayerbook on the grass as if it burned her fingers. "You want me to inform on the Scottish lady."

"No!" It had crossed my mind, but she would be forced to repeat her observations to Ned; I would not ask it of her. "I meant things of a personal nature which we might not want seen by others."

"Such as?" She gazed at me skeptically.

I bridged the distance between us, whispering in her ear, "Such as the fact that I dream of you, and will have new and better dreams when I leave. Dreams of your eyes and your lips and"—I broke off, placing one finger on the embroidered linen above the square neck of her gown—"that freckle right there."

Her cheeks flamed but she didn't pull away, instead leaning forward so that my palm rested fully on her upper chest. Through the light fabric, her skin was warm. I could feel her steady heartbeat.

"And I will dream of a time when you are able to touch me as you wish." She bit her lower lip. "And I may touch you."

Desire slammed into me like a wall. I straightened and picked up the book before I threw myself over her on the grass. "Let me show you what I mean." I produced a sheet containing the cipher I had worked up and flattened it on the ground between us. It also contained a receipt for one of those invisible inks, easily made from ingredients she could obtain from the apothecary or the kitchens.

We spoke for some time, her questioning and me explaining, and then she closed the book with a snap. "I shall read it again once you are gone," she said, "and safely dispose of your instructions. But"—her eyes sparkled—"I will not *read* the book, only use it for the purpose for which it was acquired."

I fell back on my elbows, laughing with sheer pleasure as well as at her stubbornness. "I would expect nothing else."

"I am glad." She lay back on the grass and closed her eyes. "How long do you think I am meant to be here?"

A cloud passed over the sun and I swallowed the sudden lump in my throat. "I don't know. I hope not long." Reaching out, I twined my fingers with hers. "Believe me, Kit, I will do everything in my power to get you released from this damnable contract."

"How?" she asked practically. "I was chosen because of something my parents did. While they live, Sir Edward holds power over them. And me."

"Not only that." I did not wish to stain her happiness with thoughts of what Arthur Rowan had done. "You were chosen because you are of good birth and pleasing manners, and therefore a suitable companion for both Lady Elizabeth and Mary Stuart."

Her fingers twitched. "I wish I were not, then. Just good enough that you would want me."

I rolled to one side so I could look at her. "I would have you in any state." Reaching out, I touched the silken tendrils of hair that had sprung loose around her face. "But you are here because you are unimpeachable."

Dinner was another hours-long affair where we were separated by an endless length of table and far too many courses. Kit had to briefly attend Lady Elizabeth in the late afternoon but assured me she would be in the hall for that night's music.

"Perhaps we should dance this time," I suggested, though every fiber of my being wanted to hide away with her again, ignoring the music, the Talbots, and our responsibilities.

"Perhaps," she agreed. "If we spend too much time alone, I might cease to be quite so unimpeachable."

After the dancing, once we had separated and she had gone to her duties, I went up to my chamber, singing under my breath and making plans for our ride the next morning.

Dennis took one look at me and shook his head. "You're a man condemned," he said. "May I offer my best wishes?"

"Thank you." I threw myself back on the bed—slept in in by myself alone, because Chatsworth was a castle, whether or not the Talbots admitted it—and grinned at him. "I am the happiest of men."

He gestured for me to sit forward so he could remove my shoes and unfasten my canions from my trunk hose. "Don't worry, you'll be back in London soon enough and Sir Edward will cure you of that fancy."

"Don't remind me." I peeled off my nether stockings and handed them to him.

I was trying hard not to think about Ned, but before long, I would have to. Though I held Sebastian over his head like a weapon, I could never trust Ned not to find a way to betray me. He hadn't appreciated that I went to Cecil about Kit; I would have to give him something, and that something would be Jamie Welldon. He was far too attached to both my love and the Scottish queen, and neither would bring him any happiness. Since Ned had already thought of retrieving him, it would be for the best.

"Will you be needing anything else?" Dennis paused at the foot of the bed with my discarded clothes to be taken away for brushing.

"Get off with you. I'll be riding in the morning, so I won't need anything special. Are my boots polished?"

He looked at me as if I had two heads. "Your boots are always polished." There was something slightly resentful in the way he banged the door, but I ignored it, falling back against the pillow and smiling at the prayerbook on the nearby table.

There were but three days before I had to leave. After the sweetness of this time, seeing her twice a year would be an agony relieved only by the ability to communicate privately in our letters. I had been pleased at how quickly Kit picked up my cipher; it was not complex, but it was far from her normal endeavors.

Anticipation of the morning kept me wakeful. I rose from the bed and extracted my letter-writing kit from my bag. I owed Robin a letter. Perhaps it was silly, but I wanted him to know of my newfound happiness. It would reach him sooner sent on from Chatsworth.

A page appeared at the table as I broke my fast. "You are requested to come to the lady's apartments, sir," he said softly. "As soon as you are able."

"The Scottish lady?" What did Mary want now? "I will be there shortly."

I was dressed for riding, in black hose and jerkin. My boots, thanks to Dennis, shone like a horse's flank, but it was not suitable attire for an audience with a queen, imprisoned or not. For a moment, I debated changing but decided she would have to take me as I was.

When I left the table, I murmured to Kit that I would meet her in the garden as soon as I could get away.

"Should I come with you?" She pushed her chair away from the table.

Shaking my head, I said, "Whatever this is, it will go all the faster with fewer people involved." I risked a brief touching of her hand. "I will be quick."

Having seen me twice, the guards let me through without question. The presence chamber was empty but for a scattering of her women, and the privy chamber doors were firmly closed. I caught the attention of the nearest lady. "I received a summons..."

"That was from me." Mary Seton stepped from behind a tapestry. "We must speak, William."

I spared a thought for Kit and vowed to keep our conversation brief. "How are you, Mary?"

A jerk of her chestnut head drew me to the window. "I was better," she said in a strident whisper, "before you humiliated me in front of Her Majesty, flaunting your new mistress."

Her face was flushed, and there was true anger in her eyes, in addition to a surprising sadness at being superseded.

"Katherine is not my mistress," I said gently. "But she is my love. I intend to marry her before too long."

"But you love me." Mary's hands, nearly hidden by trailing black sleeves, clenched into fists.

I stared at her. "We may have comforted each other in our loneliness, Mary, but there was no love between us. You must know that."

She made a sharp sound which caused heads to turn in the chamber.

"I could have borne your child," she said, "and yet you can say this to me. I did not take you for a cruel man, William."

My flaws were many, but cruelty was not among them. I knew with certainty that Mary had been given no cause to believe I loved her, other than the sharing of my bed. And as far as the bearing of children— "We took pains to avoid that."

"But I could have." Her voice trembled, and she sounded unlike the self-assured woman I had known for nearly a decade. "I could have given you a child. You could have given me a life!"

I gripped her upper arms. "You have a life, Mary. One that you were born into, and which will not grant you release until the lady herself is released."

For a moment, I saw the sad, trapped woman behind the mask of anger and pitied her. But she wanted my pity no more than my explanations, and I had the sense to keep my mouth shut.

"Her Majesty *likes* her." Tears welled in her eyes. "She will be here, in front of me, daily. How am I supposed to bear that?"

I dropped my hands. "The same as she must. Katherine knows of our past relations," I said. "I would prefer that the situation was different, but there is little choice in the matter for any of us."

Mary tucked her chin hard, crumpling her starched ruff. "Less for some than others, William. As you well know."

I did not repeat the conversation when I joined Kit in the garden. There was no point, and I felt sufficiently bad for Mary that talking about her felt shameful. I wanted to enjoy the limited time we had left so there would be memories enough to keep us until our next meeting.


Too soon, it was time for us to part. We met very early on Sunday morning in the small chamber behind the stairs to exchange kisses and promises to write as soon as we could.

Kit was dressed for church in one of her dark gray governess dresses with a blue kirtle beneath and her blue sleeves. I made her sit in the window so I could admire her.

"I feel ridiculous." She squirmed as I stared at her. "You're not making my portrait."

"I wish I could." I was making a portrait in my mind, though—the way the shadows fell across her face, the line of her straight nose, the curve of her neck, the sweet swell of her breasts under their modest covering. "I want to be able to see every detail when I close my eyes."

"Come here." She patted the cushion, and I joined her. "Isn't it better to be close, instead of standing all the way over there?"

It was and it wasn't. Close meant I couldn't see all of her, but I could smell her perfume, count the freckles on her nose, and feel the warmth of her body and want to hold her close. Even more, I wanted to spirit her away, forgoing all our responsibilities and setting up house somewhere without anyone to interfere with our happiness.

"I want to take you from this place," I said. "I don't want to wait until they set you free."

Her eyes softened. "That is impossible. Let us deal with reality, my love."

Hard truth was tempered by her easy use of words which I found difficult.

"Reality," I said, cupping her face with one hand, "is wanting to never leave this room but knowing we have to."

"Exactly." She leaned forward, her nose touching mine. It was intimate, and strangely soothing. "And you will ride off to France and undertake all manner of adventures, while I will walk down the road to St. Peter's church and think blasphemous thoughts during the sermon."

"Blasphemous?" I questioned her word choice, hoping she was not concealing tendencies as extreme as Matthew's.

She blinked slowly. "I don't imagine they would call it anything else when a maid thinks upon her far-off marriage bed rather than the word of God."

I drew her to me then and we stayed in each other's arms until the sound of footsteps on the stairs drew us apart.

"How are you so happy?" Despite her tears at our imminent separation, Kit exuded a quiet contentment that I found alluring and baffling in equal measure.

"Because I choose to be," she said. "We can always choose how we feel, William. You have chosen, all your life, to be hurt. Whatever comes, it will land more gently if I am not miserable."

We rode away soon after. I looked over my shoulder until she was no more than a dot standing at the gates.

"For all the years you avoided being caught," Dennis said, watching me, "you have it bad."

"I did not think it could be so easy," I admitted.

He grinned. "When you loosen your grip on the reins and stop sawing at the horse's mouth, the horse knows how to run."

# PART IV
## 1571

# CHAPTER 41

THE NEVER-ENDING ROUND OF French court to ship to English court grew wearisome, and there were times when I came to myself standing aboard a vessel with no clear memory of having boarded, but time passed more quickly now that I had my visits with Kit to look forward to. In the ten months since we had declared ourselves, we had met but twice. Thankfully, no limits had been placed on our correspondence. Letters crossed the Narrow Sea more frequently than I did.

I managed an unsanctioned visit to Chatsworth in late October. Autumn storms made travel difficult, and it was easy to make excuses for a delay. Ned looked askance at my late return from a delivery but said nothing, and I believed my brief reunion had gone unnoticed. If not, it was still worth it.

Even as a boy, I had never felt young, but I was carefree—happy—in Kit's presence in a way that was unfamiliar. Our separation, the trials of being confined within the Shrewsbury household, all landed lightly upon her. She felt sorrow or inconvenience, then chose joy. It was a marvel and a mystery, and I loved her more deeply every day because of it. I went to bed aching with desire but wanted nothing more than to protect her, from the world and my own impulses, until we were wed.

That happy time was a long way off, as far as we knew. We had discussed it, at length, on paper and in person, but no plans could be made until one of us was free.

"You do not want a dowry?" she asked on that last visit, as we communed in our small private chamber, entwined before the fire. "You are certain?"

"I knew that about you before we met," I told her. "That you would not allow your parents to dower you." I squeezed her fingers. "I have plenty for us both, and I care not how we live, so long as we are together."

"Neither do I." She nestled her head against my shoulder, and I nearly stopped breathing from the sheer pleasure of it.

Dennis's mockery was as relentless as it was expected, but my relationship with Kit meant he no longer pressed me to accompany him on his evening rounds. He was a regular at several brothels and even more taverns. It made him useful in a way that I was not, for I never seemed to be in the right place at the right time, or to find the correct person. I was good at questioning those brought in, and I'd come a fair way in breaking ciphers, but despite having spent most of my life passing unnoticed, I'd lost the knack for doing it as a profession.

Perhaps I'd finally grown up; if I could see myself, certainly others could, as well.

On my next voyage to France, I traveled with Francis Walsingham. He had been appointed ambassador in Norris's place and was entrusted with the confounding tasks of counseling patience with the Huguenots and continuing marriage negotiations between Elizabeth and the Duke of Anjou, eighteen years her junior. Neither mission had a great chance of success, and I thought ruefully that Walsingham's teeth would be grinding when he composed his reports to London.

He was far more interested than Norris in the snippets of conversation brought back by Dennis and the other male servants, and acquired, as he had in London, a group of men to send into the city. For all I knew, they listened at doors and keyholes, in addition to seeking out tavern gossip; the new ambassador collected information as a spider collected other insects in its web.

As my plans for the future grew, so too had the Catholic plots around Mary Stuart. The was an uprising in the north, recklessly supported by the Duke of Norfolk. When it appeared the rising would fail, he confessed his involvement, along with his desire to marry the Scottish queen, and was sent to the Tower for his part in the debacle.

When I received word of the uprising, I was struck with fear that Matthew had been involved, but there was no way to see him without drawing more attention to his activities. I was comforted by a terse note from my father at the Minstrel's Arms, saying that my cousin had been unwell but was grateful to be recovering.

It was one more mystery to be solved.

In early spring, the name Thomas Ridolfi began to appear in both correspondence and conversation. He was an Italian banker living in London. An ardent Catholic and supporter of Mary Stuart, he promoted a marriage with Norfolk to consolidate Catholic power in England. Norfolk, released from his imprisonment, immediately began conspiring with Bishop Lesley to accomplish the match.

Because of Ridolfi, this latest plan had support from the Catholic nobility in England and on the continent. The Duke of Alba was mentioned, along with the troublesome Pope Pius. Walsingham paced and swore and sent more men out into the countryside to listen and spread rumors.

In April, as I made ready to depart for London and my spring meeting with Kit, we received word that a man named Charles Baillie had been arrested at Dover. He had in his possession incriminating messages from Ridolfi.

"He is in God's hands now," Walsingham said with a frightening smile. "And may God forgive him, because Cecil will not."

"Will this affect my situation?" I asked carefully, not wanting to sound too eager. Ever since Kit had agreed to marry me, I had continued to campaign for a return to England. My request had recently been granted, but I feared that this latest plot would keep me in Paris.

"I think not," he said. "Replacements have been chosen. There will be two, as between issues of religion and the queen's marriage, there will be even more news to convey." His black brows knit together. "Are you certain this is what you want?"

"I am." Even though I would undoubtedly be sent everywhere but Derbyshire and Yorkshire, I would be on the same island as those I loved.

Once I had seen Kit, I badly wanted to visit Winterset. Six months ago, Sebastian had disappeared. The bookshop had been sold to a Frenchman who claimed to have no idea where the previous owner had gone. Dennis got the man's servant drunk, but he had no further information. It was not until I received a letter from Robin, sent directly to the ambassador's residence, that I knew for certain.

*Thank you, my friend, for your perfect gift. It means
more than I can say.*

Would Robin confront Ned over his betrayal, or would he remain silent?

My stomach was in a clench of anticipation, and not only because I would see Kit within a fortnight. I would not visit my father without cause, but Elizabeth would know if anything had befallen Matt, and if I rode hard, I would be able to venture into Yorkshire before returning to London.

The door swung open to reveal Dennis, wearing the beatific smile of a man whose drink had been paid for by another. He produced a damp and folded sheet spattered with wax. "You've had a letter. Marie said it came an hour ago, while you were out."

"Thank you." I opened it immediately, scanned several paragraphs from Kit, and dropped it on the table. "Nothing of note," I said, even as I smiled at the sight of her hand. "After all this time, she misses Hawkmoor."

"He's not *her* family," Dennis said equably.

"True." I drew off my sodden doublet and handed it to him. "I'm going to bed," I said. "The rain has taken it out of me. If you could see that cleaned before you turn in..."

Dennis headed for the kitchen with my muddy garment over his arm and I snatched up the letter again. Sliding the latch, I pulled my chair close to the window and spread the paper on the table. A small bottle and brush were produced from a concealed drawer in my chest. Within moments of application, Kit's second letter appeared, written crosswise over the first.

*Jamie Welldon has been recalled to London. He blames you.
Perhaps I made things worse by saying that his proximity
to me caused you no worry. But he is angry in a way I have*

*not seen before.*

*The lady has been unwell with pains in her joints. I made for
her the same embrocation which helped your father, and it
seems to ease her, though she is left with a choler that
resembles Lord Kelton in its violence.*

*When will you come? I long to lie beside you in the green
fields and pretend that we are husband and wife.*

Her first secret letters were simple expressions of affection—enough
for me, certainly—but as time went on, the stresses of her life began to
creep in, and she had begun on her own to write to me about Mary. *The
lady receives many letters*, read one. *Jamie Welldon was closeted with the
Scottish bishop, and the bishop concealed a letter in his sleeve.* Once she
simply asked, *Do you ever feel unclean because of the things you see?*

Yes, my darling girl, I did.

I found oblique ways to pass on the information without crediting
her, so her value in the Talbot household would not be exaggerated. The
news of Jamie trading secrets with the Scots prelate I took to Ned myself,
who did nothing more than nod and smile, but Ned was ever one to let
a man build his own scaffold.

Now Jamie had been recalled. For what reason? Was he part of this
nest of vipers discovered by way of Ridolfi's man? Baillie had, after
sufficient persuasion, given up the names of various co-conspirators. I
knew what form of persuasion had been used; Walsingham had a similar
chamber in the cellar of the ambassador's house where men were put to
consider their choices.

Though I did not want Jamie near Kit, I prayed his name would never
come across Cecil's desk as being involved with a plot against the queen.

Putting aside her delightful comment about green fields to think
about when I was unlikely to be interrupted, I turned over in my mind
the curious information that my father had permitted her to tend him.
My sister's guess about a pain in his hip had been accurate. I knew
nothing about arthetica or the ills of an aging body, but wondered that
Mary Stuart should be so afflicted, as she was almost ten years younger
than Queen Elizabeth.

I read her letter twice more, until I had learned the words by heart, then regretfully threw it into the fire. Normal correspondence came sealed with black wax and a black ribbon and was kept in my chest, but letters sealed with any other color contained additional information and must be destroyed for fear of prying eyes. I hated losing any of her words, but taken wrongly, a clandestine correspondence could put us in the Tower. It would not matter that most of it was words of love and desire; these occasional glimpses of her life with Mary—and my failure to report them—would be damning.

"Freedom," Dennis said in my ear as the ship rolled in a late spring storm. "Puke if you must, but we're being blown toward freedom."

"I'm not the one puking." I looked pointedly at the vomit spattered on deck. "You'll need a clean shirt before we land."

The deck pitched and he clutched the rail, his face reddening with the effort of keeping his food down. When he could speak, he said, "I think I'll wait a bit, if you don't mind."

The wind was dropping, even if his stomach hadn't realized it yet. The rain had lasted but a short time. Having feared we would have to return to port or spend an extra day trapped below decks while the crew fought the storm, I was grateful for our imminent arrival at Dover.

Once we disembarked and Dennis was arranging for horses, I made my way to the building which housed the harbormaster. He was a gruff, balding fellow with the impatient movements of someone who did not appreciate being trapped behind a desk. We had encountered each other regularly these past several years, and when I knocked on the frame of his open door, he looked up, a smile splitting his wind-burned face.

"Hawkins!" He stood, offering his hand over a spread of logbooks. "Are you here to make more trouble?"

"I'm passing through," I said. "I heard about the trouble you had."

That was all it took to start him off.

"Buffoons," he muttered, rubbing his shining forehead. "Six men waiting for the fellow, and another ten to escort him back to London. What did they think he was going to do?"

"I suppose they didn't know what to expect." There was always an element of surprise in this sort of work; better to be overmanned than under. "You'll be seeing less of me from here on out."

"Posted to home, are you?" He reached behind him for a flask nestled on a shelf. "Will you have a drink to celebrate?"

"I wouldn't say no." I settled on a chair by the window overlooking the swarming harbor and accepted a small pewter cup. "It'll be good to be back."

"Had enough of the French, eh?" He tipped his head back and drank quickly. "Sneaky bastards."

I took a sip and began to cough. The liquid scorched the back of my throat, spread to my nose and seemingly into my very lungs. Eyes streaming, I asked, "What is this?"

The harbormaster smiled indulgently. "A bribe from a Swedish captain. He calls it aqua vitae."

Life-water. I sniffed, realized that I still possessed all my faculties, and took another, more careful swallow. This time the burn was controlled and filled my belly with warmth.

"It's... interesting." I put the cup to one side and shook my head when he offered more. "Not something I could drink too frequently."

"You young men are weak," he said. "I have a cup this time every day. It clarifies the mind."

My mind felt more like it had begun to liquefy. I spent several more pleasant minutes with him and then excused myself to join Dennis, waiting impatiently with the horses.

"You took long enough," he complained, stepping away from my beast so I could mount. "And what's that I smell?"

"I shared a drink with the harbormaster." Dennis would no doubt appreciate the finer qualities of life water and thereby rot his brain. "Get on your horse. We don't have all day."

## CHAPTER 42

As ALWAYS, THE SMELL of the city reached us before we saw it. I welcomed it because it meant home—for the present. When we arrived at Whitehall, I sent a message to Ned notifying him of my return and went with Dennis to our small chamber.

"Leave everything," I told him. "I would rather you picked up my letters than unpack. I'm sure Sir Edward won't let me go quickly enough to do it myself."

He sketched a salute and ducked out, leaving me to dump my bag on the bed and root through my clothes to find something appropriate for my meeting. Everything was crumpled from traveling, but I shook out a shirt, sniffed it for cleanliness, and dragged the worn one over my head. My dark blue doublet looked well enough when fastened, but all my hose were creased and sagging. I fastened the least objectionable ones and ran a hand over my hair.

It would do well enough. Likely Ned would be so offended by my presence that he wouldn't look too closely. Singing under my breath, I ran down the stairs to the hall and made my way to him.

He was not there, I soon learned. He was upriver with Cecil and the queen and would not be back until evening. "Your name, sir?"

"Hawkins," I said. "William Hawkins."

The young man looked closely at me. "I believe we have met before."

Scrutinizing him, I recognized Ned's forger. "Alleyne, isn't it?"

"Yes." He seemed pleased at being remembered. "Sir Edward has been expecting you—he asked for you even as he left this morning. I will be here working on some documents for the next several hours. Shall I send a page when he returns?"

I retreated to my chamber to read and wait for Dennis. If I'd known Ned was absent, I could have gone myself to the Minstrel's Arms, retrieved my letters, and passed the time with the family instead of sitting and waiting to no purpose. Whenever Ned was involved, inconvenience followed.

Dennis appeared before two hours had gone by, bursting into the chamber smelling of ale and bearing two letters. "You look discontented," he said, handing them over. "Better you had come with me. The music was fine, and the drink better."

"It always is." The letters were from Margaery and my father. I opened Margaery's first, wondering why she had written instead of Robin—in the normal course, she appended a note to the bottom of his page, or folded another sheet inside his—and soon discovered the sad reason.

*Robin is ill. He had a fever last year and never*
*recovered his vitality. Though he receives the best*
*care, I am fearful. He has asked for you.*
*Please come. M*

Looking up, I said to Dennis, "We must ride for Yorkshire," while simultaneously a knock sounded on the door. Outside was a boy with a note from Ned, requesting my immediate attendance upon him.

He would never permit me to go to Yorkshire, not so soon after arriving, but I would be damned if he would stop me. Perhaps Margaery was wrong, but I would not miss saying farewell to my friend for the likes of Ned Pickering, nor even Queen Elizabeth herself.

In the network of offices, only Ned's door and one other showed a light. Alleyne was nowhere to be seen, though several other young men lingered in the outer chamber.

"You took your time," Ned complained when I was shown in. "I sent for you over a week ago."

I blinked. "I left Paris a week ago. I never received your message."

"Hmm." He looked confounded. "Well, you were needed here."

His pettishness was annoying when weighed against my worry about Robin. "Well, I am here now and at your command."

He rubbed his forehead. "I didn't want you for yourself—I thought you would want to support your cousin."

"My cousin?" All thoughts of Robin disappeared. "What about Matthew?"

"You swore he was not involved with the papists." Ned looked at me evenly across the desk. "You *said* he would not risk his family."

"He would not." He had promised, and when Anne had shown concern, Father had intervened. Nothing in my last batch of letters had led me to believe otherwise.

Ned shook his head slowly, flipping through a sheaf of papers. "He has been acting as intermediary for the Catholic nobles involved with Ridolfi." He raised thick brows. "One of the men we got from questioning Baillie gave his name. We have it in writing, Hawkins. He is convicted by his own hand."

I didn't trust Ned to tell the whole truth. "Let me speak to him."

"It's a bit late." Ned sounded regretful. "Cecil's men have already spoken to him. He can't change his story now."

My blood turned to ice at the thought of gentle, pig-headed Matt in the hands of Cecil's interrogators. He had not been brought up with harsh treatment. It would shatter him.

"I would see him anyway." I kept my voice steady. "But first, if you will, Ned, I would see your proof."

"Sir Edward," he corrected, though there were no witnesses to overhear my informality. "After our long history together, you don't trust me?"

Thinking of Sebastian, I held my tongue and waited until he pushed the letters toward me. I recognized Matt's writing straightaway but soon wished I hadn't. The letters were damning, making plain his support of the pope over the queen, and offering aid to those who would help Ridolfi secure her overthrow. He had built a gallows and woven the rope before handing the whole tidy bundle to the principal secretary to do with as he wished.

What *had* he done?

"Where is my cousin?" I pushed down my growing dread. Ned didn't have to know the depth of my fear. What further service was I going to have to promise to make them release my cousin—and how long would it delay my union with Kit?

"In the Tower," he said promptly. "Where did you think we would put him?"

"That seems hasty," I said, even as my stomach threatened rebellion. "I just received your summons."

His bulky shoulders lifted. "The case for treason needed to be made before you were involved, as I thought it likely you would do something stupid, like attempt to rescue him."

"He is my cousin," I said. "Anything else would be unworthy."

Ned gathered up the incriminating letters and shoved them into a leather folio. "I never knew you were such a believer in family."

"It galls me to say it, but if my father were in one of your cells, I would intervene on his behalf."

His laughter echoed in the empty rooms. "Did my summons find you in a tavern? You must be drunk, for I know full well you'd be happy to see Kelton in irons."

His summons had not found me in a tavern, but I had the same feeling I'd had when it occurred to me to wonder who Jamie Welldon was writing to besides Kit. But how could Ned know about Harry receiving my letters? It did not bear thinking of right now, any more than Margaery's letter in my breast pocket. She and Robin would have to wait.

"You understand it's a death sentence." Ned's voice was suddenly gentle. "Tomorrow he dies."

"Then let me see him, for God's sake." I couldn't keep the pain from my voice; perhaps that was what made him relent.

Getting into the Tower was easy enough. My credentials got me through the gates, and a further word from Ned's minion got me inside, where I was obliged to surrender both sword and dagger and suffer the indignity of having hands run over my person, searching for additional weapons.

"Darcy, you said." The oldest of the three guards, a lean fellow with a pug nose, looked at me oddly. "He's... downstairs. Follow me, sir."

The steps down from the main floor were of stone, and uneven; I ran my hand along the wall, feeling the pitted surface with my fingertips. It grew light, then dark, then light again, as widely spaced torches came and went. The air became dank. It seemed I could *smell* suffering.

"He's in here," the guard said, unlocking a barred door and stepping back. "I will leave the lamp outside so you can see. Shout when you want me to return."

The door slammed, the heavy lock turning with a sound final as death. I stifled a shudder and turned away, moving to one side to allow the lantern to cast its full glow through the door. The cell contained a wooden shelf to serve as a bed and a reeking bucket in the corner. As I stood there, the darkness stirred, resolving itself into a body. He was slumped against the wall beyond the bed, wearing only a grimy shirt. His head lolled. I thought he might be unconscious.

"Matthew?" I knelt on the mucky floor without regard to my hose. "Can you hear me?"

"Will?" He raised his head and I gasped. His eye was swollen shut. Livid bruises bloomed on his exposed neck and chest. "Why...?"

"What have they done to you?" I tried to gently help him to the bed, then realized his wrist was shackled, making it impossible for him to rise.

"I do not want you here." The words emerged unevenly from split and painful lips. "Leave me."

"You are my family." I moved to take his free hand, but he flinched. His fingers were mangled, the knuckles torn and bloody. "I will be with you until the end."

Matt shook his head, his lank hair covering his eyes. "Leave me to my God. Go and be a comfort to Anne and—" He stopped, an expression of pain crossing his face at the thought of his wife and children.

"I cannot leave you alone." I touched his bare leg, which seemed less bruised than his other parts. "They mean to burn you."

"There's little else they can do." Matt shifted, not bothering to stifle a groan. "But they have no more from me than when they dragged me from my home."

It was said with grim satisfaction. I wondered what Cecil and Walsingham—and Ned—felt about his inflexibility, and thought my question was answered by the extent of his injuries.

"Are you in pain? Can I bring you anything?" What could cure such ills but death? His hands would never write another letter, nor hold a child or caress his wife. They had broken his body, but he held firm; knowing that his life was forfeit, he would give them no others.

He took a hitching breath. "I am... sustained. Please, go to Anne."

"If that is what you want." It was not what I wanted, but I wasn't the one facing the pyre. "What should I tell them?"

Matt coughed, wracking spasms that bent him double. When he straightened, wiping his lips with his wrist, I saw blood on his filthy sleeve. "Tell them I died firm in my faith. I did not recant." Another spasm. "And my last thoughts were of them."

"I will do that, cousin." There was nothing left of Matthew Darcy but a bright and stubborn flame of belief, which would be quenched soon enough. "Would you pray for me?"

Tears rimmed my eyes, spilling over as he touched his wrecked palm to my forehead and muttered a blessing.

Soon after, I called for the guard. Making my way back through the dark tunnel from the cells, I climbed a short flight to a torchlit passage, and passed through the doors of the Tower into a day so bright it seared my eyes.

How could I leave him? It wasn't that I wished to witness the burning—I had seen one before and could make a long list of things I would rather do than see another—but Matt was the companion of my boyhood, my heart's brother. He deserved my presence and whatever prayers I could offer as the flames took him.

But he did not want that; his last thoughts were of Anne and the children. She was no doubt frantic with worry, and it was to me he entrusted the responsibility of breaking the sorry news. I had to go to her, no matter how badly I wanted to see Robin.

"Breathe in, when the smoke reaches you," I told him. "You will pass out before the flames grow too high."

I'd heard several people say that and hoped they were right. It was barbaric, burning people alive. And to think I had led numberless people to that fate before my last journey with Robin...

Dennis waited in the stables. "No luck?"

"I was able to see him," I said, "but no more. The sentence will be carried out in the morning." I let my shoulders droop. "We'll not be here." He asked me to tell Mistress Darcy of his death. Then we shall ride for Winterset."

He said nothing, only gazed at me strangely.

"What?"

"Your face," he said. "Look at yourself."

I caught a glimpse of my reflection in the stable window. A smear of blood, like the imposition of ashes, marked my forehead where Matthew had blessed me.

## CHAPTER 43

WHAT WERE THE WORDS to tell a woman that her young, vital husband had been executed? If it had been a matter of his beliefs alone, he would be alive, but his zeal had caused him to conspire against the queen. That could not be overlooked. Ned's glee about the whole affair, and his delay in informing me until after Matt had been tortured—those were matters I would deal with upon my return.

But my promise meant I had to choose, yet again, to go away from the direction of my heart. I wanted nothing more than to ride for Chatsworth, lay my head on Kit's breast, and sob out the sorrow for my cousin which I could not show his wife. And I would—but not yet.

First Anne, then Robin. Margaery's letter was now two weeks old. Anything could have happened in that time. My desperate hope was that he'd made a full and complete recovery and that I would find my friend his usual taciturn self, hidden behind a stack of books, asking why I chose to interrupt his work without warning him of my arrival.

But Margaery was not one to overreact. If she was correct, I was about to lose another important piece of my life's foundation. Could I bear that, on top of Matthew?

Three days later, we crossed into Lincolnshire, and I parted ways with Dennis. "Go straight on to Winterset. Tell Robin the reason for my delay." I hoped he would be alive to hear my excuses. "Do whatever they ask of you."

"Do not worry," he said. "With Sebastian there, they are in good hands."

"I know." I looked past him to the road heading north. "I wish I could be in two places at once."

"You have the harder job," he agreed, and clapped me on the shoulder. "Are you sure you don't want me with you?"

Having him there would make my conversation with Anne Darcy no easier, but knowing he was on his way to Winterset would lighten my burden.

"No," I said, wishing he could also be in two places. "Give aid to the Lewises and wait for me there. I'll be along as soon as I am able."

Riding through the day was a guaranteed way to lame my horse and delay matters further. In the early afternoon, I paused for an hour to feed both the beast and myself, then continued on. When I turned from the dusty village road onto the narrower track leading to the Darcy house, there were several hours of daylight left.

It was pretty country, with woods on either side opening to views across green fields and distant, bluish hills. Why could Matt not have been content with this?

When the house came into sight, I slowed my horse and then stopped entirely. Despite my constant rehearsals to Dennis and my horse, my brain was now empty of words. It did not seem possible to knock on the door and say, "Your husband died for his faith. His last thoughts were of you and your children."

I would say it, though it was false. Matt's last thoughts, until the flames took his sanity, were likely of the God whom he had loved more than his life.

If I could have seen Robin first, he would have given me the right words to soften the blow, having faced the threat of a similar end not long after having married Margaery. But I would have to manage without his wisdom. I clicked my tongue, and the horse obligingly began to move, kicking up clouds of dust on the dry ground.

As I came around to the front of the house, where a miniature version of Hawkmoor's garden was laid out overlooking the valley, a small movement made me catch my breath. Anne was in the garden.

Could I do this? It was Matthew's last request, but was I truly the right person to upend her life? Nothing would be the same for her after I spoke. I frantically tried to find words—the right words—until Anne looked up, saw me, and it was too late.

"William." There was hope on her pretty face, but it fell away as I remained silent. "William?"

"Anne, I'm sorry—"

I dismounted, watching in horror as something broke inside her. She howled, sounds more befitting an animal than a human woman. Doors opened and figures rushed from the house, but by the time they reached us, Anne was on the grass, still howling, her fists filled with crushed blooms and broken stems.

"Mistress, hush!" A maid knelt beside her and tried to help her up, but Anne pulled away, sprawling again on the ground. I caught a glimpse of her face and would have rather traded places with her husband than see that kind of pain firsthand.

I squatted beside her. "I am sorry, Anne," I said. "His last thoughts were of you. He—"

She twisted away from the servant again. There was a smear of dirt across one cheek. Her eyes looked quite mad. "Don't tell me my husband's last thoughts," she snarled, reaching out to me with claw-like fingers. "He would be alive but for you. You promised to keep him safe."

I recoiled. "By the time I reached London, he had already been sentenced. There were letters, Anne, in his hand—"

An older woman, clad in widow's black, came from the house at a sedate pace. "Get up," she said, stopping beside us. "Stop this unseemly shrieking."

Anne glared at the woman. "Matthew is dead, Mother."

"We have known that would be his fate since they dragged him from the conveyance," she said, no hint of sympathy in her voice. "Go inside. You cannot look like that when you tell the children."

Anne's eyes were fiery, then her chin dropped, and she began to cry, as noisily as a child. Two maidservants, one on either side, led her back to the house.

I rose and introduced myself to her mother.

"I know who you are," she said. "I am Lady Crane. You have something of your father in you." She exhaled an impatient breath. "He also tried to help, but my daughter's husband was a misbegotten dolt."

"You are not Catholic, then?" I ignored the comparison to my father; it was neither the time nor the place.

"I am not a fool," Lady Crane said harshly. "I would prefer my daughter to have a living husband." She paused until a wide-eyed stable boy led my horse away. "Was he attainted? Will they take his property?"

"I was unable to change their decision," I said, brushing grass from my hose, "but they granted a delay of some three months so arrangements may be made."

She drew herself up, crossing her hands over the smooth surface of her bodice. It looked like armor, or the protective shell of an insect. "That will not be necessary. Anne and the children will come to me until she finds a husband."

"A husband?" I could not imagine she would accept another man, after Matt.

Lady Crane's expression told me that there was much of the world that I did not understand. "I am a widow myself, Master Hawkins, yet I have not given up hope of making another marriage. My daughter must find a man, else how will she survive? Matthew should have thought of that."

Having imparted what remaining information I had to Lady Crane—Anne would not see me again—I retraced my path in the hopes of catching up with Dennis. Not more than an hour had passed before I realized that continuing to Yorkshire was impossible. Despite my desire to see Robin, to say farewell or celebrate his recovery, I could not arrive there in the state I was in.

I came to an inn after sunset, riding into the yard and sliding off my horse in exhaustion. I drank an excessive amount of ale, sopped up with bread, before falling unconscious. In the morning, the brilliance of the day did nothing to help my blinding headache, but the pain eased when I turned west, my sights set on Derbyshire. And Kit.

It was long past dark when I arrived at the gates of Chatsworth. Light flickered in the gatehouse and faint voices could be heard. At the sound of hooves, a dozen men flowed through the doors, hands on the hilts of their swords, pikes at the ready.

"Hawkins," I called. "On the queen's business."

Two men approached, one with a naked blade, the other holding a lantern. "'Tis him," the first man shouted. "Let him through." To me, he said, "You left it late enough. If I hadn't recognized you—"

"I'd be spending the night in the village."

He shrugged. "Or bleeding into the dirt."

"Understood." This latest plot had them even more on edge. "Thank you for allowing me entry."

The hall was deserted but for servants replacing the tables cleared for dancing. The under-steward, who was supervising, glanced up in annoyance. "The earl has gone to his rest," he said. "Must you speak to him this night?"

"I do not require him at all," I admitted. "I would speak to my cousin, Mistress Rowan. There has been a sad death in the family."

The man looked at me crossly, unwilling to disturb the peace of the house on my behalf. He turned away, speaking tersely to one of the servants, then came back. "There is a chamber available," he said. "Follow Gordon upstairs. I will see that word reaches Mistress Rowan of your presence. You may see her in the morning."

I could ask for no more; it was enough that I had disrupted them with my late arrival. I nodded gratefully. "I thank you for your help. I will be glad to see Mistress Rowan whenever she is available."

It was the same small chamber I had used before. I had little with me and no servant to unpack or keep me company before I retired. I hoped I would be able to sleep.

The servant who had provided escort paused in the doorway. "Do you require anything, sir?"

"Perhaps some wine?" I asked hopefully. Wine numbed the pain. I would not inconvenience them by asking for food, although I could not remember when I had last eaten.

A different servant returned within a quarter hour, with a cup and a jug on a pewter tray. Closing the door after him, I poured the wine, then stripped off my clothes. Dropping back on the bed in my shirt, I brought the brimming cup to my lips and said a quick prayer for my cousin.

I had learned, in the days and nights it took to reach Matt's widow, that sufficient drink could make me sleep, but nothing took away the guilt. I should have tried harder. I should have made him understand the dangers of what he was doing. My father, according to the second letter Dennis had retrieved from the tavern, had sent him on a month-long mission to inquire about some property on his behalf, but the damage had been done before his departure.

My cousin was dead. Anne was a widow and their children fatherless because of me. There should have been a way to save him.

As the jug emptied, memories began to overtake recrimination. I thought of young Matt, and how we had ridden together across the moors, pretending to fly; his love of dancing; his inability to hold his drink without giggling. I had teased him about it, and he'd only laughed harder.

A small noise in the corridor drew my attention from the past. Stealthy footsteps paused outside my door. I drew the dagger from beneath my pillow, the fuddling influence of the wine draining quickly away as I registered the threat.

The latch lifted. I put one foot on the floor and eased forward, ready to throw myself on the intruder.

"William?"

The blade dropped and I sprang forward, nearly tearing the door off its hinges to see Kit in the corridor, a cresset light cupped in one hand. Her hair was braided, and she wore the same embroidered silk robe I remembered from that night at Hawkmoor.

"What are you doing here?"

She slipped through the door, batting it shut with her hip, and set the light down on the table. "I was awakened with a message that you were here to see me."

"They told me you would not see me until morning," I said blankly. She looked like every dream I'd ever had or hoped to have.

"Perhaps that would be wise," she said, "but I am not wise where you are concerned." She put her hands on my shoulders and kissed me lightly on the lips. "Why have you come? Has something happened?"

I gestured for her to sit, then remembered my embarrassing lack of clothing and snatched up the bed cover. "It is no good news," I said slowly, wrapping it around my hips.

"I thought not, if you arrived this late." She patted the bed. "Sit by me, William. I do not mind."

How much more improper could it be, after all—we were already alone in my chamber in a state of undress. Only my instincts as a gentleman preserved her, and she knew it.

"It is Matthew," I began. Shame rushed up from my chest, clogging my throat so the words could barely be uttered. "He is dead."

"Oh, William." Her hand fluttered toward me, then returned to her lap. "I am so sorry. How did it happen?"

I hung my head and told her everything—Anne's letter, Ned's taunts, Matthew's unspeakable appearance in the cell. That image would be burned into my mind for the rest of my life.

"I could not save him." Tears ran down my cheeks and I swiped them away like a boy. "He died because of me."

This time she did touch me, taking my hands firm in hers.

"He was set on his path," she said, with a quiver in her voice. "You could not have stopped him, any more than you could have prevented yourself from coming to me when you were in distress." Her pale eyes welled with tears, but her expression was steady. "We all do what we must. Matthew put his faith above his family. You put your pain above your safety."

I raised her hands to my lips and kissed her fingers. "And what have you done, Katherine Rowan?"

She slid her hands from mine, touching my face with one and placing the other on my thigh, with no more than the sturdy brown coverlet to separate my flesh from hers.

"I am here, with you," she said, "at the risk of my reputation and my place in this house, because I cannot imagine being apart any longer. Every time you leave, I feel as if I have lost you forever. You are as necessary to me as air. I cannot see you hurt without wanting to make it better."

Warmth bloomed in my belly, and I discovered that I could feel desire even as my heart was broken and bleeding. "You should return to your chamber before you are missed," I murmured, gesturing toward the jug. "I have drunk deep this night to dull my pain, but what I feel for you cannot be pacified with wine. I am afraid what will happen if you stay here."

She rose in a rustle of silk, but instead of going to the door, she tipped the last of the wine into the empty cup. Holding my gaze, she lifted it and drank until the wine was gone. "Now we are even," she said, licking her lips. "And you will have to force me from this chamber if you want me to leave. I will cause such a disturbance that the guards will hear."

"Kit..."

Coming back to the bed, she sat not beside me but on my lap. It was impossible that she did not feel my reaction. One hand threaded into my hair, and she rubbed her face against my beard. "I am your home, William. That is why you have come to me."

Her words cut through the fog of grief and lust, and I buried my face in the sweet curve of her neck and kissed her. My tears continued to flow, and I tasted their salt on her skin even as I tasted her. When my lips brushed the hollow of her throat above the ribbon tie of her nightdress, she put her hand on the back of my head and pressed me close.

The ribbon opened and the deep gathers of linen parted at my touch, sliding back over her shoulders. Her silk robe had already fallen away without my notice. Her breasts in the flickering light were small and perfect, tipped in rosy pink. I lowered my head to one, then the other. Her breath quickened and her heart pounded beneath my cheek.

"You are beautiful," I said hoarsely, unable to lift my head and look at her. "So beautiful."

She shrugged so that the gown pooled around her hips. "I am yours, William. You know that."

I could have her if I dared. I forced myself to put some space between us, but all that did was bring her breasts into the light. I wanted to take the sweet points of her nipples into my mouth and suck them until she cried out with pleasure.

"And I am yours." I brought her hand to my heart. "But it is not fair for me to console myself with your body. I shall find somewhere else to sleep."

"You will not." She slid her hand inside the neck of my shirt and across my chest. It seemed that each individual hair registered her touch. "It must be ungentlemanly to make a woman feel this way and leave her unsatisfied."

All I could think of was satisfying her every desire, but she could not know that. Nor could she understand, I thought, the risks of intimacy. I peeled her hands away and reached for my scattered clothing. "I bid you good night. It is not what I want either, dearest, but it is for the best."

"I don't believe you." Kit stood smoothly and her gown dropped to the floor. In the candlelight she was made of gold. Her honey braid hid one delectable breast while the other invited my touch. My eyes wandered lower, over the smooth planes of her stomach, the curve of her hip, the shadowed triangle of darker hair.

"Kit."

She kicked the gown aside and came to me, winding her arms around my neck. I turned to bar the door before sweeping her up and placing her on the bed, where I proceeded to break every vow I'd made to myself in order to make her happy.

## CHAPTER 44

I WAS AT THE edge of the world, looking out at the gray-blue sea. The shattered hulk of Whitby rose stark against the fading sky, letting me know that Winterset was close. Riding all day in a blur of weariness and shame, shot through with threads of joy like the gold in a fine fabric, I had not noticed how far I had come. I paused to look up at the abbey's sad remains, wondering again why Robin chose to live so close; the monasteries and their destruction were a part of his past which he regretted to this day. It was something we had never discussed.

As I rode slowly along the uneven cliff road, I understood one reason: the unimpeded view of the North Sea. Robin had been a traveler, in both body and mind; what better place to spend his days once he was able to escape the rigors of court life. Perhaps rather than asking why he chose to live at Winterset, I should ask his advice on getting free of the court's web.

When I left Kit, she had pressed close, her voice a hot whisper in my ear. "When will we be able to live together, and do this all the time?"

I had no answer to her question. My moment of weakness had taken us to a place from which there was no turning back. While I felt shame at my loss of control, I did not regret what had happened.

She had been wonderful. Artless and passionate yet laughing once with the sheer pleasure of our coupling. Demanding everything of me—though I deprived her, spilling on the sheet to decrease the risk of her catching a child. I seemed to fit perfectly inside her.

We lay all night in each other's arms, talking quietly about what we would do—and how often we would do it—if we were free to follow our hearts. In the morning, it hurt to leave, but she was the one to insist, telling me I needed to see Robin.

Before we parted, curiosity overwhelmed me and I asked, "Have you ever given them information?"

"What choice have I?" Brightening, she added, "But I see very little that would interest anyone."

I was not so sure of that. "Who do you report to? Is it someone in the household?"

"I'm not certain," she said, after a pause. "I don't think so."

"Do you not know?"

Kit shook her head. "I've never seen his face. I find a message under my pillow telling me where to meet him—generally it's the chapel and he is behind a screen. I enter, he tells me to speak, and I tell him what I know—the lady's aches and pains, her worries for her son, her fears that her French relations will cast her off."

"You've never tried to see his face?"

"No." She considered me gravely. "I am not so curious as you. I wish the matter was done with. Until then, I will do what I must to protect my parents."

I passed through the gate to Winterset, surprised when no one greeted me. There was a movement at the window of Robin's library, then the front door opened. Sebastian stood inside, one hand resting on the smooth wooden door. His expression was solemn. "Master Hawkins," he said. "You've come."

Jumping down, I dropped my reins. The beast wouldn't go far before someone took him away. "Am I in time?"

He chewed his lower lip. "We took the master to the church two days past."

The brightness faded from the day—this, too, on top of Matt? Was I to lose all those on whom I relied? Then I thought of one who would suffer more from Robin's death than I ever could.

"Margaery?"

Seb stepped back into the shadowy hall. "I will take you to her."

Margaery looked like an ivory chess piece, brittle and very controlled. It was strange seeing her high color defeated by sorrow. Other than that, her grief was visible only in a new depth in her eyes and the lavender shadows beneath them. For the first time, I saw the faint lines on her face, etched by the happy life they had shared.

"Thank you for coming," she said. "He would be glad you're here."

"I wish I had been able to say goodbye." My voice was rough; the death of this man—prisoner, mentor, friend—was difficult to compass.

She smiled faintly. "He would not want you riding cross country on his account."

I dropped my head into my hands. "I will never live that down, will I?"

"Not with me." She put her hand on my bowed head for a long moment. "But I am grateful for your presence. Robin considered you a good friend, and so do I."

Of all the thoughts that had come upon me as I rode toward Whitby, what spilled from my lips was something else entirely, brought on perhaps by my conversation with Lady Crane. "It is perhaps too soon to ask, but at some point, no doubt you will think of remarriage."

Margaery sat down across from me in a crisp rustle of black skirts. "Robin told me you would do this," she said. "He said you would feel it your duty. I didn't think you could be so stupid." Her lips trembled, and I thought she would weep, but instead she burst into laughter. "Oh, Will, has no one ever told you not to propose to a widow before her husband is cold?"

"You said once that you could love me." Why had I spent so many years yearning for a woman who trampled my feelings without thinking twice? "I just thought…"

Margaery wiped her eyes, her shoulders shaking. "He also told me you're in love with that girl you're protecting, so you please do not fall on your sword on my account."

"I fall on no sword," I said, hearing in my voice the stiffness she found so amusing. "And Katherine would understand."

"You *are* an idiot," she said fondly. "You're as bad as Robin. He had no father, and you have the wrong one."

"I thought to offer my protection." I had always felt at home at Winterset, and I had loved Margaery—pointlessly—for years. Her claim was older, but my heart was set on Kit, especially after what had happened between us. But could I marry either of them with my heart and mind at odds? They both deserved better.

"Don't be ridiculous. We would make each other very unhappy." She busied herself with fetching wine, tactfully giving me time to collect my thoughts. "Robin left me very comfortably off," she said when she returned. "The bulk of the money was mine, anyway, because of Winterset and my property in France." She slid one of his ornate Venetian glasses in front of me, filled to the brim with deep ruby liquid. "I am—as I once told him I would be—a widow of some means. I intend to keep those means safe and direct my energies toward raising my children and making Winterset worthy of my son's inheritance."

"That is... admirable." The wine filled my senses, its complex flavor taking away the sting of her rejection. "But you are still young. Which is why I thought—"

Laughter again, and this time I joined in.

"Young enough," she conceded, "and there are aspects of marriage I will miss sorely. But I would not trade my independence and the memory of a man like none other for bed sport and contentment with someone whose heart lies elsewhere."

"What will you do?" She had always been too vivid for me. And Kit would *not* have understood. Coming straight from her bed to ask another woman for her hand in marriage was an act no young woman would accept.

"Raise my children." A shrug. "Manage the estate until Ralph is old enough to inherit. It is enough."

In the modest hall, ornamented with a bright painted hanging and the litter of a family of active children, we shared a quiet supper. Ralph and Margaret were red-eyed but calm, while young Sebastian, too small to comprehend his loss, had gone up with his nurse before I had arrived. Seb sat between Ralph and his sister, chivvying them whenever their smiles faltered.

"Will he stay on?" I asked Margaery, my voice low.

Her eyes raised from her plate. "Robin asked him to, and having sold the bookshop, he has nowhere else to go." A small flicker of animation. "He will marry my maid, Alice, as soon as the period of mourning is over. She was so happy to see him alive that she slapped his face."

It had never occurred to me that Ned's perfidy did more than deprive Robin of Seb's presence, that Seb himself had lost a life potentially far beyond that of companion to the master of Winterset.

"As sorry as I am not to have reached you in time, I am glad he was able to be with Robin." If I had convinced him to come back sooner, they would have had more time together. "Was it a long illness?"

"Long enough." She tore off a piece of bread and chewed slowly. "He was ill last year—I wrote you about it, yes?"

A servant came around the table with two jugs, filling our cups with either wine or ale. "Was it plague?"

Margaery shook her head. "An ordinary fever. But it lingered and weakened him." She dabbed her eyes with a napkin. "Sebastian was better medicine than anything the physician concocted. He was bound to the house these last months, but his spirits were high—they traded stories of everything that had occurred since they were last together and drank too much wine and laughed like boys."

She told me of Robin's uncharacteristic tears when Seb arrived one bright morning, and of Ralph summoning the memory of his old friend Sebby, which caused the entire household to weep. "They had six months," she said. "It was the best gift you could have given him." Her delicate hand clasped my wrist. "He said to thank you for making him come home."

"He was uncertain if he should return. Did he tell you that?"

"Damn Ned." Her tone was violent. She had never been fond of him and discovering that he had been behind the falsehood of Sebastian's death only deepened her dislike. "I should not say that. He will be damned, but not by me."

Ralph's ears had pricked up at his mother's anger, and Seb stood, ushering the children out of the room. A servant immediately came in to clear our plates.

"Your man told me of the reason for your delay," she said. "I am sorry about your cousin."

"Thank you." I did not mention my other stop. Despite my need to see Robin, it had been more imperative to bathe in Kit's healing presence. He would have understood. "I did not believe he would have risked himself that way."

Her mouth quirked. "Robin once told me pragmatism would never win out over the saving of souls."

She sounded so like him. Hot tears flooded my eyes, and I blinked them back. "I will miss him," I said. "By God, I will miss him."

"So shall we all." She squeezed her eyes shut and exhaled hard, bringing herself under control. "And now, tell me about your Katherine. I want to hear about the woman who has finally been able to lay claim to you."

"Later." I did not wish to speak of Kit to Margaery. Our union was too new, and Margaery too brusque. In retrospect, my hasty proposal was the height of stupidity. "What of Robin's book? Did he finish it?"

Robin had been working on his history ever since leaving court. Few wanted to think of the bad old days of King Henry and even fewer would admit to having sympathy for the displaced monks and nuns, but the book was a private expiation of guilt, written for no one else.

"Not completely." She shrugged, more interested in my love life than the work to which her husband had dedicated his last years. "Sebastian will finish it. He knows Robin's mind."

"Does it not matter to you?"

"Honestly," she said, getting up and going to the open window, "I wish it was never begun. That book took him from us." She shook her head, then straightened her cap. "But he needed to complete it for his own sake, so in that regard I am glad he was able to come so close before he left us."

I nodded, then voiced another thought which had occurred on the journey. "Did he leave anything..."

She looked at me with the same patient gaze she bestowed upon her children. "You do not need any final words, Will. He was not your father, for all that you would have preferred it. Be content in knowing that he cared and give him his peace. He has earned it, God knows."

Sebastian took me the next morning to visit Robin's grave. He was buried in St. Mary's Church in Whitby, with Margaery's family. The church, now Protestant, was stark and plain on the inside, its once glorious windows replaced with clear glass, and nary a gold candlestick in sight. I knelt and said a prayer for my friend, that whatever iteration of God he was meeting would receive him kindly and grant him rest. In the transept, a simple slab of white marble was set into the wall beside the Preston memorial. It bore nothing other than his name, Robert Gideon Lewis, and a short Latin text.

"Omnis ardentior amatur propriae uxoris adulter est," I read aloud, and laughed despite my sorrow. *Excessive affection in marriage is a sin worse than adultery.*

"He insisted on it," Seb said at my shoulder. "He said it would make the mistress smile each time she saw it."

It was difficult to think of a world without Robin Lewis holding down his odd corner. Younger than my father, he was old enough to have sired me, and many were the times I'd wished he had. I also could not let go of the fact that I had been too late to say farewell. It was selfish; he had his wife, his children, his work to think of... but still, I did not know how I would ride away from this place without some final word of comfort.

"You will miss him," Seb said as we rode back to the house.

"I will." More than I could have imagined, given our rocky origins. "But I am glad you were here."

His expression was sober. "I am glad you made me come. It was difficult to believe Sir Edward would do such a thing."

I had wondered about that—not Ned's ability to deceive and betray, but Robin's reaction on learning of it. "What did he say when you told him?"

Seb reined his horse, and we stopped on the cliff road, looking out over the water, smooth as gray silk on this summer day.

"It hurt him," he said. "I could tell, although he hid it and then refused to speak further of it. He said the important thing was that I was alive and at Winterset, and that I could help him finish his book."

Those were the important things, but Ned should not be permitted to get away with his actions and I said as much. "I just do not know at this point how to do anything about it."

"His time will come," Seb said placidly. "As every man discovers."

"What of his book?" I asked. "Mistress Lewis said you were able to help him."

"It is almost complete. I have his notes to finish it."

"Could I see them?" I did not know why it was so important. There would be nothing for me there, no letter of farewell scrawled in the margins. Robin never scrawled.

"If you wish." Seb gazed toward the horizon. "He spoke of you often, you know."

"I didn't." The words emerged strangled; my throat was tight with emotion.

"The master did not care for many people." He smiled briefly. "But you, you were one. He spoke often about your conversations, the books you'd read, the places you'd visited."

Those memories were painful now, but there would come a time when I would look back at the hours I had spent in his library, drinking and talking about books, and be grateful for what we had shared.

"You were there at our beginning," I said. "Would you have thought we would have come to such a place?"

"I would not." He grinned, the same joyous flashing of teeth he gave to the maid Alice. "You grew up, and he was a part of your raising." Sighing, he added, "I know not if I should tell you this, because I believe the mistress has already said her piece, but he wanted you to turn your eyes from her and Winterset and learn to live your life. To stop giving importance to other voices, even his."

I closed my eyes. It was not a letter, but I could hear his dry voice behind Seb's and would be content with that. Whether I would have the strength to follow his direction remained to be seen.

## Chapter 45

I SPENT SEVERAL MORE days at Winterset, putting aside my worries about Ned to enjoy Robin's family. Ralph and Margaret were bright and energetic children. The boy and I spent afternoons at the butts, and in the evenings, we listened as Margaret played on her lute. She was gifted but did not have the passion of Bess and Tom Minstrel. That was for the best; let the girl have her pleasures, which she could then pass along to her children.

Mornings were spent on horseback with Margaery. I was awkward in her presence, but that was nothing new. She ignored my discomfort and chattered or was silent, depending on her mood, and eventually I relaxed enough to keep up my side of the conversation.

"Robin and I rode as often as we could," she said, not waiting for the groom to hand her onto the horse. "Until his leg made it too painful. Then we broke our fast together and I rode alone and came back and told him about what I saw." At my sideways look, she elaborated. "The first roses or seeing a deer in profile with the morning sun behind him. Once a gant nested up at the tower and came diving at Artemis when we got too close."

"A gant?" I swung into the saddle and set off beside her, grateful that she had given up wearing those scandalous breeches.

"Some sort of white sea fowl," she said. "Its wingspan was enormous."

We rode toward the tower, but no giant bird swooped down to drive us off. Men worked in the nearby fields, and the hills beyond the house were dotted with the sheep which were Winterset's chief source of income.

"Do you want me to tell Ned about Robin?" Our horses scrambled up the last steep grade to the crumbling tower, stones scattering under their hooves. "Or do you want to write to him yourself?"

"I would send him straight to the devil, were I able." Margaery wheeled Artemis around so she could look back at the estate. "Tell him or not, as you like, only do not mention that Seb is here."

Would I tell Ned of Robin's death? Perhaps not right away. My friend would understand if I held the news until a time when he perhaps needed to be brought low.

"He knows I discovered the truth of what he did to Sebastian," I told her. "But his presence here will remain a secret."

"Good." She gave me one of her merry smiles. "He and Alice deserve some happiness."

"What about you?" My horse lowered his head to crop grass as we lingered on the hilltop. "Will you be happy?"

Her smile this time was tighter, a closer match to what I saw in her eyes. "I will be fine. If not now, then soon. I have had time to become accustomed to the idea of being without him. He made me ready." She changed the subject abruptly, as she was wont to do. "What about you? Will you marry your girl and be happy?"

"That is my intention." Margaery's sharp edges made me yearn for sweet, uncomplicated Kit. She was, as she said, my home. "Once we are extricated from Cecil's plots and plans."

"That is a very ambitious goal," she said. "I wish you well of it."


Margaery watched as Alice and Sebastian readied the table for the morning meal. Alice wore a broad smile, and she kept brushing against him unnecessarily. His teeth flashed and once I heard him laugh.

"You are certain you don't wish to eat first?" Margaery's hand was on the door; she was clearly eager to be away. Riding was her escape and I thought that perhaps she was ready for me to leave, so she could be alone to cry or scream or whatever she needed to do without anyone seeing.

"If I make an early start, I will reach Hawkmoor by dark." The cook had assembled a packet of meat, bread, and cheese and a flagon of ale which Dennis had already taken to the stable to load onto our horses.

If Father had not already learned of Matt's death, it was better that he heard about it from me. He would want to look out for Anne and the children; despite her mother's promise to take them in, his eyes on their future wellbeing would not go amiss. Also, observing both Anne's and Margaery's situations, I had come to understand that, should something happen to me, Kit was spectacularly unprotected. Although I did not wish to, I would have to ask his indulgence in that regard, as well.

"He is not so bad, Will." Something twisted in my stomach at her tone. I remembered the time she had traveled with us to Nell's wedding, responding to him in the way that women always had. It hurt even more than usual because I was so in love with her at the time.

"He is not *your* father." How many times had I been told that Lord Kelton was not so bad, or that his many admirable qualities should excuse his shortcomings? "Tell the children I'm sorry that I missed them."

Margaery kissed me on both cheeks. "There's the Will Hawkins I know best. Proud to a fault and stiff-necked for good measure." She softened. "Ralph will miss you."

Putting on my hat, I took a final glance around their happy house. "I enjoyed my time with him," I told her. "I am back in England now for good, so I will visit when I can."

"You are always welcome." She walked me out to the small courtyard, where three saddled horses awaited. The groom handed her up and she sat quietly, while Artemis took small, nervous steps, showing the impatience her rider was too well-mannered to display.

I mounted and turned to Dennis. "Have you loaded everything?"

"Of course." His gaze slid toward the house, where the children's nurse stood in an open upstairs window. She blew him a kiss and he mimed catching it and pressing it to his heart. "Now let us be off before Susan tries to come along."

"God be with you both," Margaery said. "Bring your girl to visit if you are able." She smiled wickedly. "And convey my regards to your father."

Artemis bounded forward, cantering through the back gate and up the slope toward the tower. I watched her go, understanding that the true period of her mourning had just begun. She had been right to refuse my proposal. Where would she find a better man than Robin?

The long June twilight had turned to violet shadows when we finally drew close to my father's house. I had considered pausing at The Bower and availing myself of Lady Rose's open-hearted hospitality, but the fear of Dennis's mockery made me ride stolidly on, and I prepared myself to face his vitriol and the inevitable upset stomach and headache which would ensue.

The wide front door opened before I could approach, with Terrence coming out to greet me. "I'll see to it that your chamber is freshened immediately," he said. "Lord Kelton is in his study if you wish to pay your respects"—he met my eyes briefly—"or you could take a glass of wine in the hall, if you prefer."

"Wine first, and then I'll see him."

The entry was a welcoming space, with wide mullioned windows and walls of buff-painted plaster with a simple repeating design in brown and blue. Lines and lozenges danced up the walls to where the beams took over, and those beams had diamonds of yellow painted upon them. One wall bore a small hanging which had been my mother's choice: a garden scene with a maiden and a unicorn. I had seen similar hangings in France and wondered how it had come to Hawkmoor, and why my father had let it remain after her death.

The trek inland from the coast had felt endless and my body ached from the hours in the saddle. I rolled my shoulders, trying to ease the stiffness in my back; my hips were so tight that I almost wished for my father's stick. When a servant appeared with a glass of wine on a tray, I threw it back like it was the harbormaster's aqua vitae.

I loosened my collar and ran a finger inside the neck of my shirt, wishing I had time to wash before seeing him. Father was a stickler for appearances, but he also was a stickler for proprieties, which meant that he must be greeted before anything else. Knocking lightly at the study door, I waited for his faint bark of admittance and let myself in.

"Good evening."

He was seated at his desk, one leg propped upon a stool, a glass and jug within easy reach.

"The prodigal returns," he said. "Again."

Despite the lateness of the hour and his solitary state, he was fully dressed in breeches, doublet, and a light wool robe in the rich tawny color he had always favored. By this time of year, his face was generally tanned from being outdoors; his pallor showed me, more than words, that he kept close to home.

"I come with sorry news." There was no point in delaying it. Sitting without permission, I said, "Matt is dead. Executed."

He jerked back, his brows drawing together in a remarkably threatening aspect. "The damned fool."

"I was able to see him—"

"Terrence!" he bellowed, silencing me with a raised hand. When the steward skidded through the door, he said, "More wine. And something for my son. He appears to have not had time to refresh himself."

"Yes, Lord Kelton." He backed quickly out.

"I wanted to tell you first," I began to explain, but he waved away my excuse. "As I said, I was able to see him, but he'd already been condemned when I reached London."

Father shook his head, his eyes closed. "What exactly... did he do?"

I explained what I knew of Ridolfi, his man who had been arrested at Dover, the different strands of the conspiracy, that it would again enmesh the Duke of Norfolk, and how Matt had been caught in—nay, willingly walked into—the web.

The wine arrived, along with a loaf of manchet and a pale golden cheese studded with almonds. I filled our glasses and cut a sliver of cheese.

"They had proof, I suppose." He took a healthy gulp. "Cecil and the rest?"

"Letters," I confirmed. "In his hand."

"Damned fool boy," he said again. "Have you told Anne?"

"She was most distraught." A ridiculous understatement, but I could not bear to detail her wild grief—so different from Margaery's control—nor the blame she had leveled at me. I ran my finger inside my collar again.

"That's because she married a dolt. What will become of her?"

That was what I wondered, and what I could not forgive Mattthew for not considering before throwing himself into a lost cause.

"She has some time to plan," I said, "but her mother, Lady Crane, has said she will take Anne and the children to live with her until she marries again."

"That is the way of things, William." Father rubbed his temples. "She is handsome enough, and her children are young. It will not be difficult to find a man, even with her husband's attainder."

Outside the window, Dennis was speaking cheerfully to a pretty maidservant; her company must have made a change from Susan, the Lewises' amorous nursery maid.

"Will she wish to marry again?" I asked. "She loved Matt very well."

"You have met Lady Crane. Would you wish to stay with her?" He gestured toward the door. "Go, William, and clean yourself. You smell like a stable."

I tipped back my glass, savoring every drop of his wine. "I thought you liked stables, sir."

"I like a clean stable." He dragged the plate to his side of the desk and proceeded to eat my food. "You reek like a livery that's not been mucked out in a week." Glancing up, a slab of cheese on the point of his blade, he added, "I would have you accompany me to The Bower in the morning. Lady Rose was very fond of Matthew."

CHAPTER 46

FATHER WAS DRESSED FOR riding in sturdy, dark clothes. My surprise must have shown on my face. He snapped, "Is something wrong?"

"No, sir." I hastily rearranged my features. "I thought we would take the coach."

"Tired from yesterday?" he asked with disdain. "I didn't know I raised such a delicate son."

"You had little part in my upbringing." I reached for the ale cup even before I sat. "I believe that was relegated to Mother, a series of governesses, and Uncle Henry."

His eyes narrowed. "Then I suppose I'm fortunate you did not turn out to be as stupid as Henry's son. No chance of you getting executed?"

"Not as yet." I ate steadily, already regretting my choices. I wanted to see Lady Rose, but not in his company—and not the two of them together. That was something I had avoided since I learned the truth of their relationship. "No chance of you becoming a different person at this late date?"

"My life is not yours to judge." His face wore its usual glower.

"I would not dream of doing so," I said drily, but his words jarred; for a moment, he had sounded like someone else. "Did you hear, Robin Lewis has died."

His brows raised. "He angered enough people in his span."

Though he would never compass the idea, he had also made people love him. "He died in his bed," I offered. "He had that comfort."

"I have every intention of dying in my bed," he said with a laugh. "Preferably not alone, and not for many years."

From his mouth to the ears of the inexplicably humored God who caused me to partner with the man I hated most; if my luck held, he would reach his centenary.

The short ride to The Bower passed without conversation. It was the perfect season to be there—as we descended the slope, the smell of roses reached us before we saw them. I dismounted and turned away as a boy came for the horses. His mood was foul enough without having me witness him require assistance from the groom.

Much like the scent of her flowers, Lady Rose's steely-sweet voice reached us before she came into view. "Two of my favorite gentlemen!" she exclaimed, coming from the garden with her hands outstretched. "William! It has been too long."

I kissed her on both cheeks and moved into the hall, unable to turn my eyes from their private greeting.

"Rose." She leaned against him, standing on her toes, as he kissed not her cheek but her mouth. It was strangely touching that their attraction had not faded in all these years. I pushed that thought away as they separated.

"Shall we sit in the gardens?" she asked. "It is too beautiful to be indoors, even in a house such as mine."

"Why did we bother to come inside?" Father grumbled, offering his arm.

"You complain like a child." She slapped him away while looking at him adoringly. "You know I am at my prettiest when surrounded by flowers."

He said something too low for me to catch, and her cheeks turned pink.

"Perhaps I should remain behind," I suggested. "Would you two prefer to be alone?"

"Oh, do be quiet, William." His voice had an edge like a blade.

Lady Rose's sprawling pleasure garden occupied one entire side of the house. Benches were scattered beneath arbors drooping under their burden of roses, and a seating area of pale packed gravel awaited our presence. My father pulled out a chair for her, then dragged his chair so they were side by side.

"What brings you to Yorkshire?" The sun shone on her face and, were it not for her silvery hair, she would have appeared no older than Kit.

"Nothing good," my father said. "It is sad news, my petal. My nephew, Matthew Darcy, is dead."

Her hands flew to her face, which assumed an expression of grieved shock. "Oh, not Matthew. How did it happen?"

Although my father said he wanted me there when he told Lady Rose, he sat back, holding her hand, and let me explain the whole sad business. It was no less painful to tell it again, to watch her eyes well and tears spill onto her soft cheeks.

Though I had been raised in the Darcy house after the age of ten, Matt had frequently come with me to spend the summers in Yorkshire, where he was drawn as surely to The Bower as we all were. Lady Rose petted and spoiled him as she did me and my sisters. I envied his treatment; wasn't it enough that he had loving parents and siblings? He did not need her extra care as I did.

She was sobbing now, a fragment of lacy fabric held to her eyes. "It is too terrible," she said from behind it. "What will his wife do?"

"Marry again," my father began.

This time I cut him off. "I asked Father if he would look out for them, so that Anne is not forced too soon into an arrangement which might not be beneficial for her and the children."

Lady Rose's eyes brightened. "That is exactly right, William. Nick, you must invite them to stay. The children can go into the schoolroom with Jane, and Anne can stay with me until she is stronger."

It was exactly what I would have suggested, had he been open to suggestion. Coming from his mistress, he could not argue, and spread his gnarled hands in defeat.

"I will write to Lady Crane this day," he assured her. "Having the Darcy children will be a good excuse to get Jane back from Liz."

"Why is she there?" I had not expected to see my niece last night, due to the late hour, but I'd felt her absence this morning. Father had not been conversational enough to ask, and I had assumed that I would see her when we returned.

"I haven't found a suitable governess since Mistress Katherine was taken from us."

"Darling girl," Lady Rose said. "I wonder how she is?"

I let a moment go by, listening to the birds, thinking of that day two years past when Kit and I had ridden with Jane to visit her.

"I have seen her recently." Taking a deep breath, inhaling bravery along with the scent of roses, I added, "She has agreed to marry me."

Lady Rose recovered first, launching from her seat to embrace me. "You brilliant boy," she said. "May you be very happy. Remind me to send you home with one of my jewels for her—a sapphire, I think, to match her eyes. When is the wedding?"

"That would be the question." My father remained seated, looking steadily at me. "Will they permit her to marry? And if so, will they permit her to marry you?"

"It is complicated," I admitted. "Not whether they will allow us to marry, but when. She must stay at her current place for a while yet, though I will try, when I return to London, to make them release her."

Father spiked his fingers through his hair. "What about you?" he asked. "Will they release you, or will you marry her and spend all your time away from home?"

The smile I turned on him was his own. "I have seen happy marriages where the husband is almost never at home," I said evenly. "Although I shall endeavor to do better than the example you set for me."

"Damned puppy!" He subsided when Lady Rose caught his arm.

"Don't shout at him," she said soothingly. "Let him have his happiness. You have had yours."

He turned dark eyes upon her and said, "My happiness is ongoing, petal."

There was only so much I could bear to watch. I stood abruptly. "Would you like me to fetch Jane?"

"Are we making you uncomfortable?" He leaned closer, so their shoulders touched. "I'll send word to Liz. If you're gracing us with your presence, she may wish to see you." His smile widened. "Though I'm not sure why."

"Don't be like that." Lady Rose caressed his cheek. "William is not you—"

"Thank God!" We spoke together.

"And just the same, you are not William. I have room for more than one man in my life. Now"—she raised her brows—"are you staying long enough to eat dinner, or do you intend to take your squabbles back over the hill?"

In the end, we ate with her and rode back to Hawkmoor in the late afternoon. Full of excellent food and wine, I felt more charitable toward my father, and hoped his feelings were similar, as I had one more favor to ask. "I'm glad you have decided to write to Lady Crane," I said. "Anne and the children need someone to look after them."

"You managed that nicely." He cut a glance my way. "Rose loves having someone to mother."

"It is a shame she had no children." I had worshipped her only slightly less than my own mother.

"She had *my* children," he said, "if at secondhand. The best of both. She sent you home when you grew tiresome."

No doubt we had. Perhaps girls were easier—but then I thought of Jane, playing dress-up with Lady Rose's jewels, and how exhausted she had been. One of those jewels, a sapphire pendant surrounded with pearls, was tucked into the interior pocket of my doublet, a wedding gift for Kit.

"I know my presence has disrupted your peace," I said, "but could I beg one further indulgence before I leave?"

"What is it?" He slowed his horse and looked at me. "Do you have more strays you want me to take in?"

"Yes, actually." I met his eyes, feeling his equal for the first time. "Since you plan to live forever, should something happen to me, would you take care of Katherine? Her family would be unable to adequately protect her."

"What do you think of me?" he asked roughly. "I care for the girl as if she were my own. If you fail to live up to your responsibilities, I will take her in." He paused. "And if you are leaving tomorrow, I have a stop for you to make on your way back to London."

What would a few days more matter at this point? Ned would be so furious at my disappearance that the extra time might serve to soften him. "As you wish," I said. "What is the errand?"

We clattered into the stable yard, and I jumped down, going without thinking to hold his horse's head. Father eased down from the saddle, grunting with pain as his feet hit the stones. "You heard I sent Matt to look at a property?" he asked. "Give the horse over, William, you are not a groom."

"Yes, sir, I heard." It had been a delaying tactic that failed, but I appreciated his attempt.

"I'd planned to send Terrence this week down to supervise some improvements." He paused inside the door, one hand going to his hip. "I need someone to accompany him south."

Terrence needed no supervision, having been at my father's side for over forty years. But I would leave the uneasy stillness of our familial waters unruffled.

"Then I will ride with him, and gladly."

# CHAPTER 47

DURING THE RIDE TO Hertfordshire, I felt like I'd inadvertently fallen in with a band of traveling players. Dennis and Terrence proved they were related by alternately bickering and singing, with momentary pauses at mealtimes to pursue tavern maids. Terrence, being my father's age, was less energetic than his nephew, and often kept me company while Dennis was off with his conquest.

"The boy will wear himself out," he said with an understanding smile. We sat on a bench outside the inn, having another cup of ale, while Dennis helped the maid clear the table in the hope of future favors. "His father was the same. If no woman was to hand, he'd start eyeing knotholes in the stable walls."

"An easy way to unman yourself." I stretched, resting my head against the rough wall. "I'd be surprised if my father has not done the same."

Terrence gave me a sideways glance. "Lord Kelton is particular about his women," he said. "And he has always had a more than ample selection."

I wasn't sure his carnality was better or worse for being discriminating. "Does he still…" I began. "With Lady Rose?"

"I shouldn't speak out of turn." Looking around for Dennis, he lowered his voice and spoke rapidly. "Yes, he goes over once a week, in the morning—on his horse, because he doesn't want to be seen as *old*, even though it pains him, and he needs that hip for the work he's about to undertake. He rides home again at nightfall." His lips curled into a delighted smile. "And for the next several days, his disposition is greatly improved, despite his pain."

Lady Rose had that effect; I was not immune, though I was thirty years her junior.

"What do you know of this errand he's sent us on?" Dennis ventured out the door and I raised my cup as a signal that he should bring more ale. "It's in Hertfordshire, this property?"

"Perhaps ten miles east of Kelton," Terrence confirmed. "Called Aldwych Priory, though it's nothing of the sort nowadays."

Another monastic property. What would Robin have to say about that? "Was it a gift from the king, like Kelton?"

"No, he bought it himself, at the same time he bought Wyncombe Hall for your brother."

Harry had lived at Wyncombe with his family off and on for a decade, yet I'd never heard mention of Aldwych before. Of course, I avoided contact with most of my family and tried not to listen when my father spoke; that could explain it.

"How did you become entrusted with the task?" Dennis jogged over with the ale, and we paused while he refilled our cups. "I did not think he liked to be separated from you."

"As you say, he trusts me." Terrence shrugged. "He used to send me to carry out various jobs, but as he's gotten older, he needs someone with him."

The ale was smooth and mellow, the exact opposite of the feelings engendered by any discussion of my father.

"You make him sound like a toothless ancient. First, he should not ride, and now he needs a constant companion."

"You do not know everything, Master William," he chided, becoming in a blink the stern servant of my childhood, whom I could never trust not to tell Father what I had done. "He is often in pain. It is the result of hard use of his body all his life and he refuses to admit it."

"Sorry." I had witnessed his discomfort but feeling sympathy for my father was a new and unsettling experience.

"Your Mistress Rowan was a great help." He took a contemplative sip. "She distracted him. And he likes having a pretty girl around, even if she is not for him." He looked down his considerable nose at me. "You've done well for yourself, if she's agreed to be your wife."

"I think so."

Dennis appeared again. "Are you two going to bask in the sun like turtles all day?" he asked. "The horses need less rest than you."

"Go away," I said. "Fetch the horses, if you will, or chase that poor girl if she'll have you. Let me finish my drink in peace."

Terrence snickered. "Your father speaks thus to me." His expression grew sly. "Perhaps the reason you do better apart is because you are too alike."

Thirty years ago, King Henry and Thomas Cromwell dissolved the monasteries of England, to their great benefit and that of many others. While the treasures of the ancient system reverted to the king, the bulk of the lands and buildings were granted or sold to loyal courtiers, especially men of the north, always a troublesome area for the crown.

Immediately upon purchasing Aldwych Priory, Father had most of the buildings demolished and the stone transported to Kelton for improvements. What remained of Aldwych—the prior's house and some outbuildings—lay abandoned for decades, the grounds reverting to wilderness and the foundations of the ruined buildings sinking into the soil. Rebuilding had never been a priority, since Mother preferred Yorkshire to Hertfordshire and would have refused in any case to reside in a house whose rightful tenants had been driven away.

After the king died and Father recognized his unfitness to the new, rigidly Protestant court, he retired to Yorkshire and set about improving his accumulated properties. Wyncombe, intended for his heir, came first, but in the last year he had begun work on Aldwych. Terrence and I had come south to see to its conclusion.

"You'll be able to see it in a moment," Terrence said, as we reached the crest of a hill. "Down there, in the valley."

It was not a large house, but it was pleasantly situated in the valley he mentioned, with a small wood and the beginnings of gardens set out on all sides. It was a little larger than Winterset, built in the older, timbered style. I admired it as another possession which would eventually pass to my brother, along with the title and any number of smaller manors and lodges acquired over our father's grasping career.

We were welcomed by a familiar-looking servant whom Terrence greeted by name. A minimal staff was in place, I was told, so the house was neither robbed nor allowed to fall into ruin again.

"Look around if you like," Terrence said, as we threw off our things in the snug hall. "I need to speak with Elder here about the work that's been done to the stables." To his nephew, he said, "The master's chamber is at the top of the stairs to the right. Put Master Hawkins's things away."

"I don't know how long I'll be staying." Terrence ignored me and followed the other servant from the room, already talking about the stables.

Nicholas Hawkins was a man of specific comforts: until his beasts and his bed were taken care of, he would not put forth effort in other areas. Seeing the stables from an upstairs window, I fully expected the master bedchamber to be impressive, and was not surprised to find a gracious, tapestried room with a bed wider than I was tall.

Dennis was busily stowing my things in an elaborate chest. "This place may yet need work," he said, looking up as I entered, "but the accommodations are better than any we've had outside Hawkmoor."

It was true. I decided to assist Terrence before returning to London and the inevitable reprimand which awaited me. After years of hard riding alternating with sitting about, manual labor was a welcome change.

Two days later, after I'd helped re-roof the buttery and unloaded several wagonloads of stone and lumber for the completion of the stable repairs, I felt no different. My muscles ached and the skin on my back and shoulders stung from working shirtless in the hot sun, but I was more alive than I had been since leaving Kit's arms.

"Shame I have to leave tomorrow," I said to Terrence as we trudged back to the house in the late afternoon. "I'm beginning to enjoy myself."

"That's good to hear," he said. "I've got something for you, once we've scrubbed ourselves clean of all this filth."

I did not bother to bathe in my chamber, instead stripping with the others and washing at the trough in the kitchen yard. When we reached the hall, Terrence moved ahead and brought a sealed letter down from the mantel.

"From your father," he said.

I looked at the lumpy, folded sheet in his hand. Nothing my father could say would dim the pleasure of this day. I cracked the seal, kicking the fragments of wax toward the cold hearth.

There were no greetings or fatherly good wishes, just a few lines stating that his lawyer, Thomas Kent, had effected a deed of transfer. Aldwych Priory was mine. I was a landowner.

Once I achieved her liberty, I would be able to give Kit a proper home.

"Why would he do it?" I sat with Terrence and Dennis, the letter and the enclosed deed on the table before us. "And why tell me now, when I am to leave in the morning?"

Terrence sighed. "Those were my instructions. He wanted you to get a feel for the place before you found out it was yours."

"And you obeyed." I raised my cup.

Beside me, Dennis shifted uneasily. "As I would you. For fear of my very life."

"I don't understand," I said. "He's never shown any sign of favor before. Why give me a house? And why now?"

"Because you're to marry." Terrence yawned, giving me an ample view of his missing teeth. "He's been waiting."

If I had married Cecily Farr, would he have given me this house then? I did not want to know—I barely remembered her face, and I could not imagine her in this house, which was for Kit alone.

My brain teemed with plans. Should I leave Dennis behind, to assist Terrence and Elder, or were my father's men sufficient for the work? Kit's parents resided in Kelton village, not far off—perhaps I should invite them to live in the house until she and I were able to join them; it was not large, but certainly there was space enough for the old couple. Kit would want them with us, of that I was certain.

"I will never understand him." I addressed my father's man. "Nor how you have dealt with him all these years."

"He is not so bad." Terrence accepted another cup of ale. "I have been with him since boyhood, as Dennis has been for you."

Dennis scratched his chest. "Then you are partly responsible for the man Lord Kelton became, uncle."

"I am not." He had often been on the receiving end of my father's rages, but Terrence would always stand up for his master. "Your grandsire was a terrible man. He made Lord Kelton's life a misery as a boy, calling him weak, pushing him to be the kind of man *he* was."

"He appears to have succeeded." It sounded a lot like my boyhood. If my father had suffered, he'd learned nothing from the experience.

Terrence shook his head. "Lord Kelton is hard because he sees himself in you, those parts of himself that he conceals or shouts so they are overlooked. It is hard to believe, I am sure, but he cares for you. For all his children."

I pushed away from the table. "Forgive me if I doubt your veracity, Terrence. The quality he likes best in me is my choice of wife."

He leaned back in his chair, looking at me with narrowed, appraising eyes. "Just know, young Master Hawkins, that Lord Kelton once swore to me that he would be nothing like his father. You can go wrong without realizing and find matters too far gone to be mended."

## CHAPTER 48

"WE'LL STAY AT KELTON House instead of Whitehall," I said to Dennis as we passed through the city gates. I had thought long and hard on the matter and decided that my father's gift of a house, however unexpected, meant I could also avail myself of the comforts of his other residences without asking permission.

"Thank Christ," he returned. "After the last few years, we need softer living."

The court had broken up for the summer. While Her Majesty was on progress in Essex, it took some time to determine exactly where Ned Pickering had gone, and for how long. The young men who stayed behind in Cecil's offices were divided as to whether he had gone to Surrey to visit his wife or to Hampton Court for reasons unknown.

Finally losing patience with their dithering, I left word where I could be reached and took Dennis to spend an hour with Harry Minstrel. There were, surprisingly, no letters for me. While I had not expected to hear from Margaery or my father so soon, I had sent a half-dozen missives to Chatsworth and received no reply.

When we returned to Kelton House in the late evening, a summons was waiting. Ned expected me at Hampton Court on the morrow. I looked at Dennis. "We'll take the river," I said. "What time is the tide?"

He shrugged. "I'll check with the steward and have him send someone to secure places for us in the morning."

"That will be soon enough." I rubbed my eyes and stretched, wanting to be alone in my chamber to wonder at Kit's silence.

"You'll remain in England," Ned said the next afternoon, "barring one final trip to France."

"Why?" I objected purely on principle. It was impossible to get away from them so easily.

"Because you must train your replacement." He looked up from beneath his brows, enjoying my impatience. "He's been at Whitehall, awaiting your return. You will depart tomorrow."

It was infuriating but not unfair. I had ridden with Starling for months, delaying his retirement. "How long will that take?"

He expelled an impatient breath. "As long as it does, man! Show him the routes, explain how not to get himself killed by the French, introduce him to Walsingham and the others in the ambassador's residence—including any particular contacts you may have—and then you're a free man." Again, his brows lowered, and he glared at me. "Free of the French, but not us. You're not to go kiting off all over England again." His fist struck the desk. "It surely did not take you the better part of two months to tell the widow Darcy that her husband died a traitor."

"I'm here now." I had resisted all demands to reveal my whereabouts; if he learned from other sources, I could do nothing, but I would not give myself up so easily.

"Then I'll have word sent to your second," he said, shaking off my lack of cooperation. "You are already acquainted, so it will be an easy process."

"Who is it?" I hoped for the other Sturgis brother, or perhaps Charles Mannion.

"You'll see tomorrow." Ned looked over my shoulder at the door. "Be in my office at six of the clock, in case there are any last minute messages. The barge for Whitehall leaves within the hour. I intend to be on it, and so should you."

We were rowed back to London on the same vessel, but Ned sat with several of the queen's men who had not yet joined the progress, and I lingered at the stern with others of my station.

"Waste of time," Dennis muttered as we disembarked, tipping his head toward Ned.

"Him or the trip?" I wouldn't have minded spending time at Hampton—when Nell first came to court, I'd passed a happy summer there following her and Margaery Lewis around, alternately worrying over my sister and lamenting my ill luck at being in love with my friend's wife. It felt like a lifetime ago.


We arrived at Whitehall before sunup. Dennis bemoaned the brevity of our stay in London, but I reminded him that this would be our last trip to France, and he subsided. Few people were about at this hour; even the guards looked drowsy as they nodded a greeting and stood aside for me to pass. The chambers given over to the principal secretary were dark but for pale wedges of light leaking in between closed shutters. A door was open further along, and a bar of brightness fell across the floor. I quickened my pace. It was enough that I had to do this, I did not need a lecture from Ned on punctuality.

I was not the first to arrive in the waiting area. Someone was tucked far back in the corner of the bench, his boots extending into my path. I went around him but turned to look, curious to see who else was up this early. The face, beneath a fashionable cap and a shock of black curls, was as familiar as it was unwelcome.

"Jamie."

He nodded curtly and returned his gaze to the floor. Judging by his expression, we shared a single thought—that we were the last men we wished to encounter in this place, at this time.

"You'll excuse me." I rapped on the frame of Ned's door to escape conversation. "Good morrow, Sir Edward."

"God be with you." Ned did not look as if he'd slept since he stepped off the barge. As he came closer, I caught a whiff of stale wine. If I was not mistaken, his clothes were the ones he'd worn the day before. "I'm sorry you annoyed me sufficiently that I caused both of us to be up this early."

"As am I." Even an extra hour of sleep would have made me less dull-witted. I had been up half the night composing another letter to Kit. "But here we are. Have you any further messages?"

"No." He yawned widely. "There is a report, but I'll send it by a faster courier. You'll be too slow, as you have to show your second the way of things and will not likely reach Paris before the middle of September."

His reasoning was logical enough but increased my resentment at having been dragged from my bed. I put the thought of September—September!—from my mind and concentrated on the matter at hand. "When does he arrive?" I asked. "I thought we were to leave first thing."

Ned rubbed his eyes, leaving them redder. "He should be out there," he said. "I sent him out to wait for you."

"Not—"

"James Welldon." He smiled broadly. "You said he was of little use in the Scottish queen's household. This will allow me to keep a narrow eye on him myself, to see what he's made of."

I closed my eyes, imagining the discomfort ahead. How could I spend weeks—in the saddle, aboard ship, in the same chambers—with a man who, according to Kit, held a grudge because I came between them? Perhaps she was wrong. Perhaps he had moved past it already—he was young and handsome and had likely drawn the attention of many women since his removal to London.

"What?" Ned asked. "Is there something beyond what you've already shared?"

"No..." For all I knew, he might be engaged elsewhere, though I doubted I was that fortunate.

"Then what possible objection could you have?" His arms were folded across his chest, waiting to hear why I was reluctant to spend time with one of my former companions.

"He wishes to marry Katherine Rowan," I explained sheepishly. "And she has chosen me."

Ned burst into raucous laughter, carrying on until tears streamed from his eyes. Wheezing, he said, "Is Mistress Rowan the only woman in England? Thank Christ old Henry is not on the throne, else he'd want to marry her too!"

I slammed the door, drowning out the sound of his laughter, and jerked my head at Jamie. "Come along," I said. "We're already late."

He followed, his mouth set in a stubborn line. When Dennis saw who was with me, he turned his face away to hide his laughter and left at a run to fetch the horses.

"You no longer have a manservant?" When we were in Scotland, he'd had a jolly fellow named Bright.

"No." There was an unaccustomed sneer in his voice. "I do not require someone to dress me."

I walked to the open doors. The sooner we got on the road, the sooner this journey would be over, and I would be able to see Kit again. "There is more to Dennis than his ability to take care of my clothes," I said. "Underestimate him at your peril."

Jamie pushed past me into the morning sun, shifting impatiently from foot to foot. He had lost flesh since we met at Chatsworth; he seemed composed of nothing but angles and edges, in his person as well as his personality.

We could not conduct the business at hand without speaking. Taking a deep breath, I said, "Neither of us are here willingly, but it must be done, and apparently it must be done by us. Let us put our hard feelings aside and work together until it is ended."

His chin jutted out. "I put nothing aside," he said, "but I will follow and learn from you. There is nothing now for me in England."

Our horses were brought out, Dennis and two other men already mounted. Jamie turned to me. "Do we need so many?"

"They will escort us to the docks," I told him, "and bring the horses back here once we are aboard the ferry. We'll pick up fresh mounts when we land, then ride on to Dover."

Ever since learning I would be responsible for training my replacement, I had thought back to the wealth of knowledge imparted by Starling, and how best to pass it on. That the recipient of this knowledge would be Jamie Welldon was neither here nor there—I had as little choice in the matter as he did, and in this case, the work was more important than our personal feelings.

We started off, Dennis obligingly behind with the grooms, exchanging bawdy stories while Jamie and I remained silent.

"It is not so bad, this job," I said. "I have seen parts of the world I would not have otherwise—I have been to the French court and seen the king and the queen mother."

"As I have seen our queen," Jamie responded. "And the English-woman."

"The Englishwoman *is* our queen. Remember, you are in England, and you now work for her."

In the most technical sense, he had always worked for Elizabeth, but he'd been better off not knowing that. If, in addition to stealing away Kit's affections, he discovered that I had been lying to him for a decade, this arrangement would never work.

Once we were aboard the ferry, I took Dennis aside and left Jamie at the rail. "This is going to be hell," I said. "I don't know if Ned understood what he was about or if it is terrible luck on both sides, but this will be the longest trip of our lives."

He nodded agreement. "Is he still a paragon or would it help if I tried to lead him astray at the first opportunity?"

"You have my permission to try." My shoulders and neck were tight with tension. "If you fail, perhaps he'll make common ground with me against your lechery."

"Who is the happier man, I ask you—the lecher or the prude?" He grinned. "I'll see what I can do with him. There's a brothel in Dover port..."

I rolled my eyes. "Don't tell me. Spring it on him when he's tired and unawares. Maybe he'll give in, and we'll all be the happier for it."

"There are times," I said, repeating Walter Starling's words, "when it is safer to travel as a man than a messenger."

"What do you mean?" Jamie had warmed slightly, and now, the evening before we sailed, we sat together in a tavern while Dennis sampled the delights of Dover. His vaunted ladies had held no attraction for Jamie; after listening to Dennis sing their praises for a full five miles, Jamie now regarded him as no better than the women themselves. It did not make common cause between us, but he had at least regained his power of speech.

"You develop a sense of when it is best to keep your messenger's credentials in your pocket and pay for a horse or a bed outright. Not everyone thinks kindly on England." I pushed the jug of ale across the table to him. "And not only our queen. Once we reach France, even if they are sympathetic to Mary Stuart, they are not necessarily sympathetic to *us*."

He listened intently as I related some of the close calls which had befallen me and the other Paris-based couriers. Despite our differences, I had to remember his youth—he was the same age as Kit, and with far less experience of the world than I'd had at his age.

"What about travel inside England?" he asked "We took the ferry to Gravesend because it was faster. Do you travel often by river?"

I took a contemplative sip of ale. "River travel may be quicker, but you go where it goes. A river doesn't always let out where you need to be. In many instances, it's faster to ride—unless you suspect the roads will be impassable." I told him a story I'd heard—apocryphal, but likely—where villagers had dug clay from the road to repair a wall and a man had nearly drowned in the resulting puddle. His eyes grew wide. "Land may be more efficient," I concluded, "but water may be quicker. None of them are perfect."

Jamie exhaled, dropping his chin to his chest. "How long did it take you to learn all this?"

"Longer than I have to teach you," I said honestly. "But once we reach Paris, Sturgis will take you in hand. You'll be his second until you're more prepared."

We sat together in silence after that, a world of information and one slender woman between us, while I planned the next day's ride.

It should take approximately three weeks to reach Paris the way I had organized the journey. He would learn the routes in the same way I had learned them: by hard riding and doubling back again and again until they were firm in his mind. Many of the villages and hamlets had no names, so Jamie would have to learn the local landmarks to help him find his way. I would introduce him to several noble houses friendly to the queen's men, along with inns where I had been made welcome in the past.

I recalled one particular inn and wondered, if we were to pause there, whether the innkeeper's wife would have a blue-eyed babe on her hip.

CHAPTER 49

WE REACHED ROUEN IN the last week of August. All ports are much the same, whether English or French—or Spanish or Italian, though I had no firsthand experience of those places. Noisy and bustling, filled with ships loading and unloading, and raucous with a babel of tongues from faces ebony black to pinkly pallid, we could as easily have been in Southampton as Rouen.

It took ten long days to make our way to the coast. During that time Jamie had begun to warm and seemed to be taking in what I told him with every appearance of listening and perhaps even beginning to enjoy the work. He was introduced to several contacts on the way to Dover, and they seemed impressed with his ingenuous manners.

I was pleased, but Dennis remained skeptical. "You don't see the way he looks at you," he warned. "When your back is turned or you're speaking to someone else. He has forgotten nothing."

"I wouldn't forget, in his place." Dennis's obstinate dislike of Jamie exasperated me. "All I need is for him to be capable of taking my place once we get to Paris."

"You keep telling yourself that. I'll keep an eye on him."

I had made peace with how long the journey would take, but that did not mean I wasn't looking forward to its end. We could continue on horseback, but the Seine made its way to Honfleur and the Narrow Sea through Rouen, and there would likely be a vessel which could convey us inland more swiftly and with less wear on our hindquarters—not to mention reinforcing to Jamie that leisure was not often a word that sounded well in the ears of William Cecil.

Dennis located the harbormaster and within minutes we had been directed toward the *Crescent*, a galiot set to depart for Paris within two hours. Having secured places, we retired to a nearby tavern to fortify ourselves for the rest of the journey. I was pleased to see Jamie speaking to several fellow travelers; it was good that he was coming out of his sulk.

Several hours later, I stood impatiently at the rail as the vessel made sluggish progress in the sultry air. There was little wind to assist the oarsmen, and I began to regret choosing the easy route. "This will take days," I said over my shoulder.

"It will take as long as it takes."

Dennis was perfectly happy to lean against the cargo lashed to the deck and watch the French countryside drift slowly—ever so slowly—past. Jamie was on the port side, practicing his French with the young men from the tavern. Their laughter reached me over the rhythmic sound of the oars.

By afternoon we had picked up speed, but as the sun passed its zenith and began its descent, the breeze dropped again. Each stop we made along the river seemed interminable.

"How far are we from Paris?" I called to a passing sailor.

He paused and looked at the beginnings of the town creeping up on us. "Twenty miles, perhaps a bit more."

I looked at Dennis. "I've half a mind to get off and hire a horse."

"Half a mind would be about it," he retorted. "We'll be there soon enough. Why risk a ride through the countryside as night falls?"

He had a point; the French had never loved the English, and our good heretic queen but deepened their hatred. And yet I could not bear to be aboard the *Crescent* a moment longer, watching the day pass and doing nothing.

"I agree with Will," Jamie said unexpectedly, joining us for the first time since we set off. "This is unbearable. And we have hours until it is dark."

My decision confirmed, I said, "We will disembark at this next town. Make ready."

We might not make Paris before the gates were shut, but we would get close enough for comfort. With any luck, we would reach the ambassador's residence as the household roused itself in the morning. A livery near the docks supplied us with three fast horses, and we pointed ourselves so that the sun was on our shoulders. "Four hours' ride, if that fellow was right."

"Five," Jamie said with a grin. "Let's not kill the beasts."

"All right." I returned his smile. "Five."

A roadside inn provided a late supper and respite for the horses. As we sat at the table, my attention was drawn by a small group of men clustered by the door to the kitchen. Their voices were low, and every so often they cast a glance in our direction.

A sense of unease started in my gut. "Be ready to ride," I murmured, moving my hand to the hilt of my sword. "I think we have worn out our welcome in this place."

"They look harmless," Jamie objected. "I passed them outside when I went to piss. They were quarreling about a woman."

"Nevertheless."

Dennis slid from the bench. "Tell me when an Englishman was ever welcome in this hellish country."

We had not reached the door when the knot of men broke and came after us. "Run!" I shouted, making a line through the yard for the stables. Jamie and Dennis swerved, taking a track behind the building.

The stable was dark, the iron bracket by the door lacking its torch. Sucking in a breath, I entered, placing my feet carefully on the straw. There were two men already in the box with our horses. I threw myself at them before they saw me, laying one out in the straw and causing the horses to whinny and rear up in the small space. The second fellow dropped the bridle and dove at me, pulling a knife from his belt.

I reached for my sword. He was on me before it cleared the scabbard, tumbling me backward. We slammed into the floor. I scrabbled for purchase, heels drumming, hands clawing at his eyes, trying to deflect the blade.

It passed so close that I felt its breeze on my cheek. Dennis leaped forward and grabbed a handful of the man's hair. A gurgling sound and temporary blindness. I drew my sleeve across my face and saw Dennis wiping his knife. The man was on the ground, his throat gaping in an obscene smile.

I rose to my knees but got no further as the men from the inn burst through the doorway, howling as they saw their slain compatriot.

Snatching up his knife, I hurled it at the nearest man and caught him in the shoulder. He staggered and pulled the blade free, swearing loudly. I scrambled to my feet, drawing my sword and advancing on them. "Come, if you will," I called in French. "The Queen of England has a long reach if her men are slaughtered."

Dennis was by my side, his blade held steady before him. A cut at his hairline bled freely down his face. "I don't think they care," he muttered. "Blasted Frenchies."

Two of the men faded back, but there were three left, and the fellow I had flattened was beginning to make noises. "Dennis—"

He needed no further instruction, dropping down and smacking the man's head into the boards again.

The other three advanced, backing us further into the cramped stable. They were armed with knives and short swords; I had the longest blade, and I slashed it through the air, making them skip back. From the corner of my eye, I saw movement. Dennis relieved the unconscious man of his knife and whirled to face our attackers, a blade in each hand. His teeth flashed in the dim light as he beckoned them to come at us.

And come they did. For several minutes the world was filled with clashing blades, labored breathing, and grunts of pain and exertion. My sword slid deep into flesh and a man screamed. The blade was nearly pulled from my grasp as his body fell away.

"Hawkins!"

I whirled. Dennis had disabled one man, but he was grappling with the second, each struggling to keep the other's knife away from his body. Dennis twisted out of range, and I pierced the man with my sword. He stumbled to his knees, then fell to one side. When I pulled the blade free, I saw that he was only a boy. His eyes glittered briefly, but he was soon dead.

Dennis wiped his knife on his breeches and gave me a sharp nod. "That should settle our supper. Where is—"

The knife struck him in the thigh, sinking almost to the hilt. He fell like a stone.

I looked around, but the man on the floor was unconscious. A creak from the stable's back door alerted me to the presence of another assailant. I sprang forward, my sword held high, but whoever had thrown the knife was gone.

Our horses were already saddled. I led them outside, then went back for Dennis, catching him under the arms and dragging him from the stable as he thrashed weakly and cried out. His leg was bleeding heavily. I yanked one of the laces from his breeches and knotted it tightly around his thigh so he would not bleed to death before we got clear of this place. "I have you." I tested the knot, then heaved his body over the saddle. Dennis was no bigger than I, but lifting him made me stagger, off-balance. When I attempted to mount, I understood why. In the fog of battle, I had felt nothing, but at some time during the fight, I had taken a blade to my left shoulder, and it was on fire. Lifting him had breached my limit; I could barely raise my arm. Mounting in the normal way would be impossible. I clambered on from the right side and gasped as my buttocks hit the saddle.

"Save yourself," Dennis croaked, tilting his head to look up at me. His scalp wound had ceased to bleed, but he was a fearsome sight, his eyes and teeth gleaming white in a mask of red.

"Save your strength," I commanded. Leading a second horse would slow me down, making me a target for further attacks, but assailed by memories of Starling, I could not leave him behind. I reached for his reins.

A torch now rested in the bracket by the stable door, brought by one of our attackers. I threw it over my shoulder into that place of death. As the flames bloomed, men streamed from the inn, but by then I was away down the road, riding like hell for Paris. It did not occur to me for several miles to wonder what had happened to Jamie.

I pushed the horses until I was certain we were not being followed. As the shock of the attack sank in, a trembling began deep inside and spread to my limbs. Despite the warm night, my teeth chattered, and my hands and feet grew cold.

A church tower spiked the dark sky ahead of us, but I left the road for the forest instead. Villages were risky: even if the locals were friendly, showing up in the night, covered in blood, would not recommend us.

My horse stumbled over something on the path. Half-unconscious, I nearly pitched over his head and gripped the reins hard. Only the constant throbbing in my shoulder reminded me I inhabited a body; my mind was still in the stable, wondering why we had been attacked and what more I could have done. For the last hour, I had tried not to focus on whether Dennis lived; he was at my side, as he had been since we were boys. That had to be enough until we reached a place of safety.

Another few hours would see us to the city, but I couldn't keep up my current pace. The trees were swimming before my eyes, and riding through the woods at night would risk injury to the already tired horses. Even if we reached Paris, the gates would be locked, and I was in no condition to persuade the guards to accept my credentials.

We would have to wait until daybreak. Fording a small stream, I slowed to look around. The forest was deep here, but faint light from the waxing moon showed a clearing, and the stream would provide water for the horses. It would do. I slid from my horse. When my boots hit the ground, my knees buckled, and I landed first on my hip and then my injured shoulder. Pain exploded. For a moment, I was paralyzed, then I pushed myself upright, gasping at the bright blade of agony in my arm. I could not continue like this; I had to tend Dennis before I became incapable.

His body hung slack over the saddle, in more or less the same position as when we'd fled the inn. I'd managed to shove one foot into the stirrup but on the other side, his hand was wedged beneath the girth: that was not my doing. Hope surged in my chest, nearly choking me.

"Dennis. Wake up." I touched his shoulder. He groaned, and the muscles beneath my hand twitched.

I was struck dizzy—was it joy or exhaustion or remnants of the terror I had not allowed myself to feel at the time? Leaning my forehead against the horse's damp flank, I thanked God for my friend's survival and prayed that I would be able to keep him alive until Walsingham's physician could repair the damage.

"I'm going to move you," I said. "Fall back against me as I pull, as slowly as you can. I cannot bear your whole weight."

He groaned again as I wrapped my arm around his good leg. There was a shift as he freed himself from the girth. A light tug and his body slid down against mine. My head struck the ground for the second time that night, hard enough that I saw stars. Dennis was on top of me, unmoving.

I shook my head until my vision cleared and propped myself on my right elbow, slowly dragging myself from beneath him. His thigh had continued to bleed, though not as heavily as before. Still, his breeches were soaked on that side, and the tie I had used was stiff and wet. I would need to retie it and attempt to bandage the wound.

"Stay asleep, friend," I said. "This is going to hurt." I slit the leg of his breeches, peeling the fabric back to expose a deep gash which oozed blood when I gently prodded the area around it. How much blood did the human body contain, and how much could it lose before it ceased to live?

My shoulder screamed as I lifted the pack down from the saddle and hunted through it. Finding one of my spare shirts, I tore it with my teeth until it was in ribbons, then soaked them in the stream and gently sponged blood from the wound. Once that was done, I had another thought, and stood with difficulty to rifle Dennis's pack.

His flask was buried deep, but when I removed the stopper, my nose was assaulted by a harsh scent. If the harbormaster's aqua vitae couldn't clean the wound, then it had no purpose at all. I braced his shoulder with my right hand and with my wobbling left, I upended the flask over his thigh.

His eyes flew open, and he made a sound I will never forget. I threw myself across his midsection before he knocked me over again. "Stay still, damn you. I'm trying to help."

"You're going to kill me." He panted, pawing ineffectually at me. "What—?"

"Stay still." I ran my filthy sleeve across my forehead to clear the sweat. "It's going to hurt."

"It already does." Face contorted, he fell back against the grass and did not move again as I packed the wound with strips of cloth, then prepared to wrap it.

"I'm sorry," I said, when I realized it was impossible. "You have to raise up a bit so I can bind it."

He groaned, using both hands to lift his leg far enough that I could pass a wide strip of shirting beneath it and tie a knot on my improvised bandage. When I finished, I lowered him back down, resting his head on his pack.

Now for my injuries. The pack yielded one last shirt. I slowly removed my jerkin. The shirt beneath was stiff and adhered to my skin. I wet the cloth and eased it free, feeling the wound throb deep in my shoulder. I set to tearing the clean portion and attempted a rudimentary bandage, wishing, when I saw the slash's ragged edges, that I had saved some of the aqua vitae for myself.

I picked up my jerkin but could not resume it. It was covered with blood—mine and that of the men I'd slain—and it disgusted me. The last remaining item in the pack was my blue doublet. It was a shame to ruin it, but I had to keep the wrapping in place. I eased it on and managed a few buttons before I had to rest. Leaning back against a tree, I closed my eyes and tried to summon Kit's face, but all I could see was the dead boy.

A greenish line in the eastern sky told me I had slept, possibly for hours. My shoulder burned like fire when I attempted to flex it, but I was able to use my hand. The horses were hobbled near the stream where I had left them, calmly cropping grass, and waiting to resume our journey. I rolled over and looked at Dennis.

His bandage was stained where his wound had bled in the night, but his chest rose and fell with every breath, and though his face was pale, it did not have the look of death. That was all I could ask for.

I got to my knees, my joints stiff with damp and lack of movement. "Dennis."

"Go away." He turned his head to one side, his face pinched with pain. "Ahh."

"Can you move at all?" I could barely stand; how was I going to get him into the saddle? "We're about two hours from Paris."

Dennis shook his head and flopped back down. "No."

"I can't leave you here." With a grunt, I wedged my good arm beneath him and hauled him upright to balance on one leg. "There is a village not too far ahead. I'll come back for you."

Lifting him had opened my shoulder afresh; a hot trickle of blood spread beneath the bandage and ran down my side. I shrugged off the knowledge, putting his arm over my shoulder and bearing his weight as he hopped toward his horse. It took three tries to get him into the saddle.

He collapsed against its neck, the reins loose in his fingers. I had an easier time in mounting, but the jouncing trot made every bone in my body hurt. I did not want to think how Dennis felt.

The village was closer than it had appeared the night before. Folk were beginning to move about, and when we stopped before the church, there was a candle in the window of the small house directly behind it.

"I'll ask the priest to keep you," I said, getting carefully down. "Don't move."

"I can't," came his faint rejoinder.

The priest was a gaunt, elderly man who did not appreciate being dragged from his prayers. Once he understood what I was trying to tell him, he followed me to the church door, crossing himself when he saw Dennis.

"He is alive," I said brusquely, trying not to show my fear. "And I would have him remain that way. There is gold in it for you if he still breathes when they come for him."

His head tilted doubtfully, and he crossed his arms over his chest. "How much?"

I named a reckless sum and watched his face change. "He is important, this man?"

"He is important to me," I said. "Keep him in your room, feed him, give him wine. Have someone tend his leg." I flung a gold sovereign at him. "Someone will come for him by tomorrow."

A clangor of church bells filled the air as I rode through the gates of Paris. My head rang along with them. I was grateful for my previous experience of the city because I was so dizzy and exhausted that I would not trust myself to find Walsingham's residence otherwise. I clenched my jaw against the pain and increased my speed, not slowing until I clattered into the courtyard and eased myself down from the horse. No one came from the stables, and the front door remained shut.

Hammering on the panel with the brass knocker, I leaned my head on my arm, the strength draining out of me as surely as the blood had very nearly drained from Dennis. Where was everyone?

The door opened abruptly, and I fell in, catching myself on the frame before I hit the marble floor. I looked up into the faces of three unfamiliar men with drawn swords. They gazed at me with suspicion.

"Qui êtes-vous? D'où venez-vous?"

I raised my hands as high as I was able. "I'm Hawkins," I said hoarsely, and swayed on my feet. "From London. Help me."

# CHAPTER 50

THE NEXT FEW DAYS were a blur of pain and fear and strange, vivid dreams. I was alone—or thought I was—but for my father, red-faced with rage and grown to twice his size. He roared at me for something I had forgotten, but the pain would not allow me to remember what it was. I cried out for Kit to save me. She no sooner appeared than she turned into Margaery, who laughed and became my father again.

At some point, my mind cleared enough to hear other voices in the room, and rapid footsteps that had nothing to do with me. I sensed panic, but my eyes refused to open. I fell away into sleep again.

When I next awoke, Peter Sturgis was seated beside the bed and another man—a physician by his robes—leaned over me. "How do you feel?" he asked, laying a light hand on my forehead.

I attempted to lift my head. It was strangely heavy, and I fell back onto the pillow. "I don't know."

"You've had a fever," he told me. "A very high and dangerous fever."

Sturgis's presence made me understand that I was in the ambassador's residence, but I had no memory of my arrival. "Was I ill?"

"You were injured," Sturgis said plainly. "In your shoulder and arm. Do you not remember?"

Memories came back to me—heat and darkness and the sound of blades—fire—

"Dennis."

"You gave his location before collapsing." The physician shifted and I saw Dennis on a pallet by the window, the covers raised to keep weight off his leg. He was asleep.

"Will he live?" I could not bear it if he died.

"Yes," the physician said. "The large vein was nicked. If you had not tied his leg so tightly, he would have bled to death."

My vision wavered and went dark as I considered the magnitude of what could have happened. Pushing down panic, I asked, "You are certain he will recover?"

"At first I did not believe it likely, but he is strong."

Sturgis snickered. "Probably all the ale he drinks."

"I had a fever, you said?" The physician's words didn't make sense. "But I wasn't ill."

He shook his head, thick reddish hair falling about his face. "Your arm, when they undressed you, was swollen and hot to the touch. Streaks of red to your elbow. You were at more risk of death than your man there. It is not yet certain you will keep the arm."

That made me sit up, despite the heaviness of my head and the pain that tore down my left side. "I must!"

Sturgis put a comforting hand on my leg. "Doctor Francois is doing his best, Will," he said. "The redness has faded, but you will get little use from that arm for some time."

I didn't care about that, so long as it remained attached to my body. What use would I be to Kit if I lost my arm? She deserved everything that was good—and whole—not a one-armed man, old before his time. The fight in the stables was the first time I'd truly used a blade in self-defense. I'd held my own, but I'd never make a soldier.

"Monsieur Sturgis speaks out of turn," Doctor Francois said sternly. "It is not yet certain."

I could not take it all in. Blinking tiredly at them, I asked, "Is the ambassador here?"

"Not at present. He is pretending to negotiate the queen's marriage contract."

Closing my eyes again, I said, "Wake me when he returns. I must tell him what happened." What little I remembered.

Days passed with Walsingham still at court. My fever subsided, leaving me weak but clear-headed. I grew accustomed to the pull and burn of the numerous stitches in my shoulder each time I moved. On the second day, I was permitted out of bed, and from then on, I endeavored to keep Dennis in his.

"If you open that wound again, the physician will have my hide." Doctor Francois was fearsome, and I did not look forward to explaining that Dennis wanted to walk to the jakes rather than use the pot like a child. "Tell me," I coaxed, trying to distract him, "what you remember about what happened to us."

He turned bleary eyes upon me. "I would rather not."

That was understandable. What man wanted to think about nearly losing his life? But there were holes in my memories, things that, when I tried to focus on them, slipped through my grasp like fish. One gap in particular bothered me.

"What of Jamie?" I probed. "How am I to explain to Ned that I abandoned my junior to a mob of murderous Frenchmen?"

Shockingly, Dennis laughed. "You did not abandon him. He abandoned *you*. His horse was saddled and waiting behind the stable. He was away before I even came in the door."

*My father roaring that I had forgotten something important...*

Jamie had been speaking with passengers on the *Crescent*, and he'd made a point of saying our attackers were arguing over a woman. I had thought him attentive to the French because of his attachment to the Scottish queen, but perhaps there was a deeper reason.

"Why would he do that?" Had he betrayed us? Did Ned know, when he assigned Jamie, that he was disloyal—or was that *why* Ned had assigned him to me? I had, after all, become troublesome, and Ned was no stranger to solving his problems with violence.

Dennis sat up, grunting with effort. "One, you took his woman. Two, he's as much in love with Mary Stuart as young Mistress Rowan, and you work for those who would keep her imprisoned. Three—"

"But he works for them, as well." Was Jamie capable of what Dennis was speculating?

"How well does he understand that?" he asked. "In Scotland, you let him think you were on Mary's side, and even after, you fawned over the

Scottish queen to where it seemed you were as likely to raise her skirts as Mistress Seton's."

It was a good sign that he felt strong enough to provoke me. "Enough. What was your third point?"

"Three"—he tipped his head back as he tried to remember what he'd been saying—"he's a papist, and it would be easy enough, in this damnable country, for him to find any number of men to murder you."

As I mended, I slept a great deal, but my sleep was broken, filled with disturbing dreams, fragments of which remained when I was shaken awake one afternoon by Walsingham's man.

"The ambassador has returned," he said apologetically. "I am to help you downstairs."

Sitting up, I saw a fresh suit of clothes across the foot of the bed. With his help, I maneuvered myself into them. My torn shoulder and the seeming uselessness of my left arm made dressing difficult, and I swore a good deal before the deed was accomplished.

At last, we made our way downstairs. The dinner hour had passed, for which I was thankful; I would give a great deal to be drunk, but the thought of food made my stomach turn over.

"The ambassador is waiting." The servant guided me to a closed door, rapped softly, and backed away as a voice called to enter.

Walsingham stood as I approached. "I hear you had some difficulty in reaching us."

"Indeed, sir." Seating myself with care, I gave a brief recitation of our trials, ending with gratitude for his physician's attentive care of both Dennis and myself. "Doctor Francois said this very morning that we should both recover, in time and with rest."

"That is excellent news."

A knock, and the servant entered with a tray containing a silver pitcher and two goblets. He poured wine for us and retreated.

Looking into the goblet, I saw in the ruby liquid an echo of the blood that had been spilled that night. All the things which could have been lost—which had been lost. I closed my eyes and took a healthy gulp.

Walsingham rubbed the bridge of his nose. "You have witnessed the work of the devil at first hand," he said. "It can be seen no other way."

"I'm sorry?"

"The papists." The swarthy face was drawn, confirming the rumors of ill health which had reached England before my departure. His black hair, badger-streaked with white, was dull and his eyes were puffy and tired-looking. "You were targeted because you were Protestant—or English."

The connection was easy to make, but it was a broad brush with which to paint all Catholics, as broad a brush as Mary Tudor had used to coat Protestants with the pitch of heresy. When fear takes over, it is too easy to lose the human scale of the matter. I thought of the many who suffered and died for their faith during Mary's reign. I thought—and then stopped thinking—of Matthew. I never doubted that the men for whom I worked were acting in the service of the Protestant God, the English queen, and England herself; only Ned's actions were tainted with personal ambition. But Walsingham's attitude spoke to a determination to win this holy war: light against darkness, Protestant against Catholic. It was that easy, and that dangerous.

"I assume you will be going back to England after you have healed?"

"Yes," I said. "That had always been the plan."

"But Pickering said you were bringing along your replacement."

"About James Welldon." I explained that he had been trained and could take over, if we could but discover his whereabouts. "The problem, sir, is that before we were ambushed, he rode away. My man saw him flee."

Walsingham swore. "Pickering said he was Catholic, but trustworthy."

It occurred to me then that the best way to fight Ned was with his own weapons.

"He has never been trustworthy," I said, endeavoring to sound sincere. "I told Sir Edward last year that he should not remain in the Scottish lady's household because his sympathies were too strong."

He looked at me soberly. "Then why was he sent here?"

"I don't know, sir." I took a sip of wine. "I assumed that Sir Edward had given you that information and wished for you to judge his loyalty for yourself."

My words landed as I intended. I watched them sink in, hoping they were as lethal to Ned as Jamie might have been.

"In that case," Walsingham said slowly, "I would prefer that you stayed through the end of the year. It is difficult to get men with your background, your understanding of the issues involved."

"Lord Cecil intends that my efforts be confined to England." I reached for my goblet again and found it empty. "I plan to marry, and though I cannot make a home for Mistress Rowan—as yet—I should like to be in the same country as my wife."

"Mistress Rowan who is in Shrewsbury's household?" His pouched eyes showed surprise. "You still want her?"

"Yes." Why would he doubt my affection for Kit?

"You haven't heard, then?" He gestured for me to refill both goblets. I lifted the pitcher and felt a corresponding twinge in my other shoulder. "About what has happened with her?"

"No, I've been either traveling or ill for over well over month." What had happened? "Please, tell me."

He leaned forward, elbows resting on his desk. "Your Mistress Rowan left the Talbot household weeks ago. She is as inexplicably located as your second."

The room spun. Walsingham's pronouncement echoed in my head over the sound of blades and the tang of blood on my tongue. The attack was more than a week ago, but I was still physically and mentally fractured. Every creaking floorboard sent tremors through me that I could not admit to Dennis or the physician. Now, this—Kit, vanished into thin air. It was like being thrown back into the stable to face another assailant.

My breath hitched, the paneled walls threatening to close in. Panic, that familiar serpent, coiled around my chest. Kit couldn't just disappear.

"She left?"

How many letters had I missed? What must she have thought, not having heard from me in all this time? Suspicions began to form, each one a shard of ice. What if she had been taken? Walsingham's words sounded accusatory, but my mind went immediately to Jamie. He wanted her, and if I were dead... It was unthinkable that he could have swept into Talbot's house and carried her off, but it was not impossible.

Walsingham cocked his head. "She was discovered to be harboring a certain secret," he said. "When Lady Elizabeth learned of the deception, she dismissed her."

Dismissed! I sagged with relief, then thought: Kit's entire purpose at Chatsworth had been a deception, carried out with the Talbots' full knowledge. "Why?"

"Wantonness," he said blandly, waiting for my reaction. "Lady Elizabeth could not have a bastard born to one of her ladies."

I barely heard his tone, my mind reeling with the wondrous news concealed in the insult. She was safe—but for all my care, our brief encounter had borne fruit. My poor darling! I wanted to leap to her defense, to strike both Walsingham for his judgment and Bess Talbot for her coldness. Should a woman not defend one of her own?

How could I have been so careless? My lust had put her in this precarious position. I tamped all that down, along with shame at the weakness which had caused her predicament. She was what was important right now.

"And you say that no one knows where she has gone?" I kept my voice even, speaking around the thickness in my throat. I thought I knew.

"No. Nor do we care—the queen's government will not admit to hiring a harlot." He shook his head. "This is why we do not use female agents. The most innocent virgin can turn without warning. Who would ever trust a word from her after she has so disgraced herself?"

"There is no disgrace." I drew myself up as much as my injured shoulder would allow. "The shame is mine, as is the child. Sir Edward and Lord Cecil both knew we were to be married. It was their constant delays that prevented the marriage from taking place."

Walsingham fell silent, looking down at his desk, then out the window at the empty street. Finally, he spoke. "Do you point a finger at your betters, rather than take responsibility for your lack of control?"

"They are my superiors, not my betters," I snapped, filled with rage at these men with their closed minds, who could not know what life was like for the rest of us. "And I am not so certain about one of them. Sir Edward insisted on James Welldon as my second and he has fled, leaving us in a situation that could have caused our deaths. I refuse to call the man capable of such an error of judgment my *superior*."

At the first opportunity, I sent off a raft of letters to England. Three went to my father: at Hawkmoor, Kelton, and the London house, advising

him of both Kit's predicament and my own, and asking him, if she was
in his care, to keep her safe until my return. If she had gone to her parents
instead, I asked him to retrieve her—and them, if they would come with
him. The Rowans were good people, but they had neither the skill nor
the bravado to stand up to Ned Pickering, whereas my father was replete
with both.

It was a strange feeling, to ask for his assistance and know it would be
unquestioningly given. It was Kit he was helping, not me, but Kit was all
that mattered.

Sturgis was leaving for London in three days and taking several of
Walsingham's men with him. I would join their party, and very glad I
was that our numbers were larger, as I would be of no use whatsoever in
a fight and even had some doubts about my ability to ride comfortably
one-handed.

All that remained was to rest, but rest did not come easy. If I relaxed my
vigilance even for a second, it came flooding back—the darkness and the
smell of the stables; the silver sound of my blade clearing the scabbard;
the wet, solid noise of my sword finding its home in the chest of a boy.
Those thoughts were followed by visions of Kit—pregnant with our
child—turned out, scolded and shamed.

My fault. All my fault.

She must be at Hawkmoor. She knew to go to Father in case of
trouble. I had to get back to England, find her and marry her, and then
I would do what was necessary to guarantee her safety, even if it meant
coming back to the tinderbox that was France.

"They won't let me up yet," Dennis said, as I paced our tiny chamber
and outlined my plans. "And I'd slow you down."

He was right, but I wanted him with me. Dennis had always been
there—it was when he was missing that I got into trouble.

"I'm slow enough as I am." I gestured at the arm strapped to my chest.
"You will join me when you are able to travel again."

Scratching delicately at his thigh, which itched him mightily, he
asked, "And where will I join you? Whitehall, Kelton, Hawkmoor, Aldwych—or in my lady's chamber?"

"If I am in my lady's chamber," I said, "I care not for the location, and
you had better not interrupt."

## CHAPTER 51

I RODE INTO WHITEHALL'S vast courtyard, my heart in my throat. It was eight days since we'd left Paris, almost two weeks since I'd learned of Kit's pregnancy. Just over three weeks had elapsed since the attack. I kept those dates in my head, marking them off on an invisible calendar as we traveled closer to our destination. Somehow it kept the nightmares at bay.

My disquiet stemmed in part from fear that Kit would blame me for the situation in which she found herself. Certainly, the fault was mine: because of me, she had lost her place, risking her parents' safety. She would think herself pregnant and alone. Abandoned.

I would make it up to her. I would make it up to all of them. First, I would apologize. Then I would marry her, if she would have me, and install her, with her family, at Aldwych Priory. Under guard, if need be. Dennis would not be at full strength for some time, but as I had trusted him with my life, I would trust him with theirs.

My future was less certain. I had made and discarded several plans on the journey—confronting Ned with my suspicion that he had intended my death; going over his head to Cecil with what I had told Walsingham; snatching up Kit and her family and heading for the nearest port before we could be discovered. I had the location of Margaery's French house in the back of my mind; she would allow us to use it, I was certain of that.

But running felt like an admission of guilt, and none of us had done anything wrong. Fleeing to France would give that impression, and I did not want to build a new life constantly looking over my shoulder. I had

escorted men to the Tower under an accusation of treason; I had no wish
to reverse the experience.

Cecil, I decided, would be my first visit. Hurrying through the great
hall to his offices, several people turned to stare. We had been traveling
for days; no doubt, I did not look my best, but I would not waste time
on washing that would be better spent pleading my case.

Yanking open the door separating Cecil's quarters from the more
public parts of the palace, I ran smack into Alleyne the forger. Springing
back, my hand to my shoulder, I saw his goggle-eyed expression and said,
"What? Do I have dirt on my face?"

"N-no," he stammered. "I am surprised to see you is all."

"Why? It was known that I was coming home after this last trip."

Alleyne looked around and drew me to one side. "Do you not know?"
he asked quietly. "Welldon came back a fortnight ago. He said you and
your man were killed. He was distraught—said he barely got away with
his life."

Considering he'd run away before we had exchanged a single blow
with our assailants, I was led more than ever to believe he had been
behind the attack. Whether he had worked alone was my next question.

"As you can see, I am alive and well." I put a hand on his arm. "But it
might serve if news of my resurrection did not spread further. If I leave
now, will you keep quiet?"

He nodded, intrigued by a mystery, as was everyone who worked in
these dark places. "I have not seen you."

I left by a little-used back entrance and tossed a coin to a page to have
my horse brought around to the rear gate, where I could shelter without
being seen. Now that I was a dead man, I had more time to plan my
next moves. I would conceal myself at Kelton House, where my father's
servants could also keep secrets.

That a door would go unanswered in a Hawkins house was impossible.
After I had knocked three times with no response, I pushed, found
the door unlatched, and let myself in. The house was clearly occupied.
Candles burned in the hall, and the table had been recently abandoned,
with plates and cups scattered along its length. The chairs were pushed
aside as if everyone had left in a great hurry.

"Hello the house!" I shouted, to break the unnerving silence as well as to summon a servant. A soft footstep made me turn.

Terrence stood in the doorway, his eyes wide and staring. "God's teeth, Master William!"

If he was shocked to see me upright and breathing, then Jamie's tale had spread beyond the bounds of Whitehall.

"I suppose you have heard—"

He spun away, sprinting toward the back of the house and shouting, "Stop! Wait!"

I followed hard on his heels, arriving on the chapel's threshold to face a strange tableau. In my mother's time, the chapel had retained its stained glass and statuary and her precious gold crucifix, but after her death, all overtly Catholic trappings had been stripped away, leaving only the carved wooden altar, behind which was a black-robed priest. His narrow face showed annoyance at the interruption.

In front of him stood a couple, their hands linked and their heads bowed. When the priest stopped speaking, they turned to look at me. The woman was Kit. The man was my father.

What happened immediately after is unclear in my mind. I remember roaring, "Stop!" but my next clear memory was Kit on her knees, crying, her arms wrapped tight around my legs and my father swearing loudly, held back by Terrence.

"William! William!" The sound of my name had never been so sweet. I bent and helped her up, and she pressed her wet face against my cheek. "He said you were dead."

"I am alive, my love, as you can see." I brought her hand to my lips, then cradled it against my chest. "I am injured, yes, but I came back for you." I cut a glance at my father, who was glowering and rubbing his jaw. "I came for you and found this."

"You misbegotten idiot," my father spat. "With you dead, Welldon was aiming to marry her himself."

"It's true." Kit wiped her face with one hand, keeping her other firmly in mine. "He said he'd got permission and gave me a week to summon my parents to witness the ceremony. He said marrying him would keep me safe, but I didn't—"

"She didn't want that," said Lady Rose's voice, "and so Lord Kelton stepped forward and offered his protection instead."

So blind with rage had I been at the thought of my father with Kit that I hadn't even noticed there were others in the chapel: Kit's parents, along with my sister Elizabeth, her children, and Jane, whose fist was firmly in her mouth, uncertain whether to cry or throw herself at me.

"You asked me to keep her safe," my father said accusingly. "This is what I get for honoring that request."

Had I truly struck him? For years, I had dreamed of returning his blows and harsh words with similar treatment, but I was never brave enough. There was always the knowledge that he was bigger, stronger, and far angrier; any attempt would have left me bruised for a month and would have cut off the comfortable living which he provided even as he declined to treat me as his son.

"I apologize for my overreaction," I said stiffly. "I am not entirely recovered." Though I had punched my father with my good fist, my injured shoulder throbbed. "May we get out of this room so I can speak to Katherine alone?"

There was a shuffling of feet as everyone turned, but my father reached out, clasping my left shoulder in a hard grip. "You could leave," he drawled, "or you could take my place and marry the girl before she sees sense and changes her mind."

Fire burned down my arm, numbing my fingers, but I had eyes only for Kit. Candlelight gleamed off the pale gray satin of her gown—laced, perhaps, a bit more loosely to contain the baby burgeoning within.

We would have a child. A son or a daughter. And I would learn to be a father, to both follow and diverge from the example set for me. I took a deep shaky breath, and despite all the people watching, placed my palm on her stomach.

"Katherine Rowan," I said, "will you forgive me my misdeeds and marry me, in front of all these witnesses?"

I did not specify whether my misdeeds were giving her a child, being unable to protect her in her time of need or behaving like an ass in front of both our families, but she smiled tremulously.

"Of course I will marry you, William." Leaning forward so that only I could hear, she added softly, "And not just to give our child a name. I will marry you because I love you, because you are a good man, and for all your differences, you are the son of a good man."

I needed that reminder. I kissed her cheek and handed her to Arthur Rowan, while I approached my father. Bowing my head, I said, "Please forgive me. I am in pain and weary from the journey, but that does not justify my behavior."

His dark eyes considered me, but he remained silent.

"You were doing no more than what I asked—" I stumbled, realizing he'd been willing to go further than the simple protection I had imagined. I no longer cared if he'd intended to consummate the marriage. I was alive and Kit was mine, and my father, who had never remarried, had been willing to sacrifice the peace of his final years to fulfill my request—and in front of his mistress. "Thank you," I said, my voice breaking. "Thank you for that."

His hard expression shattered, and he pulled me against him. Even as he raised his voice and called me a weak, babyish puppy, I could feel the sob in his chest. This day was, for both of us, the first step in a forgiveness that would take the rest of our lives.

We were married within the hour. Afterward, the servants managed to produce a credible celebratory meal, which almost no one ate. The others had eaten before my precipitous arrival, and I was unable to consider the thought of food from nerves and exhaustion. Nevertheless, we drank and talked—though not about my near-death or the people involved—and Kit and I were put to bed with some ceremony as the bells outside struck nine.

Alone at last, we kissed wordlessly, and cast our clothes aside in the chamber that had been prepared for us. Candles burned on every available surface, and some romantic—I thought I knew her identity—had caused rose petals to be scattered on the bed cover. It was a world to itself, and given the choice, I would never leave.

I dropped to my knees to look at Kit—my wife—seeing the new fullness in her breasts and the curve of her stomach. She was more beautiful than ever.

She touched my bandaged shoulder with one finger. "Does it hurt?"

"A bit," I admitted. "Particularly after I struck Father."

She giggled. "I cannot imagine how long it has been since Lord Kelton last took a blow."

Nor could I. We hadn't been able to speak at table, as he'd sat on Kit's other side, but before the party broke up, he caught my eye. "You intend to deal with Welldon?"

"Welldon and others." I did not wish to discuss it then.

He nodded. "You have my support if you require it. In men or funds."

I clasped his hand and wondered whether believing me lost had softened him or if it was my reappearance. Likely it was the effect of Kit, who had always made him a kinder person.

"Let us not speak of him now." I drew her close and led her toward the bed, throwing aside the cover in a drift of crimson petals. "It is our wedding night and I wish to lie with my wife."

Kit lay curled against me in the wide bed. We had made love the night before, bringing to it all the pent-up emotion that had followed us over the last weeks, both of us shedding tears in our extremity. I wanted to lie beside her forever.

"Can you not stay?" she asked, sensing my thoughts. "You said they were not aware of your return."

I ran my hand over her belly. The swelling was less noticeable when she was lying down. "They do not, officially," I said, "but I was seen. Word may have already reached Cecil. I need the element of surprise if I am to confront Ned Pickering."

She nodded, her head tucked below mine on the pillow. "Do you think they will release you?"

"No." I attempted to stretch without disturbing her; stiffness had set in, and while our careful coupling had eased my mind and heart, physically I felt like an old man. "I told Walsingham I was willing to continue my service, as long as they let you go."

Her body shook, but with laughter rather than tears. "Lady Elizabeth would have hurled me from the rooftop if it had been within her power."

"How did she find out?" In someone as slender as Kit, it would not take much for a change to be noted, but there were tricks with gowns and lacing that had concealed more advanced pregnancies.

"Mary Seton." Her puff of laughter was warm on my chest. I felt a chill, nonetheless. First Jamie, then Mary. "In the beginning, she was kind. Then she laughed at me. Men were untrustworthy and used women for their own amusement, she said. I was an innocent and could not understand." She tilted her face to meet my eyes. "I did not hold her cruelty against her, for who would not be cruel, having lost you? She must have suspected my condition, for she told the queen, who told Lady Elizabeth."

I had not thought Mary capable of such treachery. "I am sorry you were put through that. You are away from them now, and safe."

She sat up, her thick hair falling about her shoulders. Her skin was luminous in the early morning light. "I did not truly mind." Her tone was almost surprised. "I had no choice in the beginning, but it was not so bad. I like the queen."

"As do I." Mary Stuart was her own worst enemy, but she had always treated me well. An idea began to form. "I must make ready. I would prefer to spend the day in your arms, my love, but I do not believe my shoulder would allow for more than that, and I cannot just lie still beside you."

The door to Ned's office was closed. Outside, one of the young men tried to bar my entry. "He is with someone—"

I shoved past and opened the door. To my surprise and relief, the man with him was Sebastian Black. So, he had got the letter I'd sent off from France—only my father's letters had gone astray. His eyes flicked up. "Master Hawkins."

"Sebastian."

"It's a miracle," Ned said sourly, not looking at us. "Both of you, alive."

"With no help from you." Seb's voice was crisp.

Ned clasped his hands on the desk. "You have no proof," he said, turning a heavy gold ring. "You've been nothing but trouble, the pair of you—who would not believe that you brought more trouble upon yourselves?"

Would he brazenly deny what he had done? I had no solid proof as yet of any conspiracy, but as Jamie's first actions upon returning to England had been to announce my death and make claim to Kit, it might not be too difficult to tie Ned's intentions to his actions.

Seb seemed to think so, as well. "You were not the only person with whom the master corresponded," he said softly. "You knew that?"

"He was always scribbling away to someone." Ned crossed his arms, leaning back in the chair.

Something flickered across Seb's face, quickly gone. "He was observant," he said. "He noticed things."

"As one does, in our profession." He examined his fingernails, buffing them lightly on his sleeve. "Get to the point, Black. I'm a busy man."

Seb's rarely used surname felt more like a slur than a form of address. My fists tightened reflexively, but Seb remained calm.

"After he left court," he said, "you kept him apprised of what went on. Not *everything*, certainly"—he paused to let Ned understand he meant his disappearance—"but those matters you decided he should know about." He sat down and propped a foot on the edge of Ned's desk. "Others filled in gaps in his knowledge."

"I did not ask you to sit." Ned rose to his feet, a considerable personage.

Seb dropped his foot but remained in the chair. I admired his nerve.

"He corresponded with others," he said, "for your sake, fearing that one day you would go too far. The letters were kept to aid in your defense." His lips stretched in what could not be called a smile. "When he realized that you had betrayed him, he gave the letters into my keeping and told me to use them as I saw fit."

Ned's mouth dropped open, and he began to sputter. "Robin would never—"

"If you overstepped, for example," Seb said. "Or tried to hurt someone he cared for, such as Master Hawkins. He gave me permission to present those letters to Lord Cecil, or whomever might be in charge at the time."

The chamber grew so quiet I could hear the blood pounding in my ears. Drops of sweat stood out on Ned's forehead. He seemed to be gathering strength for an explosion, his clasped knuckles whitening as his face turned red.

"You cannot touch me," he breathed. "You have nothing—no one would believe what you had to say—"

"I might believe it," said a voice to Ned's left. "If I were given access to those letters."

Secretary Cecil stepped from behind a panel, his hand extended. "Good morrow again, Master Black. Welcome back, Master Hawkins." "Sir." I inclined my head, then turned to Seb. "You may trust him, Sebastian."

Ned turned awkwardly, scattering papers everywhere. "William, you can't believe these two villains! Black is a murderer who ran away to save his skin. And Hawkins—"

Cecil accepted the letters and spread them out on the edge of Ned's desk. "Hawkins has given exemplary service to the queen, so far as I am aware." He looked up, his eyes skimming our faces. "I have a report from Walsingham that suggests I should inquire into your choice of second, as the young man in question permitted Hawkins and his man to walk into an ambush."

"James Welldon has been in our employ for years," Ned stammered. "You yourself allowed him to be placed in the Scottish bitch's household, where he could be of most use."

As Ned remained standing, Cecil edged around him and took his chair. "That is true," he acknowledged. "I wanted the boy to prove his disloyalty, which he did—and yet you kept him on. I was curious to see why, and now, I apparently have my answer. Where is Welldon?"

"I'm not certain." Ned's expression was sullen, but beneath his bluster, he was frightened. "I believe he may have left London."

I snorted and caught the flash of Seb's grin. "He is at Kelton House. He appeared there yesterday morning, intent on marrying my wife." I directed my words to Cecil, but kept my eyes on Ned, adding, "Upon learning she was no longer available, he became violent, and my father's men took him in hand. I apologize if they overreacted."

"I'll allow it," Cecil said briefly. "Abuse him no further. He'll be sent for in good time."

Ned rested his palms on the desk, and Cecil whisked Robin's incriminating records from view. "You can't believe all this nonsense!" His voice was strained. "Hawkins has been trying to evade service to Her Majesty ever since he left Scotland. He is the one you should be looking into."

Cecil stroked his gray-streaked beard. "Hawkins is in Her Majesty's employ, Sir Edward. But as of this moment, your continued service is... unsettled, at best."

The only sound was Ned's harsh indrawn breath. "You would not dare—"

"Do you have something to hold over *my* head?" Cecil inquired. "If not, I would advise returning to your house to await my summons."

## CHAPTER 52

"YOU'LL STAY WITH US," I said to Sebastian as we made our way out of the palace. Ned's protestations of innocence rang in my ears.

"Thank you, I'd like that." He sounded worn through. Shadows were visible under his eyes, and his skin had an ashen cast. "If we had made London as quickly as I did upon receiving your letter, the master would not have lived to see Elizabeth crowned."

I sighed. "I regret many things, but none more than the way I burst into Winterset that night."

"Why?" He cocked his head. "It was your job. The master did not resent you for it, not even at the time. He simply set himself the task of changing your mind."

I could not think about Robin right now. "What was in those letters of his?"

Seb nodded to the groom and held my horse's head while I mounted.

"You didn't need to do that." He was no man's servant; certainly, he was not mine.

"Habit," he said with a shrug. "And what *wasn't* in those letters? There was one from the Earl of Moray, the Scottish queen's half-brother, confirming his correspondence with Sir Edward. There was another from a bishop—I don't remember his name—"

"Lesley?"

"That's the one. He wrote something that confirmed Welldon was working for Sir Edward outside of the known arrangement."

"Why did Robin really have all these letters?" He'd been happy, I thought, to get out of the center of things. "Was it to protect Ned, or did he have other reasons?"

We rode through the gate and turned onto the Strand, crowded as always with coaches and horses, with men and women darting across the street.

Seb smiled. In the sweetness of his expression, I barely recognized the angry, grieving man I'd encountered in Paris. Being separated from Robin had been difficult for him.

"He could not step away from the game board, not when so many games were happening at once, and with such interesting players."

"He would be disappointed in Ned." I'd disliked Ned ever since his 'rescue' of Robin on the road to London a dozen years ago, but I'd never imagined him capable of what I now knew he'd done.

"Disappointed, but not surprised. He read people like he read his books." Seb's face pinched. "He knew how far Sir Edward was willing to go for power. He just didn't know the extent of what he'd done."

We arrived back in time for the midday meal. I introduced Sebastian and we fitted ourselves in with the others. Kit's eyes questioned: had I solved our problem? I whispered that I would explain everything once we were alone and hoped she would understand—and accept—the solution Cecil and I had worked out.

Father held court at the head of the table. His mood, ever since he'd come down in the morning, had been surprisingly good, perhaps explained by Lady Rose's discreetly smiling presence at his side. He teased Ellen until her face was poppy red with laughter and was kinder to my sister than I had seen in some years. Even I came in for civil questioning.

"Have you sorted everything?"

I drew in a breath. "It is a process, sir, but it is underway."

"What about our... houseguest?"

Kit took my hand beneath the table, and I squeezed her fingers reassuringly. "You will not have to maintain him for much longer."

There was general laughter; everyone knew Jamie was locked in a closet near the chapel, where he had been forced to listen to the words of our wedding service. I had intended to speak with him earlier but decided against it, not wanting to spoil my happiness at finally being bound to Kit.

The meal was almost over when a knock resounded through the hall. Terrence moved smoothly through the room, followed by two other men, and within moments, we heard masculine voices.

I pushed back my chair and placed my napkin on the table. "Please continue eating. I should be right back."

Cecil had sent four armed men. They nodded to me, and the leader said, "We're here for James Welldon."

"He is in here." Terrence and I led them to the small chamber where Jamie was comfortably confined. When the door opened and he saw me, his lip curled.

"Here to gloat, Hawkins?"

I shook my head. "Here so that your escort may retrieve you."

He blanched at that, and as the men entered the room, surrounding him on all sides, he began to look panicked. "You've taken this too far. You got Katherine. Why should I be punished further?"

I leaned against the door frame, enjoying myself despite my better instincts. "Why did you feel the need to have me killed?"

His head whipped back and forth as he debated how much he could say in front of the guards. "You took her from me," he said at last. "You have everything already, and you took her."

Kit's skirts brushed against me as she entered the room.

"No one took me," she said calmly. "I chose for myself. And I would not have chosen you, even if I never met William Hawkins." She exhaled a sigh. "I am disappointed. I thought you a better man."

He ducked his head so we could not see his tears. "Get me out of here," he said to the guard. "I am ready."

I had not expected Kit to speak to him. I did not object—whatever punishment lay ahead of him, it would not hurt as much as those words—but it proved again that for all my love of this woman, I did not yet entirely know her. How would that be accomplished if we were separated again?

"I do not need more food," she said, taking my arm. "Unless you are hungry, could we walk in the garden, so you may tell me what happened this morning?"

Bees droned over fading flower beds and the sun was warm on our shoulders as we paced the gravel paths, but the vibrant copper leaves of the beech trees dividing Kelton House from the next property showed that it was October.

She listened in silence as I told her of my conversation with Ned, and Sebastian's surprising proofs.

"Is he imprisoned?" Her tone was hopeful; I imagined he'd not made a good impression during their meeting.

"I do not know," I told her. "But he has no power over us now." Cecil might not lock up his assistant secretary, but he would keep him far from the beating heart of Whitehall, which in Ned's view would be almost as bad.

"Then we are free!" Kit laughed with joy. "We are free and we can travel to Aldwych and raise our family together."

"I am not so free," I said at last, hating to shatter her dream. "Cecil was willing to release you, for a price."

She stopped abruptly. "And what price was that?"

"I agreed to take your place in Mary's household." Leading her over to a bench, I sat down and drew her onto my lap. "You never wanted to be assigned to the Talbots," I said, "so I would not ask you to return to Chatsworth. Aldwych is not so very far—I would be able to visit, though not as frequently as I would wish."

Kit laughed disbelievingly. "I did not marry you to be immediately separated," she said. "Why would you think I would not accompany you? Why would you even consider that we would not be together when our baby is born?"

I gazed at her sweet, determined face. The deeper my knowledge of her became, the more she reminded me of the best parts of Margaery, without her inconveniently pointed tongue.

"I thought to spare you," I began. "It is not an ideal situation, serving the court in the way that I must, and which you already have."

"You thought to spare me my husband." Her fingers tightened on my arm. "I nearly had to choose yesterday between an evil boy and an old man, when you were what I wanted. I will not live apart from you now that we are wed."

I could not allow her to spend her life as the puppet of Cecil and Walsingham, not for me. Not even for her parents, who had covered their tracks so badly that Ned had been able to find Kit and twist her to his will.

"I suggested it for your sake."

She leaned back, resting her head on my shoulder, and drew my hand around her middle. "You should think a little harder about what I want, William, before making decisions on my behalf."

Her sharp tone made me draw back. "What do you want, then?"

"To live with my husband," she said simply. "I will return with you to Chatsworth and serve the Scottish queen, if that is what is required. In truth, I pity her."

On my behalf, I did not care whether we lived at Aldwych or Chatsworth or on the moon, but I could not believe she would be willing to go back. "What of Elizabeth Talbot?" I asked. "After what she did, you are willing to enter her house again?"

Kit grinned, looking no older than Ellen. "If I am sent at the court's command, she has no choice in the matter. And I will not have to live among her women."

"No, we will live among Mary's people." I stopped, aghast. "Which means Mary Seton."

Kit slid off my knee. "She is a sad, unhappy woman. And she realized her wrongdoing—when I was dismissed, she gave me the money to hire transport to Lord Kelton."

There seemed to be no discouraging her from a path that would be as difficult as it would be filled with joy.

"Mary Stuart will destroy herself in the end," I said, knowing it to be true. "She cannot resist intrigue. They will find her out. They are relentless."

"I know that." Kit nodded deliberately. "And while I will not hide anything, nor will I make it easier for them. They will do as they will, and so shall I."

"You will not do it alone." As powerful as the love I felt for Kit was pain at the thought of dedicating my life to the dark arts of Cecil and Walsingham and having to find my way without her. "We will go together, if that is what you truly desire."

"You are what I desire," she said, nuzzling my neck. "And for you, I will serve the Scottish queen, and the English one."

I drew her close, felt the smoothness of her hair against my cheek. For a lifetime of Kit Rowan, I would do the same, and more. "I will speak with Cecil tomorrow and let him know of our decision." The words were halting, as all I wanted was to kiss her, but this must be said first or not at all. "When that work is finished, our ties will be severed, and we will be free of them." I brushed her lips with mine. "Will that suit you?"

She returned the kiss in such a fashion that I wanted to carry her back inside. "If it suits my lord husband."

I was proposing a life spent in the shadows of powerful men, but I understood shadows now. With Kit's light, we would find our way in the darkness.

"It suits me very well."

AUTHOR'S NOTE AND
ACKNOWLEDGMENTS

I'M SO GLAD THAT I called this *The Tudor Court* series, because book four of a trilogy would be an uncomfortable place to have put myself. I originally intended to stop with *Lady, in Waiting*, and then I got the idea for *The Son in Shadow* and a fifth book, followed by a book of shorter fiction with stories and side quests of secondary characters who interested me, but didn't have a full book in them. So... two trilogies?

Book five isn't happening. I thought it would be about Jane, but she was so young in *The Son in Shadow* that I couldn't logistically connect the two books. But she will have a story, or possibly a novella, in the eventual *Tapestry* collection.

I decided to write Will Hawkins's story not long after I finished the third book, but I needed to do significant research on the period, so he has sat—mostly patiently—on the back burner throughout the writing of my entire *Ava and Claire* trilogy. I knew he was patient, but that was ridiculous.

Because he had been in my head ever since *A Wider World*, and so many of the characters in *The Son in Shadow* were familiar, this was, in a way, the easiest book I've ever written. The story built itself in my head while I was working on other things; I knew Will and Robin and Margaery and Nick and Beth and Tom and Ned and Sebastian. It was a joy to see them all again, and I hope you feel the same.

The book actually ended before my original planned ending. I had wanted Will's final trip to Paris to coincide with the Saint Bartholomew's Day massacre in August, 1572, but timelines don't always cooperate, and thankfully—although unpleasantly for them—there was plenty of political and religious unrest in the years leading up to the massacre, so I could have Will and Dennis encounter men in that tavern and have it be believable, whether or not Jamie was actually involved. (I'm not saying he wasn't, but he could have seen a good thing and decided to jump on board.)

Mary Seymour, the identity I assigned to Kit Rowan, was real, and she did vanish from the historical record at the age of two. I've always wanted to do something with her, because historical mysteries fascinate me, and Kit was my answer.

One final note on Nick Hawkins, who has been one of my favorite characters since the beginning. Yes, he's obnoxious and arrogant and oversexed and a bad father, but he is unapologetically all those things. Also, he is pretty much a gender-swapped version of my mother, except Mom was better at parenting. Except when she wasn't. For all the people who have asked for years that I write about my mother, this may be the best you get. I'm not sure if I'm ready to face anything more straight on than a father-son version of that truth.

Thanks to my usual crew of supporters: Mario, my husband and listener to the final read-aloud edit; Marian Thorpe, for knowing my characters almost as well as I do; Laury Silvers, for seeing things no one else does; E.V. Rice, for reminding me that this is a process, and that we all get there in our own time. Eva Seyler, for late night messaging—I'm grateful to have a friend on the opposite coast when plot ideas won't let me sleep. Dianne Dichter—if you don't already know it, you are my ideal reader and the person I think of when I write these books. Bjorn Larssen—see what happens when you nag me for a story? Thanks also to Rachel Rubinstein for being a super fan and a member of my advance reader group. I wish I could clone you.

I'm not promising the *Tapestry* collection anytime soon. Short fiction is not my forte, so these stories will arrive when they're ready, and not before. Sign up for my newsletter, if you haven't already, and you'll be the first to know what's happening, when, and how to get yours.

Until next time...

## ABOUT THE AUTHOR

As an only child, Karen Heenan learned young that boredom was the ultimate enemy. Shortly after, she discovered perpetual motion and since then, she has rarely been seen holding still.

Since discovering books, she has rarely been without one in her hand and several more in her head. Her first series, The Tudor Court, stemmed from a lifelong interest in British history, but she's now turned her focus closer to home and is writing stories set in her native Philadelphia.

She lives in Lansdowne, PA, just outside Philadelphia, where she grows much of her own food, makes her own clothes, and generally confuses the neighbors. She is accompanied on her quest for self-sufficiency by a very patient husband and an ever-changing number of cats. One constant: she is always writing her next book.

Follow her online at karenheenan.com and sign up for her newsletter below to receive a free novella and updates on what's next.

Printed in Great Britain
by Amazon

51411966R00229